AWAKENING THE ZOMBIE PRINCE

THE ZOMBIE ARISTOCRACY

GENTRY LEE BURKE

Copyright © 2024 by Gentry Lee Burke

First Edition Sept 1, 2024

Edge Formatting created by Painted Wings Publishing

All rights reserved.

No part of this book may be reproduced in any form or by any electronic or mechanical means, including information storage and retrieval systems, without written permission from the author, except for the use of brief quotations in a book review.

❀ Created with Vellum

Acknowledgments

For my children, my muses. You made me believe in magic again.

Special thanks go to my editor Kate Seger, developmental editor, G. Poff, cover artist, D'Arte Oriel, Labyrinth Book Design, and my art director, G. Poff.

Also a huge hug author Alissa Lace for digging me out a hopelessly tangled plot paradox. Go read her amazing books!

CHAPTER 1

Maeve sucked in a steadying breath as she pressed her hand against the oak door of Fiona's new seamstress studio. She could not understand the foreboding that gripped her. *Shouldn't my wedding dress fitting bring me joy?*

A soft creak echoed through the castle's stone corridor as the door swung open to reveal the grand space Prince Alaric had commissioned for Fiona. Maeve gasped. The prince had outdone himself in making amends to the women who served within his kingdom. Though he had not been responsible for the atrocities Lady Elora had inflicted on them, he still felt responsible, for those things had happened on his watch.

Sunlight streamed through the tall windows, casting a warm glow over the room where numerous bolts of fabric lay in wait. Rich silks and iridescent velvets sat unfurled across the vast worktables. Delicate laces, like spiderwebs spun from moonlight, were draped over mannequin forms, and tiny pearls and crystals shone amidst the finery, as if begging to be chosen to adorn her wedding gown. *Imagine, me, a bride. To a zombie prince, no less.*

Her dear friend, Fiona, stood amidst the textiles, her violet eyes alight with creative fire. "Please, come in," she said, offering Maeve a smile that acknowledged the enormity of the occasion they were preparing for. Maeve and Alaric's wedding was more than just a union of their hearts. It also represented the hope of a new dawn for humans and zombies alike.

The air in the studio bore the faint scent of lavender incense that clung to the young woman's attire, weaving itself into the excitement of the moment. "So what should we do first?" Maeve asked as she stepped deeper into the vast, yet charming space.

"I suppose you should get out of your gown, and then we'll just begin." Fiona's voice was barely louder than the rustle of her sateen skirts as she moved toward Maeve.

Though Maeve acknowledged her friend with a nod, her widened eyes lingered on the fabrics that promised to transform her, not just into a bride—but also into a zombie princess. And someday, perhaps, a queen.

Fiona took Maeve's hand and helped her onto a round pedestal positioned before a grand, gilt-edged mirror. "You've grown thinner since your change," she remarked as she helped Maeve out of her gown, then extracted a tape measure from her apron pocket.

"As have you," Maeve said, acknowledging that Fiona, too, was now a zombie.

"Aye. On the bright side, there's no longer any need for us to worry about growing too heavy to fit into our corsets. We can eat whatever we want...and sometimes wish we didn't want," she added, the corners of her mouth turning down with distaste as she considered the raw meat concoctions most of their kind considered a delicacy.

"Good thing, too," Maeve said. "Brigid plies me with enough sweets to feed a battalion!"

Fiona's soft laughter melted over Maeve like warm butter. Her tiny hands were practiced and gentle, moving with precision as she took Maeve's measurements. As the tape measure slid over Maeve's form, she could feel its roughness even through her silk chemise. Her flesh now bore the heightened sensitivity of her altered existence, a poignant reminder of the human life she had so recently left behind and the strange yet grand future she was about to step into. *So many changes.*

As she watched Fiona work, there was a quiet acceptance in her demeanor, a silent surrender to the path fate had laid out for her. Maeve understood. She, too, had begun to see beauty in the melancholy that sometimes clung to her—one that spoke of love found in the most unexpected of places and the duty that such relationships entailed. Her marriage to Alaric would again alter the book of her life.

"Alaric chose well." Fiona's hands danced over the array of embellishments, selecting a strand of lace with care that bordered on reverence. "This one will befit a queen of peace, I think," she said, draping it over Maeve's shoulder.

Maeve's reflection in the full-length looking glass appeared somewhat ghostly, but the newly angled contours of her face were made softer by the morning light. Fiona's fingers paused for a moment, her chin lifting as her eyes met Maeve's. They weren't just crafting a wedding dress; they were weaving a new future. Yet Maeve could not suppress the shiver that racked her frame.

"Don't be nervous. Your strength will shine through, Maeve," Fiona said, her voice a soothing balm to the nervous fluttering in Maeve's chest. "It always does."

"I hope you know how much I love you, Fiona." Maeve opened her arms and drew her friend into an embrace.

Because Fiona had chosen to remain in Alaric's kingdom, Maeve would not have to be alone as she prepared for her new role.

As the morning slipped by, Fiona's needle dipped and reemerged, embellishing the lustrous fabric with delicate precision. Fiona's hands were steady, but Maeve still felt a tremor within her own chest —a faint echo of the strong heartbeat she once possessed. The silver-white cloth slipped against her skin, and each pin Fiona removed was a reminder of the ceremony that would mark her transition from a mere peasant girl to sovereign.

"Does it feel real yet?" Fiona's voice carried the weight of their shared history, of the battles so recently fought, and of uneasy alliances forged.

Maeve's gaze floated away from her reflection, finding solace in the scattered sunbeams piercing the high windows. "It's like I'm stepping into a dream I'm afraid to wake from," she confessed, her voice barely above the hush of rustling taffeta. "To be a princess, to rule beside Alaric—it is like a page lifted from a fairy tale I never imagined I'd be part of."

"Yet it is a role you already wear with grace." Fiona secured another pin with a gentle tug. "He sees that in you, Maeve. We all do."

Silence fell between them, but it was a comfortable quiet, filled with the understanding that came from close friendship, of watching the world they once knew crumble and reshape itself into something new—yet also too precarious for any of them to feel secure.

Maybe this explains my foreboding. "Peace." Maeve uttered the word like a prayer. "Do you think it is even possible?"

Fiona paused, her hands stilling. Her eyes met Maeve's with an intensity that belied the calmness of her craft. "I have to believe it is," she replied. "Your union with Alaric—it is more than a marriage. It is a beacon for all of us who have ever longed for harmony."

Maeve turned slightly, the garment molding to her like a second skin. "A beacon can guide, but it can also blind," she mused, the thought snuffing the hope kindling within her. "But I fear we tread a path lined with thorns, Fiona. One misstep could bleed us all dry."

"Then you must tread carefully," Fiona assured her, resuming her work with renewed purpose. "Together, with Alaric. He will guide you right. He always has."

"Alaric sincerely believes we will prevail in our efforts to bring peace to the lands." Maeve allowed herself to be drawn back into the measured cadence of Fiona's handiwork. "He even hopes to one day see the ferals cured of their hunger. But sometimes I worry that too much of his faith rests in me...and this wedding."

"He believes in you because you are so strong, Maeve," Fiona said, her tone leaving no room for doubt. "You made clear to him you would stand beside him not just as his wife, but as his equal. He took that vow to heart. And in that strength, you will help him to build a world where fear and hatred no longer rule us."

Maeve released a slow breath, tamping down her foreboding. She loved Alaric with a passion she never would have believed herself capable of. Surely that was enough to carry her through.

As Fiona worked, her slender fingers moved with the tenderness of a scribe illuminating a sacred manuscript. The gown's bodice depicted an olive branch entwined with a skeletal hand. It was like a silent plea that peace would find its place between the living, the undead, and those souls who had passed beyond.

"See here?" Fiona guided Maeve's attention to the burgeoning pattern with a brush of her finger. "Every stitch holds meaning. You will wear the dreams of both our worlds written upon your heart."

Maeve found solace in the thought that these symbols, so lovingly crafted by her best friend, would embrace her on the day when she pledged her life to Alaric and, in turn, to the brighter future they both envisioned.

"Let the gown you have crafted serve as our North Star," Maeve said.

Fiona paused, looking up to meet Maeve's gaze. "A reminder that love is the compass by which you will chart this new world."

Maeve squeezed her eyes closed, envisioning Alaric's face, for it was he who had first spoken those words when they'd both believed all was lost. That vow had sustained her that day. Would that it continued to serve her now, for she still felt something awful lay between herself and her wedding day.

"What are you thinking of?" Fiona asked.

"Alaric," Maeve whispered, her cheeks warming. Her mind unfurled images of him—his steadfast blue gaze, the firm set of his jaw when met with the burdens of creating change, and the subtle softening of his eyes when they turned upon her. In the quiet, she could feel the echo of his desire to heal the world beating within her own heart. But she was not as naive as he, for unlike him, she hadn't been raised in luxury's lap. She knew their path would be fraught with obstacles born from a hatred that had festered for over a century.

Fiona let her fingers brush lightly against the skin of Maeve's shoulder. "He believes in you, Maeve," she said. "And so do I. There's nothing the two of you cannot face."

Those words were more than flattery. They were a candle casting away the doubts that shadowed her soul. Eager for solace, she leaned into Fiona's touch, acknowledging their friendship. Even as their forms had changed, the essence of who they once were remained unaltered.

"Yet sometimes I fear..." Maeve began, her voice trailing off as she sought the right words to address her worries. But they were not needed. Fiona's nod carried an assurance that needed no elaboration.

"Brigid would remind us courage does not come without fear," she said. "I know my own fear has made me stronger, even driving me to learn archery."

"And you've become quite the master," Maeve said. In fact, she'd taken to the art as a fish does to water.

Fiona adjusted the last pin, and the fabric fell into place with an artist's final stroke. She stepped back and smiled. "It's time for you to look."

Maeve turned slowly and gasped. She looked like a specter caught between realms. The ethereal glow that shone behind her pupils testified to her recent transformation. The gown's elegance was a stark contrast to the raw strength that now lay beneath the surface of her skin.

"Do you like it?" Fiona's voice pulled her back from her thoughts.

"It's perfect," Maeve said as her gaze lingered on the woman she had become—a zombie warrior garbed in bridal silk. "But with our vows, all will change again."

"Yes," Fiona agreed, her hand finding Maeve's, a silent anchor. "But whatever trials that day brings, it is a path you won't be walking alone."

Maeve nodded as she gazed at herself once more, acknowledging the aristocratic zombie woman she had become.

"Thank you for being my friend." Fiona reached out, her small hands enveloping Maeve's.

She pulled Fiona into a ferocious embrace, basking in the solace of their connection. "Thank *you*."

Fiona stepped back just enough to look at Maeve, her gaze tender.

"I suppose I should get back to my betrothed," Maeve said.

Once she had changed back into her clothes, they parted, their hands lingering until the last possible moment. Maeve turned away then, the hem of her day gown whispering across the floor. She paused at the threshold, her hand resting on the cool marble archway as she stole a deep breath. "And so it begins..." she whispered to herself as she stepped into the shadowed corridor. But she also knew she could not fully embrace this role without the full support of her family. She must see them, and soon.

CHAPTER 2

Maeve's horse nickered, his hooves thumping across newly reset cobblestones as they passed beneath the archway marking the entrance to the village where she'd grown up. They moved through the recently refurbished edifice, the human guards locking their arms, forming a chain that prevented the zombie guards who had escorted her here from passing through. "I'm sorry," she called out to them as she dismounted and stroked her mount's muzzle in thanks. "Just wait there. I promise I won't be long."

Though the guard leader's fists pumped at his sides before he took her horse's reins, his chin dipped in a reluctant nod. Then he gestured for the others to fall back. To wait, as if they were less than simply because they were zombies.

Frustrated tears welled in Maeve's eyes as she turned away from the gate and took in the mosaic of stone cottages. Once ramshackle remnants of The Harrowing that had scarred the land and the people in the last century, many were now crowned with freshly sodded roofs. Some of them even boasted window gardens brimming with chives and fresh herbs. She knew she should feel heartened that the village had changed so much since the last time she was here. It was apparent that Alaric had already begun sending the village supplies, food, and medicine, as he'd promised. But she couldn't shake her encroaching sense of...fragility.

Yet it made little sense for her to feel as if everything Alaric had worked for might come crashing down any second. Though she'd never been given away to the zombies as a Tributary—a rite of passage for the village's eldest daughters which would have earned her family much in the way of food, dry goods, and medicine—her entire village now prospered because of her and Alaric's impending union. She should feel happy about that. But that creeping sense of foreboding simply would not allow any room for mirth.

Determined to reset her mood, she focused on the air, rich with the aroma of baking bread and ringing with the distant laughter of children playing between the refurbished market stalls in the main square. A soft sigh escaped her lips as the charming tableau unfurled before her eyes, each sight and sound weaving threads of nostalgia through her heart. It was still recognizable as her childhood home, but it was also different. Like her. And though she loved Alaric, she also missed her own people.

Ahead, by the old fountain where she'd once made a million wishes, stood Eamon and his friend, the archer, Loren. Backlit by the soft glow of the early morning sun, their figures cast long shadows that strained to bleed into Maeve's as she approached. Her pace toward them hastened, boots clacking with a rhythm that spoke of her urgent yearning. As the distance between them closed, a crescendo of anticipation swelled in her chest.

Eamon caught sight of her first, his sharp hazel eyes cutting through the morning haze that hovered over the street. His smile, wide and unrestrained, was a welcome place to rest her gaze. Beside him, Loren's gentle brown eyes sparked with recognition, and his lips curved into a grin that spoke volumes about the history they shared.

"Ah, there she is!" Eamon called, his voice booming with a warmth that only old friends could kindle.

"Welcome home, Maeve," Loren added. "We've all missed you."

Then Maeve was enveloped in their arms, the three of them entwined in an embrace that promised to mend the fractures wrought by her time away and the tribulations they'd all suffered since. Their hug was like a fortress—impenetrable by doubt or despair.

"Your timing is impeccable as ever." Eamon pulled back just enough to regard Maeve with eyes that danced with mirth. "The blacksmith's new apprentice nearly set his workshop on fire before dawn—he gave us all quite the show."

Loren chuckled. "And I've finally perfected the elderberry wine recipe you used to make for us. But it took a few... explosive attempts," he confessed, winking.

A smile tugged at Maeve's lips, genuine and unbidden. Here, in the simple exchange of trivial yet treasured chatter, she found the solace of a history Alaric's world could not offer her. As the trio lingered in their reunion, the quaint village around them seemed to slow its pulse, whispering tales of what once was and what she feared might never be again, for she was a zombie now.

As the trio walked together, the cobblestone path meandered beneath their feet, guiding them through the village that cradled a million memories. A canopy of amber sunlight draped over them as they navigated the narrow lanes, and Maeve's nose curled at the scent of woodsmoke lingering in the air. She found herself tracing the familiar contours of the sod-roofed cottages with her eyes, each one a chapter from her past. Only they were different now. Better. All because she'd fallen in love with a zombie prince.

"Everything seems smaller than I remember," she said, her voice barely louder than the fallen leaves that danced around their steps. "Or perhaps it's just the knowledge of what's coming that makes them seem so."

Eamon glanced at her, his brow furrowed. "You speak of the

wedding, or the hordes?" His voice carried a gentle nudge for her to unburden herself. "Because if Alaric is mistreating you..."

"Stop that. He treats me like a queen. But in answer to your question, I suppose...both." The words slipped out with a sigh. Her gaze drifted toward the horizon, and the dense woods that spanned the distance between the village and Alaric's castle. "I fear what my marriage might become in the shadow of such relentless darkness. What good is love if it's torn asunder by... by..." She hesitated, the reality of feral zombies clawing at the edges of her thoughts. Though they'd beaten them back for a while, it was only a matter of time before they reassembled and began their attacks anew.

"Things beyond our control? They are, you know," Loren offered, finishing Maeve's sentence with the ease of long-shared friendships. "You've always been the bravest soul among us—facing down your fears when others would flee."

"Only because Coralie and Nan needed me," she admitted.

"And that has not changed. Nor has your courage waned, Maeve," Eamon added, laying a comforting hand upon her shoulder. "It is stitched into your being, as much a part of you as your very soul."

"As is your determination." Loren's voice was warm and reassuring. "It's what will guide us all through. We believe in you, not just in your ability to survive, but to thrive, even amidst chaos."

Their words settled around Maeve like a quilt pieced together from remnants of her childhood. In the quiet solidarity of their presence, she allowed herself a moment to lean into their affection, allowing the tremor in her soul to be stilled by the unwavering belief they still held in her.

"Thank you," she whispered, gratitude lacing her tone.

"For what?" Eamon asked.

"For still standing with me though I have changed into the very thing we all once feared. For reminding me of who I still am and will always remain." She straightened her spine, lifting her chin toward the advancing day, where rose-edged clouds paved a path for the morning sun.

With Eamon and Loren flanking her sides, she was fortified against the tide of unease that still threatened to wash over her. But not even they could shield her from the scornful glares she caught as they passed by many of the villagers. They seared her through her skin like wildfire and she had to resist the urge to flee back to Alaric's castle, where she knew she was loved, not despite the fact she was a zombie, but in many ways, because she was.

As they traversed the heart of the village, eyes—the same eyes that once smiled upon her, narrowed in fear and revulsion. Even the librarian, Nadine, who had once helped her sort through damaged stacks of books in search of one she had not read, now tucked her grandchild behind her, as if fearful Maeve might leap forward and rip her flesh from her bones.

The villagers stood as sentinels of the life she once knew, and each gaze was an arrow aimed at her newfound identity. Her pulse quickened, and her hands trembled as her being withered under the intensity of their disdain.

"Let them stare." Eamon's voice was a low, bitter rumble. Yet his tone failed to quell the pain that gripped her heart. "Their fear is born from prejudice. But it can't change who you are, Maeve."

"Nor can their whispers," Loren added softly, his hand finding Maeve's and squeezing it gently.

Yet, it was not the warmth of their comfort that lifted the shadow from Maeve's heart, but the sight that unfolded before her as they neared the village square. There stood Nan, her silver hair limned by the morning sun, her arms outstretched as if to gather up the missing pieces of Maeve's world. And beside her, young Coralie, whose innocent brown eyes sparkled with unguarded joy at the sight of Maeve.

With a cry that pierced the dark veil of judgment, Coralie bolted forward, her small legs carrying her swift as the wind until she crashed into Maeve's open arms. Nan followed, her steps slow but sure, and wrapped them both in an embrace that felt like the bonding of fractured glass.

"Look at you, my brave girl," Nan began, her voice laced with a strength that belied her frail frame. "Standing tall and proud despite the horrors you've endured."

Maeve buried her face in the softness of her grandmother's shawl, inhaling the scents of rosemary and woodsmoke, the fragrances she associated with home and acceptance. Here, in the circle of their arms, the harshness of the outside world dimmed, replaced by the undeniable truth of belonging.

"Your love... it sustained me," Maeve's voice cracked, the intensity of her gratitude heavy on her tongue.

"Love sees not with the eyes, but with the soul," Nan replied, her thumb brushing a renegade tear that dared escape Maeve's eye. "And our souls will always know yours, Maeve. No matter what the rest of the world sees...or refuses to see."

The tender moment stretched long and sweet, a respite from the trials that lay beyond the comforting borders of the square. But as the sky painted itself in hues of gold and rose, the reality of their circumstance crept back in, whispering of the darkness that always loomed just out of sight.

"Come, let us not tarry," Nan said at last, her gaze lingering on Maeve's face, as if memorizing it. "For time is a gift we mustn't waste, and I've got a nice huckleberry pie cooling on the windowsill back at our place."

Nodding, Maeve released herself from Nan and Coralie's hold, the bittersweet tang of her lost past catching in her throat. She turned to Eamon and Loren, seeing the echo of her pain mirrored in their eyes. "Is it okay if my friends join us?"

"I would be hurt if they didn't. You know these boys are like sons to me."

"Shall we be on our way then?" Eamon offered Maeve a small smile that carried the nobility of a knight.

"Yes, let's," Maeve answered, her voice much steadier than she felt. Yet, within the tight cocoon of love and loyalty that surrounded her, she found the courage to take the first steps toward the childhood home she had not seen since the day Alaric had rescued her from the snake pit.

Things were changing, indeed. And it was high time she embraced that fact and began the work of marrying her two worlds, as was her and her betrothed's most fervent wish.

Maeve brushed a stray crumb from Coralie's riotous hair, laughter bubbling up between them like a clear spring. They sat huddled together on the worn benches that Nan claimed she had owned since time began, sharing tales woven from shared yesteryears and dreams yet to unfold.

"Remember the Great Solstice Feast?" Coralie's giggle was a light that pierced through the thick veil of Maeve's foreboding.

"You danced with Eamon until your feet refused to carry you back home!" Coralie said, as if revealing a tawdry secret.

"Indeed," Nan said, "though it wasn't much of a feast. The roasted skunk cabbage roots were tough as nails that year, and the squirrel meat naught but gristle, but in the end it didn't matter. The company was enough to sustain us." The elderly woman's eyes crinkled at the corners as she smiled at Maeve, warmth radiating from her as sure and steady as the noonday sun. "And now you stand before us, Maeve, both a warrior and a soon-to-be princess."

Maeve caught the undercurrent of pride in Nan's voice, a subtle acknowledgment of the journey that had chiseled away at her innocence, leaving behind a mettle forged by an unkind fate. The afternoon wore on and the stories continued, each a lifted from a page in their shared history. As late afternoon's shadows crept across the floor, laughter melded with tears that fell silently, marking the passage of moments they'd not known back then were far too fleeting to be squandered. They had been too busy trying to stay alive.

As the shadows lengthened, casting long fingers across their faces, Maeve could see Eamon becoming restless. "It grows late," he murmured as her gaze caught his. "We should take you back to your guards soon."

Coralie whimpered and clung to Maeve's hand, her small fingers interlaced with those that had once rocked her cradle, now marked by the harsh bites of survival. "Must you go so soon, Maeve? We haven't even talked about my flower girl dress yet."

"I'm afraid I have already tarried too long, my darling. You know as well as me the ferals roam at night. Though they have been beaten back for a while, nobody knows when they might return."

"Swear to me you will stay safe and come back soon?" Coralie's fragile voice quivered with emotion.

"I swear it," Maeve said, leaning down to press a kiss atop her cousin's mousy curls. "And if you are to be my flower girl, given how much you have grown, I shall have to bring Fiona along with me so she can take your measurements!"

"Can my gown be pink?"

"I imagine it can be any color you wish," Maeve offered. After pressing another kiss to her cousin's crown, she turned to Nan, whose gaze was moist with unspent tears.

"Keep safe, my heart." Nan folded Maeve into an embrace that somehow felt soft as a pillow and strong as a fortress.

"Until we meet again," Maeve replied, her voice thick with unshed tears.

With a final glance, a silent promise passed between them—a vow of return, of stories yet to be told. Maeve rose, feeling Eamon and Loren close behind her, their presence a tangible reminder of the strength they had found in their reclaimed unity.

As THE TRIO stepped away from the village square, Maeve turned back to give her family one last wave, but their figures had already been swallowed by the encroaching dusk. She swallowed the lump in her throat, telling herself that surely the dying flame that had been rekindled inside her this day was enough to see her through until the next time.

With each footfall they took toward the village's gate, Maeve felt the mantle of her new life's purpose settle more firmly upon her shoulders. The cool breeze carried in whispers of tomorrow, of battles to be faced, and of an enduring love that no darkness could ever truly vanquish. *Alaric...*

Eamon prepared to pass Maeve off to her guards, she gave him and then Loren a hug, then drew in a deep breath. "Goodbye," she said, then stepped through the gates and mounted her horse. The distant scent of woodsmoke mingled with the cooling evening air, a bittersweet reminder of the simple pleasures she had once taken for granted.

With her zombie guards circled around her, they stepped into the dense woods. Nan's embrace and Coralie's innocent laughter still lingered in her mind, soothing the raw edges of her spirit. As the darkening forest claimed them once again, the realization unfurled within her like the first bloom of spring: she was not alone. The bonds of kinship, unyielding and profound, were the exact reinforcements she needed to see her through the next phase of her life.

As the last sliver of sunlight was swallowed by the towering evergreens, Maeve lifted her gaze to the emerging stars. They glittered coldly from the velvet expanse, silent witnesses to the countless tales of struggle that had unfolded beneath them. And though the forest that stood between her two homes was dark and vast, it could not extinguish the warmth that bloomed within her chest—

the love of her grandmother, the laughter of her cousin, the steadfast presence of her friends. But now it was time to go home to another hearth, another home, where her beloved Prince Alaric waited. Only this time, she went to him, not by chance, but rather choice, and that knowledge made all the difference.

CHAPTER 3

Maeve's heart contracted a little as she neared the castle gates, her mount's steps in sync with the dull thud of the zombie guards' boots. Shadows stretched from the castle's towering spires, reaching for her like the fingers beckoning her back to a future that nothing in her former life had prepared her for. She sighed, the weight of her thoughts dissipating slightly as Prince Alaric came into view, his stance cocksure, his grin wide, and his expression awestruck as he stared up at a white owl soaring high above the trees.

"Alaric," she called, her voice betraying only a trace of her wistful mood.

His deep blue eyes, quick to read her, sparkled with mischief as his gaze turned on her. With an unexpected flourish, he helped her dismount and swept her into his arms, their bodies moving in an impromptu waltz across the recently reset cobblestones that paved the courtyard.

Maeve couldn't help but laugh. This boyish aspect of Alaric's personality was one she had enjoyed far too little of so far, but it was these times when he forgot his station that she loved him the most.

"Whatever has you feeling so merry this evening?" she asked, searching his eyes for clues.

"Aside from commiserating with my owl friend? True love, silly," he began, spinning her once more before setting her down. "It's the ultimate form of magic. And to celebrate our coming nuptials, we are to have a ball."

She tilted her head as she inspected his face for any hint that he was teasing her. "Conversing with owls? Planning a ball? Have you spent the entire time I was away reading your beloved fairy tales?" she chided.

"If I told you it was so, would you be jealous, my love?" he teased as he caught a tendril of her hair and pulled it through his fingers.

"Only because we didn't get to read it together. But why do you wish to have a ball?"

"Aside from it being the custom to announce our wedding date at a grand ball, we can use the occasion to begin uniting our worlds under one roof, just as we shall be united under these very stars during the spring solstice."

Maeve's heart skipped a beat at Alaric's words, her doubts and worries about the future fading into the background as she caught his enthusiasm. As he locked his arm through hers and led her toward the wide double doors that would take them into the Great Hall, she allowed herself to be swept up in his vision, imagining a future when their love would become the very thing that bridged the divide between their two worlds. The ultimate form of magic, indeed.

"And the ball," she said with a smile, "will stand as a symbol of that unity. It is a brilliant plan, my love."

Alaric's grin warmed at her praise, but behind the excitement that lit his eyes, Maeve sensed something more. Something serious and determined.

"Yes," he said firmly. "It will be a grand event, one that will bring our worlds together and show everyone that there can be another way to live. A more peaceful way. Then maybe the naysayers will finally be silenced."

Maeve's heart swelled with pride at her betrothed's passion and conviction. She knew the task he aimed to undertake would not be easy—there was more than a century of animosity and distrust to overcome. But she also believed if anyone could pull off such an enormous task, it would be him. Suddenly, she felt like the luckiest woman—zombie—in the world.

As they entered the Great Hall, dinner had already been laid out with careful precision. The long oak table gleamed beneath the soft glow of the candelabras, each place setting an intricate arrangement of polished silver and gilt-edged porcelain. The aroma of fresh meats, some roasted, some quite raw, as was Alaric's preference, intertwined with the sweet scent of freshly baked bread and the tang of spiced fruits, teasing Maeve's appetite.

As they took their seats, she admired how the crystal goblets caught the light from the chandeliers, casting prismatic dances across the tapestries decorating the stone walls. As her attention returned to Alaric, she caught him dismissing the poison taster with a casual wave of his hand.

"Is that not risky of you?" Maeve's brow furrowed while she reached for her embroidered linen napkin.

"Perhaps," he admitted, picking up his fork and eyeing the succulent leg of lamb before him. "But after studying my father's diaries and his obsession with being poisoned, I've decided the fear and distrust that consumed him are shackles I'd rather not wear. According to his writings, he'd even secreted away antidotes for the most potent toxins. Yet there has not been a drop of poison in anyone's cup since I was a boy. And sometimes," he punctuated by tearing off a piece of exceedingly rare meat with a satisfied grunt, "I just want to savor my meal without someone hovering over my first bite."

Maeve watched him for a moment, but the tension in her brow softened as she saw how he delighted in his food. Not wanting to appear unsupportive, she mirrored his actions, waving off the poison taster and taking a small nibble of the tender fare on her plate. Pushing back her last remnant of trepidation, she allowed herself to be enveloped by the flavors and take solace in the increasingly comforting routine of dining among Alaric's court. Though they had not yet accepted her as one of their own, they were at least polite, and sometimes a few were even cordial.

As they continued with their meal, she found she rather enjoyed Alaric's subtle, yet thrilling rebellion against protocol. It was a small but appealing taste of the freedom from baseless fears they both yearned for and aimed to see more of.

UNABLE TO EAT ANOTHER MORSEL, Maeve leaned back and let her finger trail along the ornate armrest of her chair, wondering if this place would ever truly feel like home to her. The chatter around her was a low hum, punctuated by the occasional clink of silver against fine porcelain. She attempted to join a conversation with one of the zombie women seated to her right, offering a comment on the string quartet that played in the corner of the Great Hall.

"Were you talking to me?" the woman said.

Maeve nodded. "The music the string quartet plays is quite enchanting, don't you think?" she proffered again, her words designed to bridge the divide she sensed still held many of Alaric's courtiers separate from her. They still saw her as human. Perhaps even less than.

The response she won was a cool nod and a quick return to hushed whispers shared with the other courtiers. Another noblewoman who sat across the table eyed her over the rim of her goblet, her perusal sharp enough to cut bone. She reminded Maeve of an ice sculpture, strangely beautiful to behold from afar, but upon closer inspection, cold and brittle as death. Like Lady Elora.

A sigh escaped her lips, but was lost in furtive whispers floating around her. *Will I ever truly feel as if I belong?* The thought lingered in her mind like the ghostly echo of a bell long after its last toll. As Alaric continued to enjoy his meal and the animated conversation he was having with the courtier positioned next to him, she felt the weight of countless eyes—judging, calculating, disapproving. Again, she felt as if she were strung between two realms, yet tethered to neither.

"Excuse me, my love," she murmured, rising with a grace that belied her aggravation.

"But where are you going?" Alaric asked, looking a bit hurt.

"If we are to have a ball so soon, I must see to the preparations for my gown." Her voice, a mere wisp, barely reached Alaric before she touched his shoulder, then turned away.

The relief of slipping out of the Great Hall was as palpable as if she'd shed a rain-sodden cloak. As she approached the wide stair-case, her footsteps quickened, skirts whispering against the stone risers as she raced toward the winding corridor that would take her to Fiona's studio.

Upon entry, she felt as if she had stepped into a sanctuary. The air was perfumed with the scent of fine fabrics and warm beeswax from the candles that flickered on every ledge. The dimly lit room was bathed in the soft glow of moonlight that spilled through the leaded windows as Fiona looked up from her work, billows of gold and crimson tulle spilling across her lap. Their elderly friend and mentor, Brigid stood beside Fiona, pinning a skirt hem with deft fingers.

"Ah, Maeve!" Fiona exclaimed, a wide smile blooming on her lips. "Come in! You must tell us everything about your visit home."

"It was like stepping back into a dream," Maeve replied, her spirits lifting in their company. "Nan, Eamon, Loren, my darling Coralie...seeing them all again brought such warmth to my heart."

She watched as a faint pinkness crept over Fiona's cheeks at the mention of Eamon's name.

"Is that a blush I spy, Fiona?" Brigid teased, her brown eyes twinkling with mischief. "Should we expect to be fashioning another gown soon, perhaps one with a bridal train?"

Fiona offered no retort, only a shy smile that spoke volumes. Maeve chuckled, her heart swelling with affection for these women who had become her chosen kin in a world where bloodlines were less binding than the ties they had forged together as they struggled to survive in a world that did not much value the contributions of women. And perhaps in time, she and Alaric could change that, too.

Happy to be away from judging eyes, Maeve trailed her fingers over the sumptuous fabrics that adorned the worktable. Each color and texture was more resplendent than the last. The bolts of silk and satin gleamed with promise, as if somehow aware of the daring purpose she hoped they would soon serve. If Alaric truly wanted change, like he said, then it only seemed fitting that change should begin within the walls of his own kingdom.

"Imagine this, my friends," Maeve said, lifting a roll of deep blue velvet that seemed to drink in the moonlight that bathed the studio, "Swirling around the ballroom floor."

Fiona nodded, her eyes alight with the creative fire that always danced within when she envisioned a new masterpiece. "It will look lovely on you," she said.

"But it will look even lovelier on you." Maeve arched a brow at her friend, delighting in the surprise that lit her gaze.

"On me?"

Maeve nodded. "And this one," she added, lifting a length of gleaming russet taffeta for Brigid's perusal, "will bring out the gold flecks in your big, brown eyes."

Brigid's jaw dropped a little, and she nearly dropped the spool of thread she'd been holding. "Have you gone daft with your transformation, Maeve? Or did you perchance drink too much wine at dinner?"

"I barely had a sip. And I promise you, after seeing my family well and safe, I'm more in possession of my faculties than ever. But you both must come to the ball," she urged, her gaze earnest. "We're announcing our wedding date."

"Of course we'll be there, Maeve. To help out, like we always do," Brigid said.

"I don't want you there hidden behind your trays and aprons, but as my guests—no, as the kindred of my heart."

Brigid's eyebrows arched skyward, a silent gasp parting her lips. "But Maeve, the lines drawn between the working class and the courtiers were set before I was even born. They are not ours to blur."

"Even Alaric agrees that those lines have grown as old and tired as his poison tasters," Maeve countered, her voice soft but her tone fierce. "So let us begin the work of erasing them. Together. And what better a time to usher in change than now, when the world itself is being reborn with the spring?"

Fiona's hands stilled on the fabric, conflict playing across her features.

"Eamon will be there," Maeve teased. "In fact, all of the people from my village have been invited...though so far only Eamon and Loren, and Eamon's father have accepted."

At Maeve's mention of Eamon's attendance, a deep purple glow kindled in Fiona's eyes, as if burning her reluctance to ash. "Very well," she conceded after a pause that stretched like the last note of a lullaby. "I will if you will, Brigid."

"For you, Maeve," Brigid added, "we will be happy to step into your world for a night."

"Excellent!" Maeve said, clapping her hands together. "Now, let us work as a team and weave some dreams with these threads."

Their excited chatter filled the space as Fiona rose, plucked a pencil from her bun, and unfurled a parchment on the work table. Maeve watched, amazed, as her friend's delicate hand danced across it with swift, confident strokes. Soon, three gowns took shape beneath her pencil: Maeve's with a corseted bodice that flowed into a cascade of layered skirts, Fiona's with a simple off-the-shoulder cut that would complement her modest figure, and for Brigid, a high-waisted silhouette that promised both comfort and sophistication.

"Three gowns, with only days to spare?" Brigid said, concern creasing the space between her brows.

Maeve scoffed. "You forget who I was before my hand was claimed by my zombie prince," she replied, pushing up her sleeves. "I've neither forgotten my roots, nor the skill with a needle my Nan taught me. Working together, the three of us can easily conquer time."

A collective determination settled among them, as tangible as the fabrics surrounding them—not just to create gowns, but also brighter futures. Not just for the zombie nobles, but for everyone.

CHAPTER 4

Just a few days later, anticipation hung as heavy as the velvet drapes framing the windows of Fiona's studio.

Maeve watched, overjoyed, as her friends primped for the ball, blossoming before her very eyes. The late afternoon sun spilled through the windows, bathing the room in prisms of color that danced upon the trio of gowns laid out on Fiona's worktable.

With Maeve's help, Fiona stepped into her garment with a reverence usually reserved for sacred rituals. The off-the-shoulder design fell into place, hugging her gentle curves with an intimacy that spoke of stolen kisses and passionate embraces. Its deep sapphire hue seemed to capture the very essence of the midnight sky.

Brigid had outdone herself with the intricate vine-like embroidery that climbed over the gown's bodice, as if coaxing new life from winter's frozen ground. "It's as if the sky itself has lent you her beauty," Maeve stated, fastening the final buttons down Fiona's back.

Brigid, her hands trembling ever so slightly, then slipped into her own masterpiece. A high-waisted dress of russet taffeta, adorned with tiny jet beads that caught the light and mimicked a field of autumn grain strewn with black diamonds. The fabric flowed around her form like water caressing the banks of a generously curved stream.

"Stars have descended just to grace your presence tonight," Maeve teased, smoothing the lines of Brigid's sleeves as if she could press confidence into them.

Maeve then turned to face the mirror, allowing her own transformation to take shape. Her gown was a layered vision composed of pale, icy purples, echoing the softness of twilight. A corseted silver bodice cinched her waist, while the diaphanous layers of her skirt cascaded down, each one a silent testimony to the long nights the women had spent under the watchful eye of moonlight, needles and thread flying in their busy hands.

With tender care, they adorned each other's hair. Fiona wove delicate braids into Maeve's gleaming locks, intertwining them with amethyst diamantes that echoed the tears of joy and sorrow shed during her recent past. Maeve, in turn, crowned Fiona's soft, brown waves with a golden circlet of twisted vines, as a symbol of her growing strength. Brigid chose simplicity, a beaded golden bloom placed behind her ear—its color a perfect echo of the warm sparks that now lit her brown eyes.

"Just look at us, all fancy-like," Fiona breathed out, a soft smile gracing her lips as they stood shoulder to shoulder before the grandeur of the floor-length mirrors.

"Once bound by our respective roles, now here we stand, poised to rewrite the stars," Maeve said.

"Indeed," Brigid chimed in, her voice steady, yet tinged with the weight of too many dark moments already lived and the brighter ones yet to come. "Tonight, we are neither defined by birth nor station, but by the courage to undertake an unknown dance."

They regarded one another, not just as women with disparate pasts, but as kindred spirits united beneath the banner of impending change—a change they would herald with every step they took on this enchanted evening.

"Now, it is time," Maeve said, her voice ringing with a determination that belied her fluttering heart. "We shall attend the ball, not as mere participants, but as tokens of a new dawn that will recognize neither the lineage of blood nor the pallor of undeath."

THE GRAND STAIRCASE flowed before the three women like a gleaming river of marble, each step a ripple that would lead them closer to the resplendent ballroom below. Arm in arm, Maeve, Fiona, and Brigid descended, their gowns rustling with every step. As they entered the grand ballroom, the music trailed off, and a sea of scoffs rolled through the throng of aristocratic onlookers; their gazes widened at these women who would dare defy the confines of their stations.

"Chins up, shoulders back," Maeve whispered to her trembling companions. "No matter how much the courtiers stare, remember that this castle is as much your home as it is theirs."

The ballroom itself was a vision of opulence. Crystal chandeliers illuminated the shocked faces of the impeccably dressed zombie aristocrats. Their finery was unmatched, save for the waitstaff and the poison taster who, clad in somber tuxedos, stood over an expansive display of finger foods, petit fours, and too many wines and softer beverages to count.

As the three women moved deeper into the room, the music resumed, rising and falling with the grace of moonflower petals pirouetting on the wind.

Eamon, his gaze alight with recognition, navigated the currents of aristocrats and what few humans had been brave enough to enter Prince Alaric's kingdom until he reached Fiona's side. With a bow that spoke of a bygone era, he offered her his hand. "May I have this dance, milady?"

Fiona, her cheeks blooming with the tender flush of renewed life, nodded as she handed her beaded reticule off to Brigid and placed her hand in his. Together, they moved onto the dance floor, their careful steps like a new map being drawn beneath the watchful eyes of history.

Not far from them, Loren's father, the village's new mayor, approached Brigid with a courteous nod. "Would you honor me with a dance?" he asked, extending a hand that bridged the divide between their worlds.

With a grace born from newfound confidence, Brigid passed Fiona's clutch to Maeve and accepted, allowing herself to be swept onto the dance floor.

Maeve felt Alaric's presence before she saw him, his hand finding the small of her back with a familiarity that sent ripples of pleasure coursing through her. "You are truly a vision, my little troublemaker," he whispered, his lips brushing her ear.

"Are you put out with me?" she asked as she leaned back into the circle of his arms. "For asking my friends to join us as guests instead of staff?"

"To the contrary, my love. What you just did was beyond brilliant, the work of a born diplomat. And tonight, I count myself the luckiest man in all the world for having chosen you as my bride."

"And lucky for you, I chose you in return." A mischievous smile danced upon Maeve's lips as she passed the items she held off to a waiter. Alaric spun her about to face him and led her into the waltz, their graceful movements testifying to their love that had rooted in the most intolerant of soils. As she caught glimpses of her friends in the arms of their partners, laughter spilling from their lips and their hands entwined with those they once thought of as enemies, Maeve's spirits lifted.

Her new world was now also their world. Everything was like clay in her and Alaric's hands, ready to be molded into whatever shape they chose.

The music paused, and the ballroom fell still as a forgotten graveyard as Alaric took Maeve by the hand and led her to the same pedestal where he'd announced their engagement just a few months past. The sounds of shushes and spoons clinking against crystal goblets filled the air as Prince Alaric raised their locked hands before the crowd, the verdant stone in Maeve's betrothal ring twinkling like the Northern Lights beneath the chandeliers.

Alaric's baritone voice, clear and resonant, soon rose to fill the expansive space. "I'm happy to announce that on the spring solstice, Maeve and myself shall be wed in the gardens where we first professed our love to each other. But know that ours will not be a traditional marriage. Maeve shall be a working royal and rule beside me as my equal in all things. Now let us all pray that our unexpected union will herald a new era where peace might someday reign between humans and zombie-kind."

The zombie courtiers and human guests listened, their expressions shocked but rapt, as Alaric and Maeve's hopes for the future unfurled from their prince's lips. His melodic voice wove an impassioned vision of hope where love would intertwine with duty, and consideration for the common good would sow the seeds of peace. Yet as he finished his speech and took Maeve's hand, a deep wave of foreboding nearly dropped her to her knees, and she found herself leaning into him for support. She'd never considered herself prone to premonitions, but the sensation was too real, too confounding for her to dismiss as a mere case of the nerves.

As she sought to steady herself, the grandeur of the ball ebbed to a hush as Alaric, resplendent in his princely attire, raised his goblet high. Maeve's trembling fingers clutched her own, the cool leaded crystal heavy, yet comforting in her grasp. The waiter who had delivered the goblets hovered at the periphery for a moment, then faded into the shadows.

"To an undying love that will bridge our worlds," Alaric proclaimed. Maeve's heart took flight, her intrusive dark thoughts defeated by the beautiful dream they had woven from their entwined fates.

After clinking their goblets together, they both drank. Heartily.

But soon after the second sip of wine kissed Alaric's lips, a deep shudder wracked his frame. His eyes, once brimming with passion, widened and clouded with horror. Maeve watched, helpless, as his hand found his throat and his body sagged, crumpling to the ground like a stone tower besieged by cannon fire.

"Alaric!" Her voice tore through the stunned silence, frantic and shrill. She was at his side in an instant, his head cradled in her lap, the frigid marble floor beneath them forgotten. Onlookers moved in and encircled them, creating a tight ring of shock and confusion.

"Dr. Reinhart! Please. Someone must fetch him now!" she screamed into the void of faces. But no one moved. They were too paralyzed by the horrific spectacle unfolding before them.

"The prince has fallen," someone finally shouted from the crowd. As Maeve stroked her beloved's mahogany hair, his body stiffened as if gripped by an invisible vise. His breaths came in thin gasps, each a ghostly whisper against the din created by her own blood pounding in her ears.

"My father...the king," he managed. "Only he knows the cure..." His voice was thin as parchment and nearly lost amidst the din of the crowd. "Must find... antidote... by the next full moon... or will sleep... forever..."

"Sleep?" Maeve's mind reeled. "No! This eternal nap shall not spirit you away from me. I promise you, my love, I will find him and cut the cure from him with my dagger if need be. I swear it to you, on every star that shines down on us."

"Careful... enemies... still out there..." His urgent warning hovered between them like a malevolent spirit, and she knew he was speaking of his former advisor, Lysander, who had been missing these many months.

"Would Lysander do this to you?" Her question was one without an answer. Alaric's gaze had turned inward, his struggle to breathe visible in the tightening of his jaw, the sickly blue-black tinge that bruised his lips.

"Guards!" A strident voice pierced the shocked whispers of the onlookers. "The humans, Eamon and Loren, were seen lurking around the wine table just before the toast!"

"Liars!" Maeve's protest went unheard as several guards descended on the two men. With his captor's hands firm on his shoulders, Eamon's eyes met Maeve's, brimming with questions and fear, while Loren stood silent, resignation to his fate etched upon his dark brow.

"Please, let no harm come to them," Maeve cried. "For I have known these men since childhood, and they are innocent." When her plea was ignored, she dissolved into sobs as she watched her dear friends, their futures being rewritten by unfounded suspicions borne from prejudice. Now, they were being dragged away from the light and into the shadow-shrouded corridor. Where they would be taken from there, she had no way of knowing. *Please don't let it be the guillotine...*

"Come now, dear Maeve." Fiona's gentle touch offered Maeve a lifeline as she and Brigid, with tears staining their faces, tried to raise her from Alaric's still form.

But no matter how hard her friends tried to pry her from him, she resisted, refusing to yield because she was not ready to leave him. "Alaric, please hold on for me," she whispered, her lips brushing his as she vowed to find the truth and heal the gaping wound this night had torn open.

But her refusal proved futile. Soon, the horrified entourage made the silent march to Alaric's chambers, the stretcher bearing his unconscious form borne by several grim-faced zombies. The echoes of their footfalls rang through the corridors like a death knell for the peaceful promise that now seemed as fragile as the gossamer layers of Maeve's gown.

As they drew near his chamber, she realized that her beloved was paying the toll for the hatred that had festered between their worlds for so long. And she found it ironic that she had only begun to practice those qualities she once relied upon to define humanity after she herself became what many would call a beast.

CHAPTER 5

Shadows hovered like the grim reaper at the edges of Alaric's room as Dr. Reinhart rushed into the prince's chambers. "Miss Maeve," he said, his eyes veiled, "I've come to help our prince."

Maeve stood by the window, wringing her hands, her gaze never leaving Alaric's deathly still form upon the bed they had shared these many months. "Please, you must do something to help him," she begged.

With a heavy, almost impatient chuff, the grim-faced doctor moved to Alaric's bedside and began his examination, his skilled hands moving methodically over the prince's deathly still body.

Moments groaned by until Dr. Reinhart heaved a long sigh and lifted his fingers from the soft of Alaric's inner wrist. Finally, he turned toward Maeve, his face a mask of somberness, his hands tightly clasped behind his back as he bowed. "I wish I had better news for you, Maeve," he said, his voice somber. "As I feared, the prince shows every sign of being in a deep coma."

"But can it be reversed?"

He shook his head. "At the moment, his prognosis is quite dire. If we can't find the formula to the antidote before the next full moon rises, Prince Alaric will never wake. And even should he be roused, you might find him quite...different."

"Different? How?" Maeve pushed past the misery constricting her throat.

The doctor moved closer to Maeve and settled a hand on her shoulder, his eyes downcast with professional empathy. "According to historical records, in some cases, patients who received the antidote returned to consciousness in an...impenetrable haze. Others woke to a mental state...not unlike that of the ferals."

"No. Please! You can't let that happen...not to Alaric."

"I promise, Maeve, I will do everything in my power to keep him safe and comfortable. But the sooner the antidote is administered, the lesser are his chances for suffering...a significant mental decay."

"Were that to happen, would there be any way to mitigate the damage?"

"I'm afraid at that point, immediate euthanasia would be our only merciful—and safe—option. So much so that the Prince has signed the order into his last will and testament."

Maeve's breath hitched, fresh tears burning at the corners of her eyes. She swallowed hard, trying to maintain her composure, but this rapidly changing reality was too much to bear. The dam burst, her shoulders shaking as she sank to the floor, violent sobs racking her body.

Dr. Reinhart hesitated for a moment before kneeling next to her and placing an awkward but comforting hand on her shoulder.

Maeve lifted her tear-stained face to look at him, searching his gaunt features for any glimmer of hope. "Is there anything more you can do for him? Perhaps there's something helpful recorded in all those old journals I saw in the laboratory. Something that might even give you a clue as to the antidote?" But even as she spoke the words, she knew she was grasping at straws.

The doctor's eyes shuttered as he shook his head. "I've already decided to consult with my colleagues, but unfortunately, coming up with any worthy avenues for research will take time." He paused, then added, "But Maeve, I take my role in seeing to the prince's well-being very seriously. You have my solemn promise, I won't give up on curing him. My assistants and I will keep searching and experimenting until someone tells me they've found it, or they've at least found something that stands even the slimmest chance of mitigating our prince's fate."

Maeve nodded, trying to find some solace in the physician's determination. She returned to the bed and bent over Alaric, gently caressing his fevered cheek. Seeing him like this sank daggers in her heart. His skin was clammy, his body still and vulnerable. Gone was the capable, kind soul she had fallen in love with, always brimming with plans to bring his lofty dream of peace to fruition.

This time, as her tears began to fall, she saw no point in trying to stave them off. Nan had told her once that the gods counted the tears of women as the most precious amongst petitions. Would that now, as a zombie, the gods she hadn't prayed to since she was a child were still keeping count. For Alaric, Eamon, Loren, and yes, even she needed their divine grace now more than ever.

ONCE DR. REINHART took his leave, Maeve found herself alone with Alaric. Not knowing any other way to comfort him, she crawled into the bed beside him, her limbs trembling as she clung to his lifeless form.

In the corner of the room, the wedding gown Fiona had so painstakingly crafted stood on a dress form, its delicate lace and symbolic embroidery seeming to mock her. Where once it had shimmered with promises of a brighter future for all, it now stood as a visible reminder of all her and Alaric's shattered dreams. Without him and his grand vision, the world was doomed.

Tears streamed down her cheeks as she buried her face in the deep well between his pectoral muscles. "I feel like my life truly began the moment you lifted me from that snake pit," she said, her voice cracking with emotion. "But now, Alaric, your absence has already filled me with terror. Your subjects still distrust me, as do my own people. And I don't know if I'm strong enough or brave enough to stitch the world back together on my own."

Until now, she hadn't known that it was their love that gave her the strength to fight even when defeat seemed imminent. "Now...the thought of never looking into your beautiful eyes again fills me with dread. More than I ever even knew was possible."

As she uttered those words, she realized the enormity of the task before her—a task that she would have to undertake without the tireless support of her beloved partner. With nothing more for her to do, she held him as close as she was able, willing herself to draw upon the memories of their magical time together, praying that somehow those memories would fortify her as she searched for the means to save him before it was too late.

SHOUTS AND CLATTERING armor roused Maeve from the restless slumber she'd fallen into as she lay with Alaric. Her eyes opened upon a snowy owl perched on the windowsill, looking at her as if he was about to speak. Wondering if she was the same owl she had seen Alaric watching, or if she was perhaps hallucinating, she reluctantly disentangled herself from Alaric's unmoving form and moved towards the window, her heart quivering in her chest. As she approached, the owl startled and took flight. But perhaps it was the events taking place outside that he had wished to call her attention to.

The courtyard below was a scene of chaos. The zombie guards

fought amongst themselves, their snarls and growls echoing through the air, while others mounted zombie horses and charged toward the open castle gates.

"Alaric, what is happening to your kingdom?" she whispered, her voice barely audible above the din. Her eyes darted around the grounds, searching for some semblance of order, but all she saw was a rapidly escalating conflict. With Alaric lost in slumber, it seemed as if more than just the fragile truce between humans and zombies was beginning to unravel. Now zombies fought against zombies. But why?

She paced the room, her despair deepening with each step. She was only one person... a female one at that. How could she possibly command the gravitas she would need to hold Alaric's kingdom together without him standing by her side? Nor did she yet have the power of a crown behind her.

The pain of his absence bore down on her, an immense, crushing force. As she struggled to make sense of it all, a knock on the door startled her out of her thoughts.

"Come in," she called out, her voice tight with trepidation.

The door creaked open, and Maeve's relief rode out with the breath she'd been holding as Brigid slipped inside. Upon seeing Maeve's tear-streaked face, the elderly woman rushed forward and enfolded her in a warm embrace. For several moments, Maeve could only cling to her, sobbing uncontrollably.

"Shh, shush now, my dear," Brigid said, her hands gently stroking Maeve's hair.

"I feel like I have failed him," she finally managed. "I should have insisted he let the poison testers continue with their task."

"Poppycock. Nobody ever told the prince how to do anything and got away with it. But Alaric does not ally himself with failures. He chose you as his betrothed because he knew you were strong and compassionate, and capable of facing any challenge that came your way. And he's relying on those qualities in you now more than ever."

Maeve sniffled and wiped her tears, trying to find solace in her beloved mentor's words. "And what has become of Eamon and Loren?" she asked, her voice quivering. "H-have you heard anything?"

"Imprisoned in the West Tower," Brigid replied, a cloud of sadness dimming her eyes. "The rumor is that they will remain there until their trial."

"And when will that be?" she asked, knowing that Lady Elora's trial still had not taken place, though she had been arrested for her crimes months ago.

"Not until Alaric awakens, or a proxy is installed in his stead," Brigid answered solemnly.

"A *proxy*?" Maeve forced down a fresh rising of panic. The thought of someone else ruling in Alaric's place made her heart constrict with fresh pain, but she knew that Brigid was right. Now was not the time to allow herself even a moment's weakness. If she meant to see Alaric restored to health, she must keep her focus fixed on the present crisis. "Alaric's kingdom needs him," she said, her voice stronger than before. "For him, I will find the strength to find the antidote, even when it feels like an insurmountable task."

Brigid smiled gently, her eyes filled with pride. "There's the brave girl we all know and love. And I have no doubt you will succeed, Maeve. You still carry within you the love you share with Alaric and the level-headed wisdom your Nan gave you. That is all you will need to help you overcome any obstacle that arises in your path."

Love was always the answer that poured from people's lips during times like these, but Maeve still had her doubts. As the chaos continued to unfold outside, she took a deep breath and locked her emotions into the depths of her soul.

For Alaric's sake, for their love, their future, and both of their peoples, that's where they must remain until she persevered in the enormous task ahead. This time, as her gaze sought out her wedding dress, it did not mock her. Instead, it glimmered with the promise of fresh hope.

The candles had burned down to wax stubs, and the restless

shadows cast by the faltering light seemed like hungry succubae eager to pounce. Yet Brigid still lingered. As the clash of arms drifted through the window, she looked at Brigid with pleading eyes, desperate for answers as to what had caused the ruckus, but Brigid's gaze quickly ducked away from hers.

"Something is afoot that you have not yet told me about," Maeve said, not quite understanding how she knew the words she had just spoken were true.

"It is just men being men and of no particular importance." Brigid waved off her concerns, but her expression darkened as her gaze shifted toward the window overlooking the disturbance taking place in the courtyard.

"Then why are the guards out in the courtyard, brandishing arms as they fight amongst themselves? Have the ferals returned?"

"Seal your lips before you conjure them!"

"Then what has them so agitated?"

Brigid hesitated for a moment and then heaved a world-weary sigh. "Don't you think you've troubles enough without borrowing more?"

"Not when those troubles sound like fresh unrest has been seeded within my betrothed's kingdom. So I must ask again, what is it all about?"

Brigid dropped her gaze, her hands twisting the fabric of her apron. "When the zombie guards went to imprison Eamon and Loren, they discovered something quite... unexpected."

Maeve tilted her head as she studied her friend. It wasn't like the woman to be evasive unless the news she bore was quite dire. "U-unexpected? How so?" she managed, though she, too, wondered whether her heart could bear any more blows this night.

"One of the cooks heard that while the chamber where Lady Elora was being held was still locked, she was no longer inside."

"Did they take her somewhere else? Or did someone suddenly realize she was the most likely culprit behind Alaric's fall and schedule her well-deserved execution?"

Brigid shook her head. "Without a trial? Of course not. Everyone knows Alaric would never have allowed such a thing."

"Then where is she, Brigid?"

"That's just it, Maeve. Nobody knows. It was as if she had faded into the walls like a phantom, leaving both her shackles and the padlocked door behind her."

"You are telling me Elora has magically vanished like a ghost? Yet Eamon and Loren are still being charged with Alaric's poisoning?" Maeve's voice was shrill, her soul shattering anew with each word.

"I'm afraid so," Brigid continued, though her expression suggested she'd rather hurl herself out the windows than divulge any more details.

"Brigid! Please do not mince words with me. You must tell me everything you know about what has happened."

"Some... not all, mind you... of the zombies suspect that you might have put Eamon and Loren up to poisoning Alaric. And that you are also the one who ordered Lady Elora's release."

Maeve gasped, unable to believe what she just heard. "To what end? Have they forgotten it was Elora who kidnapped Coralie, then tried to kill both Alaric and myself?"

"They have convinced themselves it was a tangled truce you and Elora forged to gain control of Alaric's kingdom. They offer the times they saw you conversing with her in the garden long after midnight as their proof."

"Have they forgotten Elora despises everything about me? And the only thing she loathes more than me is humanity. She would never in a million years try to enjoin me in one of her schemes. And it would seem to me that if Alaric's subjects were so desperate to brand a culprit, they would look to none other than Lysander. He was likely in cahoots with her and has been missing for months." Maeve rose from Alaric's bed and began pacing the floor, wringing her hands.

"Try not to fret, Maeve. Hatred is born from fear, and right now, nobody fears more than Alaric's courtiers. They were quite content with the status quo. But now, they accuse everyone and everything.

Even the guards who are sworn to protect us all are out there, fighting amongst each other."

Maeve's eyes filled with tears once more, and she returned to sit on the edge of Alaric's bed, her face buried in her hands as new hopelessness threatened to overwhelm her. "By agreeing to marry Alaric, I have caused nothing but trouble for everyone. The distance between humans and zombies has never felt greater. And if not for having rescued me, then fallen in love with me, Alaric might never have been poisoned in the first place."

"Please, Maeve," Brigid implored softly, a note of desperation in her voice. "You mustn't blame yourself for this. You couldn't have known when you fell in love with Alaric that any of this would come to pass. You just loved him."

Maeve shook her head, her sobs echoing in the vaulted ceiling above. Through her tears, she whispered, "Perhaps Alaric chose poorly. I do not know if I am strong enough to hold his kingdom together, much less two warring worlds. Certainly not when my focus must be on finding the antidote in time to save him."

"Listen to me, and listen well," Brigid said, her tone firm yet gentle. "You will tend to first things first. Alaric chose you because he saw something in you that you still fail to see in yourself. You are more than just his lover. Your love has remolded you into a fearsome warrior who can fight both beside him, and in his absence, for him. But now it is time for you to rise up and embrace the woman fate always meant you to become."

Maeve met Brigid's gaze, her eyes raw and stinging. As she struggled to connect with the warrior Brigid insisted Alaric always saw in her, the enormity of what lay ahead pressed down on her chest. The fate of a prince, his kingdom, and even her own village now rested in her hands. All the while, the ferals still lurked at the edges of Alaric's world, waiting for their next strike. And now, with Elora lurking out there...and Lysander, Maeve knew that strike would not be long in coming.

But no matter how daunting the task before her, losing Alaric meant losing everything and everyone she loved. So once again, fate had rewritten her path, and her story had changed. And the only one who could write its ending was her.

"Thank you, Brigid," she managed, wiping her tears away and summoning every ounce of courage she could muster. "I will not let him down. I will find the antidote and in doing so, prove true his belief that love can overcome any obstacle."

And because she loved him in return, she would do so, even if she didn't quite believe mere love could cure anything.

As Brigid nodded in quiet encouragement, Maeve pressed a kiss to Alaric's forehead and steeled herself for the challenges that awaited her.

Brigid reached out, settling a comforting hand on her shoulder, anchoring her with a warmth that seemed almost foreign. "Remember how much you've already done for everyone," Brigid urged. "You have already brought humans and zombies closer together than we ever imagined possible."

Maeve's mood was momentarily brightened by the memories of her past triumphs—the cheers of the village soldiers when she and Alaric returned to the castle, victorious over Elora and the zombie hordes that had threatened their very existence. She recalled the poor tributaries, once held captive by Elora, now freed and reunited with their loved ones.

"I cannot imagine a world without you as my friend, Brigid," Maeve said, her voice stronger than before. "I will do my best to remember your words."

"Good," Brigid replied, a small smile ghosting her lips. "Now, you need your rest, for tomorrow, you must face the challenges that lie ahead."

"Promise you will always watch over him when I cannot?" she said, twisting her betrothal ring around her finger.

"Of course, my child. The prince is like a son to me." With a final embrace, Brigid bid Maeve goodnight and left the chamber.

As Maeve gazed into the last candle's weak flame, the shadows seemed to feel a little less predatory. She lay against Alaric's side, her body pressed against his silent form. As the candle sputtered and died, moonlight streamed through the window, casting an almost ethereal light on the chamber.

Her gaze drifted to the corner of the room where her wedding gown waited. Maeve's eyelids grew heavy, and she allowed herself to be enveloped by sleep, her hand resting gently on Alaric's still chest.

In her slumber, she dreamt of their wedding day. The scene was as vibrant as life, every detail etched in her mind's eye. Beneath a flower-strewn arbor, Alaric stood tall and proud, his face radiating dewy-eyed joy as he beheld Maeve in her wedding dress. Flanking him were Nan, Fiona, and Coralie in her pink flower girl gown. Even Eamon and Loren were dressed in their finest garb, acting as Alaric's best men. All the while, the snowy owl she had caught Alaric admiring soared overhead, as if their very spirits were joined.

As the first light of dawn crept into the room, she awoke, feeling as though Alaric had sent her the dream as a reminder of what they were fighting for. She turned to him, her heart swelling with renewed intent as she twisted her betrothal ring off her finger and slipped it onto his pinky for safekeeping.

"I must go now, my love, and I cannot know where this day will take me. But know I will do whatever it takes to save you," she whispered before pressing a tender kiss upon his pale, parched lips.

Maeve rose from the bed and dressed with care, each movement filled with purpose. She returned to Alaric's side and spoke softly, her voice shaking with conviction. "For now, I will conduct business as usual in your stead. Rest well, knowing that I will not let your kingdom falter."

With one last look at her beloved, she left the chamber, her footsteps echoing down the hallway as she headed towards the great hall where breakfast would soon be served. She knew most of the courtiers would not be happy to see her, but it was time they learned to at least tolerate her presence amongst them.

CHAPTER 6

The great hall's vaulted ceiling echoed with the shushes and whispers of the zombie aristocrats as Maeve stepped through the expansive room's double doors. Their disdain for her presence was palpable as she lifted her chin, crossed the room, and took her usual seat. She held back tears as she noted the empty chair beside her—Alaric's chair. As she pressed her palm on its elegantly carved arm, where just yesternight, her beloved's arm had rested, she struggled to master her reeling emotions.

The zombie courtiers simply stared. Most of their faces were expressionless, but a few risked glaring at her, their eyes narrowed with disdain. The fire in the hearth was roaring, making the air feel hot and oppressive. As the meal began, the zombies' silence remained thick, punctuated only by the occasional clink of silverware against porcelain.

"Do any of you know where I might find King Caligula?" Maeve asked, already growing impatient with this charade of normalcy. Though she tried to maintain a brave face, her voice trembled as she spoke, turning traitor against her desire to appear more composed than she felt. And in that moment, she hated herself for her show of feminine weakness. Alaric deserved better than this. He deserved the warrior his love had awakened within her. But it seemed that part of her had fallen asleep alongside him.

"Please, I must find him," she begged of the courtier, Lord Theodor, seated in the chair beside her. The gaunt man shifted uncomfortably, his watery gaze evading hers as he stared into his plate and mumbled something unintelligible. As she turned her gaze to another, he simply stared blankly ahead, as if she had never spoken at all.

The courtiers' cold detachment sat on Maeve's chest like a marble slab. They knew as well as she that Alaric's time for being cured was running out; that she had to locate his father and obtain the antidote that could save him. Her heart ached at the thought of Alaric, all alone in his chambers, lying unconscious and vulnerable, his vivacious intellect hanging by a thread. But if his subjects loved him so much, like they said, why would they not help her to help their prince?

"Please," she implored, desperation creeping into her voice. "You all know why it is imperative I find the king as soon as possible."

"Your persistence is... noted," one courtier finally deigned to say. "But we do not feel you are the right person to be entrusted with so... momentous a task. We have spoken of this matter between ourselves and have resolved to assemble a team of our own kind to obtain the cure."

"But I am your kind now."

"Yet you still consort with humans."

Maeve's stomach churned, utter helplessness threatening to defeat her. She could not, would not give up, not when Alaric's life might depend on her keeping the promise he'd made her swear to him as the poison had worked its wicked magic.

With a disgusted sigh, she rose from the table and left the Great Hall, pacing the castle's corridors until she found herself taking refuge in Alaric's library. Perhaps here, within one of the many volumes, she might discover the King's location. As her eyes scoured the shelves, looking for a likely starting point, her eyes lit on the hearth—and then the hidden keystone she and Alaric had used to enter the catacombs where the laboratory was situated.

That was when she realized she might yet have one ally within this kingdom's walls who would be, if not eager, at least willing to tell her the King's location—Dr. Reinhart. For was it not his duty to see to the prince's wellbeing?

"Ah, Lady Maeve," Dr. Reinhart's wizened face radiated the recognition Maeve craved as she entered the laboratory. "I am glad you are here, he said. There is something I wish to show you."

"Is it something that could cure Alaric?" she asked, a fragile thread of hope trying to stitch her tattered heart back together.

"Not yet, dear, but I assure you, we are leaving no stone unturned."

"Then what did you wish to show me?"

"Something I hope will reassure you that Prince Alaric will receive the utmost care during his slumber." He placed his hand on the small of her back and steered her deeper into the laboratory. "In that vein, we have developed this..."

The doctor gestured towards a long, glass capsule. Though his wizened features radiated pride, the capsule's resemblance to a coffin unraveled Maeve's frayed hopes. As her knees softened, she couldn't suppress the violent shudder that racked her body. "Gods, is this your way of telling me Alaric is doomed?"

As Doctor Reinhart noted the tears winding down Maeve's cheeks, surprise registered on his features. "Maeve, please know my intent was not to alarm you. I never considered the pod's appearance might cause you distress," he said. "The capsule was explicitly designed to support Alaric's bodily functions in his... fragile state."

The doctor took a moment to show Maeve how the capsule would provide Alaric air and control his body temperature while he slumbered. "In this way, we believe we can help prevent the prince from suffering any significant... cognitive decline. And with your permission, I intend to have it moved to his chambers and place him inside within the hour."

Maeve nodded her understanding. "Thank you," she managed, her voice still wavering slightly. "It is a brilliant invention. And it will be much easier to leave him knowing he is in such capable hands."

The elderly man's scruffy brows shot up. "You are leaving him?"

Maeve's nod was grim. "You know it's not by choice. And I had planned to leave this morning. But now the courtiers do not trust me to see this task through and refuse to tell me the king's location."

"I don't understand. They, too, would benefit from the prince's cure."

"Yet instead of aiding me in finding the king, as was Alaric's last wish before he fell under the poison's spell, they aim to send their own team after the antidote. Given all that's happened, I cannot trust them with this task any more than they do me. That makes you the only one left who might be willing to tell me the king's location."

Dr. Reinhart hung his head. "I am afraid I cannot help you, either."

"But why not?"

"Because I don't know, Maeve. And Alaric would have my head on a platter if he knew something I said sent you off on a wild goose chase that put you in danger."

"Can you at least hazard a guess?"

"All I have heard are rumors passed amongst the staff. But I am afraid I cannot confirm any of them with any degree of certainty."

"But surely yourself and Alaric have spoken of his father's location?"

His features turned grim as he shook his head. "My primary concern was with Prince Alaric's physical well-being and leading his research team. I've never been one for chitchat, so our discussions were limited to his health and scientific matters."

Maeve's gaze lingered for a moment on the glass capsule. Tears beaded on her lashes as she realized how much it resembled an image from the last fairy story Alaric had read to her about a princess cursed to sleep forever unless she received a kiss born from true love. The irony that Alaric's welfare now depended on what could pass for the glass coffin that held the slumbering princess further darkened her thoughts. But if love could truly save them, as Alaric insisted, of that she had plenty. She should not discount its power to move mountains. "Doctor, if you cannot tell me where the King is, do you perhaps know anyone who can?"

The doctor's brow furrowed for a moment. "There is someone amongst us who may know—the crone sage."

"And does this crone sage have a name?"

The doctor nodded. "Those few who dare to address her at all now call her Lady Isolde. And as one of the original zombies, she knew the king quite well. You will not find anyone who understands the history of the first outbreak better than her, and she will spend countless hours ensuring anyone who calls on her knows it, too."

"Lady Isolde?" Maeve echoed, her curiosity piqued. "Why have I not heard of her before?" Female zombies were a rarity, and stood out amongst the courtiers like the proverbial sore thumb. She found it hard to believe one dwelled here who she hadn't seen at least once.

"Because, like myself, she chooses to remain unencumbered by... social attachments," the doctor explained cautiously. "The crone is reclusive, prone to visions, and prefers the company of books, plants, and her cats to most people. For those reasons, some call her a witch and shun her. Unless she thinks she has foreseen events we all need to know about, she has little to do with us. However, Alaric is the one exception. She is quite fond of him, and I expect she might give you the king's location if you can convince her you truly have his best interests at heart."

Maeve felt the thrill of real hope spark within her. "And where might I find this woman... Isolde?"

"*Lady* Isolde makes her home in what used to be an old chapel situated against the back wall of the castle grounds," Dr. Reinhart said, pointing towards a distant corner of the castle.

"Thank you," Maeve replied, drawing the doctor into a hug. Because of him, the prospect of finding Alaric's father and the antidote felt almost possible.

CHAPTER 7

When knocking yielded no results, Maeve pushed open the ancient doors of the vine-shrouded chapel, her heart quivering in her chest as she peered into Isolde's dim sanctuary. A hazy light filtered through the dirty stained glass windows, painting a colorful but muted mosaic on the rough-hewn floorboards. The air was laced with the scents of herbs and incense, a heady mix that made Maeve feel a bit dizzy as she ventured deeper into the repurposed chapel.

"Lady Isolde?" she called out softly. Though she'd barely whispered, her voice rang out like a bell's chime in the cavernous space, but was quickly swallowed by walls adorned with tapestries depicting figures from a religion long forgotten. No answer came forth, and for a moment, Maeve wondered if she was alone in this strange place.

But then a cat meowed near the altar, and a gasp grated over her lips as she saw her. The elderly zombie sat in an ornate chair, a large book resting in her lap. The way her head was bowed made Maeve think she must be sleeping.

A zombie cat, its orange fur littered with scars but still oddly beautiful, purred contentedly as it nestled against her booted feet. As Maeve cleared her throat and stepped nearer, the cat hissed. Lady Isolde's eyes opened, and her nearly colorless stare pierced holes in Maeve's soul.

Even in her advanced age, the woman was an arresting figure, with remnants of her former beauty still visible in her elegantly chiseled jawline and the gleaming silver curls that tumbled over her shoulders. Her bohemian clothing, composed of a hodgepodge of textures and tatter-saw layers, suggested she wasn't the sort of woman who gave a damn about keeping up with the elegant fashions deemed suitable for a courtier. The dagger handle protruding from the top of her boot reinforced that notion. Several ornate bracelets were stacked on her wrists, and every one of her gnarled fingers was graced with enormous, golden rings. The roughly faceted crystals and odd symbols that spangled her jewelry hinted she was knowledgeable in ancient wisdom that went far beyond her actual years.

"Who goes there?" she demanded, her hand reaching for her dagger. Her hardened jaw suggested she was less than pleased to have company.

Maeve bowed her head and remembered to curtsy.

"For the love of the gods, stand up straight so I can hear when you tell me your name," Isolde rasped.

"I-I am called Maeve, and Prince Alaric has claimed me as his b-betrothed," she said, hating how anxiety made her voice crack.

For a long moment, the woman looked over every inch of her. "The prince always did have a fondness for redheads," she said. "Perhaps the only trait he inherited from his father. But as you will quickly learn, prettiness buys you nothing in this world. And you hardly look big enough to carry a candlestick, much less attempt to bear the prince an heir. Is that what you are after? A potion to help you conceive?"

"Of course not," Maeve said, the corners of her mouth turning down with distaste. "The last thing I need is to carry a malformed child to term when it has little to no hope of survival."

"That at least shows you are smarter and more compassionate than most who seek me out. But you still haven't told me what brought you here. Has the prince strayed from your bed already? Or is it a love potion you seek? Because you won't find that sort of silliness here. Matters of the shallow-hearted and feeble-minded hold little interest for me."

"Lucky for us both, that is not why I have come. I am here because I need your help in other...more pressing...matters. And Doctor Rinehart assured me you were the only person who might have the information I seek."

"Pfft. That heartless old geezer should have known better. It was doctors and men of science who aspired to be like gods that brought the blight upon our world. As for the king, may he rot forever in the stew of his own making. Now leave me be, child. My time is not to be wasted on the trifling worries of a dreamy-eyed girl who is hardly old enough to be cut free from her mother's apron strings." She waved Maeve off with a dismissive flick of her bejeweled wrist and returned her attention to her book.

Maeve clenched her fists and stood her ground, fighting back tears. "My mother was killed by feral zombies before I could crawl. And my reason for coming here only to be insulted is no trifling matter. Furthermore, it is not I who needs your help. It is Prince Alaric himself."

Isolde slammed her book closed, her brows lofting with interest as she leaned forward. "What goes with the prince that he would not seek my counsel himself?"

"I'm sorry to report he has been... poisoned."

The crone's face blanched an impossible shade lighter as her eyes grew moist. "I feared something horrible might befall him, but poisoned? By whom?"

"Nobody knows for certain. Given Lady Elora went missing from her cell last night, that is where my suspicions lie. But before someone else tells you, you should know some of the courtiers suspect I had something to do with it."

"So you are both smart and honest. And did you conspire to have him poisoned?"

Maeve shook her head. "I swear to you, I did not. And if I did, I certainly would not be seeking an audience with a zombie who is also, by all appearances, some kind of... sorceress. But before Alaric lost consciousness, he made me promise I would find his father and secure the antidote."

"So why waste your time seeking the company of a batty old witch when you could be doing as the prince bade you?"

"Because nobody will tell me the king's location. Will you please aid me with the information I need to find him?"

Isolde hesitated, her gaze lingering on Maeve's face. Though tears still traced her cheeks, she did not move to brush them away. Seconds stretched into minutes while Maeve endured the old woman's icy perusal. The longer she stared at Maeve, the harder her face seemed to grow, as if she, too, had gauged Maeve's fealty to Alaric and found it lacking. It wasn't until one of the cats moved toward Maeve and began to weave between her ankles, purring loudly, that the hardness in Isolde's expression wavered.

"Please," Maeve said as she lifted the black cat into her arms and stroked the soft, velvety space between its ears. "Alaric will sleep forever if I cannot find the antidote in time. And if that should come to pass... I think I might rather drink poison myself than endure another day without looking into his eyes."

Isolde's sigh was long. "Dying for love is highly overrated, my dear," she said at last, her cragged voice softened by some hidden emotion Maeve could not quite identify. "But very well. I will assist you, only because of my fondness for Alaric and the profound depth of the love I see pouring from your eyes. And while love is usually a fool's game used only to subjugate women, your mettle, paired with your earnest devotion to the prince, interests me. I believe he might have met his match in you."

"Thank you," Maeve whispered. Relief washed over her until her knees softened, making it difficult to remain standing.

"Sit now," Isolde commanded, gesturing toward a straight-backed chair positioned opposite her.

As Maeve moved forward, she couldn't help but marvel at the strange trappings inside Isolde's dwelling. Plants and bizarre-looking vines twined around every surface, their leaves brushing against shelves laden with odd-looking potions, crystal balls, and ornately carved wands. Undead cats lounged on the ledges of the stained glass windows, strange colors dappling their nappy fur. Their glassy eyes glittered like gems, and they followed Maeve intently as she took her place in the chair across from Isolde.

"Scoot your chair closer and listen carefully, child, for I will only tell you this once," Isolde murmured, her voice taking on a melodic, almost hypnotic quality. "The path before you is fraught with danger, and not just from feral zombies. But with my guidance and your unwavering love for Alaric, you might yet prevail in your quest to save him..."

"Go on," Maeve said.

"Centuries ago," Isolde began in a voice that seemed to echo from a great depth, "the sentient zombies emerged from the ashes of their cities, seeking both survival and shelter from their human cousins. They still possessed intellect and reason, unlike their feral brethren, who were driven only by their primal hunger for human flesh."

Maeve shuddered at the thought, but listened intently as Isolde detailed the early struggles between humans and zombies. Her heart ached with empathy for both worlds as she heard of the sacrifices made by both sides in their quest to restore harmony to their respective worlds. Though there were some early whispers of a truce, distrust and prejudice between the two species had caused that pursuit to fail miserably, and each vowed to cleave only to their own kind.

"Fearful of being eradicated, our kind retreated. Alaric's line took shelter here. Yet among us even now are those like Lady Elora,"

Isolde continued, "who believe sentient zombies should reign supreme, eradicating humanity as an inferior species. And this is the very crux of the battle that lies before you."

Maeve gasped as the old woman leaned forward, her bony fingers clasping Maeve's hands with surprising strength. "You must understand, child, this is not the way of all sentient zombies. A handful of us, like our prince, truly desire to live in harmony, recognizing the unique gifts each race brings to our disparate worlds."

Maeve nodded, her thoughts racing. "But with Alaric asleep and me being under suspicion's veil, how can I unite our people and bring about peace when there are so many who would oppose me?" she asked, her voice wavering. "I am only one woman."

"Belief in the greater good, and a willingness to die for your cause is your only reliable weapon," Isolde replied, her eyes narrowing. "You must hold fast to your goal and trust that your love for Alaric will be your guiding star, illuminating the path toward unity. Only when your love is tried enough to be proven true shall you reign victorious."

"Now you sound just like him," Maeve said, unable to keep herself from smiling past the tears that still stung her eyes.

"Who do you think he learned it from?" A near smile teased Isolde's lips. "It matters not whether you are zombie or human. Though it is the rarest of gems, unconditional love is the one thing worth living for—and dying for. Only because I believe you have found that with Alaric have you won my trust. And a love such as that, my dear, is contagious."

"So you will tell me where I can find the king now?"

"I will do my best," she said. "For while any man who breached Caligula's hold would be decapitated on sight, a pretty redhead just might be granted an audience. Though I am not privy to the king's location, I do have..." her gaze slid toward a shelf displaying several crystal balls, "...other means at my disposal."

As the largest of Isolde's black cats snoozed in Maeve's lap, the two women continued to speak about the strange history of how zombies came to be. The fading light of the sun slanted through the stained glass windows, illuminating the disheveled tapestries that adorned the walls. But neither the history lesson nor the dazzling display did much to assuage Maeve's melancholy. Another day without Alaric had nearly passed. As darkness approached, she began to feel frustrated, her impossible responsibility settling again upon her shoulders. But this time, it was at least eased by the bitter-sweet knowledge that her love for Alaric would be the compass that guided her as she sought out his father—and the antidote that would bring her beloved back to her.

But each tick of the clock situated on one of the windowsills reminded Maeve that her task here was far from done. There was still so much she needed to know... not about the past, but rather the future. Where was the king? And once she knew that much, she was still only one woman. How would she journey through a revenant-infested world when she had no allies in this place willing to take up their arms and accompany her?

"You grow restless, child," observed.

Maeve nodded. "I deeply appreciate you sharing your vast historical knowledge with me," she said, her voice thick with emotion. "While a better understanding about the history of zombie-kind is enlightening, I still have no better an idea about where the king is located than when I first arrived."

Isolde's sigh was wistful, and her expression appeared...almost repentant. "My apologies, child. But I truly believe a people who cannot understand and appreciate where they have been cannot possibly choose the path they must travel next. Sometimes my obsession with unraveling the threads of the past gets in the way of tending to the present moment." Isolde's eyes grew a bit misty as she released Maeve's hands and gestured toward the sagging shelf of crystal balls. "Bring me one of those, dear," she said. "But be careful not to touch the belladonna plants. They're my own strain, and quite toxic."

"Which one should I bring?"

Isolde scoffed softly. "The one that calls to you, of course. If your third eye is as strong as I suspect, you will know the right one when you touch it, as it will, in turn, recognize you."

Apprehension bubbled up within Maeve as she settled the cat onto the floor and approached the shelf adorned with crystal balls of various colors and sizes. Each one was infused with its own sort of energy. Some sparkled with an inner glow, while others seemed to whisper to her about the secrets hidden within their translucent depths. As Isolde had asked, her eyes scanned the array, and she held her breath to stave off the scent reminiscent of lilacs wafting from the plants, searching for the orb that resonated with her.

As she let her fingertips brush against the smooth surface of each orb, thinking this pursuit frivolous, she felt a faint connection, a fleeting glimpse into the vast possibilities they held. But it wasn't until she reached the end of the shelf that she felt a subtle shift in the air, like a gentle tugging at her senses.

There, nestled on a carved, rose quartz pedestal adorned with intricate carvings of a lioness protecting her cubs, was the one. She knew it the second its surface shimmered with an opalescent glow, casting intricate patterns of light on her palm as she reached out to touch it. It wasn't just the orb's outward appearance that had drawn her in—it was the sensation of inevitability that enveloped her as she gazed into its depths. Just like Isolde had promised, she somehow knew it was hers and always had been.

Without hesitation, she cradled the crystal ball in her hands, taking care to avoid the plants. As she carried it back to Isolde, a crackling surge of energy shimmered through her veins. It was as if the ball itself was alive, pulsating with a power that was as ancient as time itself.

"This one," Maeve whispered, her voice barely audible as she held it out to Isolde. "This is the one that calls to me."

Isolde nodded knowingly as she took the orb, a small smile playing at the corners of her lips. "Of course you would choose that one. For the heart of a lioness dwells within your chest. Now, sit down and be quick about it. There is much more we must discuss. The orb demands patience, and I can sense your yearning to return to Alaric's side."

Maeve had no sooner taken her place in her designated chair when the zombie cat returned to its resting space in her lap. As Isolde chanted quietly in a language Maeve did not understand, the crone's gaze, unfixed and distant, probed the depths of the crystal ball. The glass began to fog, and a deep hush fell over the dimly lit chamber, broken only by the soft purring of the contented feline nestled in Maeve's lap. Sage incense rose up and drew slow curlicues in the air as Isolde's eyes rolled back in her head, and she appeared to drift into a trance-like state.

For a few moments, Maeve wondered if the old woman had fallen asleep. But when her eyes flew open again, they were as startling and familiar a shade of blue as Alaric's, and Maeve could not restrain her gasp.

"Trouble is coming," Isolde said at last, her voice faint as if it were an echo from another realm. "You must assemble a team and depart—very soon. The dangers posed by the feral zombies are increasing. Tarry too long, and your endeavors will end in a quick tragedy."

Maeve's heart clenched at the thought of leaving Alaric behind, but she steeled herself against the tide of emotions that rose up and threatened to overwhelm her.

"Finding escorts amongst the courtiers will prove difficult... no, impossible," Isolde continued, her tone grave. "But the answer to the help you seek lies in the most unlikely of places—you must turn to Fiona and the other women yourself and Alaric saved from the catacombs."

"But even if they were able, have those poor souls not already suffered enough?"

"Their pain has made them stronger than anyone would ever have dreamed. And should you fail to enlist their aid, they will suffer far more. Because the former tributaries now feel beholden to yourself and Alaric, they will come to see merit in embracing your cause."

"But why would they when they could live the rest of their lives in relative peace?"

"Because, like yourself," she said, "they sense that Alaric's well-being is crucial if what remains of the civilized world is to survive. His role in fostering unity between zombies and humans cannot be underestimated. And neither can yours, child. But the peace you crave is a task you can only accomplish together."

"Thank you, Isolde," she said, her voice thick with emotion. "I promise to heed your words. And by the gods, I will not fail."

"Go forth with courage, Maeve," the sage replied, the blue fading from her eyes as they lifted from the crystal ball. "And remember, this task will require more from you than you ever dreamed possible. Only your loving connection to Alaric can guide you through. You must believe that he is always with you, even now."

"But I still don't know where I'm going."

"Nor do I, but Nyx does," Isolde said, gesturing toward the cat, who now slumbered like a happy kitten in Maeve's lap. "This is why you must take your cat and your crystal ball with you on your journey."

"*My* cat?"

"You don't know it yet, but the orb recognized you because you possess the ability of foresight. And it would appear that my friend Nyx has anointed herself as your familiar. Now that you are her chosen, she will accompany you always and show you the things the gods believe you need to see. But only when the time is right for you to see them..."

"But taking a cat on such a treacherous journey seems cumbersome... and cruel."

"Poppycock. Nyx was born in the wild. She can travel unnoticed into places that are not safe for you to follow. Then, with the help of your crystal ball, you will see with your own eyes what transpires as she prowls in those places."

"Are you telling me I am some kind of... witch?"

Isolde scoffed. "Witch is a word men bandy about to diminish and demonize powerful women. I prefer to call myself a prophetess. Now take your cat and be gone, child, for I have grown tired. But remember, Maeve... if you are to accomplish your goal, you must trust in your sight and heed what your feminine intuition tells you." Isolde reached out to take Maeve's hands, her grasp surprisingly strong. "But one word of warning, child. Sometimes, the orb will not show you what you ask to see, but rather what your heart most yearns to see. You must practice before you can know the difference, or your soul may become lost in the realm of what might have been forever."

"I promise, I will use caution."

"Good. For the gods themselves have chosen you for this role long before you were born. And now they have anointed you the power to assemble all you will need to see this cause through. But you will not do it here, chit-chatting with a crazy old woman. Go save our prince."

With that, Maeve accepted her crystal ball, rose, and took her leave. As she stepped into the late-day shadows and headed back to the castle, Nyx trotted along in her wake as if they had always been together.

CHAPTER 8

As Maeve crossed the courtyard that would take her back to the towering arch leading into the Great Hall, mist curled around the edges of the courtyard. The hair on her nape crawled as the wisps seemed to close in and chase her like curious phantoms. She couldn't help but wonder if their strange behavior was Isolde's handiwork.

Though she tried to tell herself the notion was silly, witches and magic weren't real, her mind brimmed with all the fantastical things she had just learned from the elderly sage—and had seen and felt for herself. Pausing, she dropped her gaze to inspect the crystal ball she held between her hands. Isolde had said it had been hers since before she was born. That it had chosen her. Then she'd suggested that Maeve was some kind of... seer.

Me? A seer? She couldn't help but scoff, for it seemed too impossible an idea to lend any real credence. Her people had always eschewed discussions about magic as the stuff of childish fairy tales. They instead clung to the level-headed common sense that had served them quite well as they sought to rebuild their battered corner of the world.

Such things simply can't be real... As if intuiting her unspoken thoughts, and eager to prove them wrong, the crystal's shimmering surface refracted the rising moon's glow in a kaleidoscope of colors that danced across her pale hands. For a moment, she thought she could sense the orb's insistent power pulsing beneath her fingertips. She wasn't altogether sure she liked the sensation. It felt too strange... too urgent.

The zombie cat, Nyx, who Isolde had said was her *familiar*, padded silently in her wake. The odd-looking feline's ragged obsidian coat rendered her nearly invisible as she leaped into the evening shadows crawling up the castle's stone walls.

As she approached the Great Hall's wide double doors, the crystal ball crackled with static electricity, and a jarring sense of wariness washed over her. The nearer she came to the entrance, the more alarming the sensation grew. Holding her breath and not knowing what to expect, she nudged open the heavy doors. She cringed when the creak of their ancient hinges was sufficient to wake the dead.

Casting a quick glance over her shoulder to see if she was being watched—or worse— pursued, she took a tentative step over the threshold. Nyx followed along, meowing her displeasure as she charged ahead of her. Though the cat's shaggy fur stood on end, her movements appeared almost playful as she pounced on the room's shifting shadows. *No magic in that. In fact, the entire notion that she is my familiar strains credibility...*

As she turned to pull the doors closed behind her, the familiar scents of aged wood and melting wax hung in the air. These mingled with the faint aroma of spices wafting up from the scullery situated directly below. Brigid's domain. Few dishes were served in the kingdom that she did not personally oversee.

When she turned back around, Fiona stepped into the silvery light that filtered through the Great Hall's high, arched windows. Nyx startled, hissed, and spit, her back hunched and her eyes gleaming like copper shards.

And no wonder. Fiona's anxiety was almost palpable, her violet eyes flashing as they darted around the immense hall. The poor thing looked to Maeve like she half-expected a hidden snitch, or perhaps even a feral zombie, to leap at her any second now.

"What is wrong with you?" Maeve asked, the hair at her nape prickling.

Frustration played on the young woman's features as she tiptoed toward Maeve, her slipper-clad feet barely making a sound on the marble floor. As she closed the last scrap of distance between them, she pressed a finger to her lips, beckoned Maeve to follow, and then took off toward the butler's pantry.

Though Maeve still had no idea what had alarmed Fiona, the glass orb she still held between her hands hummed its approval as Nyx, then she, followed.

THE BUTLER'S pantry offered a stark contrast to the genteel, sweeping opulence of the Great Hall. Its utilitarian confines were filled with the musty scent of stacked table linens. Maeve could also detect the faint metallic tang of fresh-scrubbed copper emanating from the array of serving dishes, spatulas and spoons suspended from the low, beamed ceiling.

"Close the door behind you," Fiona whispered. "And be sure you lock it and turn the bolt."

"What is all the subterfuge about?" Maeve asked.

"Every inch of this castle has ears, and we need to get you to a place where we can speak freely."

Maeve did not miss how Fiona's hands trembled slightly as she rushed deeper into the space and reached for the door to the dumb-waiter. As her friend's delicate fingers fiddled with the brass latch, the crystal orb warmed between Maeve's palms. She took the sensation to mean they had left the danger it had sensed when she entered the Great Hall behind them.

After Maeve turned the door's lock and flipped the bolt, she turned around and watched, features tightening with confusion as Fiona slid the dumbwaiter's door open. As she did so, the crystal ball went quiet and still beneath Maeve's fingers, almost as if it approved of the young woman's actions.

When Fiona indicated she wished for Maeve to crawl inside, the idea of squeezing into the cramped space seemed so ludicrous her body shook with restrained laughter. But the urgency in Fiona's expression brooked no argument. Nor did the crystal ball do anything she could take as a warning to refuse.

"We must hurry," Fiona mouthed.

The dull thud of heavy footsteps echoing from the adjacent chamber sent a shiver down Maeve's spine. As those footfalls drew nearer the pantry door, the glass she still clutched in her hands woke. Its smooth surface hummed like an angry bee against her fingertips, and her heart quickened with apprehension. Fiona's insistent gestures were what finally spurred her into action, her muscles tensing as she prepared to hoist herself into the dumbwaiter's dark maw.

As she slipped inside the cramped space, the reek of old, damp wood forced her to push her tongue against the roof of her mouth, repressing a sneeze. Nyx and then Fiona followed close behind her. The two women's breaths came in shallow gasps as Fiona slid the door closed with a soft click, plunging them into inky darkness. The blackness pressed against them as the dumbwaiter's gears rumbled to life and began a halting pace toward the scullery.

After a swaying descent, the dumbwaiter came to a halt with a bone-jarring thud. With a hiss of released air, the door slid open, revealing the dimly lit scullery. There Brigid stood, looking utterly frantic, her matronly figure silhouetted against the faint glow of the dying embers in the stoves behind her. As Maeve stepped out of the confined space, the air was as sweltering as a late summer's day. Her nose curled as her senses were assailed by the sharp aromas of garlic and rancid grease.

As Nyx leaped from the dumbwaiter and dove beneath a low shelf, Brigid gasped and jumped back, her eyes widening in surprise. The cat retreated into the shadows until nothing of her was revealed but the coppery glow of her watchful eyes. Brigid turned her gaze upon Maeve, as if to enquire about the cat, but her brown eyes instead fixed on the glimmering crystal ball clutched in Maeve's hands. The woman's gasp was as sharp as the butcher knife she held in her hands. "Maeve! What manner of sorcery have you brought into my scullery?"

"It is only a cat," Maeve protested. "And it seems to think it belongs to me now."

"I know what a cat is. But I'm talking about that... *thing* in your hands. I hope you haven't been consulting with Lady Isolde." Brigid's voice was tinged with distaste, but her brow furrowed with concern. "There are good reasons why that one has been banished from polite company. No one amongst us knows for sure whether she is friend or foe."

As Maeve nodded, her gaze locked with Brigid's, and she could sense an avalanche of unspoken warnings hovering on the woman's lips. "I only sought her out at Dr. Reinhart's urging," she protested. "Because he seemed to trust her, I felt safe in doing the same."

Brigid's features softened at the mention of the elderly physician's name. "The doctor always did have a soft spot for that crazy old crone. But what use could you possibly have for that sharp-tongued bag of bones?"

"*Lady* Isolde has been helping guide me through... this unprecedented time. And I went to her because I hoped she could point me toward the location of Alaric's father."

"And did she?"

"In a manner of speaking," Maeve said, giving the crystal ball Isolde had given her a pointed glance.

Brigid's expression only darkened further. "Be wary of the

ground you tread, Maeve. Have you forgotten those who dared to pry into the forbidden secrets of the gods were the very architects of our current plight?"

Maeve's fingers tightened protectively around the smooth surface of the crystal ball, her mind swirling with uncertainty. Yet, she couldn't deny the tug of intuition that had led her to believe seeking Isolde's counsel was the right thing to do—and perhaps the only thing if Alaric was ever to wake. Even if saving him meant selling her soul, she knew she would do so without reservation. "I would never have gone there if Alaric's courtiers would have given me the information I sought. The refused. But please know this, Brigid. While I will tread these strange new waters with caution, this crystal ball is the very tool... perhaps the only tool... I have to guide me if I am to obtain the antidote that will enable his recovery. And for that boon, however unorthodox it might seem, Lady Isolde will forever have my undying respect."

Brigid's gaze traveled back and forth between Maeve's face and the crystal ball, which now glowed a soothing shade of blue—a hue so reminiscent of Alaric's eyes that fresh grief knotted in her throat. As a tear dropped from her cheekbone onto the strange orb balanced between her palms, it pulsed with a radiant warmth that coursed up her arms and embraced her shattered heart. A part of her wanted to surrender, lose herself in the gentle mists that whorled within. So, once again, Isolde was proven right. The orb was giving her the one thing it sensed her heart most desired—to be reunited with Alaric.

As Maeve blinked tears from her eyes, the wariness retreated from Brigid's stare. The elderly woman's perusal slid to Fiona, who had been hovering at the edge of the room. As the young woman stepped forward, her eyes darted between Maeve and Brigid. The corners of her lips lifted as if she had sensed that whatever the crystal ball had just communicated to Maeve had given her great comfort. "Not all who practice the ancient arts are bad, Brigid..." she said. "Was it not women like Isolde who gave us the means to prevent ourselves from bearing children?"

Brigid's expression softened with her nod. "That they did. And I suppose during times such as these, the beggar cannot also be the chooser."

"Fiona," Maeve murmured as her friend drew closer, "why did you whisk me away so urgently upon my arrival? And to the scullery of all places? It is sweltering in here."

Fiona's gaze swam with... not fear ...but urgency. "Because this is one of the few places in the castle the courtiers will not deign to visit."

"Is something afoot that requires we seclude ourselves from the others?"

Fiona nodded. "Th-There are new whispers among the courtiers, Maeve. Those who seek to orchestrate your downfall, to lay the blame for Alaric's circumstances upon your doorstep—and their numbers are growing. And because of our friendship and my fondness for Eamon, they believe I, too, am complicit."

"And you can confirm this is more than idle gossip?" Maeve asked, her gaze shifting between the two women.

"I believe it is more, as does Dr. Reinhart, for he is the one who told me," Brigid said. "They intend to imprison both yourself and Fiona in the tower alongside Eamon and Loren. Their goal is to try you alongside them as accomplices."

"Accomplices to *what?* The poisoning of the man I love? Have they dismissed the fact that Lysander and Elora are now both at large?"

"It would appear so. That is why the both of you must flee, dear. Take shelter far from this place, perhaps back at your village. Then stay there, at least until the dust these rumors have kicked up can settle or the real culprits can be revealed."

Maeve's breath stalled, the realization she had but a handful of allies left within the castle chilling further the icy blood that ran through her veins. "But with Eamon and Loren imprisoned, aside from Nan and Coralie, we might be hard-pressed to find any fervent support there. Not without endangering my family."

"But where else can we go?" Fiona asked, her voice laced with desperation.

Brigid produced a tarnished key from the depths of her apron pocket, its metallic surface gleaming faintly in the dim light. "You still have a few true allies here, Maeve," she murmured, her eyes blazing with unspoken determination. "But first, you must free them. And in doing so, you might just win back some measure of... if not grace... at least tolerance as you seek shelter with your kinsmen."

Isolde's prediction that it was the women who would save Alaric from his plight rang in Maeve's mind as she watched Fiona close her trembling fingers around the key. She did not need to look into her crystal ball to know the key represented their only hope for staying free long enough to save Alaric.

"Now, please. You must promise me this..." Brigid's voice was a fervent plea. "The two of will hide in the pantry until I let you out. Then you must make haste and free Eamon and Loren. With that done, you must all leave this place before dawn break and return to your village."

"Would it not be safer to go now and travel under the cloak of darkness?" Maeve asked.

Brigid shook her head. "Our scouts say the hordes have returned to haunt the woods. It is far better... safer ...if you travel by daylight."

New tears welled in Maeve's eyes, her resolve to flee wavering beneath the weight of guilt that climbed atop her shoulders. "Perhaps Fiona should go without me."

Fiona gasped. "You would sacrifice yourself?"

"I fear that by accepting Alaric's proposal, I have invited ruin upon us all. And many in my village believe the same. But if we went our separate ways..." She stared deep into Fiona's eyes. "With Eamon's endorsement, my kinsmen would welcome you with open arms. As would the former tributaries, for they already know you."

Brigid's hand found Maeve's shoulders, her grip firm and unwavering. "Stop with this silliness. The two of you are stronger together."

"But Alaric... he needs ...a guardian nearby who can be trusted," Maeve protested as Brigid set down her butcher knife and began nudging both herself and Fiona toward the pantry.

"Staying here to cry over him will serve no purpose in his healing. And I stand by my promise to watch over him in your absence," Brigid said. "Now there is a bundle of food and a dagger for each of you hidden behind the first row of flour sacks. Make yourselves as comfortable as possible. Be quiet as chapel mice. I will be back to release the both of you shortly before dawn..."

As Brigid sealed the two women within, something fell off one of the shelves and clattered onto the floor. Maeve turned to see Nyx's coppery eyes glowing in the darkness. How the feline had managed to get inside the pantry without anyone noticing was beyond her reckoning. Still, as the cat ventured forward and leaped into Fiona's arms, the crystal ball illuminated the space with an inviting, amber glow that reminded Maeve of Nan's hearth back home. For the moment, at least, they were safe.

"I suppose we should try to get some sleep," she said as she pulled out a grain sack to use as a pillow. "For the gods only know what new trials we will face tomorrow."

THE HOURS GROANED by at a snail's pace, yet sleep stubbornly eluded Maeve. Shivering, she curled her knees tighter against her chest. The pantry had long since grown too cold for comfort, and every bone in her body ached. She rolled onto her side and stared into her crystal ball, willing it to give her some sign that would offer comfort but finding none. As she fretted, Fiona snored softly, her head also resting upon a grain sack. Even Nyx snoozed happily in the nest she'd made between two of the sacks.

Finally, the silence was broken by the distant toll of the clock tower bell as it announced the last hour before dawn. Each reverberation drove the trepidation Maeve felt at surrendering Alaric to the care of others deeper into her heart. Tears fogged her eyes. Leaving him now, when he was so vulnerable, would be the hardest thing this strange new life had demanded from her yet.

"Fiona, wake up," she whispered, not wanting to startle her friend. Her words hung like phantoms in the frigid air, and her breath felt as thick and tangible as the flour sacks and preserves that filled the tall shelves around them.

As she reached to gently nudge Fiona's shoulder, the girl gasped and started. When her eyes fluttered open, they glowed like twin amethysts in the darkness. Once her gaze finally found Maeve's, her irises were still glassy and unfocused, as if she had just been yanked from a deep trance. "I must have dozed off," she admitted, her voice betraying a hint of shame as she blinked away the haze.

"You slept like a baby. And I must admit, I am more than a little bit jealous."

"Did you at least get *some* rest?" Fiona asked as Nyx wandered from her hiding place behind the flour sacks and hopped into Maeve's lap.

"Not much," Maeve admitted as she stroked her new friend—familiar?—beneath her scruffy chin. The fur there was surprisingly silky, unlike the rest of her nappy coat. Maeve could not help but smile a little as her efforts won her some contented purrs.

"Considering the task ahead, shouldn't you try and get some rest?" Concern tormented Fiona's features.

Maeve shook her head. "The clock tower just tolled the last hour before dawn. Brigid will be here soon," she said, struggling to keep her voice steady though her heart ached with dread.

"Perhaps we should discuss our plans again," Fiona suggested.

Maeve nodded, her mind racing through the details they had concocted between them. "Eamon and Loren will need arms. Once we are in the scullery, we will select a suitable blade for both men to use and sheath them under our skirts. Then, we must keep to the shadows until we have made it inside the West Tower. Once we are certain that Eamon and Loren are untended, you will keep watch while I release them with the key Brigid gave us," Maeve whispered.

"But what if there are guards?"

"Given Lady Elora's ease with escaping, it is quite possible there won't be any. But in the event there are, we will have no choice but to seduce them."

Fiona's face contorted into a mask of disgust. "Seduce them? Why would we need to do that?"

"Because they will be easier to... dispatch... with their breeches tangled around their ankles."

Though Fiona still shuddered, her lips curling at the idea, she nodded her grudging assent.

"Once Eamon and Loren are freed, we head straight for the gardener's hut," Maeve continued. "It will give us cover while we scale the castle wall and drop into the forest. But we must make haste. Brigid insisted it was imperative we make it deep into the woods before dawn breaks."

Fiona nodded, her fingers trembling as she shouldered on the makeshift knapsack Brigid had fashioned from a tablecloth. "But wouldn't it be safer if we just created a distraction and made our way through the castle gates?"

Maeve tucked her crystal ball into her own knapsack and tied it closed as she shook her head firmly. "The woods are densest to the rear of the castle. Because the forest there is west facing, it will provide us the best cover against the rising sun as we make our escape."

As Fiona nodded, a soft click signaled the turning of the lock, and the pantry door slowly creaked open. Brigid rushed in, her haggard face already taut with worry. "It is time, my loves," she said, her voice choked as she passed each girl a bundle of clothing.

"What is this for?" Maeve asked.

"You can't very well go chasing through the woods in your skirts and crinolines," she explained. "There's a tunic, leggings, a mantle and boots for you both."

As the girls changed, the clock tower chimed the quarter-hour, and Brigid's tear-filled eyes flitted frantically between Maeve and Fiona. "Stay safe, my darlings," she whispered, her voice breaking with emotion.

Both Maeve and Fiona nodded. As they emerged from the pantry, Maeve paused for a moment, her sensitive eyes struggling to adjust to the torchlight. After selecting a blade for both Eamon and Loren, they each sheathed one in their boots. Then they followed Brigid as she led them through the narrow scullery. Though Maeve's footfalls were light, as they drew near the door, her heart was leaden with a sense of impending danger.

Once they reached the door, Brigid turned back and gathered each girl into her embrace. Then she pushed open the scullery door. "Remember, my darlings," she said, her voice tight with unshed tears. "Dawn approaches. Once you have freed Eamon and Loren, you must hide beneath the last scrap of the night and vanish into the woods. It won't take them long to realize that the men are gone, so make haste toward your village."

Both Maeve and Fiona murmured their understanding. Tears spilling from her eyes, Brigid kissed both girls on their foreheads. With a soft sob, she nudged them both through the scullery door. Nyx scooted through behind them just as Brigid pushed the door closed, removing the final barrier that shielded them from an uncertain and dangerous future.

At some point during the night, Jack Frost's stubborn hand defeated spring's first hints. The air was so frigid the tears clinging to Maeve's lashes had already turned to ice. Perhaps she could blame her exhaustion for the fact that she was beginning to wonder if the gods had truly forsaken zombies, like her human kinsman often insisted. But pausing to petition for divine favor was a luxury neither she nor Alaric could afford. The only thing she cared about was saving him, for it was only because he had dared to fall in love with a human girl that he had fallen into such dire straits. Gods favor be damned, she would do whatever was needed to save him. And accomplishing that task began with freeing Eamon and Loren.

As the women locked hands and stepped away from the shelter provided by the stoop, the pre-dawn darkness eddied with snow flurries. Telling herself she had survived worse back home, she shoved her hands into her armpits. Gesturing for Fiona to do the same, she stepped deeper into the unseasonably frigid air.

She swore softly as she noticed a thick layer of snow had smothered the castle grounds in an opalescent veil. Realizing the dark clothing she and Fiona wore would make them stand out like ink stains on white lace, she motioned Fiona to move closer to the castle's walls. With any luck, the shadows stretching out from the soaring edifice would be enough to conceal them as they trekked to the West Tower, where Brigid said Eamon and Loren were being held.

With their backs flattened against the castle's icy stone walls, they began to move, inch by miserable inch. They continued on this way until they ran out of any stone or shadows to hide them.

"What now?" Fiona whispered through her chattering teeth.

"To the hedgerows." Maeve looked both ways, then moved into the clearing. But each step they clamied across the ice-glazed courtyard was more unsteady than the last. Did their every breath shatter the stillness like thunder, or had her supernatural senses just heightened to the point where even the faintest sound seemed magnified? She wasn't sure. All she did know was they would not get a second chance at breaking Eamon and Loren out. One noisy misstep, or even a small slip on the ice, could find them imprisoned alongside the men they sought to free.

Beside her, Fiona seemed to have found her center, moving forward with cautious grace. When they finally reached the protective shadows that stretched from the hedgerows flanking the walkway, Maeve drew her friend into a hug, thankful for both her friendship and her steadfast nature.

After taking a moment to collect themselves, they began reiterating their plan, like the perfectly synchronized hands of a clock. Clinging to the vegetation, they slipped past alcoves, sallyports and macabre statues that were even eerier shrouded in gloom. Now and then, they found themselves crouching low to the ground as they dodged the damning glow of the torches dotting the path.

By the time Maeve had sighted the West Tower's entrance, the entire world seemed to be holding its breath. "We're almost there," she whispered to Fiona. But as she stepped away from the hedge, her foot snagged on a metal watering can someone had left lying on the ground, and it went clattering across the cobblestones.

"Halt! Who goes there?" a voice shouted.

Bloody hell. As heavy, booted footsteps headed in their direction, Maeve's heart rose into her throat, and her arm darted out, pressing Fiona back into the hedges just as she was poised to step onto the cobblestones, perhaps intending to make a run for the tower.

As Maeve's mind struggled to choreograph an escape route, the same snowy owl she'd seen the night Alaric fell made a screeching kek-kek sound as it took off from the trees. Nyx leaped from the shadows and released a yowl that seemed hell-born as she crashed through the hedgerows, sounding more like a small army of drunkards than one crazed zombie cat.

Good kitty.

As the castle guards' advance stalled in response to the creatures' strangely convenient disturbance, Maeve scraped out a slow breath. When Fiona's trembling hand found hers, she feared the girl's rasping pants were certain to give their position away. Then Nyx's yowl, more distant this time, tore through the night again.

"Over there," someone finally cried out. "Inside the mazes."

"After them," a more distant voice demanded.

Maeve continued to hold her breath as the guards' footsteps turned toward the place where Nyx had vanished. Soon, their shouts faded into the distance like the last lingering notes of an aria.

Only when the guards were out of earshot did Maeve release her breath, tension draining from her body like wine from a punctured skin. "We must make haste. Nyx will not be able to keep them occupied for long," she whispered as she clutched the key Brigid had given them tighter in her palm.

As Fiona's chin dipped, they left the safety of the hedges and made their last, frantic break for the West Tower's entrance. Should they get there only to find the doors guarded, they were both as good as doomed. But thanks to the diversion the creatures had created, they found the tower's entrance untended.

Still, Maeve's heartbeat skipped as she gave the heavy wooden door a nudge, half expecting an ambush. A near smile hovered on her lips as it yielded. After looking over her shoulder to ensure no lingering guards were watching, she extracted her dagger and pushed the door open wider with her booted foot. The iron hinges creaked softly in protest as she motioned for Fiona to retrieve her own weapon. "Hold it at the ready," she said, then gestured for Fiona to follow her inside.

Again, nobody waited for them. After stealing a moment to catch their breath, Fiona lifted one of the torches from the wall, and the women raced up the narrow spiral staircase. As they made their ascent, Maeve's mind was plagued by a thousand things that could still go wrong. What if they were too late? What if Eamon and Loren were too weak to make their escape? What if the men were not even being held there anymore? The what-ifs were as countless as they were relentless

No, she chided herself. There was no room for doubts, not now. They had a mission to complete, their fallen prince to save. As they approached the top of the stairs, she reminded herself Isolde had already seen past this moment. She had peered into her crystal ball and foreseen that Maeve's quest to find King Caligula would be made possible by the very women she'd once saved. Aside from Fiona, all those women now dwelled in her home village. They would make it. They had to. For Isolde had insisted this was her destiny, the very reason she had been born.

When they emerged from the stairwell, the door she had last looked upon when she first discovered the imprisoned tributaries loomed before them. As she stood on her tiptoes and peered through the small, barred window, her heart stumbled, tears spangling her lashes as she took in the sight of Eamon and Loren.

The men were huddled in the back corner of their dimly lit cell, their teeth chattering so hard she feared they might crack. A rat scurried across the floor just then, and she gasped. Eamon's face was a mask of dread as his head shot up and turned toward the door. His complexion was so wan she wondered if he, too, could be turning into a zombie.

As both men's hollow eyes fixed on her, recognition dawned. But their gazes revealed no joy in seeing her. Instead, they seemed haunted by the specter of a date with the guillotine that occupied the centermost point of the garden's mazes.

"Maeve? What in the bloody hell are you two doing here?" Eamon finally rasped.

"Breaking you free," she said. "And before you tell me to turn back and lock myself in the castle because I am only a woman, I will remind you that if you remain here, you are both dead men."

Her fingers trembled violently as she inserted the key into the lock, the cold metal branding her skin with a chill deeper than an open grave. For a moment, the lock resisted her efforts to turn it. Just as she began to fear Brigid had given her the wrong key, or the guards would return, unraveling their plan before it ever began, the mechanism turned. The rusty hinges groaned as the door swung open. She could see the relief wash over Eamon and Loren's faces as they struggled to their feet and stumbled out into the dimly lit corridor.

"Now what?" Eamon asked as both he and Loren rubbed the stiffness from their legs.

"I'll explain the details later, but we must get back to our village. And if we expect to make it there alive, we need to be deep in the woods before dawn breaks. Are you able to walk?" she asked, her gaze swinging between the two men.

They both nodded, and real hope sparked in Maeve's mind. But as they descended into the stairwell, a cacophony of distant yet all too familiar wails extinguished that hope. *Ferals.*

"So the rumors Brigid heard were true then. They are back," Fiona whispered.

The distant stirrings of the ravenous undead served them a cruel reminder of the dangers that lurked beyond the safety of the castle walls. Dangers they had no choice but to face.

Maeve glanced at Fiona, finding the girl's wide with fear. "We have survived far worse," she said, placing a hand on her friend's shoulder. "And as soon as dawn fully breaks, they will likely go back into hiding. We only have to survive that long."

"And I will fall myself before I let any harm come to you," Eamon vowed, though he looked too gaunt to protect them from a kitten.

As Fiona nodded, her trembling eased, and Maeve felt a fresh surge of determination. They had come too far to turn back, and their capture would mean certain death. When she looked at it that way, braving a horde of hungry ferals seemed the lesser of two evils.

"What now?" Fiona asked as they descended the last stair and gathered at the base of the stairwell.

"First," she extracted the butcher knife she'd taken from the scullery from her boot and passed it to Eamon, "we arm these men," she whispered, despite the fear welling in her chest as Fiona pressed the knife she had procured into Loren's outstretched palm.

With the men flanking them, the women gripped their daggers, dashed out of the stairwell, and rushed toward the tower's exit, their booted footsteps pounding a frantic rhythm against the floor.

Outside, snowflakes, ashen and indifferent, descended upon the hedgerows where the group huddled against winter's biting chill, not knowing which way to turn next.

As they listened for signs indicating the guards' positions, the frigid air scalded Maeve's cheeks. The only warmth was in Eamon's hazel gaze as it fixed upon Fiona. Though Maeve had been certain Fiona was falling for Eamon, she hadn't known whether he truly shared her feelings. And it had pained her that any reservations he might have about her recently altered state were unreadable behind the snowflakes veiling his sooty lashes.

"What is our plan?" Loren asked, bouncing on his heels in an effort to remain warm.

"The guard change should be happening soon," Maeve began.

"And with it, our best chance for making it into the forest undetected. But when we move, we must remember to be swift and silent as the reaper himself."

Eamon's sigh unfurled, drawing misty serpents in the air as he tore his gaze away from Fiona. His world-weary eyes, which had witnessed the fall of a thousand ferals and, more recently, the scurrilous truth behind the Tributary's origins, scanned the perimeter with practiced vigilance. "Aye, Maeve. You know the path through these infernal mazes better than any, so for now, we shall follow your lead."

As Fiona, too, nodded, the hard set of her jaw spoke of the resolve that was burning away her former timidity. "Let us always surrender to the good of our quest." Her tone was laced with an edge sharper than any blade.

As Maeve's gaze sought Loren's, he shifted uneasily, the knife Maeve had procured for him clutched tightly in his hands. "I, too, will bow to your guidance," he murmured, though his expression betrayed his uneasiness with taking orders from a woman.

"Then let us begin," Maeve said. "For already the threat of day paints the horizon."

With a collective breath, the team stepped out from their dim shelter. The world around them lay smothered in white, the castle grounds a pale ghost of their former glory. Only the shadows reaching out from the hedgerows stretched long and deep, providing them some shelter from the guards' prying eyes.

With an ear on the guardsmen's movements, Maeve led them through the skeletal remains of the once-lush gardens where Alaric had first professed his love. Now, the place he had adored most was bereft of any promise of the early spring they'd anticipated.

The snow crunching beneath their boots seemed deafening, and they paused with each distant echo of the guardsmen's choreographed march. Eamon's hand rested on the handle of his crude blade, ready to defend, protect, and fight for the chance at a future that now seemed as elusive as spring.

A twig snapped beneath Maeve's boot, and a few rats scurried from their advance. Though Fiona's lip curled in disgust, she maintained her silence, knowing well even the slightest gasp could betray them all.

With each step toward the gardener's hut that would conceal them as they scaled the garden's wall and fled into the woods, the bitter cold bit deeper into Maeve's marrow, a cruel reminder of Mother Nature's indifference. Yet it was the frantic pounding of Eamon and Loren's hearts that truly marked the passage of time. The men were only human... and their mortality far more fragile than her own and Fiona's.

But finally, the hedgerows' sanctuary dwindled, and Maeve's eyes peered across the last open courtyard, fixing on the gardening hut's sagging silhouette.

The snowfall had cloaked the world in an eerie hush, muffling the scant breaths that escaped her lips in ghostly puffs. She glanced back at her companions and found their faces etched with the same ferocity that steeled her heart. With a silent nod, they began their perilous crossing.

Loren moved away from the hedges first, his lithe form casting a damning shadow as he stole across the ice-encrusted stones. But his archer's grace betrayed him as his boot found treachery beneath the snow. A startled cry ripped from his throat as he fell, the ragged sound shattering the stillness. The gasp that followed was not his own, but a collective intake from the group.

"Guards," Eamon hissed as distant male voices stirred in response to Loren's outcry. He moved instinctively toward Loren, but Fiona was already in motion, closing the distance between them and bending to pluck the blade from his hand. With a swift, practiced movement, she drew her arm back and sent it sailing deep into the mazes.

A few seconds later, the blade's impact echoed—a metallic clang that drew the attention of patrolling boots, redirecting their purpose. In the fleeting respite that followed, Eamon hoisted Loren from the ground, the grimace on the lad's face betraying the immense pain he suppressed in his effort to stand.

"'Tis now or never." Maeve's voice was barely audible above the frantic thud of her human counterparts' hearts. Knowing they had only this fleeting moment to make their escape, the team surged forward once more and raced toward the gardening hut's protective shadow.

THE HUT LOOMED before them like a dilapidated monolith, brooding against the backdrop of winter's last stand. Maeve's breath materialized before her like specters, each pant crystallizing faster than the last. The hut was a mere waypoint on their journey, yet her steps faltered as Nyx veered into their path, her eyes smoldering like embers.

"Wait," she whispered, fingers tightening around her dagger, her gaze transfixed by the feline's assured movements as she mewed and darted off to the left. There was purpose in that cat's agile trot; she was sure of it.

"What is that wretched creature up to now?" Eamon grumbled beneath his breath, but Maeve barely heard him. A peculiar sensation unfurled within her—a pull that seemed to weave through her very marrow, guiding her toward a destination yet unseen.

Isolde. As her mind uttered the sage's name, it carried the weight of prophecy. "We must change course and go to the chapel."

Fiona cast Maeve a dubious glance, then scowled at the cat, now a mere shadow blending into the darkness. "Are you certain? That way is where the witch—"

"You must trust me," Maeve insisted, her voice imbued with harsh conviction that silenced any further protest. So they changed course, following Nyx's silent lead, the crunch of their boots on snow charting their passage toward an uncertain fate.

As the neglected form of the abandoned chapel carved itself out of the darkness, it stood as solemn as a grave marker—a dilapidated relic of a world that had forgotten how to pray. Yet, there was no mistaking the hunched figure who stood at the threshold as if she had known they were coming.

"Lady Isolde," Fiona whispered, her voice laced with awe.

The elderly woman beckoned them inside the chapel with a quick flourish of her age-worn hand. Her eyes reflected the last scrap of moonlight with a deep glow that spoke of ancient spells long since outlawed by mortal and zombie men alike. "Come, now, boys, don't be cowards," the duchess demanded as the men stepped back and hesitated. "And be quick about it."

"By the gods," Fiona exclaimed as they crossed into the chapel, the door closing behind them with a thud that felt like the sealing of their fates. "I... I had my doubts about your claims about visions, Maeve, but standing here now..." As she took in the strange paraphernalia, glowing elixirs, and undead felines that occupied every surface, her voice trailed off, the skepticism that had armored her expression when Maeve had told her she was a seer crumbling away.

"Your cat's intuition has led us true yet again." Eamon's roughened features softened as he looked upon Maeve with an expression that bordered on reverence.

Loren simply nodded as he touched his wounded shoulder, a reminder of his mortal fragility in this world where death seemed to stalk every soul that still breathed. But here, in this once holy space, now forsaken by the old gods, they had found an unexpected ally; a strange old woman whose undead visage seemed as eternal as the stone walls themselves. Her charismatic presence promised them guidance through the perils that still lay ahead.

Even Maeve's eyes clung to the crone as if she were the only lighthouse visible in a storm-besieged sea.

"Time and tide wait for none." Isolde's raspy voice was nearly defeated by the encroaching ruckus outside. With steady hands that betrayed no fear, she bolted the door and rushed toward the altar to press upon an unseen mechanism hidden beneath. A low grinding sound reverberated through the floor as the altar gave way to reveal a steep stairwell shrouded in cobwebs and pitch.

"Through here," Isolde said, her gaze locked with Maeve's, "lies an underground pathway, as old as the forest itself. It will shield you from prying eyes and lead you into the deepest heart of the woods."

Maeve nodded, casting an inquisitive glance at Fiona, Eamon and Loren. "Are you ready, then?"

Their reverent nods indicated their intent to follow her wherever her newfound sight led them.

A heavy pounding on the chapel door rattled the glassware on the shelves. As the guards' shouts sliced through the tranquility of Isolde's strange sanctuary, her eyes blazed with the defiance of a thousand torches. "You will find a stash of weapons hanging on the wall at the base of the stairs," she said. "Now go, with the swiftness of the wind." Though her words were tinged with urgency, the tired lines time had carved in her face reflected something akin to sorrow.

"But would it not be wiser if you came with us?" Maeve asked, fearing for the sage's safety.

Isolde brushed off her concerns with a wave of her bejeweled hand. "Even zombie men fear women like me too much to risk suffering a curse. May the goddesses watch over your steps and cloak you in their protective shadows," she said as she passed Maeve a small torch.

With a final, lingering look, Maeve descended into the darkness. The others followed close behind, the musty atmosphere foreshadowing an uncertain fate from which there could be no turning back.

"Be swift, be silent, and above all, be safe," Isolde's voice called after them. Nyx leaped through the opening just as Isolde sealed the entrance, leaving only the lingering echo of her blessing to guide them.

CHAPTER 10

Just as Isolde had promised, swords, bows, shields, and even loaded quivers were suspended from metal hooks that had been driven into the cavern's walls. Maeve's team wasted no time arming themselves as heavily as they dared. After they'd slaked their thirst from the waterskins Maeve and Fiona carried, they were on their way, each of them chewing on strips of dried meat Brigid had wisely stowed in the women's packs.

The soggy path before them wound ever downward, spiraling into earth's rancid bowels like a serpent. But sequestered here, in the cavern's dark embrace, Maeve found a rare sense of camaraderie, and that gave her some solace.

As they moved forward, her boots met the damp earth with a soft thud, and her breaths haunted the stale air like phantoms. The narrow beam of her torch danced over the moisture-slick walls, casting shadows that contorted with each step. Beside her, Fiona's wide-eyed gaze swept the fulminant darkness, while Eamon's hand rested on the hilt of his sword. Loren still limped slightly beneath the weight of his newfound quiver and bow, the ice having betrayed his sure-footedness. Yet his determination to forge onward appeared unyielding. Though a wave of foreboding washed over Maeve as she studied him, her admiration for the young man's stoic nature grew.

Nyx slinked silently before them, looking back at them now and again with eyes that gleamed like coals stolen from a furnace. The silences between them grew longer as their procession delved further into the earth's dark maw. The deeper they descended, the more stale the atmosphere became, damp with the scents of decaying moss and moldering bones. As Maeve yearned for the moment when they left this strange sanctuary and lifted their faces to the morning sun, the hair at her nape began to crawl. Nyx yowled her agreement that something sinister awaited them.

"Hold your arms at the ready," Maeve announced as the muddy path before them began to slope upward.

Time seemed frozen as the icicles clinging to the cavern's bat-encrusted ceiling. As the weary group hastened through the darkness and struggled to scale the muddy, frost-glazed path, Eamon and Loren's breaths came in ragged gasps. Just as she thought of suggesting they all take a rest, the insistent weight of Duchess Isolde's voice pressed upon her mind, a spectral whisper that seemed to drift from the walls that hemmed them in.

Hurry, Maeve. The sage's voice whispered in her mind like an urgent susurrus rising over their labored footfalls. "Though dawn has broken, the ferals have grown more restless. Nor will the guards relent in their search. Even now, they invade the same cavern that conceals you."

She could feel the chill of her blood as it sang through her veins, and could hear Eamon and Loren's mortal heartbeats drumming in time with the frantic cadence of their escape. Finally, the steep path before them began to level out. And then, as if answering the urgent wishes she'd whispered within her mind, a sliver of light cut through the gloom. It grew, inch by inexorable inch, until at last, they emerged from the earth's bowels into the morning's first light.

Just as Isolde had promised, they stood on the threshold of an opening in the forest's canopy. On the far side, the trees began again, looking like a fearsome line of giants silhouetted against the awakening sky. Dawn break had smudged the heavens in melancholy hues of lavender and rose, a bittersweet canvas that denied the urgency still roiling within Maeve's mind. Something was out there. Something *awful*. Yet turning back only to be arrested by the castle guards was an even more unpalatable choice.

With the first rays of sunlight touching her skin, she turned to gaze upon her comrades. The fatigue of their ordeals etched their faces, yet their eyes were alight with relief over their too-narrow escape from the guards. Together, they had defied the iron grip of their pursuers, and together, they would face whatever perils that still lay ahead. But then they did not know what she did—their flight was not over yet. Far from it.

"Keep moving, for they still pursue us," she admitted.

"I heard nothing to indicate we were being chased." Loren's brow knitted with irritation that the sharp senses he'd honed during his years as an archer might have been bested by a woman.

"You forget, my senses are no longer human," Maeve insisted.

Fiona, too, opened her mouth to agree with Loren. Before she could speak, Maeve raised her hand to silence her. She was not ready to admit the message she had heard tolling like a bell within the cage of her mind, for they might think she had lost her faculties. "Perhaps you are right and I heard nothing. But can any of us afford to assume my concerns are unfounded?"

One by one, they each shook their heads no.

"Then we must move deeper into the woods, for they will provide us some cover," she managed, her voice steady despite the tremor that crawled along the length of her spine. "Once we are more sheltered, we will take a short rest, then make for the village before the rest of the world fully wakes."

She cast a glance at Nyx, the zombie cat padding silently at her side. Aside from her emergent skills as a seer, which she did not yet trust, the feline's otherworldly presence was their only talisman against the ravenous beasts that prowled these woods. If the mindless creatures were out there, Nyx would be able to detect them before anyone. *And then you will warn us, my friend.*

The cat looked up at her, blinked, and flicked her tail.

As the weary group trod deeper into the thickets, the trees seemed to close around them, an embrace that should have felt more sheltering than suffocating. But all too soon, Nyx came to such a quick halt that Maeve nearly tripped over her. The feline arched her back, hissing at some unseen predator.

And then she heard it, too, the rasping sound of feral zombies screeching in the distance—a guttural chorus that spoke of insatiable hunger and the relentless pursuit of anything that still lived. And it was coming at them from every direction.

"Bloody hell," Eamon swore softly as he, too, detected the disturbance. But even as those cries clawed at the fraying edges of Maeve's courage, she remembered the love that had driven her this far, and Isolde's promise that it would save them all.

"Be ready to defend yourselves," she said as she extracted her dagger from her boot and urged her companions to keep moving with the same unflagging determination that had brought them this far.

So they pushed forward, the forest's canopy thickened until they were shrouded in shadow.

As if birthed from the forest, several feral zombies clawed their way into the weak light, their haphazard ranks like those of a macabre army. Their putrid flesh hung in tatters, revealing raw sinew and the gray-white bones situated beneath. Eyes, clouded and devoid of humanity, fixated hungrily on human and sentient zombie alike.

As if driven by an invisible puppeteer, the ferals lumbered forward in unison, ravenous and relentless, each shuffling step an exercise in agony defeated by an insatiable craving for flesh.

If there had only been a few, they could easily have outrun them. But the sheer numbers that composed the horde made cutting around them an impossible feat.

Loren had barely loaded his bow when chaos unfurled like the petals of a dark bloom, the scent of their rising stress mingling with the fetid stench of decaying flesh.

Maeve's breath hitched as she stepped into the clearing and clutched her weapon tighter. The world seemed to slow, each second stretching taut as Loren's bowstring. Rank after rank of drooling, snapping creatures encircled them.

"Maeve, Fiona, stay at my back. Loren, you stay to their rear," Eamon growled, his voice a low rumble of contained fury.

He ducked his head and plunged into the fray, his blade singing a grim dirge as it arced through the air, finding purchase in the rotting face of a snapping zombie.

Then, the battle began in earnest.

Each swing of his weapon was a desperate bid for survival, a dance with the demise that dripped from the gory edge of his sword.

Behind him, Maeve fought to quell panic that threatened to swallow her whole. Though her dagger felt inadequate in her hands, she willed it to become an extension of her will to protect, to endure. As feral after feral came at her from every direction, she swung her blade with grim determination, severing limbs that twitched and writhed even after being parted from their owners.

Fiona, too, had joined the battle with a vengeance Maeve would not have believed her capable of, her own weapon glistening with fetid ichor as it whistled through the air.

The scents of copper and rot assailed Maeve's nostrils, bitter reminders of how thin the veil between life and un-life was. Each zombie that crumpled to the ground was a small victory, but the horde seemed as vast as an ocean. Revenants advanced in relentless waves, crashing upon them time and time again.

In the heart of the fray, Maeve caught distant sight of Eamon. His shoulder muscles coiled with the intent to shield them all from the bloody tide. His movements were quick and precise, a testament to countless hours honed in battle and his blade never once wavered amidst the oncoming tempest.

"Keep fighting!" Maeve shouted, her voice weaving through the sickening squelch of metal cleaving flesh. She struck again and again, her thoughts a whirlwind of fear for her companions, for their mission to save Alaric. But she could not ignore the creeping sorrow for the human lives these poor, twisted husks had once led. Once, they, too, had loved. And had been loved in return.

Yet she could not allow herself to be felled by pity. Alaric needed her and this was her duty—to fight, to survive, to carry the weight of hope for a world that had been besieged by nightmares for far too long. And so she kept fighting, alongside her friends, who, like herself and the undead they fought, had asked for none of this. But even as she did so, every heartbeat felt as if it were sinking daggers into her soul.

Behind her, Loren's scream pierced the cacophony, a jagged shard of terror. She dispatched another feral, then whirled around, her breath hitching as she saw a zombie, its jaw unhinged like a snake's, revealing a maw of blackened gums and broken teeth as it clamped down on his arm. The creature's eyes were bottomless voids, yet they appeared to roll back in its fractured skull, brimming with grotesque glee.

"No!" she cried, her voice half-strangled by the dread unfurling in her chest. The image of Loren's anguished features seemed to stall time, burning into her soul the possibility of his transformation into a feral.

Her legs propelled her forward, but it felt as if she moved through a sea of mud, each step a battle against the fate that clung to Loren like a shroud. In her mind's eye, she saw not just the man he was, but the grotesque premonition of what he might become.

Blood seeped between Loren's fingers as he clasped his wound, his eyes wide with dawning comprehension. Maeve's hand reached out, as if she could somehow pull him back from the bottomless precipice upon which he teetered. But there was too much distance between them.

Then, amidst the bedlam, Fiona erupted into motion, her

diminutive form a graceful blur that belied the fragility they had all believed was her immutable nature. The timid seamstress they once knew dissolved before Maeve's eyes and was replaced by the sinuous grace of a ferocious warrior.

With each fluid movement, Fiona's blade sang a dirge for the undead, its keen edge severing limbs and carving paths through the relentless tide. When she approached Eamon's side, a raucous symphony of destruction played out in arcs of silver as the pair danced among the monsters until the last remnant of Fiona's old self was discarded into the bloodied slush.

Maeve watched, torn between the unfolding tragedy of Loren's bite and the awe-inspiring metamorphosis of her friend. In Fiona's swift strikes, there was a poignant reminder of the sacrifices they had all made and the strength that had been born into them by sheer desperation.

Maeve pushed another foot nearer to Loren, renewed by the real-ization that this battle had sowed seeds of change within them all, even as it threatened to steal Loren's life. But that dawning aware-ness was bittersweet. For in their shared struggles, they had become more than survivors—they had become guardians of each other's humanity and defenders of an all too fragile dream they refused to let shatter.

"Loren has fallen," Maeve shouted to Eamon over the ghastly din as his gaze caught hers. "I need you to make space for me to tend him."

His answering roar reverberated through the clearing, a din of defiance that drew the horde's attention as he raced toward the tree line. His flight granted Maeve a scant moment of reprieve to check on their friend. But she knew this chance was as slender as her waning hope that Loren would not only survive, but also not be turned. His accepting the fact she was a zombie now was one thing. Accepting the same transformation taking place in himself was quite another. He would probably much prefer to fall on his own blade.

With her blood roaring in her ears, she locked gazes with Fiona, desperate to know she understood what Maeve was about to do. But that was all the time it took for the zombie who had assaulted Loren to charge at Maeve.

"Protect him," she shouted to Fiona through clenched teeth as she nodded towards Loren, who still lay writhing on the ground, looking pale, crumpled, and vulnerable.

Fiona gave a scant nod, and in that quicksilver second of intuitive understanding, the two women moved as one. Maeve lunged forward, her weapon severing the throat of the same zombie that had threatened to claim Loren's life. As the creature's grotesque head thudded to the earth, it erupted in a putrid spray of worm-eaten brains. Its gruesome body danced a ghastly jig for a few horrifying seconds before it, too, let go of its existence and crumpled to the ground.

Though Maeve knew she had no other choice but to defend herself, tears glazed her eyes as she recalled Alaric's hope that the research he was sponsoring might allow the ferals to be at least somewhat cured. But there was no antidote for a true death, and whatever hopes and dreams this beast had once harbored had been vanquished along with him.

Beside her, Fiona took on two stragglers, her sword carving through sinew and bone. Each stroke of her blade proved her metamorphosis from waif to warrior, and Maeve had never been more thankful to call her a friend.

The forest seemed to be holding its breath as the last of the zombies fell, dispatched by Eamon's unyielding onslaught. They all spent a long moment panting amidst the devastation they'd wrought, their exhausted bodies heaving with exertion and their expressions taut with disbelief.

Her gaze swept over the sea of fallen ferals, her mind refusing to accept their victory as anything more than a temporary lull in the maelstrom that had become their existence. For there would be more killing in her future, of that she was certain.

"Are you two alright?" Eamon approached, his voice cutting through the deathly silence, ragged with exhaustion.

Loren moaned as he sat up, his trembling hand still clutching at the torn flesh of his arm.

Blinking back tears, Maeve rushed forward and knelt beside him, her fingers trembling as she assessed the damage. The bite he'd suffered was deep, its edges ragged, but it was the wound's blackened edges that made her heart sink. Already, the tissue was necrotic... and the rot was spreading fast. If the infection made it to his heart...she feared he would surely turn feral.

"We need to stop the advance. Eamon, give me your shirt," she instructed, her voice tinged with an urgency that mirrored the fear thrumming in her veins.

"Will he—" Fiona's words trailed off, unable to give voice to the dread that hung over them like a death edict.

"We can't know for certain. Not yet," Maeve replied, her eyes never leaving Loren's pallid face as she used her dagger to cut a sleeve off the shirt Eamon had proffered, then tossed it back to him as he'd need it for warmth.

"For now," she said as she used her dagger to cut the sleeve into strips, "I will lance the wound. That will help keep the infection from reaching his heart. Then we must keep moving toward the village."

As Maeve worked to score Loren's wound and stem the fresh blood that spurted from the freshly lanced tissue, the reality of their situation settled upon her. Each strip of fabric she wrapped around the dazed man's arm was both a prayer for his soul's survival and an acknowledgment of the high toll a journey such as theirs could take. And this time, that toll might well cost Loren his arm... if not his very humanity.

CHAPTER 11

The group moved onward only because turning back to let Loren rest in the cavern's shelter would be tantamount to serving themselves to their pursuers on a silver platter.

With Eamon half carrying, half dragging Loren, their collective footsteps drummed a soggy cadence against the forest floor. But at least for now, Maeve saw no sign of lingering ferals. Apparently, neither did Nyx. The feline seemed oblivious to her diminutive size as she ambled before them, like she had always known the path to her human friends' destination and was happy to lead the way. For the moment, Maeve was content to let her, and she found herself wishing she could thank Isolde for gifting her with such a useful and vigilant familiar. She'd never felt more tired than she did now, and with remnants of snow transforming the forest's landmarks, she wondered if she could even find her way back to her village left to her own devices.

Though she knew it must be approaching midday, the shadows cast by the towering pines stretched long and forlorn as the group traversed the uncertain terrain, each one clinging to the other. Not just for physical support, but for the strength to endure the long road ahead. For they all knew the same thing she did—her village was but a waystation on this journey toward saving Alaric.

But hope wasn't lost just yet. They were still free and alive. And in the restless quiet that had followed their harrowing escape, Maeve could feel the delicate threads that bound them tightening. Love and duty toward their own peoples was what had first brought them together. But now, their union was also tempered with their shared sorrow for the fate that might have befallen Loren.

Even as the forest loomed over them, Maeve clung to the belief that within their fragile alliance, they would somehow find the strength to face whatever new trials might await them in the village she'd once called her home. For the rising of the hair at her nape told her there would be quite a few.

Finally, the woods began to thin, giving way to the same soggy fields Maeve had spent many of her childhood days working to clear. In the distance, sunset had begun to fall over the small village where she'd been raised. As they crested the last rise on the dirt road that would lead her back to her family, the last rays of sunlight clung desperately to the sod rooftops. It felt to Maeve like they, too, dreaded being swallowed by another feral-infested night.

With wistful tears for her lost innocence glazing her eyes, she led her companions over the rise with a weariness that seemed to suck the marrow from her bones. She was aware of Fiona's watchful gaze as her eyes scanned the dirt road ahead for any signs of threat. She didn't have to ask Fiona to know what she was thinking. Given how she'd been received on her last visit here, she doubted most would be glad to see her return. And assuming the news of what had befallen Eamon and Loren at the ball had preceded them, some might even wish to see her and Fiona dispatched from this life.

As if intuiting her thoughts, Fiona's grip on her weapon tightened, proving that she, too, anticipated an unwelcome reception from their human cousins. Only Eamon was too distracted to share their concerns—but then he was not a zombie. His attention instead lingered on Loren, whose pallor had grown even more pronounced against the dimming light. "Hold on, my friend," he murmured, righting Loren as he stumbled. "We're almost there."

"But first, we must get past the guards," Maeve said. "They were none too happy to allow me entrance last time, and if the village has suffered a feral attack, they will be all the more vigilant."

As they closed in on the village gates, every rustle of the wind, every creak of a snapped twig, was another admonition for them to tread lightly lest they draw any unwanted attention to themselves.

Even Nyx's ears were peaked, her tail crooked and twitching as if she was attuned to the tension that hummed through the air.

A feral screamed in the woods behind them, and someone fired a warning shot into the air. Three of the guards charged toward the armory to sound the alarm bells, leaving only one still tending the gate. With a sudden arch of her back and a hiss, Nyx sprang forward, bounding toward the village gate with a spectral grace that belied her undead status.

She roared like a lioness, appearing larger than life as she bounded through the gate, leaped, and clawed the face of the startled guard. He cried out as he threw her to the ground and gave chase, his shouts receding into the background as Nyx parried and weaved, a phantom lure intent on leading him away from Maeve and her company.

In the wake of the diversion, the group slipped past the distracted guards, each step carrying them deeper into the village's familiar yet foreboding embrace. But Maeve's pace did not lighten with the relief of her homecoming, and she took on the rushed urgency of a fugitive.

While they wove through the narrow alleyways that would take them to Nan's cottage, Loren's staggered breaths were a grim accompaniment. Maeve found herself praying to the gods who had likely abandoned her that it was caused by some treatable infection, or blood loss, not the dark threat of his impending transformation hanging over him like a guillotine's blade.

They navigated swiftly through the dimly lit streets. The occasional sound of laughter or a voice lifted in song proved the villagers oblivious to the chaos they had left behind in the forest. Maeve's gaze flitted from one darkened window to another, her mind fraught with concern, not just for Loren's condition, but for the safety of those they sought refuge among. Should Loren be changing, nobody could know whether he would be transformed into a sentient zombie or a feral one.

The familiar cobblestones paving the alley that would dump them into the square near Nan's cottage suddenly felt alien beneath her feet, as if the village had become a mere echo of its former self. As they finally stepped into the square, her instincts begged her to shield her companions from the dangers her alliance with Alaric might summon. Not just upon them, but upon her family, too.

Maeve rapped on the timeworn door of Nan's tiny cottage. But the usual joy she should have felt upon visiting her family was tempered by trepidation. If Nan and Coralie weren't home, they had nowhere else to go.

When familiar, shuffling footsteps sounded within, she blew out a relieved sigh. "The rest of you should probably stand back," she whispered to her friends, her voice tinged with urgency. "My grandmother won't be expecting us, and we look and smell like fetid meat." She didn't want to speak aloud what they were all thinking—Loren's appearance was growing more shocking by the moment.

As her friends nodded and slipped into the shadows, the door groaned on its hinges with a sound that Maeve found as world-weary as it was welcoming. The familiar scents of drying herbs and frying meat wafted through the opening, greeting her like a tender embrace from less complicated times. So much had passed since Maeve had last seen her family, and she had no idea what her grandmother already knew about what had occurred at the ball or what, if anything, she ought to tell her first.

But in the end, it did not matter. Nan, with her silver hair cascading over her knitted shawl, gasped and rushed through the door with her arms outstretched. Maeve could not help but fall into their protective circle, the weight of her worries momentarily suspended. Within seconds, Coralie had joined them.

"Welcome home, child," Nan murmured, her raspy voice falling over Maeve like a comforting quilt.

"We missed you so very much," Coralie chimed in, her words flitting around Maeve like fireflies chasing away the shadows.

"I missed you, too, more than words can say," she replied. Her eyes glistened with tears born from gratitude that her transition had not broken their familial bond. She could only hope that should Loren be changed, too, they would treat him with the same care and respect. In fact, she was counting on it.

"Did you come to measure me for my flower girl gown?" Coralie asked, her amber eyes wide with excitement. "And will it really be pink, like I asked?"

"I fear there won't be any time for a dress fitting this visit, my love." Maeve's heart constricted as the child's bright expression melted into a pout. With a soft sigh, she threaded her fingers through her young cousin's soft, brown curls. "But I promise you, when the time comes, your gown shall indeed be pink. As shall the flowers we will weave into your beautiful hair."

Coralie squealed, her hands clasped beneath her chin. "Swear it before the gods?"

Maeve nodded as she drew an x over her heart. "And you will be happy to know that Fiona, Eamon, and Loren have accompanied me." She beckoned her friends into the light. "I hope it's alright that we came here unannounced," she added, her gaze sliding toward Nan. "I'm not sure how much you have heard about the goings-on in Alaric's kingdom," she explained. "But know that we had nowhere else to seek refuge."

"Coralie," Nan said, shooing the child inside. "You're going to catch your death of cold. Now be my big girl and go stir the gravy before it turns to lumps."

"I have indeed heard some troubling things," Nan whispered hoarsely as she waved them all inside and pushed the door closed. "But until the whole truth came from your mouth, I did not think it wise to share those rumors with Coralie. Is it true that Prince Alaric was poisoned?"

Maeve's eyes misted with her nod, as did Nan's. "Leaving his side was the hardest thing ever, but there was no other choice. There is an antidote, but without any allies in the kingdom, it was left to me to find it."

Nan's expression turned grim with her nod. "While I am always happy to see you, you all look and smell like you've been through a battle. And by the looks of Loren, he barely survived. What happened?"

"I could not let the charges waged against Loren and Eamon after Alaric fell stand. After Brigid, Fiona and I hatched a plan to break them free, we had to make a run for it."

"Then you've chosen your destination wisely. So long as I breathe, you and your friends will always be welcome here."

"Nan," Maeve said, wincing as she watched Eamon help Loren inside. "Before you agree to give us sanctuary, there's something else you should know."

"Go on."

"Along the way, we were accosted by a horde. Loren was gravely wounded."

"And was he bitten?"

Maeve nodded.

"Then we must feed him, tend to his wounds, and find him a safe place for him to rest until we know how dire the situation is. So please," she said, waving them all inside, "make yourselves comfortable. Dinner is almost ready, and thanks to Prince Alaric's generosity, there's plenty of food, bandages and medicine to go around..."

"Then you should dole these things out sparingly," Maeve said as she followed Nan inside. "For as soon as Alaric fell, all the progress we had made in bringing his courtiers and our villagers together was replaced with the same fear and distrust that has kept us at odds these many years..."

Nan's face tightened as if this information had left a sour taste in her mouth. "We still have to eat. So go wash up as best you can, and we'll assemble at the table after."

THE HEARTY CRACKLE of the fire struggled to penetrate the melancholy that dulled Maeve's senses, but her proximity to Nan and Coralie finally thawed the icy shield that had encased her heart since Alaric had fallen.

Though she struggled to hold back tears, the hearth's glow danced against the walls, casting soft shadows that seemed to dance in silent celebration of their reuniting. Even Fiona's eyes, still bright with the terrors they had faced, softened as they took in the quaint trappings of the room.

Maeve's breath escaped in a quiet sigh—a physical release of the fear that had been coiled within her like a spring wound too tight.

Eamon, his forehead lined with fatigue, let his guard down for a moment, allowing the mantle of protector to slip just enough to give Fiona a soft smile as her gaze sought out his.

Even Loren, pale and drawn as he was, managed a feeble smile as Maeve's attention fixed on him.

As they all assembled around Nan's rough-hewn wooden table, which occupied the heart of the cottage, Maeve felt the tension in her shoulders ease. Here, amidst the creaks and sighs of the old wooden beams, lay memories that anchored her to Nan and

Coralie's, to the very reasons they fought—and to Alaric's hope for unity that still twinkled in her mind like the last star at dawn.

Her gaze drifted inadvertently to the door they'd just passed through, where a small, shadowy figure crept toward them with silent purpose. Nyx slinked into the room like an apparition. Her copper eyes shimmered with an otherworldly intelligence, reflecting a knowledge that went far beyond her feline appearance.

Maeve watched the cat approach, her heart caught between wonder and wariness as the creature that defied nature itself wound around her legs. "Look who followed us inside," she said, her voice a mix of incredulity and affection as she bent to stroke the cat's coarse hair. The feline nudged against her palm, accepting the gesture with a rumbling purr that belied its macabre form.

"Is she your kitty?" Coralie asked. "May I pet her?"

"I suppose she is mine. She has given me no choice in the matter. But she is a zombie cat and may never have seen a child, so only touch her if she will come to you first." She couldn't help but smile as Coralie clamored to the floor and cooed when Nyx nestled in her lap and began to bat at her curls.

"What's her name?" Coralie asked.

"Nyx," Maeve answered.

"It would seem we owe that ugly little beastie more laurels than we ever would have thought," Fiona said, her tone laced with a newfound respect as she observed Coralie's interaction with the cat.

Eamon nodded, his eyes never leaving Nyx. "In these times, even the most unlikely of allies can become gifts."

But Maeve knew Nyx's presence here was more than just luck. The bond between herself and the strange feline had deepened, perhaps because of the unspoken understanding that existed between those who walked the edge of two worlds. As the cat held her in its unwavering gaze, there lay a silent assurance that for now, in the uncomplicated serenity of Nan's cottage, they had been granted a brief reprieve—a chance to breathe before they were called upon to face their next trial.

Judging by Loren's face, that time would come all too soon. His features contorted as he pushed away the steaming plate Nan set before him. Groaning, he leaned forward in his chair, his trembling arms clutching his belly. His breaths came in ragged pants, and the bite on his arm had oozed through its makeshift dressing. That the putrid-smelling stain was black did not bode well for his fate.

"That wound should be cleaned," Nan said, then ordered Coralie to procure bandages, clean rags, and antiseptic from the storage pantry.

As Eamon stood up from his chair and approached his brother-in-arms, Maeve watched, her chest tightening as Loren's tortured gaze lifted to meet Eamon's. "Help me get away from them before…" he mouthed, the trembling in his hands underpinning his plea.

As Maeve noted his eyes were growing clouded and distant, she thought of Nan and Coralie, of the warmth and laughter they had brought to this place. She would not have them or their home endangered by the specter of a potentially violent creature lurking in their midst. Even if that creature wore the visage of one she had known for as long as she could recall.

"I care for him, too, Eamon, but Loren is right. We must get him away from the others until we know his fate," she said, her voice barely above a murmur, yet laden with an urgency that brooked no argument.

Eamon agreed with a curt nod. With Coralie's return, he hauled Loren to his feet. As his body took the bulk of his friend's weight, there was a contrived steadiness in his gaze, the unyielding resolve of a man who had seen too much heartache, yet refused to falter. "If it's alright by you," he said to Nan, "I'll take him to the storage room. After I have tended to his wounds… well, we can board it up if need be. In the meantime," his gaze sought out Maeve's, "Fiona can place your dagger blades and my sword's blade into the fire. The heat should sterilize them in the event that…" Though the balance of his words caught in his throat, Maeve did not need to hear them to know what he was thinking. An amputation might be the only way to save Loren's life—and with any luck, perhaps even his soul.

As the two men started toward the pantry, Eamon's hands, calloused and scarred from battles past, cradled his friend with a gentleness that spoke of a bond forged in fire and tempered by shared perils. Maeve's heart stuttered as she watched her friends disappear through the aged oak door. "When the blades have been glowing for a while, bring them to me and knock," Eamon called over his shoulder. "Then find some boards, nails and a hammer to drive them in with. And do not hesitate to do so should I command it."

The click of the latch echoed like the note of a requiem. Now, only the gods could decide Loren's fate. As Maeve turned away, her gaze first fell upon Fiona, who stood by the fireplace, wide-eyed and silent, her own turmoil barely hidden beneath the hastily assembled visage of her newfound courage. In her violet eyes, there shimmered a reflection of the warrior she had become, a transformation that had been wrought from necessity and the will to survive. But Maeve thought she also saw something else blooming there as Fiona cast her gaze upon the pantry door, something as fragile and new as it was lovely—the deep love she now felt for Eamon. And because she loved him, she now feared losing him, just as Maeve feared losing her own beloved.

CHAPTER 12

As Maeve went to tuck a bubbly and babbling Coralie in for the night, Nyx hopped into the bed to join them. Normally, she would have protested. There was no telling what manner of vermin the feline had gotten into today. But she looked clean enough, and with her cousin content to cuddle her strange new bedfellow instead of insisting on her usual never-ending story, she let herself sink into the worn chair positioned beside the bed. She was grateful for a moment to just bask in the rare and simple pleasure of her cousin's company. Only tonight, the fraying cushion's familiar embrace offered little comfort.

The starless night pressed against the windowpanes, a reminder that darkness was never far away and was always waiting to claim what scrap of light they still held onto. As she watched Coralie's eyelids flutter and grow heavy, she realized for the first time how very exhausted she felt. Not just in her aching body, but in her spirit, too.

As Coralie began to snore softly, she let her thoughts reach out to Alaric, and to finding the antidote that might yet snatch him back from the precipice. While she wondered how on earth she would ever find the means to procure it in time, her gaze fell to the white circle where her betrothal ring had been. In her mind, its verdant glow shimmered weakly as if it, too, carried a hope as delicate and fragile as a spider's web.

Gods, how she missed him. She'd give anything, even her soul, to find herself held in his cornflower blue gaze. His heavy-lidded perusal never failed to illuminate the darkness that had stalked her since the day he had first pulled her from the snake pit and taken her back to his castle.

"Tomorrow, we will speak to the tributaries," she whispered, more to Alaric than to herself. "For Isolde insists they hold the key to your resurrection. And no matter how thin my faith might grow, so long as I breathe, your hopes for our world will not die. So please know this, my love. I undertake this quest not just for you, or even myself, but for a better future for all of us."

In her mind's eye, she saw Alaric framed in the doorway, the candlelight striking copper sparks off his mahogany hair as he held her in his beautiful gaze and nodded. "You will find a way, my love. You always do. And then we will be married."

She so desperately wanted to believe those words had truly come from him. But as a restless quiet settled over the deceptive sanctuary of the cottage, his image faded, and a fresh sense of unease wove itself into the homespun air she breathed. Outside, she thought she heard the beating of great wings, and the atmosphere suddenly grew heavy and pensive, like the stillness before a storm, the deep quiet that spoke of things left unsaid and the destruction of paths yet untrodden. Paths such as poor Loren's.

Maeve's gaze drifted to where Nyx now lay curled at the foot of Coralie's bed. The feline's steadfast presence offered her a peculiar comfort amidst the brewing tempest she sensed. As if bidden by her gaze, the zombie cat, with eyes that seemed to hold the wisdom of the ages, seemed to whisper to her about the secrets of survival against all odds. But she could barely resist the urge to bark out a laugh when the cat seemed to whisper that the best weapon against all of the horrible things that had transpired wasn't witnessing more death, but rather mantling herself in true love's unrelenting embrace.

Now you are starting to sound like Alaric, she mused, and the cat mewed thinly as if in affirmation.

Then, an owl hoot-hooted outside the window, reinforcing the idea that Alaric was somehow with her. Guiding her. Or perhaps she was losing her mind. And though she knew her mood, combined with Loren's plight, meant sleep would elude her tonight, that silly fairytale notion that love would conquer all caused her resolve to solidify like the steel blades that even now were being tempered in the roaring flames within her grandmother's hearth.

As if bidden by this thought, Fiona nudged open the door to Coralie's tiny room. The young woman's eyes were wide and flashing with worry. "It is time to take the blades in to Eamon," she whispered. "And judging by the sounds that have been emanating from the pantry, the job before him will be tedious and fraught with danger..."

With a last pensive glance at Coralie and a silent prayer to the fickle gods to always keep the child safe, Maeve heaved a wistful sigh of lamentation for the simple things that might never be again. Then she rose from her chair, braced her shoulders, and followed Fiona back into the main room to see what, if anything, could be done for poor Loren.

Nan's stooped form hovered over the crackling fire, her weathered skin flushed and gleaming with moisture as she tended the cast iron pot hanging from the spit. The rhythmic clinks of metal against metal accompanied her movements, blending with the soft moans emanating from the pantry where Eamon was locked in with Loren.

Billows of steam carrying hints of medicinal herbs wafted up and gathered around Nan's head like a halo, giving her the appearance of an angel. And perhaps that is exactly what her grandmother was, a stalwart soul who had been dropped into this realm to show them how grounding the relationships shared between family and friends were.

A near smile touched Maeve's lips as she remembered to count what few blessings she had left. Nan, Coralie, Eamon, Loren... and of course now, Fiona and her beloved Alaric... they were her touchstones and always would be, no matter how far away this harrowing journey took her.

"Stop with your daydreaming and carry me that stack of rags," Nan directed as she caught Maeve hovering at the edges of her vision. The urgency in the woman's voice cut through the faint howls of wind outside. "And be quick about it. Even now, Loren's sickness advances."

"So you believe he will lose his arm, then?" Her voice was barely above a whisper as she handed the rags off to Nan and watched her dip them in the boiling liquid.

Nan nodded as she draped some rags over the spit to steam. The hiss and sizzle of moisture meeting heat added a tense accompaniment to their conversation. "It will prove a grave loss given he is an archer, but if Eamon feels amputation is the only way to save Loren's life... perhaps even his soul... then so be it."

"Do you think Loren is cognizant enough to know what is about to happen to him?"

Nan's shoulder lifted. "I have no way of knowing. But if Loren is aware and able, he has surely agreed. And should things turn for the worse, he would be the first to insist Eamon lop off his head while he has the chance."

Maeve was unable to contain the dry sob that scraped past her lips, for the inevitability of her grandmother's statement was overwhelming.

"Try not to fret. Given the lad rages with fever, it is quite possible... even likely ...he might not know his own mind. Either way, if Loren is to stand any chance of being saved, this is how it must be done."

"But what about his pain?" Maeve's voice wavered as sympathy for her friend rose up, clogging her throat. "I can't imagine how much misery he could suffer. Perhaps even enough to speed his... fate."

"Eamon is dosing him with spirits and sedative herbs as we speak," Nan replied, her tone heavy with concern. "I take the fact the shrieks emanating from within the pantry have gone more scarce as proof they are doing their work. I only hope the steam rising from the pot is sufficient to sterilize these rags."

"But if Loren should wake while Eamon is working on him... and turns... then Eamon, too, could be in grave danger," Fiona interjected from behind them, her voice shrill.

"Aye," Nan agreed, her gaze flickering between the younger women. "But what other choice is there? If Eamon does not act, Loren could turn...and perhaps for the worst. Then we will all be in grave trouble."

"But Fiona's concerns can't be dismissed," Maeve murmured, her thoughts racing as she considered the weight of their decisions. "Should Loren manage to turn Eamon, too, all here besides Fiona and myself would be in mortal danger. And should he get out into the town..." No. She could not, would not let that happen, or Alaric's dream of peace would be undone, perchance forever this time.

"But we can't just let him keep suffering," Fiona said, her voice taut with sorrow.

"Of course not," Maeve agreed, struggling to keep her tone firm as she reached for one of the glowing blades. "Like Nan said, it's possible—

likely—Loren's arm must be sacrificed for his greater good."

"But Eamon..." Fiona's voice trailed off, her eyes reflecting her rising terror. "We could well be sacrificing him, as well."

"That is why we must be the ones," Maeve said, her voice steady despite the turmoil railing within her. We will take Eamon's place and ensure that doesn't happen."

Though Fiona's eyes swam with horror, her nod proved her assent.

"May whatever gods still watch over us be with you both," Nan murmured, her voice thick as she drew the two women into a fierce hug.

"Please, keep yourself and Coralie safe," Maeve whispered as she pulled away and bracketed her grandmother's weary face between her palms.

"Perhaps it is best if I retreat to Coralie's room while the two of you tend to Loren. Should things go badly, we can escape out the window and warn the neighbors there is a feral zombie in our midst. But should that happen, swear to me you will both break for the woods before the watchmen and scouts can assemble in the square. For at that point, they will care not whether you are sentient or feral zombies."

"I promise," Maeve said. "Now you must go, quickly, before Loren's sedative leaves his body."

"I love you, Maeve. Always have, always will," Nan said.

Overcome with emotion at the sound of the endearment they'd shared so often, Maeve kissed her grandmother's cheek and gently nudged her toward the room where Coralie still slumbered, oblivious to the horror about to take place beneath the very roof she'd always trusted would keep her safe.

Nan's words echoed in Maeve's mind as she watched her grandmother scuffle off to her cousin's room and waited for the metallic click that proved she had remembered to lock the door behind her. Turning back to face Fiona, the enormity of their task settled heavily on her shoulders, mingling with her worry for Loren's fate. The gravity of what they were about to attempt—assuming Eamon would even let them—was overwhelming. "And now," she said to Fiona, "it is time."

As the women rushed about, gathering their makeshift medical supplies, the weight of the sword in Maeve's hand felt both familiar and foreign. Though she had wielded weapons many times before, she'd never had cause to use her blade in such a life-altering manner. The blade's polished metal seemed to wink at her in the firelight, as if mocking the enormity of their task. Though in her world, weapons were precious, she already knew that this one would be buried alongside Loren's arm, for once this deed was done, she would not be able to bear looking at it again.

With their supplies gathered, the girls exchanged a solemn glance. Maeve saw no need to ask Fiona what she was feeling—her determination to help Loren, laced with sadness for what was about to transpire, was written on her face. The moisture that welled in her eyes was surely mirrored in Maeve's own. After this night, a poor young man's life would never be the same. All of that was assuming he even survived their homespun attempt at an amputation. Yet this was a far better fate than idly standing by while he transitioned into a feral or died of a rampant infection. No matter how she turned this situation in her mind, Maeve could see no other choice than to proceed as they had planned.

"Are you sure you are prepared for this?" she asked Fiona, whose eyes had grown impossibly wide and luminous, dominating her tiny face. "There will be much bloodshed."

Though Fiona shrugged, the gesture was far from flippant. "Slaying zombies in the woods was one thing. They were trying to kill people I care for. But Loren... he is our friend. Watching him bleed from an injury I helped inflict... will not be easy. And to be honest, I have no idea where to begin."

"Have you ever helped butcher a deer?" Maeve asked of her friend.

Fiona shook her head, no. "I've seen that sort of work, but given the courtiers consider butchery to be men's work, I never had an opportunity to assist."

"Well, lucky for you, I have. Amputating an arm shouldn't be much different. So you can assist, but when I warn you the time has come, it is fine to close your eyes and leave the actual amputation to me. But before any of that can happen, I might need you to use any charms you can muster to convince Eamon it is in all of our best interests if he lets us be the ones to remove Loren's arm."

Fiona's terse nod was all the confirmation Maeve needed. As the clock chimed the midnight hour, they approached the pantry where Eamon waited with Loren. The seriousness of Maeve's role as Loren's surgeon by necessity caused her throat to constrict. The deed could be done in one cut, but that cut must be swift, strong, and true. There could be no room for error.

Rapping gently on the pantry door, she steeled her heart for the harrowing task ahead, knowing it was not only Loren's fate that hung in the balance this night, but also Eamon's. Surrendering his role as Loren's protector to women he'd rather protect might not come easily for him. Yet, somehow, she and Fiona must convince him to cede control. Unlike them, he was still a mortal. Should Loren turn despite the amputation, Eamon could well lose his life, or worse, be turned himself.

As she pushed the narrow door open, Maeve peered through the dim light to where Loren lay on the floor, his entire body shuddering. No matter how hard she tried, she could not swallow her gasp. The poor man was barely recognizable, with his normally dark complexion pale and gaunt, his breathing rapid and ragged. During the short time he had been confined to the pantry, his wounded arm had swollen to twice its size. The makeshift bandages Maeve had applied now dripped with blood and oozed blackness. As she moved closer and knelt to feel Loren's cheek, her lips curled at the rancid smell emanating from his dressings, a vile combination of gangrenous flesh underpinned with something sickly sweet, like honeysuckle, only far more cloying.

Her eyes welled with tears as she realized her friend's transition was imminent, and she wondered if leaving him in his cell to face the guillotine would have offered him a kinder fate. Now, the only question left was whether he would change into a sentient zombie like herself, or a feral one. The had to keep that infection from reaching his heart.

"Perhaps we are already too late," Fiona murmured as she stepped in beside Maeve. Eamon sat cross-legged on the floor with his dear friend's head cradled in his lap, holding a compress to his forehead.

Maeve bit back a sob, fearing the worst. If the infection spread, if Loren turned feral—she could not bear to think of the repercussions, and neither outcome represented a kind fate for their friend. Worse, it was possible he could suffer both miseries at the same time. But gods be damned, she couldn't bear the thought of losing him. They had to do something... try anything. She owed him at least that much.

"Has he been lucid within the last hours?" she asked of Eamon, gesturing with a tilt of her chin toward Loren.

Eamon's face was taut, his expression grim. "Up until the minute I dosed him with spirits and soporific herbs. But the fever grows worse by the minute. And judging by the swelling, the infection still advances." The oil lamp's scant flame illuminated the moisture brimming in Eamon's hazel eyes as he ran a hand through his hair and looked away for a moment. "I don't know how much longer we have before whatever is going to happen..."

He did not bother finishing. Nor did he need to. They all knew what was at stake. "His best chance is to keep the infection from reaching his heart. For us to amputate. Here." She touched her shoulder joint.

Countless emotions flurried over Eamon's face. "Maeve, I know it makes logical sense to do so, but I've reconsidered," he finally managed. "He is an archer, the best this village has got. But without his arm... no. We can't. If he was able right now, he would be the first to tell us, given he has no family to mourn him, he would be better off dead."

"But we have no other choice available to us!" Maeve cried, her voice growing shrill. "When the infection reaches his heart, he will die in misery while the rest of his body follows. And we both know that is the least of his worries..."

Fiona moved in behind Eamon and pressed her face between his shoulder blades. "Eamon," she said, not knowing how to begin. "Judging by the looks and scent of him, he's already turning. But if we get that arm off now, perhaps we might at least mitigate the impact of the bite."

"But what if it doesn't, and he wakes up during the procedure? Should he wake as a feral, I would likely be turned myself before either of you could blink."

Maeve scooted closer to her friend's side and settled her palm on his forearm. "That is why you cannot be the one to do the amputation. But Fiona and I.... we are already turned. So though Loren might bite us, he cannot infect us again."

"You would have me leave two small women alone with a man who could transform into a monster and tear off your heads at any second? That is insanity, Maeve. It defies everything we were taught about the rules of decorum..."

"Decorum left this world long before we were born, Eamon. And you damn well know it."

"Maeve is right," Fiona murmured, her tiny hands working the muscles in Eamon's shoulders. "The idea is only slightly less insane than leaving Coralie and Nan unprotected. While mine and Maeve's trials have hardened us, they still depend on men for their protection. That is why we need you to guard them, in case he turns after we..."

His silence, paired with the stubborn set of his jaw, did not bode well for her plea. Desperate, Maeve placed her hands on his shoulders, pinning his gaze with her own. "Please, Eamon. You have to let us be the ones to do this. Not just for Loren. But for all of us."

Eamon silence was long.

Maeve could see anguish welling in his eyes, the longing to protect his loved ones, even though he had been there as she and

Fiona helped him fell a horde of ferals as efficiently as any man. But at last, he relented with a sigh and a nod.

"Do what you must," he said hoarsely. "But gods... please stay safe. He might not be able to infect you, but as a feral, he could easily tear off a limb. And know if you need anything, I will be but footsteps away, armed and guarding the door."

MAEVE PUSHED the door closed behind Eamon and focused on her breathing as she turned back to face the grim task ahead. Loren's life now depended on her and Fiona's ability to see this thing through. She could only pray she would not fail him, that there was still a chance to save him.

She steeled her jaw, willing her hand not to tremble as she lay her sword upon one of the clean rags Fiona had brought in with her. All too soon, the time would come to wield it once more—only this time, in hopes of saving a life rather than ending one.

With Eamon departed and Nan and Coralie tucked behind a locked door, Maeve helped Fiona clear one of the wooden pantry shelves. Together, they wrenched it free of the wall and used some wooden crates to create a makeshift operating table.

"We still need something to restrain him," Maeve said with a grunt as they lifted Loren's limp form onto the table.

"What for?" Fiona's brow was knitted with confusion.

"In case he should wake... during."

The edges of Fiona's mouth tightened as she gave Maeve a sharp nod and started rummaging through a crate in the corner, producing several leather straps that should serve their purposes.

After they secured Loren, Maeve took his pale, clammy hand in her own, feeling the thready, irregular race of his heartbeat. "I'm so sorry, my friend," she whispered as she gently unwound the putrid dressing off his arm and swallowed back the bile the stench drew into her throat. "I would give anything to spare you this, but it's the only way I know to try and help you."

"Will you be needing anything else?" Fiona struggled to keep a brave face, her voice strained, and her trembling hands clenched into fists at her sides.

"Just your faith," Maeve said gently. "And your courage."

Fiona met Maeve's gaze, her eyes glistening with tears. But her voice was sure and steady as she replied, "And you will have it. Loren deserves no less."

As Maeve wrapped her hand around her sword's handle, she took a deep, steadying breath, pushing aside her fears. Loren's life now depended on her steady hand, her unflinching will.

And now the time had come. "Close your eyes if you must," she said quietly. "But please, no matter what happens, do not stop holding his free hand. He deserves that much."

Holding back tears, Maeve watched as Fiona knelt and curled their friend's hand within her own. Then Fiona gave a small nod, indicating it was time to proceed.

As Fiona's eyes slid closed, Maeve drew in another deep breath and raised her sword. Heart heavy, she whispered a silent prayer to gods she scarcely trusted for strength, surety, and guidance. With a guttural cry, she let her sword fall in hopes a single swing would do the job.

But it was not meant to be. Thankfully, Loren only stirred with a muted groan, and Maeve took this as proof he had been spared the worst so far, thanks to Eamon's careful administration of soporific herbs and spirits.

Bracing her nerves and holding back tears that begged to be spilled, she swung again. And again. The task proved increasingly arduous, the sounds of snapping bone and the sight of spurting blood causing fresh bile to rise in her throat. But she continued to weld her blade with determination until, finally, the deed was done.

Loren's arm lay severed on the floor, but she still needed to staunch the bleeding. Though Fiona's eyes were still closed as Maeve moved to apply pressure to the wound, she still held fast to Loren's hand. While Maeve wrapped the jagged flesh with twine and tied it off, Fiona began singing a lullaby, perhaps in hopes he would remain calm as they waited for proof that the last ring of darkness that stained his flesh was receding.

Maeve sat back on her knees, swiping tears and sweat from her brow, her hands still trembling from exertion. As Loren began to softly snore, Fiona rose and stood beside her, a silent pillar of support as they stared at the gruesome outcome of their desperate gamble.

Minutes stretched into eternity before they saw the first signs of fate's intent. The blackness that had threatened to move beyond Loren's arm began to advance from the fresh wound Maeve had made, crawling toward his heart like a never-ending nightmare.

Then, without warning, Loren's eyes flew open. A ragged scream tore from his throat, his leather restraints groaning against his struggles. As he strained against his bonds, his unseeing eyes glowed crimson. A guttural snarl gurgled in his throat as the hand on his severed arm that lay on the floor clawed at the air.

The Loren they had all known and loved was gone. All that remained of him was a beast, foaming at the mouth and snapping his jaw as he fixed his gaze on Fiona. Maeve's heart shattered into a thousand pieces as she gazed at the tormented ruin of their friend. And for a moment, she could only stare at the proof of her failure, hating herself more than she ever thought possible.

"Eamon!" Fiona's scream echoed through the pantry, ragged with grief and anguish. "Help us!"

The door burst open. Accompanied by the sound of splintering wood, Eamon raced inside, his eyes widening at the otherworldly sight before him. At Loren, his friend, his brother in arms, thrashing and snarling against his makeshift restraints. At the severed arm lying discarded on the floor, its blue-black fingers still grasping at thin air. At Maeve and Fiona, who were both clinging to each other, drenched in blood and tears.

With a roar of fury and a sob laced with sorrow, Eamon launched himself across the small space to take the sword from Maeve's hand. With one swing of the blade, Loren's head thudded to the floor, his body going limp and still against the makeshift operating table.

Silence fell over the pantry, broken only by quiet sobs. Maeve leaned heavily against Fiona, what remained of her strength leaving her until she felt as limp as Coralie's favorite ragdoll.

The deed was done.

There was no going back.

All that remained now was to mourn the passing of their friend, then carry on with their quest to save Alaric, one dear man shorter than when they began.

CHAPTER 13

Silence gored Maeve's heart like an iron maiden as she, Fiona, and Eamon trudged from the dim confines of the pantry, their shoulders sagging and expressions somber. Each footfall seemed to bear the weight of their combined sorrows, and Maeve's ears rang with the ghost of her old friend's laughter, now forever silenced by a swing of his best friend's blade. The smell of copper and putrid flesh still lingered on their bloodstained clothes, a stark reminder of the macabre act of mercy that had claimed Loren's life, yet had also saved his soul. But it mattered little that they had done what they believed served the common good, for they had all grown to love the young man like family.

Maeve's heart felt as though it were encased in stone, each beat a dagger stabbing her ribs. She could sense Eamon's grief as tangibly as if it were her own—loss dueling with undirected fury boiling beneath his features. Fiona's small hand, though still trembling, was a constant presence at the small of his back, a silent show of support amidst the maelstrom of his angst. Maeve almost envied their connection, for she would give anything to have Alaric here with her now. But then again... if he was here, none of this would need to have happened. Loren would still be alive and well. *This is all my fault. I should never have let myself love him.*

"You have done nothing Loren would not have wanted from you." Nan could have been reading Maeve's mind as she emerged from the shadows, like the quiet appearance of the moon through parting storm clouds. Though her voice was raspy with age, it somehow spoke both of resilience and the tenderness of old wounds that had been reopened by Alaric's fall and made deeper by Loren's senseless loss.

"You cannot grieve properly with the poor lad's lifeblood still clinging to you," Nan said, her bleary eyes soft and moist as they passed over them. "There is a barrel of fresh rainwater on the back stoop. Grab some rags from the stack by the back door and wash yourselves up. It will help clear your heads for what is yet to come."

Maeve nodded, her throat too tight with emotion for any words to push through. She watched as Eamon and Fiona, bound by their as yet unspoken affection for each other, made their way towards the back door. Though Maeve worried for them, the gentle clasp of their hands spoke volumes. Already, the couple shared a silent language that suggested shared strength and solace. And again, witnessing their growing connection made Maeve long for Alaric that much more.

"Go ahead," Maeve managed as Fiona paused, casting a questioning glance over her shoulder. "I will have my turn shortly."

As her friends departed, her eyes, brimming with unshed tears, swung back to meet Nan's as she silently pleaded for time—time to gather herself, to weave her splintering thoughts into some semblance of order.

"Take all the time you need, child," Nan replied, the lines of her face etched with the wisdom of years and the knowledge of countless goodbyes whispered to loved ones lost, Maeve's own parents being among them. The woman's hand, gnarled yet steady, reached out to gently squeeze Maeve's forearm—a gesture that anchored her to the moment, to the necessity of facing what still lay ahead.

Somehow, they must lay Loren's body and soul to rest, then move on.

As Eamon and Fiona disappeared into the darkness beyond the back door, Maeve felt the walls of the small room press in closer, as if bearing witness to the turning of a page in yet another treacherous tale being spun by sinister forces. Later, there would be time for tears, for whispered regrets and tender memories—but not now, when duty called with a voice as insistent as the wind.

"Nan," Maeve finally began, her voice a thready whisper in the encompassing stillness, "there is so much we need to discuss... but there is not much time."

Nan's chin dipped, her eyes steady on Maeve's. As always, she was the matriarchal pillar amidst the crumbling ruins of their village's recent flirtation with peace and prosperity—all thanks to Alaric's effort to restore trust between her former village mates and his equally distrustful kingdom. "Peace is a worthy cause to die for, child," she said, as if reading Maeve's mind. "For none will survive long without it."

Maeve could only nod. But as she and Nan sat at the table, two generations weathering the same storm from different ports, the sorrow in the room took on a new shape, one of shared burdens and the quiet determination to do their parts to help set their broken world right. She only needed to remain strong until Alaric awoke and folded her in his arms. Only then would she feel safe to properly grieve Loren's loss. So she sat next to her grandmother in the kitchen where they'd shared countless meals, her heart a churning maelstrom of guilt and despair.

The scents of drying herbs and curing meats that once bespoke of sanctuary now threatened to sicken her. Struggling to avoid upending the contents of her gut, she pinned her focus on tracing the grain of the wooden table with a trembling finger; each swirl and knot mirrored the chaotic din whirling within her soul.

"Alaric," she murmured her beloved's name, a talisman against her fracturing spirit. "What have I done?" Her thoughts betrayed her, tumbling out as words and falling from her lips like stones, too burdensome to carry any further.

"Child... please, don't blame yourself." Nan's voice was like a warm shawl wrapped around Maeve's shoulders. "You cannot bear the brunt of so many burdens alone." The old woman's eyes brimmed with a resigned sorrow that stretched back through the ages, yet the arm she looped around Maeve's shoulders still found the strength to offer her loved ones sanctuary and solace.

After giving Maeve's shoulders a comforting squeeze, Nan rose and retrieved a pitcher of water, a basin, and a clean rag. She poured the water into the basin and dipped the rag in, wringing it out slightly. With tender motions, she began to wipe the dried blood from Maeve's hands, gently cleaning away the scarlet remnants of Loren's sacrifice. "Please, child. Surely, you must know your troubles are safe with me."

"Nan," Maeve finally began, "I fear indulging my love for Alaric has brought us all to ruination. If I cannot save him, if I am the cause of all this suffering..." Her words trailed off, unable to express the utter desolation of enduring a future without him. Now, with Loren fallen, it seemed their shared dream to bring peace back to their world had also lost its power to serve as her guiding light.

Nan sighed as she dipped her rag again, using it to softly wipe the drying streaks of blood from Maeve's face. "Love is a force far beyond our reckoning," she said, her tone soft as silk but unwavering as steel. "Yet it has shaped destinies, birthed nations, and felled evil empires. But you, Maeve, do not hold the power to be the architect of anyone's fate."

"But if Alaric perishes anyway, what is the point of all this bloodshed?" she pleaded, searching the depths of Nan's eyes for the source of her wisdom.

"Life will go on, child, with you or without you. Even when it seems hope is but a wisp of smoke on the wind," Nan crooned, cradling Maeve's hands in the nest of her own. "We must do right by Loren and send him on his journey with grace, yet in a place where his remains will be undisturbed by the prying eyes of those who do not yet understand what we fight for."

Maeve nodded. "Loren's death... I cannot let it be a sacrifice made in vain."

"Nor shall it be, unless you lose hope and quit," Nan affirmed. "But for now, we must give his soul peace by laying him to rest. And in doing so, we will honor the sacrifice he made for those who are still living."

Though Maeve agreed, the weakest of nods was all she could manage.

"There is still much strength left in your heart, Maeve. But you must find in yourself a way to hold fast to it. Not just for your dear Alaric, but for us all. Including yourself."

Maeve wrapped herself in those fortifying words while Nan continued with her gentle ministrations, cleansing Maeve's skin of Loren's lifeblood. In silence, Maeve acquiesced to her grandmother's care, watching as she dipped her rag and wrung it out again until the water inside the bowl bloomed with the color of roses.

As Maeve extracted herself from Nan's embrace, a flicker of movement caught her eye. Eamon and Fiona stood huddled in the back doorway, their expressions etched with sorrow at the conversation they had unwittingly eavesdropped upon. As their gazes connected, the air lightened with their unspoken understanding, and Maeve's breath hitched. She had not meant for her fears to spill over, for her doubts to be laid bare before those who had been looking to her for guidance since they had left the castle grounds. Yet there they were, witnesses to her most vulnerable confessions.

Eamon stepped forward, the lines of his face softened by the empathy illuminating his hazel eyes. "Maeve," he said, his voice a steady fortress against her tumultuous emotions. "You must not blame yourself. Nor do we blame you. But Nan is right. We must think of what is right and proper for Loren. We must tell the others so we can see him into the next world."

"Then I will help you tell them."

Eamon's expression grew sadder as he shook his head. "The townsfolk cannot know of your presence; it would spell danger for us all—especially Nan and Coralie."

Maeve heaved a tremulous sigh, and he moved closer, placing a hand on her shoulder. "It is best if I am the one to announce Loren's passing."

"But how can you possibly explain the nature of his... wounds?"

"I cannot so long as his body remains here. But if I can take him to the edge of the woods under night's cover..." His words died off, his struggle to master his emotions clear in the set of his jaw.

"But what of the ferals?"

His brows merged, irritation lancing his features as he raised his hands. "I was protecting this village from ferals long before you learned to wield your blade. I would ask that you quit with your fretting while I perform this last act for my friend. He will have a proper send-off."

"Of course," Maeve murmured, demurring though her cheeks flamed with the realization he might still find her newfound skills... ill-suited for a woman. "But what will become of Loren's body once he has been placed at the forest's edge? By the time anyone discovers him—"

"That is why I will hasten back to the guard tower and lead them back to Loren's body with the claim we were ambushed by ferals after our escape. They will assume I was forced to dispatch him. Then everyone in the village will be eager to give Loren the hero's funeral he deserves."

"And you are comfortable taking such liberties with the truth?"

His chin dipped. "It is not wholly untrue, and those parts which are... less than forthright... I shall carry with me to my grave. If letting the villagers assume what they may serves to protect all of you," he said, his gaze warming as it fell upon Fiona's, "then I shall happily seek forgiveness from our creators in due course."

With his plan laid out before them like a map of necessary deceptions, Maeve felt a tremor of dread ripple through her. Once again, this had become the currency of their survival—secrets and little falsehoods, to be traded in the shadows. She had never felt more removed from Alaric's idealistic ambitions than she did now.

"And when the time comes for Fiona and me to return to Alaric's kingdom," she said, "will you still feel right about shouldering this guilt alone?" Maeve's voice was barely audible, yet it carried the weight of the world.

Eamon gave her an earnest look that bore the marks of his steadfast soul. "Loren loved his village, your Nan, Coralie... and you. He would not have it otherwise. His soul will find no rest, knowing he might yet bring harm to those he most cherished. So I will think of these necessary untruths as his legacy's shield."

"Then let it be so," Maeve said at last, her voice steadier as she, too, embraced the path Eamon had laid out before them. It was a road paved with sorrow, but it was one they would at least walk together.

A SHORT TIME LATER, Eamon stood by the linen-swaddled burden of Loren's lifeless form, his posture strong and erect despite the emotions lancing his noble features. Despite Alaric's talk about the redemptive power of love, all the love in the world couldn't have done anything to help Loren.

Fiona reached out, her hand trembling as her palm lightly brushed against Eamon's sleeve. "You needn't do this tonight," she whispered, fear pricking at her features like thorns. "You are already exhausted. The toll upon your wherewithal could prove a deadly distraction."

"Shush now." Eamon's voice, but a gentle murmur, bore the strength of iron wrapped in velvet. "Loren's peace is worth more than any peril to myself. I will not have his soul wander, restless and perturbed, should his passing become the cause of any further misfortune."

As Fiona's protests died on her lips, Maeve saw in Eamon's eyes the acceptance of a fate chosen by that thing she was beginning to doubt most... love. And in that, he reminded her of Alaric. Fiona would do well in his care, if only their world would allow their union to unfold in peace.

A pang of envy swelled in Maeve's throat as Fiona's hand reached for Eamon's with an urgency that betrayed the depth of her affection. Their fingers entwined, and for a brief heartbeat, the world seemed to pause, admiring the affection that thrived between them despite the misery they had shared this day.

"Please stay safe," Fiona implored, her voice thick with unshed tears. "Every step you take away from here... let it be one closer to your return."

"Always," Eamon assured her, the promise hanging between them like a sacred vow. He pulled her into his embrace, and for a moment, they simply clung to each other in a heart-wrenching display of untried passion.

With a final, lingering look that held all the words they could not speak, they parted, and Eamon knelt to cradle Loren in his arms, lifting him as if he were a sleeping child. As they watched him move to the back door and vanish into midnight's dark embrace, Maeve and Fiona stood side by side, their clasped hands speaking of the sisterly love that both bound them and fortified them to keep fighting.

CHAPTER 14

The mourning bells that had been sounded for Loren had long since stopped tolling. Though they proved Eamon's ruse successful, that knowledge brought Maeve little solace. Loren's senseless death still crushed her heart, a profound sense of loss still gripping her.

No matter how many times she tossed and turned on the pallet Nan had set out for her, sleep would not come. But she took great comfort in the rasp of Fiona's soft snores emanating from her own pallet situated across the room. It gave Maeve some solace, knowing that at least one of them had found rest.

After all that had transpired, Maeve did not know if she would ever again be able to surrender her worries to slumber's call. There were too many questions regarding her quest Isolde had left unanswered, and now that the cottage had fallen quiet, those questions clanged in the cage of her skull, each of them demanding attention—and answers.

How fared Alaric?

Where was Lady Elora… and her presumed henchman, Lysander,

who had been missing since the day Maeve, Alaric, and Eamon had released the tributaries from the West Tower?

Most important, where was Alaric's father, King Caligula? She knew no more about the banished king's location now than the moment when she'd first asked this question of Dr. Reinhart, and then later, at his bidding, of Lady Isolde. Though the wizened zombie sage had been short on answers, she had at least gazed into her crystal ball and foreseen that Maeve would indeed find him. But the ball had also portended that Maeve would not know the king's actual location until the time was right.

Maeve hissed out a frustrated sigh. She wanted that time to be now, but she and patience had an uneasy alliance. Entrusting Alaric's fate to an inner sight she scarcely trusted, much less understood, not only felt like a bridge too far—it also felt reckless.

As her ears scoured the winds weaving around the cottage for answers, Nyx materialized out of the shadows. Fixing Maeve in her copper-eyed stare, the zombie cat mewed like a delighted kitten and crawled into the crook of Maeve's knees. Acting as if she had performed this ritual a thousand times, the cat turned around three times, then fussed as she set about kneading the coverlet into a nest.

Soon, the feline's rumbling purrs were accompanied by Fiona's gentle snores. As Maeve began to drift on the strains of those soothing sounds, she was aware of a strange tug at the edge of her consciousness. Then she heard the soft hoot-hooting of an owl. Though she felt as if she were falling through layer after layer of darkness, she was not afraid. Giving up her hold on conscious thought, she succumbed to the notion that she and Nyx were one and the same and the owl, a kind soul who had been sent by Alaric to watch over her, guide her. With the owl's wings flapping overhead, she saw through Nyx's eyes as she stole silently through the restless darkness on four legs. Then a surge of vivid images flooded her senses.

There, amidst the whorls of color and emotion, stood Lady Elora, her figure poised and elegant as she stared into an ornate, gilt-framed mirror. As the zombie admired herself, her lips stretched into a thin, cruel smile as she settled Alaric's crown on her head.

With her head thrown back with laughter, she began chanting in a language Maeve could not comprehend, much like the one she'd heard when Isolde had peered into her crystal ball. The zombie's graceful hands wove through the air in complex patterns, and it seemed to Maeve as if Elora was a conductor, directing the dark tendrils of chaos that snaked through the air around her.

Though Maeve could comprehend no words, nor speak any, her intuition detected within those tendrils a chilling pattern, revealing Elora as the source of all the discord festering within Alaric's kingdom. Maeve knew then that the zombie's intent was to maintain a world that was cleaved in two by fear and subjugation.

But she also sensed Elora was not alone in her pursuit. Another form moved in the shadows behind Elora, and Maeve turned, expecting to see Lysander's golden eyes shining in the darkness. But instead, the eyes she saw were as gray and hard as ice. Though Maeve could not see any details of the man's face, she somehow knew him to be Alaric's own father.

Moisture painted her eyes as she realized how much treachery and betrayal was afoot... and perpetrated by those Alaric had once loved and trusted more than any others. A pang of grief clawed at her spirit as she began to understand the enormity of Alaric's opposition and the heartache he would feel when he realized his own father, along with Lady Elora, had somehow enacted his downfall—within his very own castle.

With a sob and a deep breath, Maeve opened her eyes, the ephemeral strands of her strange vision dissipating. But now she understood at least part of the truth: Alaric's father would never willingly surrender the antidote that might hold the power to save his son, for he and Lady Elora were the very ones who had orchestrated his poisoning. As for and role Lysander had played in all of this —there, her vision had failed her.

But she knew one thing to her very marrow—

somehow, she would have to find the means to seize the antidote. And whether she procured it by hook or by crook mattered not.

As dawn's first blush crept through the cottage window's warped panes, Maeve's eyes fluttered open. Though every inch of her ached with her stretch, the gentle half-light painted her surroundings in rose-tinted hues, contrasting against a night that had been marred by so much bloodshed and sorrow. And now, her suspicions about Lady Elora had caused her grief to swell twofold.

Had her dream been fear-born, or was she truly prescient, like Duchesse Isolde had said? She supposed only time would tell, but for now, her visions and intuitions were the only compasses she had to guide her.

As Nyx roused and hopped onto the windowsill, Maeve lay still for a moment on her pallet, staring up at the thatched ceiling as if the answers she still sought might be encoded in its golden weave. Her mind, still weary and bruised from grief, wandered back to the grim events that now seemed a world away from the quiet hush of Nan's front room.

Loren, her brave and unwavering friend, was now but a specter of the past. Her heart clenched at the thought of beginning this day without hearing the familiar sound of his laughter as he uttered another one of his terrible jokes. A single tear wound down her cheek, tracing a path through the remnant salt of yesterday's grief before disappearing into the rough fabric of her pillow.

Seeking anything else on which to pin her thoughts, she turned her head slightly until her gaze settled on Fiona, who still slumbered on her own pallet across the room. Maeve sighed softly as she noted the rise and fall of Fiona's chest. Though faint, as she was a zombie like herself, the movement brought a small measure of comfort to the gaping pit where Maeve's heart had once lived.

Gratitude for their friendship swelled within that seemingly hollow space. The fates had long since been cruel, but they had not machinated entirely without mercy, for they had at least given her

Fiona. Maeve did not know what she would do without her, and she prayed she would never have a cause to find out.

The paling sky, with its rosy fingers teasing aside the darkness, glowed like a portent. A near smile played at her lips as she considered perhaps Loren's spirit was soaring free now, unshackled from the torments of this fractured world. Surely, if there were still gods who loved them, they were welcoming him home with the same warm embrace that now hugged the skyline.

As she lay there, allowing herself to bask for a moment in dawn's fragile solace, she thought she could still hear the distant cries of ferals. Only this time, she felt neither fear nor rage. These weren't the agitated screeches she'd grown up dreading. Today, their other-worldly voices threaded through the morning's stillness like a somber lamentation. Once, even these sounds would have stoked fear in her heart, but today, they stirred something else within her—empathy.

Memories of the previous day's brutality surfaced unbidden. She winced as she considered that each feral they had felled was once someone's beloved, someone's kin, like her own parents, assuming they, too, had been turned feral after the zombies took them.

Were these plaintive howls a dirge for their own fallen? Could it be the ferals retained echoes of their former selves and still possessed hints of the love and familial bonds that had once defined them?

A lump formed in her throat as she considered the possibility. All her life, she had been taught zombies were devoid of any semblance of humanity. But now, grave doubts gnawed at her convictions. If she still felt love, could it be possible that even those poor, damned souls grieved, just as she did now?

These ruminations on mourning led her back to thoughts of Eamon. Though grief-ridden himself, he had taken on the unenviable task of deceiving the villagers, convincing them he alone had ended Loren's misery after he'd been turned. And he'd done so only to protect herself, her family and Fiona. But it was a heavy and untimely burden for him to bear, and Maeve could not help but wonder at the toll the ruse had exacted upon his noble conscience.

Her musings were interrupted by a soft, rhythmic tapping at the door—a sound that seemed too deliberate, too controlled, to belong to a casual passerby. As she rose from her pallet, her heart skipped a beat. With careful motion, so as not to disturb Fiona, Nan, and Coralie, she approached the door.

"Who goes there?" she demanded as her trembling fingers fumbled with the latch, though she believed she already knew the answer.

"It is me," came Eamon's hushed reply from the other side. His presence both soothed and alarmed her—she was comforted because he was safe, but also alarmed because his arrival at this hour could only mean that the fragile thread of peace she'd just as soon cling to a while longer was about to fray.

Her fingers shook as they grazed the cold metal and threw the latch, her heart pulsing with a rhythm that echoed the urgency in Eamon's knock. She opened the door just wide enough to peer outside, where the dim light of dawn was just beginning to seep into the village streets, casting long shadows on the porch. Without a word, she gestured for him to wait as she stepped out, letting the door close softly behind them.

"Where have you been all night?" she asked as she sat on the top porch stair, her voice a mere whisper lost amidst the chilly morning breeze.

Eamon sighed as he leaned his shoulder against the porch post. His eyes held the moisture of unshed tears, and his features were drawn in the dim light. "After I led the guards back to Loren's body at the edge of the woods," he began, "I thought it best to return to my own cottage near the guard towers. It would have raised too many questions if I was seen coming back here at so late an hour."

Maeve nodded, though the gesture went unnoticed. She wrapped her arms around her torso, seeking to stave off the unseasonable chill, her gaze turning to the horizon, where the sky glowed with the promise of a new day. Another pang of lament for Loren filled her chest, but it was also accompanied by a wave of sorrow for the ferals they had slain. She was beginning to believe those wretched beings also deserved their moment of silence and a patch of unmolested earth to call their final resting place. She found herself wishing they had taken the time to bury them.

"His soul will find peace now," Eamon murmured, as if reading her thoughts. But Maeve caught the tremor in his voice. His young face was lined with the strain of bearing his burdens with his characteristic stoicism. And for a moment, she wondered where the law was written that men were not allowed to purge their agony with tears.

As silence swelled between them, she could see the sun's glorious ascent, its rays painting the sky in hues of gold and rose. Though it was a daily resurrection, it felt almost personal this morning. The beauty was a strange backdrop for against the darkness they had endured. As Eamon's gaze followed in the wake of hers, this moment of shared rapture seemed to bind them. "I shall miss him, too," she uttered as they shared witness to nature's relentless cycle.

But as the light grew stronger, she noted the deepening furrow in Eamon's brow, the way his jaw clenched when their eyes met again. A fresh knot of dread climbed into her throat. She didn't have to ask him to know there was something more that burdened him, something so heavy and ominous that he was reluctant to let it spill from his lips.

"You have heard something," she stated, her voice tighter and more tremulous than she had intended.

A muscle at his temple twitched as his chin dipped in the slightest of nods. "But whether it is born from rumor or truth, I cannot yet say."

"You have heard news," she uttered, more as a statement of certainty than a question. "From Alaric's kingdom."

He hesitated, his hand running through his disheveled hair. "Like I said, Maeve, it is quite possible it was just a rumor."

"Well? Do you intend to share?"

He shook his head. "Not yet. I fear if I tell you, it might upset you, distract you from your path."

"Upset me?" Maeve's eyes narrowed as hurt and indignation welled within her. "After everything that has passed, you still think of me as too... fragile? Why? Because I am just a woman?"

A blush stained his skin from his collar to his forehead, but his show of contrition was not enough to mollify her.

"You, of all people, should know better, Eamon. After Loren... after all of it, you should understand by now I am far stronger than I appear. As is Fiona."

Eamon's shoulders slumped, defeated by her resolve. "I would not hesitate to have either of you flank me in battle, but I would rather spare you this. At least until I am certain..."

"True friends do not keep secrets," she continued, her tone softer now but no less determined. "Especially not ones that involve the affairs of loved ones. Your silence is not protection."

He let out a breath, heavy and ragged, and his gaze returned to the sunrise as if seeking courage from his fallen friend. "Alright, Maeve," he whispered as he shoved his hands in his pockets and cast his eyes toward his booted feet. "You win. I will tell you everything. But please do not take it to heart. Not yet. For much of it defies credibility."

Eamon's tale began as a husky whisper, barely breaking the hush that clung to the early morning air. "One of our scouts said he made it into Alaric's kingdom," he began, his eyes not quite meeting Maeve's. "He swore to the gods he had seen the things I am about to reveal with his own eyes. And though they sound fantastical, I have never known him for a liar."

Maeve could only nod as a slow breath slipped from her. As Eamon paused, parsing his next words, she watched a solitary leaf spiral from a branch overhead, its descent as slow in coming as the story Eamon still seemed so reluctant to reveal.

"But why?" she asked, her fingers absently tracing the grain of the porch wood. "Why would one of our scouts go there when every-thing is in such upheaval? He could have been killed—or impris-oned, like yourself and...." Her voice trailed off with Loren's name hovering on her lips.

"Necessity. Supplies are growing short again," he said, his gaze also following the leaf as it settled on the ground, caught on the breeze and skittered across the cobblestones. "The last delivery Prince Alaric promised has not arrived. Though there had been rumors of Alaric's fall, the elders wanted to know for certain what was amiss before they told everyone else and risked inciting a panic."

His revelation filled Maeve's heart with dread. Without those supplies, her village would soon fall back into decay. Deprived of the sustenance they brought, Nan and Coralie would go hungry again.

"Surely that is not all?" she prompted, feeling the leaden weight that sat on her chest grow heavier.

Eamon looked at her then, his eyes dark and inscrutable as lake water reflecting the last remnants of the night. "This is where the story begins to sound like a fairy tale. The scout reported that... everyone there was... asleep."

"Well, of course they were sleeping. I'm sure the scout had the good sense to approach under the cover of darkness."

"No, Maeve. You do not understand. The entire kingdom was motionless, silent as a grave. Not in their beds, but exactly where they had been standing when whatever happened... did. Even the animals. The birds. The lowliest insect. The gardens were withering and untended, with strange brambles springing up and creeping toward the castle walls at an... unnatural rate. And every last soul who dwelled within the kingdom's walls was sleeping. Save for two."

"Who?"

"The first, a zombie woman, ancient and alone. She was creeping about, perhaps keeping watch over the others under the cover of darkness and shadows."

A deep chill passed through Maeve, stealing the scant bit of warmth the rising sun had offered. "That would be Isolde," she whispered.

"Agreed."

"But why would she do that?"

Eamon shrugged. "Perhaps she believes she is protecting them with her so-called magic, believing she can keep them safe from whatever vile influence has befallen the kingdom."

Maeve's thoughts turned inward, her mind picturing the still forms of the courtiers and servants alike, locked in a slumber so profound it bordered on death. *Just like Alaric.* As the melancholy of the scene wrapped around her heart like a shroud, she knew the story Eamon had heard was no rumor. Nor even a half-truth.

"You appear dazed... or distraught. Are you sure you want to hear more?" Eamon asked as he noted the tears trailing down Maeve's cheeks.

She could only nod as she swiped her arm across her face. "Yes. You must tell me everything," she urged, steeling herself against the tide of despair that threatened to overwhelm her.

"The scout revealed there was another person there who did not slumber like the rest," he said, the morning light casting harsh shadows on his face. "A white-haired zombie woman... somehow commanding a band of ferals. Under her watch, the beasts appeared organized, purposeful. And they behaved as if they were preparing the kingdom for something... significant."

"Preparing?" Maeve felt the edges of reality blur, the fantastical vision playing out in her mind now encroaching upon the waking realm. "Like for an event?"

Eamon nodded. "Perhaps for a dignitary's arrival... or even... a coronation." Eamon's admission hung between them with the weight of a dire prophecy.

"Lady Elora," Maeve murmured, certainty lacing her tone. "She covets Alaric's crown. But the only way she can have it is to ally herself with the former king." *Just like in my dream...*

"That would be my first guess," Eamon added.

"That bitch!" Maeve spat. "She is a puppeteer pulling at the strings of the undead for her own dark purposes."

Eamon nodded again, his face now etched with concern. "And whatever was happening there appeared to be gathering momentum. The person they are waiting for will likely arrive soon... if they have not already."

Maeve's hands clenched into fists, her nails lancing her palms. Yet, in the heat of her growing rage, a seed of determination took root. Though she still did not know the deposed king's current location, she at least knew his future one. All she needed to do was rally her forces. And this time, she would not give Lady Elora another chance to unravel the fragile hope for peace for which Alaric had sacrificed everything. She had felled that bitch once, and she would do so again. But this time, she would not let Alaric's belief in love's power cause her to make the mistake of showing Elora any mercy.

Her breath hitched, a cold mantle of terror enfolding her as this new truth, which in her mind was stark and undeniably real, settled upon her. *King Caligula is already there.* Even thinking his name was like invoking a curse that sapped the warmth from the nascent dawn.

Her heart and her thoughts raced towards Alaric, laying vulnerable in his perpetual slumber. If Brigid and Alaric's physicians were also cursed, then her beloved was utterly defenseless against the machinations of a conniving woman and a king who was so loathed by his own subjects that he had been sent into exile to pay penance for his crimes. And according to Alaric, the man had borne little love for his only son. A sob unwrenched itself from her soul's depths and clawed across her lips. She would not be surprised if that bastard intended to behead his own son, thus ending his life. "Eamon. We have to stop him."

"Who?"

"Alaric's father. King Caligula."

"Look at me, Maeve." Eamon's voice, gentle and steady as an April rain, cut through the fresh turmoil raging within her.

As her gaze found his, his hand, calloused from welding his sword, came to rest upon her shoulder. As had been true since they were but children, that stalwart, familiar comfort helped ground her.

"You cannot know for certain it is the return of Alaric's father they are preparing for," he said. "It could just as easily be Lysander, who has remained at large all this time. As for Prince Alaric and the others... they are only asleep, not dead. So long as that is the case, there is still cause for hope."

"Hope?" She bristled, his words doing little to quell the tempest raging in her heart. "For what, exactly?"

"Unexpected blessings, for one."

She tilted her head and perused him through narrowed eyes. "Have you perhaps gone daft?"

His chin lifted as if she'd slapped him. "Is it not a blessing that Alaric may still have Isolde watching over him? Though I know little of magic, and have been taught to dispel its worth, we owe that old woman our freedom. I also believe she is a force our foes have not counted on meeting and would underestimate even if they did."

"But what if Lady Elora truly is preparing for the king's return? Isolde might have access to powers we can't understand, but she is still only one woman, elderly and frail. Once the king and his entourage reach the kingdom, what will become of Alaric then?"

Eamon's hazel eyes dulled to agate as he gazed at her, his confidence wavering like an ebbing candle's flame.

"In the event that proves true, perhaps we can intercept the entourage before it ever reaches the kingdom," he said, the conviction in his voice doing battle with the doubt that lay beneath. "Force the antidote from him in return for his life. With that in your grasp, you may yet turn this wretched tide."

"For that, we would need an army," she whispered, the word tasting of bitter defeat on her tongue. "You can be sure with Elora on his side, he will be traveling with a legion of undead."

"An army..." Eamon echoed, his darkening gaze drifting towards the horizon where the rising sun fought valiantly to vanquish the night's last remnants. "If only that were possible."

"But is that not why we came here? To find not only refuge, but help in our quest?"

"Yes, but judging by the mood of the guardsmen, the village is short on manpower that harbors any sympathy for the zombie aristocracy."

"Then forget them. For this village is not short on women who do sympathize. Women who owe Alaric their very lives. So that is who we must turn to in order to raise our army."

Eamon barked out a dry laugh. "And you would call me daft?"

"Do you have a better plan?"

He shook his head, no. "But you would have a band of untrained women challenge a king's cohort? That is the very definition of madness, Maeve."

"Then let my madness become the thing that saves my beloved's soul," she retorted. As she stared down her friend, her jaw set firm, her spirit unyielding as the ancient trees spanning the forest between the village and Alaric's kingdom. "You said it yourself, Eamon. We have no men-at-arms, nor knights in shining armor to call upon. But if I turn to the women—

perchance, they will rally around our cause."

"Will they now? And will they tow their children on their backs as they weld their knitting needles?" Sarcasm laced Eamon's words, but Maeve saw the briefest flicker of something else in his eyes, a spark of light that defied the encroaching despair.

"Remember, Eamon, the same cause that binds us, binds them. Like ourselves, they would sacrifice anything for those they love, for a future free of tyranny and sorrow."

He nodded slowly, the gesture one of reluctant acquiescence. "All will be saved in love's name then, then? I suppose your zombie prince would tell us he would not have it any other way."

"Exactly," she said, ignoring the sarcasm that tinged Eamon's voice. With newfound determination, she left Eamon still shaking his head and turned back towards the humble abode that had become their temporary sanctuary. She would awaken Fiona, Nan, Coralie—they needed to know, to understand the gravity of what awaited them beyond the threshold of safety.

But first, there was one more ally to consult. One whose ancient wisdom transcended the bounds of mortal reckoning. Before she woke the others, she would surrender her doubts and study the crystal ball that Isolde had entrusted to her. If the time was truly right, as she believed, its crystalline depths should confirm this new path she had chosen was both true and right. Otherwise, of what use was it to her?

CHAPTER 15

Maeve's relief manifested with a sigh as she pushed closed the cottage door and found the dim interior as quiet and still as a graveyard. Though grief would normally drive her to wrap herself in the comfort of family and friends, she was somewhat heartened that all were still fast asleep. The quiet that had greeted her would serve her purpose well.

Desperate for confirmation of her path, yet still doubtful of her role as a seer, she lifted the crystal ball from her pack and settled it on the table where she'd shared countless meals with her family.

Disappointment tried to drown her hopes when she found the crystalline orb's surface silent as death. Wondering whether the sphere had become damaged during her travels, she held it aloft, seeking the elusive truths Isolde had promised she would see hidden within its depths.

"Please. Show me something," she implored, her voice barely above a whisper. "Show me *anything*."

But the crystal remained as stubborn and enigmatic as the strange crone who had given it to her. No matter how deeply she stared into its murky depths, it yielded nothing until a frustrated tear wound down her cheek and dripped onto the glass. Just as the urge to hurl the damnable thing across the room welled within her, she sensed a stirring at the orb's innermost core.

Her hands shook violently as her palms cradled the crystal ball, blood ringing in her ears like choir bells. Gasping, she leaned closer. The world around her blurred as she contemplated the amber sparks that swirled and eddied within the glass. Drawing in a ragged breath, she whispered another desperate plea for its guidance. "Please, do not forsake me in this."

Static crackled beneath her palms, the familiar world around her dissolving until she felt her very being fade into the undulant mists. Once they cleared again, she was no longer safely tucked in the familiar confines of her grandmother's cottage.

She found herself back in Alaric's bedchamber, looking onto a scene that drove a spike through her heart. She saw Elora, naked, beautiful, and brazen, standing over Alaric. Her eyes simmered with lust as she opened the glass capsule Dr. Reinhart had designed to protect him in his slumber.

Maeve was paralyzed, unable to scream or cry out. She could only watch the zombie's beautiful face contort into something dreadful and hungry as she stared down at Alaric's vulnerable, unsuspecting form.

Her innards twisted in revulsion as Elora worked open Alaric's robe, rendering him nearly as nude as she. While Maeve stood paralyzed, unable to mitigate this fresh horror as it unfolded, Elora attempted to arouse him with increasingly intimate touches, her long fingers tracing over his unresponsive body until they reached his manhood. Refusing to be dissuaded, the zombie resorted to attempting the most intimate of kisses along his limp staff. Despite her obvious mastery of the carnal arts, Alaric's flesh remained unresponsive and utterly unexcited. If Maeve was able, she would have dissolved into peals of triumphant laughter.

"Gods damn you, Maeve!" Elora cursed, her gaze swinging toward Maeve as if she'd always known she was being watched.

"What sorcery have you worked over him that his man flesh would recoil from my attention? Or," she murmured, her eyes narrowing to slits, "is this perchance the work of that batty old witch, Isolde?"

Elora's mouth twisted into a snarl as she turned away from Alaric and donned her discarded robe. Still cursing Maeve's very existence, her hand found the doorknob. As she stepped through the heavy, wooden frame, Maeve longed to remain with Alaric and watch over him, but her spirit was seemingly pulled into Elora's wake.

Then, another scene materialized. Elora was prowling through Isolde's abode, her dagger lifted and her displeased voice echoing through the empty rooms. "Show yourself, hag. I know you are here, for I can scent you. But unless you reveal yourself and give me that which I seek, your sleeping prince shall be the first victim of a most bloodthirsty revenge."

A leaden silence filled the air before Isolde slowly materialized from the shadows, her bleary eyes wary, and her demeanor defensive. "What could you possibly want from me that you have not already taken?" she demanded.

"I am in need of magical... assistance. Whether 'tis a spell I require... or a potion, I do not know."

Isolde's laughter was dry as bone as she gestured toward the oddly colored vials and leather-bound spell books that lined the nearby shelves. "Fine. Help yourself."

"You know as well as me I cannot use those. I have been taught to eschew any art whose merits cannot be proven in a laboratory."

"Yet the fact that you are here begging me for favors would make it appear your opinion of my craft's worth has changed. So I must ask, Elora. What has made you desperate enough to resort to magic?"

"Science cannot yet provide me with the means I seek. Trust me, I have tried. And my results have been... volatile... at best."

"And exactly what is it you could want enough to seek me out?"

"I need a potion... or a spell... anything that will allow one to... assume the countenance of another," Elora demanded coldly.

Isolde's scoff was not delicate. "I believe you are well-educated enough to recall guise magic is the stuff of dark forces and exacts a lofty toll. Are you prepared to lose your soul in the trying?"

Elora scoffed. "You speak as if I have not benefitted from such a ruse before. Yet here I stand, still alive, still beautiful, and closer to getting my heart's desire than ever."

"You say you have already accessed such magic, so it would appear you have no need of me. So why are you really here?"

"Do you think me stupid, old woman? If I possessed the means to enact my desires, I would not be here. So give me what I seek, and perhaps I will yet consider sparing what remains of your son's pitiful existence."

A tear slipped from Isolde's eyes as she shook her head firmly. "Even if you were to offer me my son in exchange, I have neither the means nor the will to tamper with dark forces…"

As Elora growled with rage, Isolde vanished once again, leaving the would-be zombie queen slashing at the air with her dagger.

Isolde has a son? Maeve gasped and staggered backward, fear gripping her heart. Whether these events had transpired yet or not, she had no way of knowing. But it was now clear what Elora was after— power. And she was willing to resort to dark magic to cut down anyone who stood in her way. But if that was the case…when would the time come when keeping Alaric alive no longer suited her?

As the vision faded, the realization of how much danger such a fate would pose to her loved ones filled her with rage. "They must be stopped," she whispered fiercely, her grip on the crystal ball tightening. "Please, you must show me the rest of her plan. For Alaric's sake, and for the sake of our people."

But the only thing Maeve saw within the glass was the reflection of Fiona's face, her delicate jaw dropped open with shock.

The dying embers of last night's fire spit as Maeve pushed back from the crystal ball, her heart breaking into a thousand pieces. She was no stranger to being taken against her will, and the sordid liberties she had seen Elora take with Alaric in his most vulnerable state filled her with disgust. What kind of gift would force her to foresee such a dire event when she had no power to intercede? She would do anything, even sell her soul, in exchange for the means to spare him this fate. But what hope did she have of getting to him, when everything was still in such disarray?

"Maeve, sweetie. What is this about?" Fiona pressed her palms on Maeve's shoulders, turning her away from the glass to fold her into her arms.

"I saw... things. Inside the crystal ball. Horrible ones."

"I do not know what events you glimpsed just now," she whispered as she stroked Maeve's hair, "but it does not require a sage to sense the despair they have caused you."

"It was all her," Maeve choked out between sobs. "And I do not know why the orb would show me such things when I am powerless to stop them."

"Sadly, I cannot read your mind, Maeve. Of whom and what do you speak?"

"E-Elora. She... and the King... are the masterminds behind... all of it."

"All of what?" Fiona asked.

"Alaric's fall. Eamon and Loren's imprisonment. I also know Elora will not stop choreographing events until she is the only one left in line to wear Alaric's crown. Once that happens, she will have no further cause to keep Alaric alive."

Fiona set Maeve away from her and bracketed her face with her palms. "Look at me, Maeve. Elora is of noble blood, but she'd have to remove half the Kingdom to take the crown."

"But she could *marry* into it."

"She *could* do...anything. But just because your glass has foreshadowed these events, it does not mean they must come to pass. I cannot believe the shape of our future is determined by the whims of fate, but by the actions of people. And perhaps it would behoove you to consider the foresight you have been given as a gift instead of a curse."

Maeve swiped her tears, her brow furrowed in thought as she glanced back at the crystal ball, its depths no longer revealing any evidence of the treachery she had seen.

Could she truly have been granted the power to change the course of destiny? It sounded like something she might have read in one of Alaric's fairy tales. Yet the things she'd seen felt as palpable as an anvil sitting on her shoulders. At the same time, Fiona's words sparked the tiniest ember of hope. She had already bested Elora once. If what Fiona said was true, her gift could become the secret weapon that would give her an edge over that bitch's dark machinations. *Isolde has a son...*

As Maeve considered this new insight, and why her crystal had chosen now as the time to reveal it, creaking door hinges announced Nan's entrance. The elderly woman's bleary gaze caught Maeve's, and she gasped, noting the tears tracking down her granddaughter's cheeks. Her scruffy brows knit as she rushed toward the women and gathered Maeve into a fierce embrace.

"My darling child," she began, "what has worked you into such a state, and so early in the morning? Is it Loren?"

As Maeve pulled away and swiped her eyes with her palm, Nan's eyes traveled to the crystal ball, her brows lifting with surprise. "Maeve! Where in the world did you get that thing?"

Sensing her grandmother's concern, Maeve's gaze flitted between Fiona and Nan. Feeling utterly drained, she dropped onto one of the chairs and spent a moment twisting her hands in her lap as she worried her bottom lip between her teeth. "I... I suppose I must confess some things."

"What is it, child?"

"In my quest to find a cure for Alaric, I befriended an elderly zombie sage in Alaric's kingdom... Lady Isolde."

"A zombie... sage?"

Maeve nodded. "When I sought her out, she foretold many things. Then she said I was a seer. That's when she gave me... that."

She gestured toward the orb, its depths now swirling with shadows and light. "She said it chose me... as did Nyx."

Nan gasped. "By the gods, are you telling me you have the ability to foresee events in that—

thing?"

"Yes, Nan, that is exactly what I am saying." Maeve dropped her gaze back to her hands, not wanting to see if disappointment, shame, or, gods forbid, anger registered on her grandmother's features. "But please know I would never have touched it if Lady Isolde had not gifted it to me," she added when the silence that stretched between them became unbearable. "When I tried to refuse, she put it in my hands and told me it had always been mine. That it had somehow... chosen me. Then she insisted it did so because I had the sight, as well."

"And you have reason to believe that is the truth?"

Maeve's body shuddered with her nod. "But the visions I have seen within, they are... overwhelming, terrifying. Yet no matter how hard I try, I cannot make myself look away."

When Nan said nothing more, tears sprang to Maeve's eyes. "I know you taught me that magic is a forbidden art. And the last thing I would wish is to bring dishonor onto our family. But what if my skills could be used to save lives? Because Loren... poor, dear Loren... I cannot help but wonder if I could have done something to prevent his demise had I embraced this gift sooner."

Nan listened intently, her eyes filled, not with the disdain Maeve had anticipated, but with empathy. As she finished speaking, the older woman reached out to nest her shaking hands in her own. "Just because we no longer speak of such things doesn't mean they don't exist. But even if you had foreseen Loren's fate... well, you know as well as I the men who dwell here will not tolerate even the slightest rumor of magic," she murmured. "Loren, in particular, loathed any talk of it. If he had known your advice was magic-rooted, he would never have given it any thought. The hour of his end would still have been the same."

Maeve nodded. "Are you angry with me, Nan? For toying with magic, I mean?"

The elderly woman heaved a soft sigh, then shook her head. "I only worry it could cause people to distrust you more. Though it's true magic has been deemed taboo by our elders, many of our women have continued to nurture its practice in the safety of shadows. But to this day, no one dares speak of it in mixed company."

"Anyone I know?" Maeve asked as someone rapped on the front door. "That would be Eamon, I imagine," she said, feeling more than a little disappointed that, at least for now, their conversation must end.

"It is just as well," Nan said. "Coralie will be awake soon, and famished. And I'm sure Eamon would like a good meal after his labors of last night. Let me get breakfast started. We shall retreat to my room to discuss this matter further after."

THE BUTTERY MORNING light filtered through the kitchen windowpanes, casting a gentle glow upon the table as Nan busied herself with preparing the day's first meal. Soon, the comforting scents of fresh biscuits and brewed chicory mingled in the air, providing a soothing balm for Maeve's troubled heart. As she watched the elderly woman work, an unexpected calm settled over her, offering a brief respite from the worries that plagued her. But as she noted Eamon's somber expression, she could not stop a fresh stream of tears from slipping down her face.

"Maeve, your face is longer than a haunted mile," Nan began, expertly slicing slivers of pork jowl and setting them on a skillet to fry, "I know you still grieve for Loren; we all do. But remember, he chose to be an archer because he took his hero's calling seriously. It was his choice to heed that calling, and his alone. While it is right to mourn his passing, you cannot keep blaming yourself for the life path he chose."

"You should heed your grandmother's words, for she speaks the truth," Eamon added. Then his gaze swung to Fiona, and he extended his hand to her. "Would you care to join me on the back stoop? I would take in some more of the morning air before the villagers start moving about."

"Breakfast will be ready shortly, so do not tarry long," Nan advised.

Fiona's eyes shone like amethysts as she nodded and settled her small hand into Eamon's. "I would be honored," she whispered as she peered up at him through the soot of her lashes.

"And I do not need to ask to know you have not washed your hands and face," Nan said, turning her gaze on Coralie, who had just emerged from her bedroom, oblivious to all that had taken place since Maeve had tucked her in. "So march."

"Yessum," Coralie grumbled as she scampered off to do her grandmother's bidding. As Nan watched Coralie depart, she gasped softly, her eyes gazing into the distance as if remembering something from long ago.

"Nan, you look as if something just crossed your grave," Maeve said.

"A memory, perhaps triggered by our conversation of earlier. It was said my own grandmother was a seer," she continued quietly. "She also excelled in the healing arts. I remember my mother telling me the elders forced her to stop practicing, lest she be banished."

"They would have sent her out into the forest to fend for herself?"

Nan nodded. "The elders feared she might invite dark forces into the village. But like many women of her time, she continued her practice in secret, using her gifts only to help other women and their young when the doctor could not...or would not when matters of bearing children were involved."

Maeve listened intently, her heart aching for the sacrifices the strong, resilient women had made in order to feel safe within their own community. She wondered how many more stories like theirs remained untold, buried beneath men's fears and prejudices?

After Eamon and Fiona returned, Coralie bounced from her room and rejoined them at the table. With Nyx purring beneath the table, they turned their attention to a breakfast none of them but Coralie felt much like eating.

But the sound of the child's laughter invoked its own brand of magic, and Maeve felt a ray of brightness coursing through her veins. No longer would she allow herself to be consumed by guilt or doubt; instead, she would embrace her newfound abilities and use them to forge a brighter future for all those she held dear, for they still lived.

A somber silence settled over the small room as they forced their focus on the meal they barely had the heart to eat, set to the accompaniment of Coralie's incessant chatter about wedding gowns, satin slippers and circlets woven from flowers picked from Alaric's gardens. As Maeve battled tears for things that simply could not be right now, she smiled, nodded, and picked at her food.

But Nan knew Maeve's heart too well. She leaned back in her chair to study her face. After a moment, she ordered Coralie to go outside and draw a pail of fresh water from the pump.

"You know it's always a joy to see you, Maeve," Nan said as soon as the door swung closed behind Coralie. "But why have you really come to our village, child?" she asked softly, her voice filled with concern and curiosity. "There's got to be more than what you've told me."

Maeve sighed softly and spent a moment blotting her mouth with her napkin. "As always, you can see straight through me, so I will cut to the chase. After Alaric fell, I was shunned by the courtiers," she began, her voice nearly as tight as the fist that seemed to clutch her heart.

"Why would they shun their prince's future bride?"

"They thought Eamon and Loren were complicit in his poisoning. And because they believed I was the one who invited them to the ball, they harbored suspicions about me, too. They distrusted me so much they refused to provide reinforcements so I could seek out the king, who Alaric managed to tell me holds the antidote. They said they would much prefer to handle the matter on their own."

"It could well be a journey fraught with danger, and, in their minds, one better left to heavily armed men. Could that be why they would not entrust you with this task?"

Maeve shook her head. "Alaric spent his last words to me insisting it must be me who found the antidote."

"But why would he charge his beloved with so dangerous a task?"

"I suspect he already feared something was amiss in his kingdom. So much so that he was studying his father's diaries. But sadly, whatever he knew was information he had not yet shared with me. After Fiona and I released Eamon and..." her voice trailed off as she swallowed a fresh knot of grief. "L-Loren," she finished, "we decided this was the safest place for us to regroup. We also hoped we might find kindred spirits willing to help us find the king... and, in turn, the antidote that could rouse Alaric."

Her gaze flickered to Eamon, who had returned with Fiona. He offered her a small, sad smile, acknowledging his agreement with her description of the events that brought them here, and the enormity of their shared heartache.

"Now, I have reason to suspect the king may be returning to Alaric's kingdom even now, eager to reclaim his throne," Maeve continued, her voice growing stronger with each word. "We might well have to face him on the very ground where Alaric sleeps."

Fiona's brows lofted as her gaze narrowed. "How is it I've not been made privy to this particular detail?"

Maeve dropped her gaze to her plate and stabbed at an uneaten bit of pork jowl with her fork. "There was hardly time, Fiona, between battling ferals and trying to save Loren," she murmured.

Fiona's nod satisfied Maeve that she was at least momentarily mollified by her answer. "We have come here to recruit the reinforcements I was denied, for without them," she said, returning her attention to Nan, "we stand no chance of confronting the king and forcing him to divulge the antidote."

"In that vein," Eamon said, shifting in his chair, "I have a bit more to add." He blew out a measured sigh before beginning, as if he, too, parsed his words. "It seems many, if not most, of the villagers also distrust Maeve. They feel her union with the prince has invited danger back into our midst." He paused for a moment, his eyes pinned to the biscuit he tortured between his hands. "Those who I trusted enough to query fear helping us will only unleash more terror upon our village."

Nan nodded solemnly, the lines on her weathered face deepening with her frown. "I, too, have overheard such whispers. The villagers seem to have forgotten that real change never comes without casualties."

Eamon and Nan's words weighted the air, choking the life from Maeve's hopes like a noose. Not even the steadying weight of Fiona's hand upon her own could assuage her hurt.

"Then we will have to find another way," she declared, her voice firm despite her trembling hands. "We cannot abandon Alaric nor our people to tyranny. For that, I will keep searching for the antidote, even if I must do so alone."

Fiona pressed a hand to her mouth to restrain her gasp.

"But I also believe I will not have to," she continued, remembering Isolde's vision even as Eamon scoffed softly.

Nan regarded her with an expression that suggested both admiration and sorrow, her eyes brimming with unshed tears. "Such courage and loyalty are rare, my child," she said, reaching to clasp Maeve's hand in her own. "Whatever the future holds, know you all have gained the love and respect of at least one old woman—and perhaps many more who hide their true hearts behind walls of fear and doubt."

"Those people are the exact people I am counting on finding," Maeve said.

After the group had finished picking at their meal, Nan ordered a displeased Coralie to clear the table and beckoned Maeve to follow her into her bedroom. There, she retrieved a small wooden box from a hidden compartment in her dresser.

"This little trinket belonged to my mother," she explained softly, as she opened the box and placed the talisman it held within into Maeve's hand. "Because of what the symbols on it represented, I kept it hidden. But since it had belonged to her mother, she always carried it with her," she murmured as she curled Maeve's fingers around the talisman. "Then it was passed to me... and now it belongs to you."

As Maeve clutched the strangely etched trinket near her heart, she whispered her thanks as they shared a tender embrace. "But why would you want to give me this when it is a keepsake from your own mother?"

"To keep with you so it will always give you the same reminder my mother gave me. Though the menfolk refuse to admit it, women have long been the keepers of magic," Nan told her gently. "And it lives in all of us. But we must always remember to be discreet with our abilities, for it is also true that ambitious men fear nothing more than a powerful woman. Let this talisman be your reminder when it feels as if men—even those you might love—seem to have forsaken your best interests. For they only do so out of fear."

"Isolde said much the same." Maeve's thoughts drifted back to the enigmatic zombie who had set her upon this path. Was her refusal to hide her abilities the reason she had been outcast from the castle's walls? Or was that a choice she had made on her own? And what of her son? Who was he? Why was he not with her, protecting her? It saddened Maeve to know how isolated her friend's existence was. "I have seen firsthand the proof that what you say is true, both here and in Alaric's kingdom. The women there also practice their magic craft in the shadows, using it only to take care of one another when their men either cannot... or will not."

Nan smiled, her eyes shining, but her chin lofted. "It does my heart good to know you are surrounded by such brave women, Maeve. And I have no doubt that whomever you might rally to your cause, you and Fiona will find the means to face whatever challenges come your way."

Patchy sunlight danced on the wooden dresser top, casting lacey shadows across Maeve's hands as she gathered the courage to say the rest of what was on her mind. Her heart ached with her burdens, but she knew she could not falter now; too much was at stake, and her grandmother's opinion of what she intended to do next meant everything to her. "Nan," she finally began, her voice soft yet unwavering, "Isolde believed... and said she foresaw... that it would be women who, in the end, saved Alaric. What I cannot understand yet is how they could possibly have the means to accomplish such a feat."

Nan nodded, her eyes reflecting the filtered sunlight like polished stones. "It would not surprise me one bit if that proved true," she admitted, raising her gaze to meet Maeve's own. "I believe there are stronger forces than ourselves at work here, my child—forces even the mightiest army may be powerless to defeat. And you, my dear, have been called upon by a higher power than ourselves to lead them."

"Tell me more," Maeve urged, sensing some critical bit of wisdom was hidden within Nan's words.

The elderly woman leaned forward, her gnarled hands enfolding Maeve's. "I believe when you rescued the lost tributaries, you set something unprecedented into motion. Instead of blending back into the town, marrying and beginning families of their own, those women have clung only to each other. They even built a compound on the village's outskirts, secluded within a grove of brambles and deadwood. Then, to the elders' disdain, they devoted themselves to learning the art of weapon-wielding, completely shunning the company of men."

Hope swelled within Maeve. Perhaps these women really could provide the reinforcements she needed. "Do you think they would join our cause?" she asked, struggling to keep her desperation in check.

"Perhaps," Nan replied. "They hold you and the prince in the highest regard for setting them free. But remember, those in Alaric's world have caused them great suffering. They may be wary of trusting anyone to lead them back into the midst of their captors. Even you."

"Then I shall have to prove myself worthy of their trust," Maeve vowed. "I will remind them we share a common goal. And Alaric's dream of unity will not be realized until it includes us all."

"Be cautious, Maeve," Nan warned, her eyes bright with concern. "While their loyalty could prove invaluable, the path you have chosen is ridden with danger. Every choice you make will bear consequences—both for yourself and those who will follow in your footsteps. There are bound to be casualties amongst you."

Maeve took a deep breath, her body shuddering as the gravity of grandmother's warning settled upon her shoulders.

With a tender smile, Nan reached out to cup Maeve's chin, her grip firm and reassuring. "You must go to them. You won't find peace until you do," she murmured, her eyes damp and shining. "The rest is up to the fates to decide.

"Yes. And I shall, as soon as possible."

"May the stars watch over you and all the brave women I already know will be standing by your side."

KNOWING they were unwelcome to attend Loren's burial, Maeve and Fiona gave Eamon their wistful best wishes. And perhaps their absence was for the best. With the rest of the village distracted, now was the perfect time to make their appeal to the former Tributaries.

Taking care to avoid human eyes, they made their way to the

place where Nan had said their hold was located. Just as she'd said, they found them within the gnarled grove of brambles they'd claimed as their own. But this morning, their makeshift stronghold did not appear as intimidating as they probably hoped. The light pierced the branches, casting ephemeral patterns on the ground that resembled the fragmented memories of the lives they had all known... before. But just as it was with Maeve and Fiona, these women, too, had been transformed by their trials.

As Maeve stepped into the grove, the largest and most stout of the women—Ingrid, if she recalled correctly—palmed her sword's hilt and stepped forward. "Maeve! What in the gods name brings you into our company this fine morning?"

"A leap of faith, I suppose," Maeve uttered, acutely aware that her own form was an uncanny echo of her former self. With her transformation complete, she must now look to these women like the semblance of death's handmaiden. "And in that vein, I have come here bearing a plea. One I sincerely believe might help restore our shattered world to... if not unity, at least the possibility of such."

As Ingrid regarded her with a narrowed gaze, Fiona's presence at her side was as solid as an ancient oak. Refusing to be intimidated, she scanned the faces of the former tributaries, some of whom had known Maeve in her vibrant youth. But now they and their apparent leader appraised her, not as the innocent young woman she'd once been, or even as the zombie maiden who had helped free them from their prison, but with a mingling of awe and apprehension.

But they had changed too. No longer were they frightened, half-starved women desperate for a knight in shining armor. They now wore the trappings of warriors, the skirts they had once donned replaced by tunics and leggings, swords, and quivers. And if Maeve did not watch her step, sundown might just find her with her head mounted on a stick.

"My friends," Maeve began, her voice threading through the thick silence, "I come before you as your ally against a common threat. I am sure you have all heard that Prince Alaric has been poisoned."

The women nodded, some of them joining hands or looping their arms around their partners' shoulders, conducting themselves as lovers might console one another. And somehow, this heartened Maeve. For it seemed good and right that these women, who had been so damaged by men, would forge bonds of the heart amongst themselves. And in some ways, she almost envied them.

"Now," she began again, "much of the zombie aristocracy counts us as their enemies. They have allied with those who would seek to divide us and rule over our fragmented spirits. And if we do not raise an army, and face them on their own ground, we stand no chance of saving Alaric. Nor ourselves."

Ingrid scoffed and turned her head to spit on the ground. "And what of the men, Maeve? Have they not proclaimed themselves the only souls fit to serve as lords of war?"

Maeve shook her head. "Eamon reports the men here also distrust us. Because of this, they would refuse us the reinforcements we need to recover the antidote that could save Alaric. But all of us, united, might prove a force our enemies can neither fathom nor anticipate. And should we prevail, perhaps then, men will finally begin to see us, not as their chattel, but as true equals."

Whispers rustled through the grove like brittle leaves scraping over cobblestones. Skepticism furrowed brows and lips parted only to close again without words.

"Why should we risk the peace we have forged for ourselves to save those who turned their heads while we were imprisoned?" the woman Maeve remembered as Diana demanded.

It was Fiona who stepped forward then, her gaze locking with each person in turn. "Maeve may wear a visage reminiscent of what your trials have conditioned you to fear," she said. "As do I. But our hearts beat with the same love and courage they always have. We ask you to look beyond appearances to see the truth she and I still embody—that together, we can still find the means to heal Alaric.

Only then can we help him save this fractured land so we might reclaim a peaceful future for us all."

One by one, the walls erected by doubt began to crumble, as if the idea of giving unity a fresh start was already taking root in their minds. A shared nod here, a whispered concession there, until a chorus of assent began to rise above the fear. For these women knew better than any the cost of division; it was etched into the very faces that still bore the scars of their past trials.

Ingrid cast a glance, first at Diana, then at her comrades who were gathered behind her. After a moment spent gauging their expressions, she nodded, then turned back to Maeve. "Where goes one, all will follow. We must speak for a moment amongst ourselves. Please give the privacy to do so."

Maeve retreated and stood with Fiona at the edge of the grove, her gaze cast on the distant tree line that marked the boundary of her village. As the moments the women spent conferring drew out, her fingers laced together, knuckles whitening with the effort to anchor herself in the here and now, against the tide of doubt that threatened to sweep her into an ocean of despair.

"Can I truly navigate this path?" Her voice was scarcely more than a sigh carried off by the breeze.

"Only if you trust yourself, Maeve, "Fiona's voice cut through the fog of her thoughts, steady as the ground beneath their feet. "Your love for Alaric and your sight has led you... and us ...this far. I refuse to believe those things will forsake you now."

Maeve turned toward her companion, observing the soft lines the last days had etched into her young features—evidence of the battles they'd endured and somehow survived. This alliance they sought was more than a coalition; it was the melding of spirits wearied by their trials, transformed, yet still unbroken by the whims of thoughtless men.

"Look at them." Fiona gestured toward the former tributaries, many of their faces scarred with their tales of loss and defiance. "Whether or not they choose to stand with us, they have already prepared themselves to fight for a world where they can feel safe and free. They are already your and Alaric's legacy."

The air hung heavy with the scent of impending rain, a promise of renewal amidst the blighted land. Maeve nodded and let out a slow breath, allowing the rhythm of her heartbeat to sync with the pulse of the land that still cradled them all despite its wounds.

Ingrid gestured her closer just then, and she stepped forward, her movements deliberate, reclaiming the conviction that had momentarily slipped through her fingers like grains of sand.

"We will stand with you, to the bitter end," Ingrid murmured as she extended her calloused hand to Maeve.

"Then let us be united," Maeve declared, her voice clear and resonant as she settled her hand into the nest of Ingrid's. The other women approached, one by one, forming a circle around Maeve and Fiona. Their clasped hands became a fortress against an unseasonable chill, their collective breaths the wind that would carry them back into their enemy's stronghold... together.

"When do we travel?" Ingrid asked.

"At dawn's first light tomorrow," Maeve said. "But tonight, we must join together and plan our siege. Preferably in a place that is free from prying eyes."

"I know just the place." Ingrid gestured toward a long, low hut that was buttressed against the rear wall of their brambly hold.

"It will serve our purpose well. And I hope you know that no matter what happens, the prince and I are beholden to you and yours always." Maeve pulled Ingrid into a quick hug, then turned to go, with Fiona following close behind her.

But as they stepped beyond the threshold of the tributaries' refuge, Maeve did not feel as heartened as she should. Perhaps because the familiar landscape that greeted them tugged at the remnants of her heart. This battle had begun long before she was born. The fields where she had been told children once played within the shelter of summer's wheat still lay barren. Even the trees that had surely looked over them and witnessed their childish secrets still stood silent and skeletal.

Still, this fractured land was her home, and one she loved dearly, despite its lingering scars. It did not matter anymore that the villagers wanted no part of her and her ilk. She still cared for them and wanted them to be safe. As did Alaric.

Each footstep she and Fiona took nearer the village heralded a new pulse of bittersweet memories, every familiar sight now forever tainted by the grim veil of her new existence. Only because of who she had become—what she now was—did many of her own people either despise or fear her, or perhaps both at the same time. And that knowledge hurt, for there was nothing she would not do to ensure their peace and prosperity.

"What are you thinking of?" Fiona's voice cut through the haze of Maeve's thoughts, her cool fingers threading through Maeve's to give them a reassuring squeeze.

"Just remembering gentler times," she said, a wry smile tightening her lips. "Do you have any memories of living here before you were... taken?"

Fiona's eyes darkened as she shook her head. "Only a few. Fleeting. Vague."

Maeve nodded, beginning to understand why Fiona seemed mostly unfazed by the villagers who had so openly shunned them. "See that field of brambles over there?"

Fiona's eyes followed the wake of Maeve's and she nodded.

"Coralie and I used to race across it like it was covered with grass instead of burrs," she said. Though her eyes misted with the memory, the corners of her mouth bowing in a semblance of a smile. "That little stinker always cheated, though, cutting across the stream that once ran alongside the road to win the game while I was busy picking a path over the cowgate. And I never once called her on it."

"Spoiled rotten, that one," Fiona added, gently elbowing Maeve's ribs. "But that's probably all your fault for letting her get away with murder."

"Guilty as charged," Maeve affirmed, the bittersweet acknowledgment wrapping around them like a shawl. She had spoiled Coralie, and she had enjoyed every second. Gods, how she missed the simplicity of her old life. But that failing to hold back some bit of herself had probably played a part in her becoming the zombie woman she was now. She had loved too much and, fearful of the day when she and Coralie might be parted, had given in to the child's careless whims too easily.

As Maeve acknowledged her own failings, and realized she would do it all again if it meant Alaric would be healed, that deep sense of foreboding once again seized her. But she trudged onward, their impossible cause pressing down on her with each step they took. What once would have been a carefree journey, filled with laughter, games, and idle chatter, now stretched out like an endless path to redemption—or certain doom.

As a tear slipped from her eyes, she lifted her face to the sky just as a great white owl lifted off from the trees and circled overhead. As it dipped toward them, a cool rain began to fall, as if the gods themselves tried to balm the proof of her angst. The sky that had been a merry blue just moments before had transformed into a boiling cauldron of grays, the rising wind singing a dirge as it scraped through the bare branches. Even the dust beneath their feet appeared to recede, as if the very land also despised what its two lost daughters had become. But the owl... he seemed not to care that they were zombies now.

Fiona tracked Maeve's gaze to the sky and gasped.

"I've been seeing him everywhere," Maeve admitted. "It started the night Alaric announced we would have our engagement ball. He was watching him as he soared above us. He practically claimed he could converse with the creature." And that made her wonder. Isolde had said she and Alaric were close. Had she taught him, too, the ways of magic? If so, why had he kept it from her?

As the owl circled ever lower. Fiona reached out, her hand finding Maeve's arm in a steady, grounding gesture. "Maybe it's a sign, Maeve. Perhaps Alaric sent him to tell us we will get through this," she murmured, her words heralding a lull in the rain.

"Perhaps," Maeve uttered, still scouring her soul for the where-withal to keep going. "And I shall be counting on you and those big violet eyes to help me convince Eamon the tributaries are as fit an army as we will ever find."

"Fiddlesticks," Fiona feigned with a roll of her eyes. "I hope my job doesn't involve kissing, for I may need much practice before I am successful in swaying him."

Maeve found herself laughing, despite the gravity of the task looming ahead. But if this quest were to cost her Fiona, too, she did not think her heart could possibly go on beating.

HIDING BENEATH THEIR CLOAK HOODS, Maeve and Fiona threaded through the last narrow walkway that ended at the back stoop of Nan's cottage. As they approached, the hair at Maeve's nape began to crawl. A deep shudder worked over her as she sensed the cloud of tension hanging over her childhood home. She did not need her crystal ball to know something awful was amiss.

Maeve and Fiona entered the dimly lit room to find Coralie huddled in the farthest corner, her small arms clenched tightly around her knees, shivers rattling her slight body. As Nan tried to offer comfort, the child's eyes were wide and glassy. Tears ran unchecked down her cheeks, and her breath came in frantic gasps.

Eamon stood nearby, his fists pumping at his sides and his brow furrowed with anger as he glowered out the window.

"Wh-what happened?" Maeve asked, her voice barely a whisper as she moved deeper into the room.

"She slipped out," he said. "As soon as I opened the door, your cat made a beeline toward the castle gates. I found Coralie screaming for help as she tried to climb a tree on the other side," Eamon explained, his gaze never leaving Nan and Coralie.

"Did she fall and hurt herself?"

Eamon shook his head. "Just as I spotted her, a feral came out of nowhere. It was nearly upon her when... this huge, white owl swooped in and..." He squeezed his eyes closed as if staving off images of how badly things could have ended. "Well," he continued, "thanks to the gods for sending that creature. Only because of its vigilance did I get to her in time."

"It's as if she had a guardian spirit watching out for her," Fiona uttered as Maeve rushed forward and knelt beside her cousin.

"I am glad you are here. I can't get a word out of her," Nan said. "Perhaps you will have better luck."

Silently uttering her thanks to the owl—to Alaric?—Maeve nodded, gently stroking Coralie's tawny curls, offering what comfort she could. The child's crying eased as Maeve lifted her trembling form into her lap and began to rock her like she had when she was a wee tot. The ferals were growing bolder, and she couldn't shake the feeling that they were seeking revenge for the zombies they had felled in the woods. If that were the case, this would not be the last close call her loved ones would suffer.

"We cannot delay seeking the antidote much longer," she said, determination steeling her voice. "But Coralie has no sense of her own mortality, and Nan is only one person." She swung her gaze to Fiona before speaking again. "I cannot possibly justify leaving them here *unguarded*."

"Agreed," Fiona said, swinging her gaze to Eamon's. "They need someone with them who knows Coralie's ways and understands what is required to fend off ferals."

"Who do you have in mind?" Eamon asked.

Fiona moved nearer to Eamon and settled a hand on his arm. "You, Eamon. You must stay here and protect them."

"But what of our quest for the antidote? Is that not more pressing?"

"It is. And our quest will continue as planned," Maeve said.

"You and Fiona would be better off traveling alone into a bear's den. Yet you would go without reinforcements?"

"You'll be happy to know Fiona and I have managed to raise a force of our own." Maeve's chin hardened as her gaze met his.

Eamon's jaw dropped, silently working until he found words. "Amongst the villagers? I find that rather hard to believe."

"No. You were right about them. But the former tributaries have agreed to assume their mantle. Tonight, we meet to plan our advance. Then, at dawn tomorrow, Fiona and I will lead them as we infiltrate Alaric's castle."

"And you seriously believe this is wise?" Eamon asked of Fiona, his green eyes searching hers as if he doubted her sanity, too. "You have seen firsthand what is required to dispatch ferals, and my heart could not bear it if I were to lose you, too."

"You have already seen that Fiona is agile and adept with her weapon," Maeve protested. "And I would take damage on myself before I let anyone harm her."

"But look at her. She's hardly bigger than a church mouse."

"'Tis true, I am small," Fiona said. "But so are badgers, yet they are renowned for their ferocity."

"I can't argue that point," Eamon said, though he still looked unconvinced.

"And Loren would not have made it out of the castle grounds without her," Maeve added, "much less back here."

Eamon began to pace as he raked his hand through his hair. "But for the two of you to lead an untrained pack of women into battle... flies into the face of... not just convention, but sanity."

"You underestimate those women, my friend," Maeve said, her tone firm. "Because of what they have endured, the tributaries have spent their time in seclusion honing their weaponry skills. I realize this idea flies into the face of your assumptions about women, but I have no doubt they will prove themselves as fine a force as any," she argued with far more confidence than she felt.

"Please don't worry, Eamon," Fiona added. "I have seen with my own eyes that those women have the wherewithal to fight as well as any men. And we will also have the element of surprise on our side. Nobody will suspect our garments hide blades until it is too late to counter. And if Maeve is to keep her focus on saving Alaric, you and your experience are needed more here."

"Alright," he conceded, though his voice still wavered with uncertainty. "But promise you will be careful and raise a signal fire should you need reinforcements. I will send what few men who won't try to dispatch you themselves."

"I promise," Maeve assured him.

"Then I would have a moment alone with Fiona," he said as he placed his hand on the young woman's waist and steered her toward the back door, the lingering concern on his face evident. As the door slid closed behind them, Maeve's heart began to flutter, her eyes flicking from Nan's worried face to Coralie's now sleeping one to the worn floorboards beneath her. Her responsibility to keep all those she cared for safe pressed down on her with an almost unbearable force.

"Alaric would have faith in you," Nan said, her voice firm yet gentle. "He would trust you to lead them back to the castle."

"But what if I fail them? And you?" she whispered, her eyes brimming with unshed tears. "What if Eamon is right, and we are not strong enough a force to take down the King and Elora's army of ferals? I will have endangered you all for nothing."

"You forget that we were already in danger; we just did not know.

Should you fail to penetrate the castle the first time, you will regroup and come back stronger, just as you did before," Nan declared, her grip on Maeve's hand tightening. "You are a warrior, Maeve, forged by love and loss. Embrace your gifts, both the obvious and the hidden, for they were given to you for a reason. Let them be the things that lead you through the darkness."

She nodded and blew out a soft sigh. "Could I borrow your room for a while?"

"What is mine is yours, Maeve. Take as long as you need. I have plenty to occupy me out here."

Determined to heed Nan's advice, she lifted Coralie and carried her to her bed. After tucking her in and ensuring she was asleep, she retrieved her knapsack and retreated to her grandmother's room, Nyx already slinking silently at her side. With a deep breath, she lifted her crystal ball from the sack, sat on the bed, and settled it on the mattress. "Show me the best way home," she murmured.

After sucking in a few slow breaths, she focused her energy on the orb's center, willing it to reveal the path forward. Isolde had told her the glass would only reveal its secrets when the time was right. Would that the hour of her knowing had arrived, for her time to save Alaric grew short.

As the orb's swirling mists began to clear, Maeve found herself transported to a different place and time. Alaric stood before her, alive and whole, his cornflower blue eyes shining with love as he extended her his hand and swept her into a dance beneath a sky spangled with stars. "I thought you would never join me," he said.

As she pressed her hand to his chest, the scents of moonflowers and night jasmine clung to the air, mingling with the soft strains of a haunting melody that seemed to emanate from the stars themselves. *Home.*

They twirled amidst the lush garden, their steps fluid and graceful, their laughter ringing out like wind chimes. Alaric's fingers brushed against her waist as he pulled her close, his voice thick with emotion as he whispered, "I am so proud to make you my bride, Maeve. You are everything I have ever wanted and more."

The moment was intoxicating, a dream she had longed for in the depths of her darkest nights. Her troubles fell behind her as she lost herself in the vision, her heart aching with the fierce yearning to remain by Alaric's side for all eternity. For this moment to be the one that was real... and that other world, naught but a nightmare.

"Promise me," she murmured, her gaze locked on his, "that I will not have to leave you. That we can be together always, just as we are now."

"Forever and always," Alaric vowed, pressing his lips against her forehead in a gentle benediction. "We can remain out here forever, but only if that is your choice."

As they swayed together in a starlit embrace, Maeve felt a rare sense of peace envelop her, cradling her weary spirit, and she could not help but wonder if all the trials she believed she and her friends had suffered were indeed nightmares inspired by her deepest fears. Perhaps it did not matter anymore. She was with Alaric. He was whole and well, and she knew if she let go and surrendered those specters, this perfect night could... and would ...last forever.

As Alaric and Maeve continued their dance, a soft mist began to roll over the garden. Somewhere in the distance, Maeve heard the insistent mewing of a cat, the beating of great wings. Then, in an instant, Alaric grew as intangible as the starlight now sifting through her fingers. As his form grew ephemeral before her very eyes, the three-quarter moon broke through the clouds, and her anxiety peaked, her mind struggling to recall the thing she was supposed to accomplish before the next full moon.

Alaric's form dissolved into the mists, and Maeve choked out a sob. "You promised we would be together always." Something swooped over her head just then, its expansive wingspan blotting the moon, plunging the entire garden into pitch.

Maeve's eyes snapped open as the same snowy owl that she and Fiona had seen yesterday crashed through the oil paper window, toppling everything in its path, leaving her gasping for breath and clutching her fractured heart.

"Alaric? Where are you?" she cried out, part of her still caught in that gentler place, her voice choking with confusion and heartbreak.

The owl came to rest on the dresser, its wide eyes gleaming with...recognition. The creature seemed to regard her with a mix of sadness and concern, as if sensing the turmoil within her. But as she reached to touch it, confirming it real, it startled and soared towards the open window, a single perfect feather drifting down and landing gently in Maeve's outstretched hands. *I have always been with you, and no matter what happens, I always shall be...*

"Wait!" Desperate for answers, she rushed toward the window, her eyes scouring the sky.

But the owl had vanished into the night, leaving behind only the faintest echo of a melody that sounded hauntingly familiar.

Feeling caught between worlds, not knowing which was real, she stared at the snowy feather in her palm, a strange warmth embracing her as she realized the truth: the owl was somehow connected to Alaric's spirit and had been guiding her and protecting her on her journey. She could feel his love surrounding her like a shield, and she knew then that she was not alone, nor had she ever been.

"Thank you, my love," she whispered to the empty night, her eyes brimming with tears as they lifted to behold the three-quarter moon. "I will not fail you, Alaric. I promise."

She turned to Nyx, who eyed the ruined window warily, her eyes like copper coins reflecting the fractured moonlight. "I should clean this mess up," she said softly, determination burning in her chest like a flame. "Time grows short, and Fiona and I must prepare ourselves to meet with the tributaries."

As Maeve reset the room, her mind raced with plans and strategies, weaving together a tapestry of tactics that would ensure their survival. She would trust in her newfound abilities, in the wisdom of Fiona and the tributaries, and most of all, in the love that bound her to Alaric. They were connected by more than just their hearts; they were united by an unbreakable bond that transcended time and space. Surely, a force such as that could bend even the darkest will.

By the time the room was righted, her doubts had receded. She was no longer the scared, helpless girl who had feared nothing more than zombies; she was a warrior, a leader, and a future queen. And she would do whatever it took to bring her people—

and herself—the peace they truly deserved.

"Are you ready, Nyx?" she asked, her voice steady and strong. A rap sounded at the door just then, and the cat looked up at her, her tail flicking with anticipation. *Always*, the creature seemed to say, echoing the same vow Alaric had made from the depths of her vision.

"Maeve," Fiona called out. "What are you doing in there? The hour grows late. It is time for us to say our goodbyes and go."

CHAPTER 16

The three-quarter moon made its weary ascent, bruising the clouds with purple and gray. Maeve and Fiona bid Nan, Coralie and Eamon a tearful goodbye, then made their way to the bramble-encased fortress the tributaries now called home.

As they approached the fortress of brambles, the air hung heavy with the scent of woodsmoke, its pungent aroma mingling with the distant howls of feral zombies.

Maeve shuddered with this reminder of the dangers that lurked in the woods, for it testified to the peril inherent in their quest to save Alaric. No doubt she would face them again. And by the sound of it, their numbers were growing. She suspected she had Lady Elora to thank for that.

Ingrid was waiting to receive them and escorted them into the long, low hut she had pointed out yesterday. Within, the struggling light of a small fire cast shadows upon the faces of the women who were already gathered around it. These were the same women Maeve, Alaric, and Eamon had once saved from the clutches of a cruel fate, and it heartened Maeve that their eyes were no longer hollow with the despair of their prolonged captivity. Now, they glinted with good health and a stony determination that spoke of the strength they had forged in the crucible of their shared traumas.

Maeve's gaze swept over the group, taking in the scars that marked many of their faces. Some bore the evidence of blades, thin silver lines that gleamed in the firelight, while others carried the mottled remnants of burns, proving the cruel treatment they had endured under Lady Elora's watch. Had the king already been her master then? Somehow, she already knew the answer was yes. Yet, despite the physical reminders of their shared past, the women's faces radiated a quiet determination, a quality Maeve knew would be invaluable in the trials yet to come.

"Please. Join us in the circle," Ingrid said. Though her voice was rough, like gravel underfoot, it carried an undeniable air of authority as she waved Maeve and Fiona forward.

As they, too, settled in around the fire, it was Ingrid who broke the silence first. "Maeve, Fiona," she began, her eyes reflecting the dancing flames, "as promised, we will abide by our promise to stand with you in your quest to save the prince. But first, we would all like to know what your plan is."

Maeve felt Ingrid's gaze upon her, a tangible probing that seemed to bore into her very soul. She was protective of her friends, and rightly so. So, she drew in a deep breath, the scent of burning wood filling her lungs as she gathered her thoughts.

"I have reason to believe the exiled king is even now ensconced in Alaric's castle," she said at last, her voice steady despite the tremor that ran through her hands. "There is where we will find the antidote and, with it, the key to breaking the curse that has befallen the prince."

"And what of those who reside within the castle? Are there any allies amongst them?"

Maeve shook her head. "Sadly, aside from Lady Isolde, there are none within the castle walls who will help us. Even if there were... one of the village scouts reported to Eamon that the courtiers, too, are all... sleeping, much like Alaric."

At the mention of the king's name, a murmur of apprehension rippled through the group. Some of the women exchanged glances, their eyes speaking volumes in the language of shared experience and unspoken fears. But it was the youngest of the tributaries, a striking, ebony-skinned girl named Ilyana, who voiced the question that seemed to be on everyone's mind.

"But what of the golden-eyed zombie, Lysander?" she asked, her melodic voice barely above a whisper. "The one who was imprisoned with us? Was he, too, freed? For if he was, I have no doubt he would return to help us."

Maeve's breath caught in her throat, the memory of her vision slamming into her like a blade. Lady Elora's words echoed in her mind, a sinister confession of the dark magic she coveted to help one assume another's countenance. She pressed a hand to her mouth to suppress a cry, a sickening suspicion threatening to shatter her already fragile composure. *Perhaps it wasn't Lysander. I might have this all wrong...*

She fixed her gaze on Ilyana's wide, obsidian eyes, plundering them for any hints of artifice or subterfuge. But she might as well have been staring into the eyes of a doe. "You must tell me, Ilyana. How long was Lysander confined there with you before you were freed?"

"Quite a while, milady," she said, her gaze never faltering.

"And you are certain he called himself Lysander?"

Ilyana nodded. "We grew quite... close, milady."

"Golden eyes. Dark hair. Handsome as a god?" Fiona asked.

Ilyana's ensuing blush began as a mahogany shadow at her neckline and raced toward the crown of braids piled atop her head. "Yes. He was all those things."

Fiona's hand found Maeve's, the coolness of her skin a balm to the feverish heat that seemed to radiate from her own. *I have never felt so confused.*

"How is that possible?" Fiona asked softly, her eyes probing Maeve's.

Maeve swallowed hard, the truth like a bitter poison on her tongue. "I swear to you, I saw him, Fiona, clear as day. And my body did not pluck the wounds he left on my flesh from thin air. Nor did I turn into a zombie all by myself." Maeve's voice trailed off as replayed the vision. Of a spell that could make a person assume the face of another. She broke out in a cold sweat, remembering how adamantly Alaric had defended him. It had almost torn them apart. *But maybe I was mistaken.*

"But both of those things cannot be true unless he can occupy two spaces at once," Fiona said.

Ilyana's chin lifted, her jaw hard with conviction. "I assure you, I am not mistaken in this. He was with us. And during the time we were chained next to one another... well, say what you will, but I learned enough about him to know he would never take that what is not his to claim."

"Then perhaps he did not," Maeve conceded, but not because she believed it. Some sort of trickery was afoot, she knew it to the pit of her soul. "For in a vision, I saw Lady Elora begging Duchess Isolde for a potion that would allow one to assume the appearance of another. She spoke of having resorted to such means before. Now I fear the man you saw was not Lysander, but someone else entirely. A spy posing as a prisoner to keep tabs on you, perhaps."

A collective gasp rippled through the group, their faces etched with a mix of horror and disbelief. Some of the women clasped their hands over their mouths, their eyes glistening with unshed tears, while others clenched their fists, their knuckles turning white with the force of their anger.

Ingrid leaned forward, her brow furrowed, and her lips pressed in a hard line. "But if not Lysander, then who?" she demanded, her voice like the crack of a whip in the silence.

Maeve shook her head, her heart heavy with the weight of her suspicions. "I do not yet know," she admitted, her words barely audible over the crackling fire. "I do not even know if my insights can be fully trusted. But I do know what I saw, felt."

"As do I," Ilyana said, her chin firm and her eyes flashing with indignation. "One thing I do know is the kindness he showed us was not faked."

"I agree," Ingrid said. "But if it the man we knew was not Lysander, then our quest has been complicated. For without any other allies in the castle, we might just need that kind soul's help."

"So, there is another mystery in our quest to vanquish the treachery that has festered in the shadows of Alaric's kingdom," Fiona said.

As the night wore on, the maps Maeve had scratched into the earthen floor with a stick had been consulted, and the plan they hoped would stitch together their fractured world was made. They would leave at dawn break.

After dirt was thrown on the fire to quelch its flames, the tributaries bade them goodnight and settled into their bedrolls, the soft rustling of woolen blankets and the gentle snores of the sleeping women soon filling the air.

But no matter how long Maeve stared into the fire's dying embers, she knew rest would not find her this night. Though her body and mind ached with exhaustion, she found her thoughts being pulled to her crystal ball. As she sat up and pulled it from her pack, its swirling depths flickered to life with a promise of answers to the questions the mention of Lysander had caused to plague her mind.

With Fiona and Nyx curled beside her, their presence provided stalwart comfort, and Maeve felt safe enough to gaze deep into the orb. Her breath caught in her throat as the mists beckoned her within, then parted to reveal a scene that forced her to swallow the cries gathering in her throat.

Lady Elora and King Caligula stood before her; their faces contorted with a malevolence that seemed to seep from every pore. The strange glow cast by the mists only served to amplify the cruelty etched into their features. Though Maeve's heart contracted with horror, she could not pull her eyes away, for she was transfixed.

She recognized the scene as the laboratory situated in the catacombs beneath Alaric's library. In Elora's hand, a vial of shimmering liquid pulsed with a dark energy that made Maeve's skin crawl. The sight of it filled her with an oppressive sense of foreboding, and as Elora tipped the vial to Caligula's lips, Maeve's heart rose into her throat. The liquid spilled into the exiled king's waiting mouth like a sadistic communion, and in an instant, his hawkish visage began to shift and blur.

The cruel lines of his face rearranged until Maeve found herself staring into the handsome, golden-eyed features of Lysander, the man who had once been Alaric's closest advisor, the one whom he had felt safe telling the kingdom's most sensitive secrets—as well as a few of his own.

The truth of what may have really happened to her that night hit her like a physical blow, knocking the air from her lungs. It may have been Caligula all along, disguised by Elora's dark magic, who had gained entrance into her chambers, then drugged and violated her wearing Lysander's guise. To what end, she did not yet know. Perhaps he had thought infecting her, then immediately taking her might make her provide him what the Tributaries could not—a vessel able to conceive and gestate his vile spawn. Or, perchance, he had sought to regain his throne by posing as his son's most trusted advisor, then turning his own kingdom against him. It was even possible—no, likely—both of those were true.

But Caligula's intentions mattered little, for the damage was already done. Yet the revelation she had seen was both sickening and strangely liberating; had she not taken pains to ensure she would not conceive, she might have born Alaric his own malformed half-brother. Her hands balled into fists, nails digging into her palms. *That would have been a far more horrible a fate.*

As she forced her thoughts to disconnect from the horrific vision, a twisted knot of betrayal unwound in her chest. Caligula hated his son and wanted him dead.

Her hands began to shake, a scream of despair building in her throat, but no sound escaped her lips. Her mind reeled as she tried to process the magnitude of what she had just witnessed, and she found herself clinging to Fiona as if she were the only stronghold in a world that had suddenly turned upside down. Tears streamed down her face in salty rivulets, and she found herself pressing ever closer to her friend. With her face buried between Fiona's shoulder blades, her body shuddered with silent sobs.

Fiona turned, her sleep-glazed probing Maeve's. "Maeve, what has you so distraught?"

"I might have been mistaken after all." Her voice was raw with emotion. "I saw it in my crystal ball, Caligula, but wearing Lysander's face. All this time, I thought... I may have blamed... an innocent man for ravaging me. And now nobody knows where he is... or how he fares.

Fiona turned and held her close, her arms a fortress of comfort and understanding. "Even if that's true, you had no way of know-ing," she murmured, her own tears mingling with Maeve's. "But now, armed with the truth, justice can finally be delivered. We can still set things right, for Alaric, for Lysander, and for you, as well."

Maeve nodded, something that almost felt like relief unfurling in her chest. But the assault she had suffered, the pain, shame, and confusion that had plagued her for so long, none of that faded in the face of this new knowledge. She tried to be heartened that at least she knew now who her true enemies were. She would stop at nothing to see them fall.

Just as they had planned, they would infiltrate the castle, seize Elora and the king and force the antidote from them, shattering the web of lies and treachery that had ensnared them all. Hopefully, there they would find the clues that would lead them to the real Lysander... for there was no telling how many others in the kingdom might be hiding behind the guise of another.

She could trust no one. Nor did she intend to.

Maeve's heart pounded in her chest as she imagined the confrontation to come. Still, she knew that with the power of her visions, the strength and intuitions of her feminine allies, and the unwavering love she held for Alaric, they could emerge victorious.

As the night wore on, and safe in her best friend's arms, Maeve lay awake, her mind racing with plans and possibilities. She doubted she would rest again until they had put an end to the evil that had plagued them all for far too long.

WITH THE FIRST rays of dawn swathing the sky in pastel ribbons of pink and gold, Maeve rose from her bedroll, eager to begin.

As the sun's first light crept over the horizon, Maeve and her small army prepared to set out. Though it was possible some of them might meet their ends this day, each woman moved with a sense of peace... and purpose. Their steps were sure and their heads high, as if the very act of readying their swords and loading their quivers was a declaration of their intention to prevail. Maeve's heart swelled as she looked upon this small assembly of women, their eyes bright with the fire of their shared cause. They were more than just survivors now; they had risen from the ashes of despair like phoenixes and transformed into warriors.

Would that I be made fit to lead them, Maeve prayed to the same gods she still feared had forsaken her and her kind. *If not for mine and Alaric's sakes, then at least for the humans who stand as much to gain today as any.*

And deep in her mind, she could hear Loren's voice tolling, clear a clock's chime. *You were born fit, my friend. And while I cannot be with you in body, my spirit shall march alongside you. And in doing so, perchance, my fall, too, shall be avenged.*

"So, mote it be, my friend." Maeve sheathed her spare dagger in her boot, shouldered on her pack, and moved to join the rest of the group. As she drew near Ingrid and Diana, Fiona appeared at her side, her small hand clasping Maeve's own, not as a show of fear, but rather unity.

"So, it is time, yes?" Ingrid asked as Nyx, eager to be their ever-watchful scout, wound between their legs, her copper eyes gleaming with an anticipation that seemed almost human.

"That it is," Maeve said, not missing the sparks of passion that danced in Diana's eyes as Ingrid sought out her gaze. And the knowledge they had found safe harbor in each other's arms reinforced her notion that love truly was the most transcendental force in the Universe. "Now let us go forth and remember with every step we take that no one person shall guide us today, but rather, love."

"For love!" the women chanted as they stepped out into the light of the new day.

The slushy dirt road ahead stretched before them, a winding path that would lead them to the forest, fraught with danger and uncertainty. But when Maeve saw the pale owl circling overhead, she knew, with a certainty that resonated deep within her soul, that Alaric was somehow with her. And they would walk into this fire together, bound by a love that even the darkest magic could not extinguish. *I am coming, my love...*

By the time they approached the dense woods, the sun's warmth had eased the worst of the night's chill. One by one, they marched into the shadows toward Alaric's castle, where Maeve was certain lay the key to all their salvation. And with each step taken, she felt the weight of her destiny settling more firmly upon her shoulders. Only this time, it did not feel like too heavy a burden to bear. For she was more than just a peasant girl now, and more than a zombie prince's betrothed. She was first a woman, once violated and afraid, but now a force to be reckoned with righting a world whose factions had forgotten how to love one another. With the support of her friends, the strength of their shared convictions, and the power of her gift, she would lead them all into a future where the lines between human and zombie, love and hate, would be forever blurred.

And should she die trying?

Suddenly, she knew either outcome was fine with her, for her mark on this world had already been made in the hearts of these fine women who marched with her, determined to save the zombie prince who loved them all.

If she could not save him, she did not have to ask to know those who remained standing after this day was done would. And in that, Alaric's vision for a unified world had already won. Nan, Coralie, Fiona and Eamon... everyone she held dear would finally know peace.

CHAPTER 17

With the sun's rays barely piercing the forest canopy, Maeve and her unorthodox army began their trek toward Alaric's castle. Though Maeve only had her visions to assure her, there lay her best chance for intercepting the king, and thus the antidote, her faith in her abilities grew stronger by the day.

If the elements conspired to foretell any ominous turn of fate, they were doing a poor job. Portents of spring had returned with a vengeance. The air was crisp with the scents of dew and newly sprouting evergreens, and the earth that had been glazed with frost just two days ago was soft and yielding beneath their feet. It seemed to Maeve that the spring goddess herself was urging them forward, perhaps even hastening their quest.

As they moved through a sea of towering evergreens, she sometimes spied the snowy owl circling overhead, as if he was somehow... guarding them. Though she kept her silence, knowing he was still there heartened her.

"Might I suggest we take a wedge formation for as long as we are able, with you at the lead?" Ingrid offered.

A chill breeze whipped over them as Maeve nodded and took her place at the head of the group. With the others assembled behind her, her braids whipped about her face like fiery banners in the dappled light. As they paused a moment to listen for any disruptions in nature's music, Maeve was flanked on one side by Fiona and on the other by Ingrid. "All seems well enough," Ingrid whispered.

"Agreed," Maeve answered. "So, we will continue."

With all remaining silent, they moved forward with cautious purpose, their steps sure but their eyes always sweeping the thickets. Each of them held their hands ready to raise the weapons they had forged from the same pain and resilience that had brought them together.

"Stay alert," Maeve cautioned as they journeyed deeper into the forest, the vegetation growing more tangled and treacherous with each step. "Whether it be a feral horde or a booby trap, we cannot know what dangers might lurk behind the next tree. Given I've no clue how numerous the booby traps are, I suggest we tighten our wedge."

Fiona nodded and fell back, the bow Eamon had given her from Loren's belongings at the ready as she passed Maeve's order on to the others. "We all must move closer to one another and guard each other's backs," she whispered. "Pass the order to those behind you with as little noise as possible."

After the soft murmurs shared amongst the group died, Ingrid hefted her battle axe, the blade glinting in the sunlight, and fell in again behind Maeve. They moved forward in this manner, each of their eyes scanning the shifting shadows between the trees.

One hour passed, then two, and all remained unperturbed. Suddenly, the birds fell silent, and the world seemed to pause, as if holding its breath. Nyx leaped ahead of Maeve, her mottled fur rising as she arched her back and hissed at a thicket of bushes. As she did so, a bone-chilling shriek pierced the air, and the women froze, their hands instinctively reaching for their weapons. From the shadows of the distant trees, two feral zombies emerged, their sunken eyes gleaming with a hunger that knew no bounds. The creatures were in various stages of decay, their flesh hanging in tatters from exposed bones, their maws dripping with foul ichor.

"Form a circle, facing out, shoulders touching," Maeve shouted, her sword ringing as she drew it from its sheath. "Then leave enough room in the center for Fiona. And you, Fi, must occupy the circle's center so there is sufficient room to draw your bow. And no matter what happens, keep the ring closed. Do not let even one feral break through until their numbers are at least manageable!"

The tributaries moved as one, heeding Maeve's instructions and preparing to face the oncoming horde.

"Now, Fiona!" Maeve shouted.

As the ferals advanced, Fiona let loose a volley of arrows, each one finding its mark. But it wasn't enough. The beasts came from everywhere, all at once. As one leaped at Ingrid, she charged, her axe cleaving the air as she met her attacker head-on. But their circle could not, would not hold. There were simply too many revenants to count.

Maeve broke formation next, dancing among the horde, her sword a blur of silver as she struck out at creature after creature, always aiming for their necks to sever their heads. Their rotten flesh yielded beneath her blade, sending putrid sprays of black blood arcing through the air.

"Behind you!" Diana cried as a feral lunged at Fiona from the shadows.

Fiona stumbled back, her bow falling from her grasp as she tried to evade the creature's grasp. Maeve and Diana rushed to her aid, their weapons striking as one. Maeve's blade sliced through a zombie's neck while Diana's spear found its mark in another creature's throat. But they were no closer to Fiona than when they began.

Just as Fiona was pinned to the ground by her assailants, a great flash of white broke through the forest canopy and descended into the fray, pecking out eyes and pulling flesh.

The distraction proved the exact boon Maeve needed to dispatch the creatures.

"Thanks," Fiona gasped as they pulled her to her feet. "That was too close."

"We've got you," Maeve reassured her before turning to face the remaining zombies. "Now, let us finish this before we are the ones who are finished!"

The women fought with renewed vigor, their movements coordinated and precise. They called out warnings to each other, their voices rising above the clash of metal and the wet snarls of the ferals.

As the last zombie fell, Maeve's sword struck true, severing its head from its shoulders. But as the creature collapsed, its hand reached out, grasping at the hand of another fallen zombie beside it.

Maeve's heart clenched as she watched the two creatures, their final moments spent in a macabre display of human-like connection, and she could not keep herself from bursting into tears.

"You would grieve for them?" Ilyana asked, her head tilting with confusion.

"I-I can't help but feel sorry for them," she whispered, her voice heavy with emotion.

"They are soulless and mindless," Ingrid reminded her. "I doubt they can even feel pain."

"Everyone knows that, Maeve," Diana agreed. "Please don't waste your grief on them."

"But is that not what you once believed about zombies like myself? Can any of us really know for certain what happens inside their shattered psyches?"

"Certainly, Lady Elora has devised the means to control them," Fiona offered.

Maeve nodded. "And Alaric once told me his researchers were close to finding a way to ease their suffering, perhaps even reintegrate them into society."

The other tributaries exchanged glances, their expressions surprised.

"But is forgiveness even possible?" Ingrid asked, her brow furrowed. "After all the lives they've taken?"

"Have we not taken at least as many of theirs? Can any of us say for certain they do not feel, cannot mourn? Or is that something men we trusted simply said was true to position themselves as the world's saviors, knowing others would follow suit?"

Fiona laid a hand on Maeve's shoulder, her touch a gentle comfort. "If it is true, then it means there's still hope for them to have a better world, too," she said softly.

Diana nodded, her eyes bright with unshed tears. "It's hard to fancy, but if we could all find a way to coexist," she mused. "To heal the wounds that have divided us for so long..."

Maeve felt a warmth surge in her chest, a spark that burned brighter with each passing moment. "And that is exactly what we're fighting for," she said, her voice ringing with conviction. "Not just for Alaric, but for all of us. Maybe even including them."

The women voiced their agreement, their faces set with new determination.

"Then let us keep moving," Ingrid said, hefting her axe once more. "We have a long way to go, and we will need all our strength to see this through."

As they set off again, the sun at their backs, a renewed sense of purpose flowed through Maeve's veins. With these brave women by her side, anything was possible. They would find the antidote, break the curse, and bring Alaric back. And in doing so, they would light the way for a brighter future, perhaps even one where the living zombies and the truly undead could find a way to, if not coexist, at least live in peace.

THE WOMEN VENTURED DEEPER into the forest's dark heart, spring demurring to winter's chill. The castle's spires loomed above the snow-dusted treetops, but this time, Maeve didn't experience the ease she had grown accustomed to at sighting the place where she had made her home with Alaric.

Something more than the weather had changed. She could sense it in her marrow as her mind whispered about the dangers that lay ahead. With each step, her discomfort grew, a prickling at her nape that spoke of a malevolence more ancient than time itself.

Suddenly, Maeve halted. Nyx's fur stood on end, and she spun about, their gazes locking. Once again, Maeve's mind tumbled through time and space, stealing the breath from her lungs. As she stumbled, her head struck the ground. The world around her blurred and was replaced by a scene of such vivid clarity that it seemed to unfold before her very eyes. She saw Elora and the King rummaging through Dr. Reinhart's offices...a scarlet banner of blood unfurling across the floor. She cried out, the vision already fading. Fiona and Ingrid were at her side, their hands steadying her as she fought to stand on legs that felt disconnected from her body.

"Are you harmed?" Fiona asked, her face etched with concern, as if she feared speaking too loudly might shatter the heavy silence that had descended over the forest.

Maeve shook her head. "I saw them, Elora and the king, as clearly as I see you now."

"Your visions have proven true, then," Fiona said.

Maeve twisted one of her braids, willing the haze to clear from her mind. "If I am to trust what I saw, the king has already arrived. And that means... his coronation is imminent."

"But at least now you know where he is. Is this not good news?" Fiona's eyes softened as a rogue tear trailed down Maeve's cheeks.

"They were pillaging Dr. Reinhart's office. The antidote must have been secreted there all this time. And if we do not make haste, they might well destroy it before we can intervene."

Ingrid's face hardened, her grip tightening on her ax. "Then we haven't a moment to lose," she said, her tone urgent. "We must breach the castle before it is too late."

But as they approached the castle's gates, Maeve's heart dropped like a stone. The once-grand structure was now encased in a thick cage of brambles. The vines writhed like malevolent serpents, their razor-sharp barbs glinting like fangs in the wan light. The tributaries dropped back a little, talking amongst themselves.

"How will we ever get inside?" Diana asked, her regal brow pinched with worry.

Maeve stepped forward, drawing her sword from its sheath with a steely rasp. "We have no choice but to hack our way through," she said, raising her blade. "It's the only way."

"So much for slipping in unnoticed," Ingrid grumbled as she hefted her ax. With grim determination, the women drew their blades and set about slashing the vines. But for each one they cut, two more appeared in its place, thicker and more twisted than before. The harder they worked, the more the brambles fought back, their thorns drawing blood that spattered the frosted ground with crimson stains.

Minutes stretched into hours as the women labored, sweat and blood mingling until Maeve's muscles burned and twitched. Yet still, the brambles grew back, a living wall that defied all efforts to breach it. Despair began to set in as Maeve and Fiona exchanged hopeless glances, their initial determination giving way to frustration... and, for Maeve, grief.

"It is no use," Ingrid panted, the arm that wielded her ax trembling. "We will never cut through at this rate."

"There has to be another way in," Maeve insisted, but a tremor of doubt crept into her voice. The brambles twisted and writhed, seeming to mock her, forcing her to accept a bitter truth—the castle where Alaric slept was now beyond her reach, and barring a miracle, there was no way in.

She sagged against the brambles, ignoring the thorns that pierced her skin, silent tears tracking through the grime on her face.

Behind her, Fiona and the others stood in silence, their quest now thwarted at the gates of their goal.

The sun sank lower, the snow continuing to fall, giving the illusion they'd stepped into another realm. Disheartened and exhausted, she fell back a few paces and considered the brambles from a new perspective. With her arms clutched around her body to stave the shivers racking her frame, she scrutinized the strange network for any point of weakness.

Just as panic began clawing at her dying hopes, something overhead caught her eye, a flicker of brightness amidst the branches. There, perched on the brambles, was the snowy owl, huge and magnificent, its ivory feathers gleaming like stars against a midnight sky. As she gasped, the creature's eyes fixed on her with a quiet intensity that stole the breath from her. Her heart stalled with her realization its eyes were not golden, as was true with all the other owls she had seen. Rather, they were a vivid cornflower blue, as soft and inviting as Alaric's gaze. And there, winding between the thorns, a flash of copper eyes. Nyx, her movements graceful as a deer's as she scaled the gnarled branches, looking as if she was trying to climb up to greet the owl. "Look!" she cried out, lifting her finger to point toward the creatures.

"Perhaps he really was sent by Alaric to guide us," Fiona murmured, her eyes growing wide.

But Ingrid didn't look ready to be swayed. She arched a brow, her gaze darting between Maeve and Fiona. "This is the plan now? You would pin the prince's fate to the whims of two dumb animals?"

"You know as well as me this isn't the first time since we left that a creature has saved us," Fiona insisted.

"Where would any of us be if Nyx had not been there to alert us to the ferals?" Maeve added. "Surely their unwavering presence is a portent."

For a long moment, the women watched the creatures, some with awe, others with disbelief. But soon, the restless whispers they passed amongst themselves died, their stares unwavering as the owl and the cat began to advance along the perimeter of the brambles. Their movements were sure and purposeful, imbued with an urgency that caused Maeve's breath to catch.

The women followed their path until the owl lifted off and soared toward the same woods from which they had so recently emerged—and where Fiona had nearly died. Nyx followed, moving away from the castle and racing toward the trees.

Ingrid came to an abrupt halt, her arms crossing over her chest as she set her gaze upon Maeve and chuffed. "Now what?"

"We must make haste, before we lose them," Maeve said.

Diana fell in with the others behind Maeve, but Ingrid just as quickly pulled her back. "Have you not noticed they are leading us away from the castle?"

"You may stay here if that is your choice, and nobody would not fault you," Maeve said. "But I, for one, intend to heed my intuition."

Though she grumbled still, Ingrid fell in beside Diana and followed.

When the creatures came to a halt at a small opening in the thickets, dry laughter tore from Maeve. As she leaned forward to part the thickets, exposing the dark recess that seemed to lead into the bowels of earth, joyful tears welled in her eyes. "Of course this would be our way inside," she said, her voice ringing with certainty. "For few beyond Isolde would know of its existence, much less that the path within these caverns ends at her abode."

"But how can you possibly know it will lead us into the castle?" Ingrid asked, ever the skeptic.

"Because this hidden cavern is the same means we used to escape the zombie guards just a few days ago," Fiona said, her lips bowing toward a smile.

"But will it lead us to friend or foe?" Ingrid's reservations still marred her brow.

"If memory guides us true, it should lead us right back to the same person who revealed it to us—Lady Isolde," Maeve said. "And now it is the path we will take to get back inside the kingdom."

Ingrid nodded slowly, her eyes never leaving the spectral forms of the owl and the cat as they lingered by the entrance. "If what you say is true, I suppose your strange guardians are wise souls indeed."

"To ignore such a clear sign would be the height of folly," Diana added.

As if on cue, the owl launched itself into the air, its powerful wings beating. Just as Maeve thought the creature was done with them, it turned and arrowed toward the hidden opening. As it soared into the tunnel's dark maw, Nyx bunched her haunches and leaped in after it.

An exultant grin lifted Maeve's cheeks. "It seems our scouts grow impatient. And I, for one, do not intend to keep my prince waiting a moment longer."

As they ventured into the tunnel, the temperature plummeted until their breaths clouded in the frigid air. Maeve bent to retrieve the torch she had left by the entrance just days ago, and the ice-slicked ground made each movement a treacherous gamble.

"Too bad we haven't the means to light it," Fiona said. "You and I can see well enough, but our human friends lack our heightened senses."

Ingrid's mouth tipped into a near grin as she reached into her pack and retrieved a strike box, its surface worn smooth by countless uses. With a practiced motion, she struck the flint until a shower of sparks illuminated the darkness. The sparks caught on Maeve's torch, and flames sputtered to life, casting a warm glow on the frost-glazed walls.

Maeve held the torch aloft, its dancing flames reflecting off the jagged icicles that hung from the ceiling like a thousand glittering blades. The shadows retreated before the advancing light, the tunnel slowly revealing itself in the wavering illumination.

"Watch your step," Maeve warned, her voice echoing through the passage. "The ice is everywhere. One false move could send us tumbling."

Something rustled just ahead as Fiona nodded, her bow at the ready, her keen eyes scanning the shadows for any sign of danger. "I don't like this," she murmured, her voice tight. "There's something about this place that feels... different. Wrong, like we're walking into a trap."

As if in response to her words, a sudden gust tore through the tunnel, threatening to extinguish Maeve's torch. The women cried out, but their voices were soon defeated by a howling wind.

"Stay calm," Maeve called out, willing her voice to remain steady despite the trepidation that clawed at her throat. "Night falls, and with it, the ferals will search for sustenance. We have to keep moving, no matter what obstacles might befall us."

Maeve shielded her torch with her body, but the flame still ebbed as it danced in the wind. Yet, by the grace of the gods, it refused to die. The other women followed her lead, their hands joined in a human chain as they bent their heads against the biting chill.

With Nyx and the owl leading the way, they moved cautiously, their boots crunching on the icy ground, ears straining for any sounds that might signal danger.

A loud crack echoed through the space, followed by a sharp cry. Maeve whirled around, her sword at the ready and her heart in her throat. There, on the ground behind them, lay Diana, her leg twisted at an unnatural angle, her face contorted in agony.

"I slipped on the ice." She gasped as she clutched her leg, her voice tight with pain. "It's everywhere, and I couldn't see."

Maeve rushed to her side, her hands gentle as she examined the injured leg. "It's broken," she said softly, her voice filled with quiet urgency. "And bleeding."

"We have to splint it, we can't leave her behind," Ingrid said, concern torturing her features.

As the women set to work, tearing strips of cloth from their cloaks to splint Diana's leg, a new sound filled the tunnel, a sibilant hissing that set Maeve's teeth on edge. "What manner of dark enchantment is this?"

"Gods only know, but it's coming from the ceiling." Fiona loosed a disgusted cry as she notched an arrow and pointed it at a fissure above them. "And it's moving!"

The sound was joined by a rattling din that filled Maeve with terror, for she had heard that sound before. And if not for Alaric's intervention, she would have lost her life because of it.

"Snakes!" Fiona screamed, giving voice to Maeve's thoughts as she pointed at the cavern's roof, her features torn with terror. "Dozens of them!"

Maeve's eyes widened as she took in the slithering knot of serpents that swelled from the fracture, a cold sweat breaking out on her brow as she realized the true nature of the trap they had stumbled into. The ice, the snakes... all of it was designed to stop them, to prevent them from reaching Alaric.

But her and Alaric's story wasn't meant to end like this. She wouldn't allow their love to be defeated by the machinations of their twisted enemies. With a fierce cry, she hooked her torch between two stones and launched herself into the first tangle of snakes as it fell.

As her sword flashed in the torch glow, a white blur streaked past her. The owl she was coming to believe was Alaric's spirit incarnate had joined the fray, his eyes glinting with a ferocious intent. *I've got you, Maeve. Now and forever.*

"Look!" Fiona cried. "They're helping us!"

The owl swooped again, its beak shredding through snake after snake. As if rallied by his presence, Nyx darted between the writhing bodies, her furious yowls echoing through the cavern.

Emboldened by their unexpected allies, the women fought, their vigor renewed. Maeve's blade whipped through the air while Fiona's arrows found their mark again and again, each one a deadly strike against their foes.

The owl and Nyx moved in perfect sync with the women until the serpents began to fall, their bloody carcasses littering the ground.

"I never thought I'd be so glad to have a zombie cat on our side."

A near smile softened Ingrid's lips as she watched Nyx take macabre delight as she devoured a snake.

"Or an owl," Fiona added, her eyes shining as the majestic bird soared overhead, its pale wings casting an angelic silhouette on the walls.

"We did it, my love." Maeve's whisper was filled with quiet pride. "Because of you, we beat them, and you proved to me once again our love will always make us stronger than those who hate us."

The owl cooed, its eyes appearing almost human as they met hers. Even Nyx seemed proud as she wound herself around Maeve's legs, her nappy tail held high.

The other women looked on, their faces seeming to shine with the same fierce joy Maeve felt. "Now," she said, her voice ringing with determination, "let us keep moving. Alaric needs us, and I do not intend to let him down."

CHAPTER 18

Maeve did not recall her last trek through these insufferable depths having taken so long. They had been following this subterranean path for what seemed like an eternity. The only thing about this place that had changed was the air they breathed as it grew thicker and staler. Now, even the wavering flame on Maeve's torch appeared too weary to continue.

As she and Fiona rounded another bend, the earth beneath Maeve's boots began to tremble. Shuddering, she raised her hand, and behind her, the exhausted crew took her cue and slowed.

"Stop," Fiona's voice cut through the murk, her tone as sharp as the arrows in her quiver. "And do not move so much as an inch."

"What alarms you?" Maeve asked.

"Look ahead," she whispered as her trembling finger pointed into the shadows.

As Maeve's gaze followed in the track of Fiona's gesture, her heart plummeted. Before them, a jumble of rocks and debris choked the passage, the visible remnants of a recent collapse. One that had cut them off from the owl... perhaps even from Alaric himself. Whether this new obstacle was created by nature's hand or not, she couldn't know. But for the moment, it mattered little, for the end result was the same. Aside from Nyx, who sniffed at the rockfall, they were now on their own. Their only way forward, which had promised them safer passage than battling the cursed landscape above, was now an impenetrable wall.

She choked back a sob as she moved forward and lay a hand upon the unyielding rocks, feeling the enormity of this, their newest predicament. For the first time since they had sallied forth, she had no idea what to do next.

"Do you think if we teamed up, we could clear it?" she asked Fiona, though her voice betrayed the futility she felt.

Fiona shook her head, her slim silhouette sagging with resignation. "Not without risking more raining down upon us. Unless we turn back, we are as good as trapped."

As Maeve tracked back to speak with the women behind them, Diana leaned heavily against Ingrid, her face pale and drawn from pain. The sight of the women's mortal vulnerability struck a fresh note of panic within her.

"Why have we stopped moving?" the woman Maeve knew as Tilda demanded. "Diana needs rest, medicine, none of which she will get down here."

Maeve nodded and cast her gaze into the darkness behind them. There was no going back—the horrors the darkness concealed saw to that—and now, the path forward was barred by an even crueler fate.

"The tunnel ahead has collapsed. So, we must find another way," Maeve uttered, the words a hollow comfort in the face of Diana's obvious agony.

Desperation clung to them as tightly as the dank air, and the weighted silence that followed was broken only by the distant drip of water. Surely, the women knew the same thing Maeve did. They stood at the crossroads of hope and defeat, and right now, the balance was tipping precariously toward the latter.

Already, her human allies' breathing grew shallow, their eyes darting amongst themselves in the dim light. Their whispers swirled like a rising wind before a storm. And Maeve could scent their panic as surely as she could smell her own in the beads of sweat that gathered on her forehead.

"We should go back to the castle," Tilda urged, her voice trembling. "We can yet cut through the brambles—there has to be a way."

"Are you mad?" Ilyana retorted. "Even if we got past the ferals, those thorns would shred our hides before we claimed an inch!"

Their arguments swelled, words colliding in frantic dissonance. Within the cacophony, Maeve's gaze remained fixed on the impenetrable barrier before them. She knew the path back meant more death and bloodshed. But they had to do something, try anything.

"Maeve, come here!" Fiona's sharp command sliced through the tumult. Her frame was bent over the ground where she examined the tunnel wall as if she sought to divine a solution from the small stones piled at the wall's edge.

As the women continued to bicker amongst themselves, Maeve knelt beside her. The air shifted, fresher now and laced with the scent of damp earth. A small opening, not much wider than a hare's burrow, beckoned from the base of the tunnel's wall.

"Here." Fiona's finger traced the outline of the gap, then began to move up. Her touch was gentle, as if she were divining secrets from the stone, her fingertip tracing the suggestion of a larger opening. "There might be a passage through—a doorway—if only we could find the means to open it."

Maeve's breath caught at the possibility, but she also knew false hope was a treacherous companion. As she crouched lower to peer into the dark void beyond, her ear was met with an ominous sound. A groan, low and guttural, emanated from the unseen chamber. Something akin to the rattling of chains followed, speaking of confinement and despair.

Maeve stilled, her every instinct screaming for caution. The others moved in closer, their curious voices mingling in whispers. But she did not need to hear their words to know they echoed her own thoughts. What manner of soul lay beyond? Friend or foe? Zombie or human? And even if they found the means to broach that space, was it their path to salvation, or further peril?

"Shush for a moment," she whispered, her words barely more than a sigh. The anguished keening continued, accompanied by the relentless clinking of metal. "Could it be something—an animal perhaps—is trapped?" she offered.

"It sounds more like a person, perhaps imprisoned, just as myself and the others once were," Fiona murmured, her voice steady despite the uncertainty that gripped them both. "And if so, are we not honor-bound to try and help them as you and Alaric helped us?"

Maeve nodded, her mind racing. Neither of the choices before them felt palatable—they could push forward into the unknown, or they could stay here, as Lady Elora surely must expect and face whatever fresh doom she had in store for them.

With a glance at her companions, their stricken expressions hardened her resolve. Fresher air awaited them inside. And if someone needed their help, love demanded they must do all they could to provide. Even if they could not give aid, at least they would know they had tried. But first, they had to find a way inside.

Maeve's heart pounded a rhythm that matched the clinking from beyond the wall. The shadowed chamber called to her with an eerie siren song, but its mysteries remained shrouded in stubborn darkness.

"If we all pushed at the stone, it might yield. This could be the exact boon we need." Fiona's voice was a lifeline amidst the waning air that conspired to choke the life out of the humans amongst them.

"It is a treacherous plan if we cannot see what awaits us," Maeve murmured, her gaze locked on the thin fracture etched into the stone.

As she considered options, her fingers felt in her pocket, and she found the talisman Nan had given her, its surface warming against her skin. Nan's gift—a symbol of their secret lineage and a tangible reminder of the magic coursing through her veins, silent yet potent. She squeezed it tight, wishing it could somehow anchor her to the legacy of her matriarchal lineage.

Magic has always been within you, Isolde's voice echoed in her mind, a mantra that fortified her to keep trying. She closed her eyes, drawing upon the wellspring of power that lay dormant, waiting for her command.

Nyx nuzzled against her leg, her plaintive whine piercing Maeve's veil of concentration. She opened her eyes and looked down at her faithful companion who Isolde had said was her familiar. The feline's copper eyes reflected a world unseen, and a vision that had been shared between them once before.

She drew in a deep breath, reminding herself that her own ancestors had walked this path in secrecy, their gifts cloaked in shadows lest they draw the ire of those who feared the arcane.

"Guide me once again, my friend," she whispered, granting the creature permission to delve into the unknown. A silent understanding passed between them, an unspoken pact that transcended words. The talisman in her grasp hummed with energy, its resonance a melody only she could hear, a song of courage woven by the hands of those women who had come before her.

The darkness beyond beckoned, a canvas painted with hues of uncertainty. Yet Maeve now knew that within her lay the flame to illuminate their path. With her ancestors' wisdom as her shield and Nyx as her sentinel, she would use the feline's feet to step into the chasm so she could know whether it was monster, friend, or foe that awaited.

The tunnel's musty air grew ever heavier, forcing her to push down panic as she realized the women's breaths grew more rapid. But beneath their panting, she could also hear something they could not—an all too familiar, yet faint, scuffling. The dreaded sound set her preternatural nerves on edge. Though quite distant, their steps moved ever closer, carrying the unmistakable note of impending danger—the ferals were stalking their scents. And in just moments, the others would hear it, too. Then, an unquenchable panic would ensue.

"Listen," Maeve whispered to Fiona, her voice barely louder than a breath. "Is that what I think it is?"

Fiona's body shuddered. "All the more reason why we must make haste," she whispered back. "If you expect to push through to the other side, we will need their help. It is time to tell them."

Maeve blew out a slow breath, then rose and turned to face the others. Their eyes, widened with trepidation, all fixed upon her as if they depended on her for their souls' redemption. And perhaps they did.

"What are we to do now?" Ingrid asked. "Idly sit here until we all run out of air?"

"I understand your angst, for I feel it, too. But the passage is blocked, yet we are certain to encounter a more dangerous threat if we turn back."

"So, it is over, then," Ingrid uttered her statement as grimly as an executioner's reading their death sentences.

"Not yet. But in order to know we will not escape this place only to face an even greater danger, I need you to quiet yourselves and allow me a few moments to use my sight." She had barely finished speaking when a feral's faint but unmistakable screech wafted from the shadowed depths. The women moved closer together, readying arms that barely had the strength to swing, and a murmur of uncertainty rippled through them.

"There is no time for that. They have already found us," Ingrid rasped, her grip on her ax firming as encroaching panic threatened to devour her forced calmness.

But it was Fiona who stepped forward, her jaw tight with the sort of determination that was born from desperation. "I would remind you all that Maeve's insight is what has brought us this far," she said, her words cutting through the rising tension. "So quiet yourselves and let her do what she must."

Ingrid's gaze scanned the faces of the others, gauging their expressions. "Fine. But they're getting closer, so be quick about it."

Nods of reluctant agreement followed the women's silent surrender to the unknown, echoing louder than any spoken word ever could.

"Thank you for trusting me," Maeve said. With her heart thrumming in an irregular cadence, she spread her cloak on the ground, knelt, and reached into her worn pack until her fingers brushed past the familiar contents and closed around the cool surface of her crystal ball. With great care, she drew the shimmering orb out, cradling it in her hands like it was the last precious relic excavated from the ruins of a world long forgotten.

"Keep watch, all of you," she instructed, her gaze lingering on the faces before her.

Closing her eyes, she inhaled deeply, allowing the scents of mossy earth and damp stone to ground her spirit. She envisioned a radiant web of energy swaddling the world, and she knew it to be the gossamer threads that connected all living things. As she sought the thin, silver strand that bound her to Nyx, her consciousness wove toward her familiar, tendrils of intention entwining with the essence of the loyal creature now curled up in her lap.

As her body began to rock, the boundaries between woman and beast blurred. She felt herself gasp as her being expanded beyond the limits of her perception. With a gentle tug and a thudding sensation, her spirit left her body and seated itself within Nyx's.

The feline began to move, her lithe form slipping easily through the narrow opening, gliding like a wraith into the hidden chamber.

Through their shared vision, Maeve scanned the space, searching for signs of life and the metallic clink of chains she had heard rattling in the darkness. Though the air here flowed freely, it was tinged with a pungent stench that intensified with every silent step, a foul miasma of decay that clawed at their unified senses.

As their eyes adjusted, she saw that the stone walls were lined with metal chains and shackles, each set whispering about torments long endured.

Torture devices lay scattered about—a rack stretched out like the death's gaping maw, an iron maiden with its spiked innards standing ready to embrace its next victim, and a bloodstained wooden table boasting rusted thumbscrews that spoke of countless turns.

A creeping dread wrapped icy tendrils around Maeve's spirit as she and Nyx delved deeper into the vermin-infested depths. As they rounded the first bend, mice scurried from the flickering torchlight, squealing in protest as the conjoined pair invaded their dominion. A pile of human bones and skulls lay heaped in a corner, white and stark against the stone, remnants of the many lives that had been consumed by this abyss.

The moans of that poor damned soul echoed through the tunnels, growing ever closer, a chorus of agony that resonated with Maeve's encroaching dread.

Turning the next bend, Maeve's gaze fell upon a chained figure— a tall man with long, dark hair that cascaded over broad shoulders that, in good health, would have been heavily muscled. His long beard was thickly matted, and his massive body emaciated.

Gods help me...this can't be. Maeve wished she could avert her gaze, but seeing through Nyx's eyes, she could only keep looking..

Nyx, sensing Maeve's shock, let out a plaintive mew. The man's head jerked up, his tormented eyes flashing with a golden fire that cut through the gloom.

Recognition seared through Maeve; it was Lysander, but he no longer appeared like the cruel predator she had feared for so long. He was now himself made prey, ensnared and weakened from months of imprisonment. But because he was a zombie, not even death held the power to grant him reprieve from his ghastly plight.

His gaze could have torn holes in her. The knowledge she knew it was not him who hurt her warred with her body's need to run. Hide.

Nyx, we must leave—now, she commanded through their bond. But as they turned to flee, another figure loomed into view, casting a sinister shadow across the dungeon floor. Dr. Reinhart approached with deliberate steps, his medical bag in hand and a whip coiled at his side. The placid man Maeve had known was gone, replaced by a savage countenance that chilled her to the core.

Lysander groaned as he recoiled from the doctor's approach, but he was no match for the whip's lash, which forced him into silent submission. Dr. Reinhart's lips bowed as he drew forth an enormous leech and pressed it to Lysander's jugular.

Maeve watched, petrified, as the truth crystallized within her— the bigger monster was not the man shackled before her. It was Dr. Reinhart, the very person she'd entrusted to care for Alaric in her absence.

In the space of a heartbeat, a distant commotion pierced the trance that held Maeve's body captive. She felt a jolt, a sudden and urgent pull, and with a wrenching force, her spirit disengaged from Nyx's, her consciousness recoiling back toward the others, who needed her more.

Maeve's physical form shuddered awake amidst the chaos, her mind reeling, her heart racing with the echoes of the dungeon's horrors.

Confusion clouded her thoughts as she struggled to piece together the fragments of what she had witnessed. The stingy light of reality was harsh against her eyes, yet it could not dispel the darkness that clung to her soul.

Her body twitched as her mind wrenched free from Nyx's grasp. The dank scent of rotting flesh assailed her nostrils, and she knew— the feral zombies were nearly upon them, their shambling forms already casting eerie shadows on the cavern walls. She could hear their rasping breaths, the scrape of bone against stone, and the wet, sickening sound of rancid flesh sloughing off their bodies.

"Steel yourselves," she hissed to the others, her voice a blade cutting through the restless silence. "And weapons ready! I promise you, we shall not fall here."

Fiona stretched her bowstring, arrows whistling through the air and finding their marks with deadly precision. Several ferals stumbled and fell, but more surged forward, their eyes glowing with feral hunger. Maeve could feel their desperation, their unrelenting need to feed, and it chilled her to the core.

The darkness seemed to throb with the anticipation of more bloodshed. The feral's advancing shadows danced as if mocking their plight, while the distant groans of more revenants swelled into a dreadful dirge.

"Advance!" she urged, her dread transmuting into a desperate resolve. From the corner of her eye, she saw Fiona notch another arrow, her lithe form poised with a grace that belied the terror they all felt. Her violet eyes met Maeve's for a scant moment, sharing an unspoken promise—she would fight until her very end.

"By the gods, let my aim be true," Fiona cried, her fingers deftly sending arrow after arrow into the advancing horde. But as each fell, another rose up to take its place, an endless sea of rotting flesh and gnashing teeth. Fiona's arrows were as futile as whispers uttered in a gale.

A sudden rumble overhead drew Maeve's gaze upward. Ingrid's attention followed and she wasted not a second in swinging her weapon with a might fueled by desperation. The ax arced, a silver flash in the dim light, striking the cavern ceiling. "Duck!" she cried out as a cascade of ice shards rained down, a glittering barrier crashing between them and the relentless advance of the ferals. The impact sent shockwaves through the ground, the ferals howling in pain and rage as the razor-sharp fragments tore through their rotting flesh.

Maeve felt a fleeting triumph until she realized several ferals had been spared the deluge Ingrid had created.

"Take them!" she commanded, more dust falling as her voice

echoed off the stone ceiling. She lunged forward, her own sword a silver streak of vengeance. As she and the others met the remaining ferals head-on, the stench of their putrid breath filled her nostrils. She could feel the chill of their grotesque bodies as they pressed in around her. Her blade sliced through tendons and bone, sprays of black blood splattering across the ground.

Beside her, the others fought with an equally desperate ferocity, their weapons flashing in the darkness. They moved as one, a well-oiled machine fueled by the primal need to survive.

As the zombies were cut down one by one, their decapitated bodies twitched in a grim dance that spoke of their will to survive. But each life Maeve extinguished began to pull at her soul, as if tethering a part of her spirit to this cursed place. Though her blade found its mark, again and again, pity welled up within her. These creatures, once human, were only doing as their instincts bade them, and they, too, deserved to rest in peace. She vowed silently that once Alaric was saved, she would return here to grant them that dignity, assuming the fates allowed them safe passage through this nightmare so her beloved could be saved.

And he will be saved, she pledged inwardly, her will hardening like ice. *For if we have survived this long, surely, we are meant to endure.*

With their realization, their subterranean refuge was now blocked from both directions, new angst unfurled amongst the tributaries. Even Maeve's breath came in sharp rasps as she turned to face the cryptic door Fiona had found etched into the stone—its existence barely visible to untrained eyes. "We must find a way to open it. Help me."

The others gathered close and pressed against the stones, shoulders braced against the cold, unyielding surface. But no matter how many times they pushed, the damnable thing did not yield so much as a finger's breadth.

"Push harder!" Fiona's voice, usually so steady, now trembled with the urgency of a cornered doe. The air grew thicker and danker by the moment, and Maeve knew the human women could not survive much longer. But their combined efforts were to no avail. Their only reward was a fresh rain of dust falling from the disturbed ceiling over their heads.

"Fall back, lest we create another rockslide," Fiona said, her slender fingers tracing the intricate carvings. Maeve joined in her quest, searching for a catch, a lever—any means for opening this door they might have missed. But the edifice stood firm, indifferent to their rising desperation.

It was Diana's agonized groaning that inspired them to keep trying.

"Push again. Gods damn it. Harder this time!" Ingrid grunted, her muscular frame straining with effort. Veins stood out on her temple like a gruesome map as Tilda, Ilyana, and the others joined her. Yet, despite their collective might, the door remained as immutable as the passing seconds they could ill afford to lose.

Maeve stepped back, heart hammering against her ribcage. She scanned the grim faces of her companions, seeking to rekindle hope's fire. But she found only ashen countenances etched with despair. Wordlessly, the women slumped to the ground, conserving what little air their lungs could claim within the grasp of this miserable tomb.

The silence that followed was every bit as suffocating, as if fraught with certain doom. It was then a subtle metallic click resounded through the chamber, a sound so soft yet profound that it sliced through the gloom, dispelling their apathy like a gunshot.

The doorway slid open with the ease of a ghost passing through the stone, and from beyond the threshold, Nyx trotted forth. The feline's copper eyes gleamed with a smug intelligence, her intervention offering them yet another testament to the unseen forces at play.

"By the gods!" Maeve's gaze fixed on the majestic creature as it wove around her legs, purring like a happy kitten. "We are not yet forsaken."

Her companions cheered, their eyes reflecting the light of their renewed spirits. But the revelry was broken by Diana's moan as Ingrid lifted her from the floor and carried her toward the opening as one might a beloved child. The scraping of their boots rasped against the stone floors as the women filed one by one through the doorway.

Maeve fell in behind them, each step cementing her silent vow to survive, to fully reclaim the power evil men had once sought to steal from their daughters.

CHAPTER 19

The leaden thump of the door sliding shut behind them ensured there would be no turning back. Though the air moved more freely here, the smell was even more rancid. Yet the human women paused, seeming not to care as they braced their hands on their knees, raking in deep breaths of life-saving air.

Maeve felt almost hopeful as she watched it emerge through their open mouths in small clouds, haunting the dim light like apparitions of the poor souls who had suffered here until they lost their lives.

As they straightened, her gaze trailed over their grime-coated faces. The exhilaration of their narrow escape soon drained from their expressions, replaced by a grim understanding as they took in their surroundings.

"By the gods," whispered Ilyana, her eyes wide as coins. "We have emerged into the very hell from whence Maeve and Alaric freed us."

Tears flowed freely, recognition dawning on each woman's face like a collective nightmare. Maeve didn't need to ask to know this was the place where they had been held captive and endured unspeakable horrors. She had only witnessed a hint of the hell they had suffered here. Now, because they had trusted her, they found themselves having traveled full circle. How could they ever trust her again?

"Remember what happened to Clara?" Tilda's hands twisted together as she relived the memory. "She—she refused to be experimented on. They forced her onto the rack until she agreed to bear one of those poor, doomed... things. Not a one of those cursed babes she carried survived."

Their bitter memories hung in the air like a dark incantation as they joined hands, recalling the desperate cries of agony and the helplessness that had consumed them as their bodies were turned into vessels to gestate horror. Each of them had faced a horrible choice: submit to twisted experiments or suffer a far more terrible fate.

"Marjorie's baby... born with his innards on the outside. Though that poor babe had the face of a cherub, he didn't last a week," someone else added, choking back a sob. "They wouldn't even let her kiss him goodbye or utter a petition for his soul before they took him away."

"And they always took them away..."

"Unless they chose to cut them out first..." Diana said with a sob. "Like my own conjoined babes."

Maeve blinked back tears, envisioning strange, tiny creatures, their mouths opened wide with their last screams, forever suspended in jars of formaldehyde in the name of advancing someone's twisted idea of science. And she knew then that Marjorie's babe—all of them, most likely—had fallen victim to even crueler experiments once they were spirited away from their broken-hearted mothers. Experiments Maeve now suspected were carried out by Dr. Reinhart himself.

As the women gaped at the bloodstained chains and shackles, they stood frozen, their shoulders sagging and their heads bowed, heavy with rekindled grief.

"If we lose faith in our cause now, they will have won," Fiona finally said. "For this is how evil works. And I, for one, did not escape this torture chamber for naught. I must believe—

do believe—the fates had another job in mind for us and still do."

"And even if I found the means to open the door we just passed through and lead you away from recalling the travesties that were inflicted upon you," Maeve added, "you would only be turning back so Fiona and myself could hold your death watches."

"Maeve is right," Ingrid said, shoulders braced and jaw hardening. "It would be a greater tragedy if we let this place break us again. Nor can we forget it was Alaric and Maeve who risked their very lives to retrieve us from evil's maw. We have a toll to pay, and we have come too far and lost too much to give up now. And we've done it all together."

"Right," Maeve said, her voice firm despite the empathy that threatened to undo her. "You faced your darkest moments here, but because you cared for each other as you endured beyond hope, you also survived."

The women exchanged glances, drawing new strength from one another's presence, their shared pain forging a bond that could not be broken. They had been through the worst, but they had also glimpsed hope in their darkest moments. And as long as they clung to the fragile faith enduring once again offered, they could face whatever lay ahead.

"Let us keep moving, then," Maeve said, her voice now steady. "We need to take turns helping Diana and get out of this damnable place."

As the women fell in behind Maeve, they ventured deeper into the darkness. The dim glow of the torch Fiona had lifted from its mounting cast strange shadows, as if the past itself was reaching out, reminding them again of the agonies they had endured.

Though Maeve still could not shake off the feeling that something was amiss, she dared not say so aloud. But she felt as if she was viewing the remains of a map that had been torn and reassembled with some of its pieces missing. *Elora claimed she had used guise magic before...*

"Would you believe it?" she whispered to Fiona, her voice barely audible. "If I told you that through Nyx's eyes, I saw Dr. Reinhart? And I suspect he was involved in everything the former tributaries suffered?"

Fiona, who had been uncharacteristically quiet, nodded. "It is hard to accept, but if you say that is what you saw... well, I have already seen with my own eyes the power of your abilities. And if everyone else in the castle is sleeping, as Eamon said, why has the doctor been spared?"

"My exact thoughts. So I must ask... can we really trust anyone within the castle who is not asleep?" Maeve's eyes darted around the labyrinth, her gaze flitting over the faces of their companions. All of their fates now hinged upon her choices. "And what about Isolde? Eamon reported that she, too, was awake. So, can we really trust her?"

"Let's not forget," Fiona said, her chin firming, "that without her assistance, we wouldn't have made it this far. She also gave you Nyx. Only because of the bond you share have we endured. Is it possible she cast a sleeping spell for Alaric's protection?"

"Perchance. But what if she helped us for some darker reason?" Maeve sighed, trying to focus on the task at hand. As the sensation that nothing was what it seemed gnawed at her, Ingrid stepped forward, her features torn.

"What is the holdup?" the woman asked, her words clipped. "Diana grows weaker. She needs help soon."

"Of that, I am well aware," Maeve snapped, "but neither do I wish to lead us into another disaster."

Ingrid scoffed. "We are not the same women who once quaked in these very depths. We have since faced unimaginable horrors and survived. We have grown stronger, braver, and more cunning than we ever thought possible. And now, Diana is depending on us to save her, just as she fought to protect all of us."

Ingrid's passionate words stirred something within Maeve. As she looked back at the former tributaries, now her fearsome allies, she realized there were still souls in this world she could trust, and they were all right here with her. So long as that remained true, her hope for Alaric's recovery was not lost. Ingrid was right. Their trials had made them stronger. "Let us press on then."

As they ventured deeper into the labyrinth, they moved as one, alert to the possibility more danger awaited. But only the shadows chased them as Maeve led the way, Fiona's torch casting a faint glow to illuminate their path.

Approaching the place where she had seen the man she believed could be Lysander, the air grew rancid with the sour stench of bile. A deep tremor worked over her as she sensed his emotions, their oppressive weight gripping her chest like a vise. He longed to perish yet could not, for he was a zombie. And Maeve was beginning to understand his agony, for she felt it, too.

"Stay close," she warned as they approached another sharp bend. "And keep your wits about you. For I have a feeling you will all recognize the shell of the man who is shackled to the walls up ahead."

"Who do you think it is?" Fiona whispered, her eyes lighting on Maeve's taut visage.

"I hope just this once, my sight is proven wrong," she admitted, her thoughts racing as she tried to piece together the kaleidoscopic fragments of information she had uncovered through Nyx's eyes. She would much rather be proven wrong than face the dark memories Lysander's visage would invoke. "But whoever he is, we must remain cautious. Dr. Reinhart could still be lurking in these depths as well."

Her words died off as they rounded the corner, the moans growing louder, echoing through the maze-like corridors like the last wails of the damned.

Fiona's eyes grew hard as agates as they peered into the darkness. "Whatever happens next," she said, her hand gripping her bow, "we face it head-on or die trying. For none of us wishes to spend another moment longer in this repugnant hellhole than necessary."

"Indeed," Maeve agreed, her spirit filling with pride at the fierce loyalty that kept them all bound. No matter what lay ahead, her unorthodox army would prove a fearsome front against the dark forces that sought to end Alaric's reign.

"Look!" Ingrid whispered, pointing into the shadows. Just as Maeve had seen, a broken figure was slumped against the wall, his wrists shackled to the filthy stone walls. Though he appeared to be unconscious, even from a distance, she could see the marks of suffering etched across his face—the hollow cheeks, the sunken eyes, the tight slash of his parched lips.

"Is it him?" Fiona asked, her voice trembling as they approached.

As they drew closer, Maeve felt icy fingers of dread crawl down her spine, clawing at her very soul. She replayed what she'd seen through Nyx's eyes, feeling the same sense of sureness then that she did now "By the gods," she rasped, barely able to believe her own eyes. "I believe it really is..."

"Who?" Tilda demanded, her gaze fixed on the prisoner. "Who would be locked away down here? And why?"

Maeve braced her shoulders and stepped forward, her torch held high. As she reached for the man, she felt her breath catch. His head dropped, denying them a clear view of his face, and she tucked her hand beneath his bearded jaw, lifting his face into the light.

The second she saw the hint of gold flickering between his half-closed lids, she knew that their journey to unveil the truth had just begun, for this man... this zombie ...was indeed Lysander.

CHAPTER 20

Lysander groaned, a dry and ghastly sound. A cry gathered in Maeve's throat, and she jumped back as if his flesh was made of fire. Fearful she was spinning into the past, she reminded herself she was not the only one here who had endured traumas. It was here where the innocent women who had taken up her cause had been shackled and abused. Women of worth and potential, treated like they were worth less than common breeding stock.

Do not falter now, my love. For knowing the truth will strip these secrets of their power to harm you. Tears pressed the back of Maeve's lids as Alaric's voice echoed in her mind. She could go to him now, escape within their shared dream. And there, he would be healthy and whole. As would she. And a part of her screamed to go while she still could, for that place had seemed more true to her than all of this relentless misery.

Not knowing what to do next, her gaze swept the empty shackles that had once bound her allies, and her mind wailed with the distant echoes of their grief. The residue of their terror was still imprinted on the walls, an unbearable weight crushing her soul. But she also felt something else—their abject refusal to surrender hope. Those tiny embers of faith that, in the end, goodness would somehow prevail were what had fed their weary souls and sustained them.

Alaric needed her. But so did they. As she needed them.

It was Fiona who finally roused her from the choice between escaping into her dreams or staying here to relive past horrors no amount of time could erase. Fiona, too, was forever changed by the miseries she had suffered here. Yet now, she was somehow better. Stronger.

"Maeve?" Fiona uttered again, her small hand providing an anchor in the storm that railed through her mind. "Should we try and wake him? Find out what he knows?"

Maeve pulled herself away from her vision of Alaric standing in his garden, his hand outstretched...

But going to Alaric in a vision will not save him. Instead, she focused on the zombie—Lysander.

Though his once striking face was smeared with dirt and blood, the sight still elicited a torrent of bitter memories—that horrid night when shadows and a soporific elixir had played tricks on her mind.

Maeve backed away, averting her eyes. Her hands trembled as she took in his face, trying to reconcile the man before her with the treachery that had been wrought in his image. When she thought the man Alaric trusted most became an instrument of defilement and degradation.

She took a deep breath, steadying her nerves, as she willed her heart to reject that path. *It was not really him, she told herself.*

Yet her stubborn heart stumbled as she relived the moment. She was unable to align the man Ilyana comforted with the man who had brought her such pain. Those wounds had first stripped her dignity, her childish innocence. Then, later, they had risen anew to turn her into a zombie... like Alaric.

Alaric...

Maeve squeezed her eyes closed, summoning his image. Though she sensed the intensity behind Fiona's gaze, she couldn't bring herself to answer her question. The betrayals she'd felt that night still festered like an open wound left untended. Was she prepared to acknowledge this pain now?

She'd give anything to find herself in Alaric's arms, where anything felt possible. But she also knew he would tell her the only person who could vanquish her demons was herself.

Instead of dwelling on things she could not change, she forced her focus back to the task at hand—finding a way out of this place so she could awaken Alaric before it was too late.

"Yes, rouse him," she said

"You are certain of this?" Fiona's eyes narrowed as she scrutinized Maeve's expression.

With Ilyana already reaching for the waterskin Fiona held, Maeve could only nod. Her mind still dwelled on the delicate scents of the strange blossoms in Alaric's garden, beckoning her back. It had been spring there, and warm.

Alaric, please wait for me...

She was answered only by the cavern's chill searing her damp cheeks as she stepped nearer to Lysander and the others.

Ilyana uncorked the waterskin and poured a ration over Lysander's face. But he did not stir.

"Try something else." Maeve's throat ached as she pushed out the words. "But move cautiously."

Fiona ripped a length of fabric from her tunic and handed it to Ilyana.

Tears staining her scarred face, Ilyana took the cloth, wet it, and then began dabbing at the thick grime coating Lysander's cheeks. He stirred, a tattered moan escaping his lips as his tongue darted out to wick the droplets trickling down his chin.

"Careful," Maeve said as Fiona inched closer to Lysander. The words had no sooner escaped when she realized the sharpness of her tone.

But the sight of Lysander, so thin and vulnerable, yet reminiscent of that dark figure from her past, caused her gut to clench. She stepped back, overwhelmed and struggling to stay in the here and now. She curled her palms, using the pain from her fingernails digging in to ground her.

"Should we stop then?" Fiona asked, her brow taut as she looked toward Maeve.

Maeve shook her head. "Let him drink," she instructed, her gaze fixed on the shadowy corners of the cavern, half-expecting a cadre of demons to emerge. "I need him alert enough to answer some questions."

Lysander's hands strained against his chains until his wrists bled, his head craning toward the source of water. As Ilyana continued ministering to his face, Fiona took the skin and tipped it into his mouth.

Maeve almost felt sorry for him as she watched him lap it up with a desperation that spoke of prolonged deprivation.

She watched him, still warring with herself. Italicized thought. *But what if I am wrong. What if this is all still a trick? How can I be sure?*

"Enough for now," she said as he began fighting his restraints.

"Understood," Fiona replied as she stepped back, her expression laced with unspoken questions.

Maeve could not deny the affection Ilyana held for this man. Nor could she keep herself from cringing at the woman's soft crying as Fiona withdrew the waterskin.

Not understanding her own actions, Maeve backed deeper into the shadows, her blood pounding in her ears. But the judgmental stares of her companions still bored through her. *I need to be sure.* Even if they thought her actions cruel. She reminded herself it was not her need for vengeance that was in play, but rather the fragile balance of trust and survival within their group. Her decision about how to proceed would be the fulcrum upon which all their futures would hinge—including Alaric's. Was this man truly Lysander?

Diana, pale and weak, caught Maeve's eye with a look that mingled concern with question. Maeve offered a curt nod, the gesture a silent promise she would do what she felt was best to shield them from further horrors. Especially those that might come disguised in familiar forms.

"I would have a moment to collect my thoughts." She turned away from eyes that burned with judgment for depriving Lysander of the right to slake his thirst. With each step she took away from them, the chill around her seemed to deepen. She needed some time to pull herself together. Then, with a better understanding of her own actions, she would return.

A duel began inside her. She didn't understand how she could feel such compassion for the creatures that had felled a world, but not for a man who had been tortured beyond belief. But she could not deny these women knew Lysander in a way that she never could. And they cared for him.

As had Alaric.

Her shadow receded as she turned back to the light, her decision made. She would allow the women to proceed, but she would remain wary. Once again, she faced the prisoner, her eyes narrowing. As she approached him, the flickering torchlight cast a warm glow that seemed to mock her distrust. "Tell me, Lysander. What transpired between you and Lady Elora that night I saw you together in the hedgerows?"

Lysander sighed as he lifted his bloodshot gaze to meet hers, the torchlight igniting something unreadable in his eyes. "She was... enticing me," he began, his once melodic voice hoarse from disuse.

"How so?"

"She led me to believe she desired my company and that her intentions were of an... intimate nature. I fear the needs of the flesh overtook my usual prudence."

Maeve's grip tightened on her dagger's hilt. Though Lysander's reputation with women had gained him near notoriety, she didn't yet know if she believed him. "And then?" she pressed, her tone insistent.

"She drew me into a kiss. I responded in kind. And next... just darkness," he continued. "I remember naught but waking here, in this gods forsaken tomb, with chains biting into my flesh.

"But why were you not rescued with the women?"

"I was confined in the iron maiden when the rescue took place. After the women were gone, Dr. Reinhart visited often, delighting in finding new ways to torment me. I presumed he and Lady Elora were conspiring to tip the scales of power in their favor. But I must ask, Maeve. Why are you here, dressed in a warrior's garb instead of Prince Alaric and his guards?"

The sound of her beloved's name crossing his lips forced Maeve to close her eyes, damming tears she did not wish him to misconstrue as a show of feminine weakness. She focused on her breaths, scouring her memory for any scrap of truth that might have escaped her. Had she seen Lysander since that night when she had caught him and Lady Elora cavorting in the gardens? She couldn't quite recall, but she thought not.

"Maeve," he rasped, concern creasing his brow. "What is amiss?"

Maeve chuffed softly at his casual use of her name. In her confusion, the familiarity felt too much. "That is a conversation for another time. Just be thankful you have been found," she said once she had regained control, "for no one knew of your location. But to what avail would the doctor hold you here?"

"At first, he sought knowledge—secrets about the inner workings of Alaric's kingdom I convinced him I did not possess. When he realized I would sooner perish than betray our prince... that's when the torture began. Only later did he impress me into service as a subject for his... experiments."

Whispers rippled through the group, but it was Ilyana's voice that sliced the tension. She stepped forward, her ebony face a strangely beautiful tapestry of scars and conviction. "It is true, what he says," she interjected, her voice imparting certainty.

Maeve's gaze shifted to hers, studying her with renewed interest. "You can confirm his tale?"

Tears shone in Ilyana's eyes as she shook her head. "No, milady.

I can only attest to his character. Lysander's songs and stories were what kept hope kindled within our hearts. When despair threatened to claim us all, he spun epic tales of the prince's valor, promising deliverance." Her dark, doe-like eyes, bright with the memory, poured into Maeve's. "He gave us hope when we had none left. Please, Maeve... you must free him from this torment at once."

Maeve's heart thrummed against her ribs, a cadence of wariness. Could she trust words delivered by a man who bore the face of her attacker? Yet, in the haunted eyes of the woman who clearly loved him, she saw a different man and a spark of devotion and fealty that could not be feigned. He'd clearly done something noble to be held so high in her esteem.

"Very well," she conceded, hoping her voice betrayed none of the turmoil churning within her as she returned her attention to Lysander. "We shall consider your release... with certain conditions." As she uttered the words, the echoes of the past whispered a warning. In the depths of this forsaken place, she feared the line between ally and enemy had grown as treacherous and uncertain as the path ahead.

"Anything. Just release me," he pleaded, his voice rasping with urgency. "I know this place as if it were my own shadow. Let me slake my thirst and lead you out, for I do know the way. And Alaric must be beside himself with worry..."

Maeve suppressed a gasp, realizing Lysander behaved like he did not know what had happened to Alaric. She studied him, her suspicions now tempered by hope. Yes. Genuine concern simmered in his eyes.

It really is him! And perhaps there lay the pawn she needed should the gamble she was considering turn sour. "Help us, and I will see to your freedom," she decreed, knowing full well the risks she took. "Betray us, and I swear on Alaric's life, you will be returned here. Forever."

"Thank you," he whispered, relief written across his features.

"But Maeve, why would I betray the woman who is betrothed to the prince I have sworn to serve?"

She stared into his eyes for a moment, noting how their spectacular shade dimmed to ochre, still not knowing whether she could trust the confusion and hurt that brimmed there. "We'll speak of this later. There are more pressing matters at hand."

"Such as?"

"For starters, do we need to fear Dr. Reinhart's return?"

He shook his head. "Days... sometimes weeks pass between his appearances. He left not long before you arrived. But something else confuses me, Maeve. Why would you bring these defenseless women back to the very scene of their undoing?"

"Love," she said, her gaze never leaving his face. "Ingrid. Take your ax to his chains. Then we'll offer him as much sustenance from our packs as we can spare while we prepare Diana to endure the rest of our trek."

With a roaring cry, Ingrid hefted her axe and struck it against Lysander's shackles. With a shower of sparks, the rusted chains clattered against the stone floor.

Ingrid's blade winked in the scant light a second time as she welded it to release his other hand. As Lysander grunted and sagged into Ilyana's waiting arms, every muscle in his body twitched from disuse.

As Fiona and the others helped him to sit, Maeve's eyes tracked his movements, searching for any sign of deception or threat. But she saw only the broken remnants of the former zombie aristocrat, seemingly desperate for salvation. Yet Lady Elora had taught her better than any that good looks and the trappings of nobility could deceive. Nor could she deny the unease that prickled beneath her skin at the sight of him unshackled.

Tears sparkled like diamonds on Ilyana's lashes as she knelt beside him and began fussing over his wounds. The way his eyes warmed beneath her tender attention reminded Maeve again how infectious she, too, had once found his charm. And it still startled her how very rapid a sentient zombie's ability to heal from almost any wound was.

True to the Lysander she had known—had even once felt a brief moment of attraction to—his presence soon commanded the chamber. As he drank greedily from the waterskin, the others rushed forward, presenting him their cloaks and what meager sustenance they could spare, even knowing the trials ahead would demand all their strength.

Only Ingrid held back, her noble face etched with worry as she tended to Diana. A knot rose in Maeve's throat as she watched the woman rewrap Diana's twisted limb and ensure she, too, ate and drank her fill. The pair loved each other, and seeing them together, treating one another with such tenderness and devotion, reminded Maeve again why they simply must prevail. Loves such as theirs also deserved the chance to take root and blossom freely. *Love sees not with the eyes, Maeve, but with the soul.* How right Nan had been. About that. And about everything that truly mattered in this life.

"How does she fare?' Maeve asked as she watched Diana snuggle closer to Ingrid, her lids floating closed.

"She's a fighter," Ingrid murmured, her gaze not leaving Diana's flushed face. "She will survive so long as we get her to safety soon," she added, but her voice was taut and uncharacteristically tremulous.

"What can I do to help her now?"

"Mostly, she needs warmth."

Maeve nodded, her mind already racing ahead as she took off her cloak and draped it over Diana's quaking form. "Ingrid, what she most needs right now, aside from warmth, is rest. What if you and some of the others remain here until we know what awaits at the far end of this labyrinth? And as soon as possible, we will return with some manner of stretcher so she does not have to walk even a step further."

Ingrid's chin dipped in reluctant assent, a fierce light burning in her eyes. "And what of you, Maeve?"

"I will take Fiona, Tilda, and Ilyana, and we will press on," she replied, her gaze sliding to Lysander.

"And what of him? I need not be a seer to sense the trepidation you feel every time you gaze upon him."

"Lysander will soon be well enough to go with us. If he truly wishes to prove his loyalty lies with his prince, now is his chance. Should he fail... well, you have already seen I am quite capable of dispatching zombies."

Lysander met her stare, his demeanor unflinching. "I would gladly pin my honor on this cause, Maeve. But first I would like to know why Prince Alaric would need a savior when he is a fearsome warrior in his own right? Where is he?"

"Given I am the lady in this conversation, I believe you are bound by the honor you profess to give me the benefit of the first question," she said, her gaze never leaving his. "Tell me all you know about Dr. Reinhart. And should I sense you have left anything out, or have embroidered your tale to cast yourself as the hero, I will see it in your eyes and act accordingly."

As Maeve awaited his response, shadows slipped like wraiths along the damp stone walls, illuminated only by guttering torchlight.

Lysander grunted as he rose and stood before her, his once proud frame now gaunt, his face tired and drawn. Yet his gilt eyes glinted with a feverish intensity. "As you wish, Maeve." He heaved a sigh, dragging a trembling hand through his matted hair.

Still, Maeve's hand tightened on her dagger's hilt, unease crawling up her spine. Was he stalling, carefully choosing his next words—or was he ruminating over his escape plan?

"I have no recent experience with the doctor's affairs in the kingdom," he finally began, his sonorous voice echoing off the close walls. "Save for times he has come here to torment me. And it is important to note that before the tributaries were rescued, he and his assistants wore hoods to shield their faces from their victims. It wasn't until the women were freed that I realized our tormentor and Dr. Reinhart were one and the same."

Maeve's eyes narrowed as she studied Lysander, trying to divine truth from lies. Her gaze flicked to Ilyana, taking in the woman's adoring expression as she stared up at him, her hand lacing through his. "Does he speak the truth?" Maeve asked, her words sharp as flint.

"Yes, milady," the girl whispered, her hand white-knuckled as it gripped Lysander's. "We never once saw the faces of those who..." Her voice cracked and faded, choked by horrors Maeve could only begin to imagine.

Satisfied for now, Maeve gestured for Lysander to go on. Even if he spoke the truth about this one thing, she could not yet fully trust him. But if she meant to navigate these catacombs—and his intent was true—she also needed his help. "Go on," she said.

"Those moments, the things I have seen him do..." Lysander shuddered, his breath quickening.

Maeve could almost smell the fear on him, acrid and cloying.

"Dr. Reinhart is not the kindly physician we all thought. His science is the only master he serves. And of late, his pursuits have grown in fervency and are evermore... twisted."

"I have had my own suspicions about the doctor's complicity in the kingdom's ills," Maeve said, watching him carefully for any hint of reaction.

A grim, knowing look passed over his haggard features. "I believe the doctor to be obsessed with unlocking the same forbidden secrets the king coveted. I fear his experiments now venture into realms that should never be explored, perhaps to produce an heir he deems more suitable than Alaric. And though she never said it, I suspect my own mother has long since harbored similar fears."

"Your mother?"

"Lady Isolde. The outcast Duchess."

A jolt went through Maeve as a vision of the aged crone flashed through her mind. The many years that stood between her and Lysander did not quite add up. "The crone sage is your mother?"

Lysander flinched as if struck, his sunken eyes flying wide. "You know of her?"

Maeve stepped closer, crowding him against the damp wall. "If Isolde is your mother, which seems doubtful given her age, then why were you forced into Alaric's service when you, yourself, were born a duke!"

"I... I fear I spoke out of turn."

"Enough with your riddles! Alaric is in trouble. I need the truth, and if I am to infiltrate the castle, I need your help. But I cannot trust you unless you give me sufficient reason."

Lysander sagged back against the wall, his face lined with despair. "You presumed too much, Maeve. I am not the duke's son. I am a bastard, conceived after my mother believed age had rendered her barren. I was unacknowledged by the late duke. And like my mother, I was shunned by the courtiers until King Caligula himself took a personal interest in me..."

As Lysander unspooled a tale of being raised caught between worlds, realization slowly dawned on Maeve. The tension that once festered between him and Alaric... Isolde's fears that under Caligula's zealous rule, science had exceeded the bounds of their hearts... all the pieces began to fit together, painting a dire picture. The world Alaric envisioned had never been under greater threat than it was now.

"Lysander," she said, gripping his arm. "Alaric has been poisoned and is comatose. With his last strength, he told me his father held the formula for the antidote. Without it..." She swallowed hard. "While I still do not know if I can fully trust you, I need help to navigate these catacombs and find what I seek. There isn't much time."

Moisture shimmered in Lysander's eyes. "No... it cannot be..."

"Yet it is. And I fear the doctor is merely the king and Lady Elora's henchman. So please, if any shred of fondness for Alaric remains in your heart... help me save him.."

Lysander closed his eyes for a long moment. When he opened them again, they were gilded with conviction, banishing the remnant shadows of his misery. "For Alaric, I will do anything. Let us tarry no longer."

CHAPTER 21

As Maeve and her weary team trod onward, time seemed to stand still. She had no idea of how long they had been down here. It could have been hours...or it could have been days.

With no way of sighting the moon or gauging its shape, she could only hope they would find the antidote in time. And most of all, that her tentative trust in Lysander had not been misplaced.

But it is him. I was tricked. What an extra layer of cruelty. Yet even though she was firm now in this deception, she found herself still struggling to make eye contact with him. To walk next to him. Not to blame him for actions he did not take. Not knowing what else to do, she fell in behind him and doggedly placed one foot in front of the other.

"Are you alright, Maeve?" Lysander asked as he paused, casting a glance over his shoulder. "I swear I can feel your eyes boring holes through my back."

"I'm fine." She knew her answer was too terse, and she sensed Lysander knew it as well. Though she tried to focus on the immediate moment, her thoughts still churned with the revelations he had shared.

As they pushed on, the air began to thicken with the stenches of rot and excrement. As Lysander moved beyond her torch's reach, she quickened her pace, determined to stay close enough to keep him in sight. Fiona, Ilyana, and Tilda trailed behind, their hands joined.

When they finally approached the maw of an open chamber, they were greeted not by the wails of tortured souls, but by a soft mewling sound.

Lysander and then Maeve stepped into the cavernous space. They'd only taken a few steps when Nyx slinked from behind a pile of rubble, her copper eyes glowing like coals. Maeve couldn't restrain her gasp as the undead feline began rubbing against Lysander's legs like she was greeting a long-lost friend.

"Strange to see you down here, little one," he murmured, lifting the cat into his arms. As he held the creature close and scratched beneath her chin, her tail waved in a slow arc, rumbling purrs filling the silence.

The cat's reaction erased the last bit of Maeve's doubt and her jaw went slack as she watched the scene unfold.

"Does that look like the work of a villain to you?" Fiona whispered as she fell in beside Maeve.

"Not any I have seen."

Fiona nodded. "Given how connected you are to that little beastie, perhaps this is her way of telling you the man you believed to be a villain can be fully trusted after all."

"Perhaps."

With Nyx now flanking Lysander, the group began moving again, the meager light transforming innocuous shapes into nightmarish specters. Eager to be free from this place, they delved deeper into the winding catacombs.

Chamber after dismal chamber unfolded, each more horrifying than the last. Strange instruments of torture leered from every corner, their cruel purposes unmistakable. Maeve's breath caught as her eyes fell upon a pair of iron cages dangling from the ceiling, their rusted bars caked in what could only be dried blood.

All gasped as they passed by heavy wooden workbenches cluttered with filthy restraints. Dirty scalpels glinted wickedly in the dim light, their edges still sharp despite the rust embedded in their handles.

But it was the sight of aged bones and putrefying flesh strewn carelessly about the chamber that sent Maeve's stomach into spasms. Bile seared the back of her throat,

the horrific images before her blurring and warping. Past became present, the walls seeming to pulse and contract, as if the very stones were alive. Sweat beaded on her nape, and she longed to claw her way back to the surface and never look back.

It was Fiona's grounding touch that freed her from her encroaching paralysis. "Maeve. Is your mind trying to travel again?"

She nodded, struggling to maintain her composure, to cling to some semblance of reality. But with each passing second, she felt herself slipping further into an abyss of ugliness.

"By the gods," Ilyana whispered as Lysander tucked her into the crook of his arm. "What manner of evil has taken place here?"

"Dr. Reinhart must have been serving a dark master for a very long time," Lysander rasped, his golden eyes hardening.

In silence, they continued. But soon, the shadows revealed something even more unsettling: tiny brambles creeping towards them like malevolent snakes.

"I thought we were done with these wretched things," Fiona muttered, her voice tight with unease. As Nyx arched her back and hissed, Fiona's eyes darted from one twisting vine to another. "It's like they're stalking us."

"Stay alert," Lysander warned. He cursed and scooped Nyx up just as one of the brambles struck at her like a viper. "The damnable things seem to have minds of their own."

"You have no idea," Maeve murmured. As if confirming her words, a vine suddenly drew back and lashed out toward Fiona, coiling around her ankle. She let out a sharp cry as Ilyana rushed to her side, drawing her dagger to slice it away with a swift stroke.

"Thank you," Fiona rasped as she gaped at the severed vine still creeping along the floor only to rejoin with the mother from which it had sprung.

"Are you alright?" Maeve asked as she knelt next to her friend.

Fiona nodded, but Maeve could see the other women who clung to each other in a tight not. The near miss had shaken them all, a stark reminder the perils that awaited them would only increase—especially for those they had left behind. If they were in danger of being ensnared, what of Ingrid and Diana? They had no way of knowing what was about to happen.

"Fi, take Tilda and go back for Ingrid and Diana," she ordered, unable to contain the urgency that had seeped into her voice. "We need to get them out of there before they are cut off from us."

"Right away," Fiona replied, beckoning to Tilda and another Tributary. Without argument, they fell in step behind her and jogged back the way they had come.

Maeve watched them go, concern gnawing at her insides. But time was too precious a commodity to squander. They could not stop to wait, even for the sake of the others.

Dodging brambles made progress slow. The reeking air seemed nearly impossible to breathe, even for Maeve and Lysander.

"Wait," Fiona called out from the shadows, as she and the others she had gone back for filed into the chamber, Ingrid carrying a moaning Diana in her arms.

The semi-conscious woman's face was pale as the moon. "I don't think I can carry her another strep," Ingrid said as she passed her beloved off to Tilda.

"I have an idea." Lysander crossed to a wooden table, its surface scarred and stained from years of unspeakable acts. With a determined grimace, he let out a roar and wrenched the top free from its supporting frame. "We can better distribute Diana's weight if we use this as a stretcher."

Maeve couldn't help but smile, her heart swelling with newfound trust that he was indeed who he said he was. She nodded, feeling a surge of relief. "Thank you," she said as she drew him into an awkward hug. "It is a brilliant idea."

With Diana secured on the stretcher, the party continued, their sense of urgency driving them forward despite their exhaustion. At last, they came upon a massive wooden door adorned with intricate carvings and gleaming brass fittings that made it feel out of place amongst the backdrop of gore and ruin that filled the catacombs.

"Could this finally open into Alaric's kingdom?" Fiona asked, her voice hushed.

As Maeve looked to Nyx for guidance, the feline brushed up against the door and began to purr. "I guess there's only one way to find out," she replied. "But hold your weapons at the ready."

The words had no sooner crossed her lips when Lysander turned the knob and shouldered open the door like he knew exactly where it would lead them.

Hang on, my love, we're almost there. Drawing in a deep breath, she steeled her nerves. Joining one hand with Lysander's, she readied her dagger and stepped over the threshold.

CHAPTER 22

Maeve's nose curled at the metallic scent of fresh blood. The foul aroma was underpinned with something reminiscent of lilacs, setting her nerves even more on edge. The hair on her nape crawled with the realization they'd emerged in Dr. Reinhart's office. At least what was left of it. Papers, books and the contents of overturned shelves were scattered everywhere. Even Nyx showed alarm, her hair bristling as she leaped onto the massive desk, hissing and spitting.

Circling the desk to see why the cat was so wary, she froze. Dr. Reinhart's decapitated body lay sprawled on the floor, fresh blood pooling around his severed head like a crimson halo.

Maeve pressed a hand to her mouth, repressing a scream. She retched as Lysander gripped her upper arm and tried to pull her back from the carnage. But she twisted away, bristling at being treated like a delicate blossom, rooting herself to the spot.

Only her desire to shield the others who rushed through the door behind them prompted her to jump back. Several cupped their hands over their noses, complaining about the scent that seemed to cling to everything.

"Stay back," Maeve said, raising her hand. "There's been some... trouble."

"What has happened?" Fiona asked, her brow creasing as she watched Lysander drag a shaking hand through his tangled hair. "And what is that gods awful smell?"

"Dr. Reinhart." Maeve pushed from her constricted throat. "He has been... murdered."

"Murdered?" Fiona repeated, her expression incredulous. "By who?"

"Whoever committed this atrocity is long gone," Lysander said before Maeve could give voice to her suspicions.

Dr. Reinhart... murdered. Maeve needed to think clearly, seek evidence that could prove Lady Elora was behind this. But as she knelt beside the doctor's lifeless form, Lysander pulled her back to her feet.

"Let him lie for now, Maeve. He isn't going anywhere, and Diana looks awful." He glanced back toward their friend, his features torn. "I doubt this infernal scent is helping."

Maeve wanted to dig in, argue, but one glance at Diana's bluish lips confirmed why Lysander was right to be alarmed. Diana needed help, and decapitated zombies did not rise to tell their tales. So, on this point, at least, she would demur.

"Perhaps the laboratory has something that can ease her misery," she said, turning away from the carnage to gesture toward the door. "It is that way. But be wary. We have no way of knowing what fresh horror might await."

Taking the lead yet again, Lysander nudged open the door just enough to glimpse the room beyond. But Nyx pranced right through, her tail waving behind her like a banner.

He opened the door wider, beckoning the others to follow. Together, they crept into the vast space, their weapons readied.

Instead of the hostilities Maeve feared, several laboratory workers were scattered across the stone floor. The wreckage of their ruined equipment was strewn around them. Maeve struggled to assemble their story, her nose curling at the cloying fragrance, even more overwhelming than before.

Lysander nudged one of the nearest workers with his foot. "Do you think they are also dead?"

Maeve shook her head. "They can't be. They still have their heads attached. I imagine they're just... asleep." *Like Alaric.* Her brow furrowed as she recalled Eamon's assertion the entire kingdom had fallen victim to some sort of soporific. "But to what end would someone do this when they could just as easily have murdered them, too?"

"Perhaps they just wanted them out of the way, intending to awaken them later," Lysander offered.

"Then it makes no sense it would be the work of the same poison that felled Alaric. Could this damnable scent be the culprit? Should we do something to help them?"

Lysander's brows merged as he considered the possibility. "I suppose the odor could be to blame. I guess the best thing we can do for them is find its source."

A shudder shook Maeve as her eyes darted around the room, seeking the scent's origin, wondering if it could also be behind Diana's turn for the worse. "Either way, we won't find anything to ease Diana's suffering by standing around talking. We need to get her to Isolde."

"Agreed," Fiona added.

"Damn you, Lady Elora," Maeve muttered, recalling her vision of Elora and the king standing in this very room, feeding journals into the fire. But judging by the number of journals that littered the floor, that had not yet happened.

"You really believe she's capable of masterminding this?" Lysander asked, not looking convinced.

"You underestimate the power of a woman with a cause," Maeve said. "There's no time to rehash history, but know she and the king are the only ones who would benefit from preventing Alaric's cure."

"Look!" Ilyana pointed toward the room's farthest corner. "Nyx is trying to climb up to the vent."

"I think my mother's cat may be seeking the source of this damnable odor," Lysander said as Nyx lost her footing and fell to the floor.

"You should know she is my cat now," Maeve barked, closing the distance between herself and Nyx. "Mine," she whispered, scooping the cat into her arms and cradling her like an infant. But the creature's soft snores suggested she was only sleeping... like the workers. Still, seeing her like this sent daggers through Maeve's heart. She couldn't bear the thought of losing Nyx, too.

Fiona stepped between Maeve and Lysander, as if to redirect their attention. "I think we can all agree we need to get out of here. But where can we go without getting ambushed?"

"Somewhere with better ventilation," Maeve agreed. "A room with windows. Or... outdoors, perhaps."

"That is a feat easier said than done." Ingrid's gaze fixed on Diana, who had now surrendered to sleep... or worse.

"Do you have any place in particular in mind?" Tilda asked as she knelt by Maeve to stroke Nyx.

"At least here, it's warm, and we have a door standing between us and danger," Ingrid said.

Maeve shook her head. "Fiona's right. We can't stay here. Lysander, Fiona, and I might be immune to this madness for a while, but a human's body processes are far more... robust." Her eyes darted around the room, gauging the demeanors of the other women in their party. "I fear soon, all of you might drop where you stand."

As if cursed by Maeve's words, Ilyana stifled a yawn, her heavy lids shuttering until her eyes looked like crescent moons. She swayed on her feet and might have fallen had Lysander not rushed to her aid.

And then Maeve knew. It was not lilacs that poisoned the air they all breathed. It was belladonna—in large enough doses, toxic. And if not for the brief time she'd spent with Isolde, she never would have been able to make this connection. "Staying would mean we all fall. I believe the atmosphere is laced with belladonna. We must find a place that will afford us fresh air."

"I know just the place." Lysander looped his arm around Ilyana's shoulders, her slight form melting deeper into him, giving Maeve a stark reminder of the vulnerability they might all soon default to if they did not prevail.

"Where?"

"My chambers have plenty of windows." With Ilyana in tow, Lysander started toward the door leading into the catacombs beneath Alaric's library. But as he reached to pull it open, he paused and turned back to Maeve, uncertainty playing on his features. "But given how long I was imprisoned, could my chambers be occupied?"

Maeve lifted a brow, wondering if his confinement might have addled his brain. "Not to my knowledge," she replied. "But have you forgotten this is an invasion?"

His scoff caused her next words to tumble out, clipped with frustration. "It isn't as if we can go rushing through the corridors with a sick woman on a stretcher without being noticed. Or worse, attacked."

Lysander's eyes roamed over Maeve's disheveled appearance— her torn clothes, the smears of dirt and blood marring her skin. "If I'm to gauge by your appearance, you've managed far worse today and survived."

"Did I mention Fiona and I are both *wanted*?" Maeve's voice cracked slightly, betraying her fear.

A hint of a smirk played at the corners of his mouth, a jarring contrast to the gravity of their situation. "That is a story I'm eager to hear, but if nearly everyone in the castle is sleeping, as you believe, then being detected should not pose a problem."

Maeve's eyes narrowed, her jaw clenching. She did not need a man to explain their obvious circumstances to her. "Yes, but who knows if the spell extends to Elora's cadre of ferals? We've no way of knowing where they might be lurking."

"Her cadre of... ferals?" Confusion and disbelief warred on

Lysander's face. "Are you saying she has asserted some sort of control over the undead?" He looked at her like he thought the notion ridiculous.

Maeve pinched the bridge of her nose, frustration rumbling in her throat. Everything that had transpired since Lysander's disappearance pressed down on her like a physical force. "There is no time to fill you in," she snapped. "Just know she indeed found a way to make them do her bidding."

Lysander scoffed again, the sound harsh in the tense atmosphere. "But that defies everything we know about ferals."

"Have you forgotten you and Alaric defied everything I once thought I knew about zombies?" Maeve's words were sharp enough to draw blood, but she was sick of propagating the baseless assumptions that only served to keep all of their worlds at war.

"Touché," he said, raising his hands in surrender.

"If Lady Elora's minions are patrolling, they are sure to catch us before we can get to your chambers. Our only real power here is our ability to surprise our enemies."

Lysander's eyes darkened, his expression wounded. "You forget Alaric and I were raised here during The Harrowing," he countered. "With the forest overrun by danger, the catacombs were our favorite playground. As were the secret passageways that connected them to the castle."

New hope welled in Maeve's chest. "And you know of one such point of access?"

"I know them all as well as the back of my hand," he replied, another hint of the arrogant zombie Maeve remembered creeping into his voice. His gilded gaze softened as it plundered Maeve's. "Please, just quit arguing and trust me on this?"

The silence stretched between them, taut as a bowstring until finally, Maeve relented. "Fine," she breathed, the word barely audible.

"Fine, then," he echoed. With a determined set to his shoulders, he pushed open the door. The ancient hinges groaned in protest, another gush of sickly sweet air rushing in to greet them.

Lysander took Ilyana's hand and led her through the door, the darkness beyond swallowing them whole.

THE MEAGER TORCHLIGHT scarcely illuminated the catacombs, casting uncertain shadows that meandered like snakes across the floor. They had only traveled a short distance when Lysander paused and traced with his index finger a symbol carved into the stone wall. With a soft groan and a shower of dust, a hidden door swung open to reveal a steep stairwell soaring upwards until it was swallowed by pitch darkness.

"Each step will bring us closer to safety," he assured, though his expression suggested uncertainty as two of the women struggled with the first rise.

As they began their laborious ascent, a dirge composed of groans and grunts accentuated every step. They hadn't gone far when Ingrid cried out as Tilda stumbled, nearly dropping the makeshift stretcher. With concern torturing her features, Fiona rushed to their aid. Maeve passed Nyx off to the woman behind her to follow suit. Together, they suspended the stretcher between them, relieving the exhausted women of their precious burden.

"These stairs seem without end," Maeve grumbled as they continued to climb, but after what felt like a century, the weary group emerged into a large linen closet.

While most of the women stumbled into the space, bracing their hands on their knees as they gulped for air, Tilda soldiered on, defying her exhaustion as she began gathering clean linens. "We can tear them into strips to better support Diana's leg," she explained.

All the while, Ilyana swayed, her lids fluttering in the effort to remain open, but it was clear the belladonna would claim her next.

"Stay here and rest while Lysander, Fiona, and I locate his chambers," Maeve told the women. She had barely finished speaking when Ilyana's knees gave way, and she sagged onto the stone floor.

"But where are you going?" Ilyana's pleading gaze latched onto Lysander's, and Maeve could not help but feel Ilyana had forgotten the capability her trials had afforded her. And it made her fear that when all was well, the world would soon default to the same customs that had torn it apart.

"We must confirm my old chambers are unoccupied," Lysander explained to Ilyana. "It won't take long."

Though Maeve concurred with a nod, she sighed as she watched Lysander press a kiss atop Ilyana's braids.

CHAPTER 23

Maeve, Fiona, and then Lysander slipped out the linen closet door, the sharp tang of their anxiety hanging in the air. After ensuring they were alone, the trio crept through shadowed corridors, their rasping breaths tearing the silence.

Soon, the familiar shuffling of undead feet echoed nearby.

Maeve's arms shot out, pulling the others behind a marble pillar just as two feral zombies lurched past, their swords drawn and their vacant eyes sweeping the hall. She held her breath, feeling Fiona's trembling from behind her. For a heart-stopping moment, one of the zombie's footsteps paused, and she could envision its ghastly head tilting, as if sensing their presence. Then, mercifully, it also shambled onward.

"That was too damn close," Lysander whispered, his voice tight.

As they continued through the once-grand halls, tears glazed Maeve's eyes. Cobwebs draped the eaves like shrouds, and a thick coating of dust dimmed the once grand tapestries. With each step they took, mice scurried in and out of piled debris. Even the creeping brambles that had cocooned the castle's exterior now sought to infiltrate the heart of Alaric's domain, as if they sought to squeeze the life from his vision of unity. How so much decay could occur in the space of a few days was beyond her reckoning.

For the first time, she knew that magic was not only real. It was also sometimes deadly.

"Almost there," Lysander whispered as they approached his chamber door.

Relief washed over Maeve as they cautiously entered, Lysander pushing the door closed behind them. But she gasped, realizing they weren't alone. Lady Isolde sat by a roaring fire, her back turned to them. She wept, feeding dark berries into a bubbling pot.

Maeve's suspicion rose as she watched tendrils of steam rising toward the vent, recognizing it as the source of the lethal belladonna that had permeated the entire castle.

"Mother?" Lysander managed, his voice cracking with emotion.

Isolde stood from the stool she'd been perched upon and whirled around, her eyes widening in disbelief. "Lysander? Sweet goddess, is it really you?"

A lump rose in Maeve's throat as they rushed into each other's arms, tears streaming down both their faces. Isolde choked out a sob as she buried her face in her son's broad shoulder, inhaling his familiar scent.

"I've missed you so much," Lysander choked out as he recovered himself and set her away, his palms settling on her shaking shoulders.

"Oh, my darling boy." Isolde sobbed, cradling his face between her palms. "What have they done to you? You look so thin, and your eyes are so... haunted."

Lysander managed a near smile. "I'm alright now. And I have Maeve and her friends to thank for setting me free. But Mother, what are you doing here?"

As Maeve wondered the same, Isolde gasped, her eyes darting toward the pot she'd been tending. Pressing a hand to her breast, she cried out. "We must dispose of this poison immediately."

As Maeve and Fiona worked to remove the pot from the spit, Isolde explained Lady Elora used Lysander's safety as leverage, forcing her to keep the kingdom asleep while they prepared for some grand event.

"The coronation I foresaw," Maeve whispered.

Wondering how they should dispose of the cauldron's contents so it could do no more harm, a flutter of white drew her gaze to the doors leading onto a small balcony.

The snowy owl perched on the balcony's wrought iron rails, its cornflower blue eyes meeting hers. Relieved he had escaped the catacombs, she reached for the door, eager to thank him. But as she pulled it open, he blinked once, his gaze seeming frantic as he took flight. She watched him soar toward the rising moon, serving her a grim reminder: the full moon would rise tomorrow night.

As her mind searched for a plan to find the antidote in time, a sudden crash echoed through the hall. Fearing Alaric was in danger, she bolted toward the door. She flung it open, then skidded to a halt as she passed through, her entire world tilting on its axis. There, just a few feet away, stood Alaric, locked in an embrace with Lady Elora.

Maeve's vision swam, her legs trying to collapse, betrayal crashing over her in waves. She could only watch, her tongue turning to lead as Elora's hand wound behind Alaric's neck, deepening their kiss.

As Alaric groaned with obvious pleasure, a glint of green caught Maeve's eye, yanking her heartstrings tauter. The same emerald betrothal ring Alaric had given her, the one she had left on his pinkie for safekeeping the day she departed, now adorned Lady Elora's elegant hand. A fresh wave of hurt cleaved her soul, leaving her breathless.

"Why?" she mouthed, no sound slipping past the knot in her throat. Tears sliding from her eyes, she gripped the rough stone wall for support. Her mind flared with the image of Alaric falling to his knees and slipping the ring onto Elora's slender finger, tormenting herself further. Had all they'd shared, overcome together, meant nothing to him? "I don't understand," she whispered.

At the sound of Maeve's plea, Fiona burst into the hallway, her dagger at the ready. "What the bloody blazes?"

As Elora looked past Alaric's shoulder, she disengaged from his embrace, her black eyes wide with shock. For a moment, she looked as if she were seeing an apparition. But ever cunning, she recovered herself. Her lips curled into a sly smile as she murmured into Alaric's ear. "Darling, as much as I would love to retire to your chambers and finish this, it appears we have an audience."

Maeve gritted her teeth, struggling to contain a whirlwind of emotions. She knew she couldn't afford to lose control now, not when so much was at stake.

Glancing at Fiona, who stood next to her, stance wide and features taut, Maeve realized they needed their allies now more than ever. But even with the belladonna no longer tainting the atmosphere, they needed time to awaken and regain whatever strength they had left.

"Elora," Maeve said, her voice laced with steel. "What have you done to him?"

"That's what I would like to know," Fiona said.

For a fraction of a second, Elora hesitated, uncertainty marring her face as Alaric spun about to face Maeve.

But gone was the soft, cornflower blue gaze she had poured her heart into a million times. The stare he beheld her with now was hard as steel. Wondering if she was caught in a nightmare, she braced herself for the words that contorted his features. But he said nothing.

"Alaric," she rasped, her voice taut with heartache. "Say something. Tell me this is a jest. Tell me anything that can make me understand."

"There's nothing to understand, Maeve," he began, "for Elora has already told you the truth." His words were too cool, too clipped, and the once-loving stare that beheld her now glinted with so much disdain she couldn't help but shrink from it.

"You would have that witch wear my betrothal ring?" she demanded, tears burning the corners of her eyes. But she refused to let them fall—she could ill afford to show more vulnerability when everything she believed to be true was falling apart around her.

"Ah, but you see, dear, sweet Maeve..." Elora stepped forward, a triumphant grin playing on her lips. "After you abandoned our prince, the spell you cast over him was broken. With his senses restored, he realized this ring you so carelessly discarded"—she wiggled her fingers, making sure Maeve couldn't miss the emerald glinting in the dim light—"should always have belonged to me. Or perhaps your former betrothed forgot to tell you we were chosen by the king to be wed before we could even walk?"

"The exiled king, you mean," Fiona spat. "The very one who Alaric detests."

A knowing arch lofted Elora's brow, forcing Maeve to clench her fists so she didn't take a swing at her. Her mind raced, seeking some way out of this twisted web and wondering if the belladonna could have impacted her, too. For surely this was a nightmare. She couldn't believe that Alaric would so readily accept Elora's twisted version of events.

"Alaric, please," she began, her voice barely audible above the roaring of her own blood. "You must know I would never have abandoned you, not willingly."

But as she searched his face, seeking any glimmer of kindness, she saw only cold indifference... and dismissal. It was as if the man she loved so fiercely had been replaced by a stranger, leaving her with nothing but the bitter taste of betrayal.

"I have heard enough from you, woman," he snapped, his tone dagger sharp. "Surely you can see your presence here is unwelcome. I would ask that you both leave my kingdom now. Go back to those whose welfare you cared for more than mine."

The finality in his words fell like a death sentence, threatening to shatter her. But she couldn't give up, not now. She needed answers, but she also needed the support of allies. The obvious names like Ingrid, Ilyana, and Tilda echoed in her mind, reminding her that in the spaces behind her were still those who believed, as Alaric once had, that love must always prevail. But they could not intercede yet. They needed time for the belladonna's effect to dissipate.

Stalling seemed her only option, and she could only hope that Fiona sensed what she was about to do. She would give the appearance of leaving, then double back to rally the others.

"Fine, Alaric," she whispered. "I will go, but know this: I will uncover the truth. And when I do"—she lifted her chin, her gaze steady and unwavering—"perhaps you will recall that I have never been the enemy here."

With that, she turned on her heel, hooked her arm through her Fiona's and urged her a few steps down the corridor, determined to give the appearance they were doing as he had demanded.

"You cannot just free her," Elora's voice sounded from behind them. "One who has committed treason once will have no qualms in doing so again. Let my guards imprison her and that clinging vine she calls a friend."

"You bitch!" Fiona twisted away from Maeve, starting for Elora. If Maeve had not grabbed her by her belt to yank her back, she might well have sunk a dagger in her.

Gasping, Lady Elora clapped her hands. As if bidden by the sound, shuffling gaits filled the distant shadows.

"Fear not," Maeve said to Fiona as she extracted her dagger from her boot and braced herself for Elora's revenge.

Her eyes flickered again to Alaric, seeking respite, but finding none. Instead, he regarded her with fresh contempt, and the dagger of his apparent loathing plunged deeper into her wounded heart.

"Elora makes an excellent point," he said, his voice hard as flint. "Abandoning me after my poisoning was indeed an act of treason."

Though tears wound down Maeve's face, his once gentle eyes remained empty and lifeless as a statue's. "Trusting you to meddle no more in my kingdom's affairs is folly. So you can wait in your cell until tomorrow's wedding and my coronation have passed. Then we will consummate our nuptials to the music of your screams as you and your lowborn bloodhound are executed."

The dagger slipped from Maeve's hands and clattered on the stone floor. She had hoped whatever spell had been cast over him would dissipate, and he would see past Elora's lies.

"Alaric, please," she implored, her voice cracking. "I never meant to betray you. I was only trying to save you."

"Save me?" He scoffed, his scornful laughter echoing throughout the hall. "By poisoning me and leaving me to die while you hid behind your precious family? Your actions have already spoken louder than your empty words."

With his judgment bearing down on her, Maeve's resolve to set these things right threatened to crumble. But deep within her, a spark of defiance still burned—a stubborn refusal to give up. Something here was not right; she knew it to the seat of her soul. Clinging to that dying ember, she steeled herself for the battle ahead.

"It is clear your mind has been poisoned," Fiona retorted. "But truth shall always prevail."

"If not revealed by me before the moment of my execution," Maeve added, emboldened by Fiona's support, "then by the gods themselves." She locked eyes with Alaric, her gaze unwavering. "Then perhaps you will recall the woman who loved you enough to put her own life aside to save yours."

"Enough!" Elora's voice was shrill as a banshee's as she secreted the glowing vial she wore around her neck into her decolletage. "You and your ilk have no place in the zombie aristocracy," she said. With her ghastly minions assembling behind her, she stepped aside and signaled them to advance.

As the revenants lurched forward to do their mistress's bidding, the futility of resistance stung like hailstones pelting Maeve's flesh. She cringed as their foul hands disarmed her friend, her sister-in-arms.

As they were herded forward, she vowed that before her sentence could be carried out, she would use every iota of sight she had to reveal the truth. Only then could she find the key to unraveling the tangled web that had turned the world's destiny on its ear.

"Fear not," she said, her hand finding Fiona's in the last second before the guards surrounded them. With their captors shoving them down the corridor by their broadswords, Alaric's scorn seared a hole through Maeve's back. But she also saw something else, something that made her hope the fates were not yet done writing their story.

CHAPTER 24

Maeve's breath came in painful pants, her steps faltering as the door to the linen closet where they'd left the others creaked open. She slowed, holding her breath. She sensed a friendly presence, and hope blossomed that the sound heralded her friends who were waging an assault.

One second passed, then two. When no movement came forth, she could only put one foot in front of the other as she and Fiona were roughly urged down the corridors by Lady Elora's guards. But faith refused to die until a few moments ground past with nothing happening.

Her optimism seeped out with a sigh as she surrendered to the fact that the miracle she had dared hope for just wasn't meant to be. She forced back a sob, and the walls seemed to close in on them, suffocating any evidence of her fraying hope that still lingered in the air.

Unhappy with their pace, two of the zombie guards moved forward, flanking her and Fiona.

Fiona was wretched, for they were a grotesque sight to behold, with their skin a mottled patchwork of greens and grays, stretching taut over bones and protruding in places where decay had taken hold. And Maeve could not help but wonder if these lost souls she had been so foolish as to pity would soon become her executioners. Perhaps she had been a fool, believing that love alone could save them all.

As they left Maeve and Fiona no choice but to move, dried sinews and tendons creaked, each step a reminder of the horrific state The Harrowing had inflicted on them. But it was the smell that assaulted Maeve's senses most violently. The acrid stench of decay wafting from these animated corpses was nauseating. Their proximity only amplified the odor, creating a miasma of death that seemed to seep into every pore. Each labored breath she took was a struggle against the urge to gag, but she would not give her tormentors the satisfaction of knowing her suffering. A dark part of her almost wished she had dispatched more of them when she had the chance.

Her panting breaths became shallow as they advanced down the tight corridors that would take them to the most wretched fate she could have imagined. Casting one last desperate glance over her shoulder before they turned a corner, her stubborn heart hopeful for a reprieve, her eyes locked on Alaric. His once-vibrant presence had been reduced to a statue representing only the shell of his former self. He seemed deader to her than the ferals Lady Elora had remanded her to. The sight of him not looking at her, but through her, undid her further. But seeing him like that and having heard the uncharacteristic words he'd used to describe Fiona caused a new concern to gnaw at her insides. Perhaps once again, some sort of guise trickery was afoot.

Or perhaps that was only her broken heart talking. She'd been right when she believed love was a currency exchanged by fools. She'd learned that lesson once before, with her assault. But its barbs had been smoothed by the glow of Alaric's presence.

One of the guards growled, shoving her as she lingered. His touch between her shoulder blades was pure ice, causing her flesh to crawl.

"Hands off! We're going as fast as we can." Fiona's eyes threw flames at the undead soldier who had dared manhandle her. Her demand echoed off the stone walls, amplifying and repeating her small act of defiance until it faded into nothingness.

Just like their quest.

Maeve gritted her teeth, trying to shove aside the dread that threatened to consume her. They were being led to their doom, and there was nothing more she could do about it unless she could get a message to the others. She swallowed hard, her throat tight and the bitter taste of her own fear poisoning her tongue.

But then, something else caught her eye; a small, dark figure lurking beside them, clinging to the deepest shadows. Nyx! The cat's copper eyes gleamed in the dim light, twin suns offering warmth within the chaos. As she wondered whether she might be hallucinating, the encroaching threat of fresh hope caused her heart to stumble.

"Look, Fiona," she whispered, tipping her chin toward the cat. "Do you see what I do?"

Fiona's eyes shone as she, too, caught sight of Nyx. "Do you dare think...?"

"That perhaps all is not lost?" Maeve finished, her voice barely more than a breath. "For if Nyx is awake, then it stands to reason there must be the others." As she spoke, warmth spread through her chest, melting the icy dread that had gripped her.

Nyx continued to slink along, stubbornly cleaving to the shadows, her movements graceful and fluid. The soft padding of her paws was almost imperceptible, yet to Maeve, it heralded hope's return. It was clear the creature intended to follow them to their destination. And if that was the case, perhaps she could urge her familiar to alert their friends and rally them to their aid.

Maeve allowed herself a small smile, the muscles in her face relaxing for the first time since she had rushed into the corridor only to find her betrothed embracing her nemesis. Regardless of where this dreadful trek led them, they would not be facing their plight without the hope they'd live to wage yet another fight.

"Come, Nyx," she murmured beneath her breath, her words carrying the faintest wisp of hope. "Do my bidding once more. Follow us, so you can then alert our friends."

As they continued down the dimly lit corridor, Maeve's thoughts turned to their friends: Lady Isolde, Ingrid, and the others. As the lurching torchlight cast long shadows on the stairs, she imagined them transforming into her awakened allies, preparing to free them so they could yet wage the assault that had brought them all back here.

"Even if the worst happens, at least we still have each other," Fiona said grimly, her hand trembling in the nest of Maeve's palm.

"Indeed," Maeve agreed. "Together until the bitter end. But from the moment we met, that has always been enough to get the job done, has it not?"

THEIR DISMAL MARCH SEEMED INTERMINABLE.

As they trudged into the next corridor, she gasped at the once-lively courtiers, now mere shells of their former selves. They were strewn about the stone floor like so many discarded rag dolls. An unnatural stillness clung to the air, and that foreboding sent shivers coursing through her. Alaric's castle, which had once vibrated with activity, was now as still as a mausoleum.

But if Nyx, who still stalked after them, was awake, Maeve could not help but wonder how long the belladonna's effect on the courtiers would last. Worry tightened her brow as she recalled the last time she had seen them. Their harsh words and wrongful accusations had proven she could not count them as allies. Chances were, should they wake now, they would point the finger of blame at her for the strange spell that had fallen over them.

But if the magic Isolde had woven continued to wane, it wouldn't be long before they stirred. More chaos would ensue. Knowing this caused her to pick up her pace, putting distance between them.

As they finally exited the castle and made their way toward the looming West Tower, she noticed something else... while if not exactly heartening... peculiar. The twisted brambles that had encased the castle walls in their suffocating embrace were now wilting. The dark magic that had fueled them appeared to be dissipating, and she suspected Lady Elora had forced Lady Isolde's hand in this as well.

"Damn these cursed brambles," Fiona hissed, her eyes narrowed as she watched them. "This mess has to be Elora's doing. And because of her, Alaric, too, has become some kind of... monster. I am starting to question whether our quest to save him is still worth our lives."

"Remember," Maeve said as they were nudged onto the tower's sagging stoop and urged through the door. "When it comes to Lady Elora, nothing has ever been as it seems."

Their conversation was cut short, Fiona's retort still playing on her lips as they were pushed up the dank stairwell leading to the same cells where they'd found Eamon and Loren. With their final destination looming before them, Maeve's steps became more purposeful, her posture straightening as if shedding a shroud of despair. She need not fear, and as soon as they were alone, she would explain to Fiona why she, too, should let go of her anger toward Alaric.

They scaled the dilapidated stairs, slowly outpacing their guards, and Maeve paused, her eye drawn to a faint glimmer of light spilling through the small, vent-like window. The realization that it emanated from the chapel where Isolde had made her home after being shunned by the courtiers served her a reminder that a secret world she had only scarcely begun to understand still existed. *Cling to your magic, Maeve, and let your heart manifest a new path*, the crone's voice echoed within the confines of her mind. *For that is all that can save our world now.*

As the guards closed the space she and Fiona had put between them, Maeve fixed her gaze on that distant glow for as long as she was able, remembering she was—and always had been—the benefactress of her ancestor's magic. She was no longer only a girl. She was a woman connected by an invisible cord to all the women who had come before her. Through them, and the insight they had bestowed upon her, a new future, nay, a new world would be born this day.

And she no longer cared whether the price for helping bring Alaric's vision to fruition was her life. For she knew deep in her soul the ancestral magic she had inherited would someday manifest in Coralie, and she could not think of a purer vessel to contain such power.

Nyx darted ahead of them, seemingly unnoticed by the ferals. The feline's stalwart presence further bolstered Maeve's confidence. Her companionship was a testament to the enduring bonds that could connect all living things if pride was surrendered and prejudices set aside long enough to let them.

They passed the last of the windows dotting the stairwell, and Maeve gasped, seeing the snowy owl's regal silhouette pressed against the silvery moon, its massive wings spread in flight. And then she knew. Alaric still loved her and wanted her safe. *Love has always been the cure for what ails this world, Maeve. And somehow, that love must be bestowed upon all the gods' creatures—even those we might fear.*

She and Fiona were herded into their cell, the heavy clank of the bolt vibrating through the tight space. Yet the air now carried shimmers of possibility, and Maeve drew it in deeply, fueling her determination to endure. Their trials may seem endless, but somewhere beyond the darkness, an ember of hope waited to light a new fire. Alaric was now and always had been with her. As she plunged her hand into her pockets to find her talisman, something beneath it brushed against her fingertips, pushing a peal of maniacal laughter past her lips.

THE SOUR TANG of Fiona's rising desperation tinged the stale atmosphere within their cell. From the courtyard below, the ominous scrape of metal against stone wafted through a narrow window far too high for them to reach. Already, the guillotine was being prepared in anticipation of tomorrow's executions. Each grating sound of the falling blade made Fiona jump, a cruel reminder of the fate that might soon await them both. But still, Maeve could barely control her mirth.

"How can you laugh at a time like this?" Fiona's voice trembled with a mixture of rage and disbelief. "Have you forgotten your betrothed just sentenced us to death? And that Lady Elora's undead puppets prepare the guillotine as we speak?"

While Maeve struggled to contain her glee, a hysterical smile battling her forcibly grim expression, Fiona seethed. Spewing expletives, she paced the moldy floor, her footsteps creating a frantic rhythm that matched her expression. With each turn, she growled like a caged animal, her fingers biting into her fisted hands.

"Just look at us, Maeve," she spat, her words dripping with venom. "Prisoners in our own kingdom! And all because of that vile witch, Lady Elora." She whirled on Maeve, eyes flashing dangerously. "You should have killed that bitch when you had the chance. And what good is your so-called sight when it has helped nothing?"

"Nor can hindsight can help anything. Call me crazy if you will, but it is quite possible Alaric may not be fully... himself." Her words hung in the air, heavy with implication, while in the distance, the creaking of rusted gears added to the dreadful symphony outside.

But when it came Fiona's turn to laugh, her tone was sharp and bitter. "So that licenses him to have us beheaded?"

"Of course not," Maeve replied, her fingers confirming the item hidden deep in her pocket was indeed real. "But we do know Lady

Elora is a master of deception. I only ask that you be cautious in assigning blame where none may be warranted."

Fiona stopped pacing abruptly, her jaw dropping as she stared at Maeve. She studied Maeve's face, and her brows lifted, suggesting she believed her friend had lost her grip on reality. "I know what I saw, Maeve," she hissed, her words barely audible over the distant sound of shuffling footsteps. "And I certainly know what I heard that turncoat cur say to you. How can we possibly discover the whole truth when we are trapped like rats in this gods forsaken place? And all while your betrothed prepares to marry another?"

Maeve smiled grimly, her fingers brushing against the slick stone walls. The cold seeped into her bones, slowing her racing mind as she desperately tried to formulate a plan. "We will find a way, Fiona. We must. For ourselves, for Alaric, and for all those depending on us."

When Fiona said nothing more, Maeve paused, her hand dipping into her pocket. "And perhaps," she continued, lifting the item into the scant moonlight filtering through the high, barred window, "the means to save ourselves has been with us all along."

Fiona tilted her head, confusion momentarily replacing her wrath. "What do you mean?"

"Hold out your hand," Maeve instructed, curling her fingers around the cool metallic object.

As Maeve deposited the item into Fiona's trembling palm, a gasp escaped her friend's lips, her eyes widening like twin moons. "Is this... a key?"

Maeve nodded. "And not just any key. It is the same one Brigid gave us to release Eamon and Loren from this very cell."

For a moment, hope dawned on Fiona's features, but as she cast a glance at the cell door, it just as quickly melted into a mask of despair. The grind of a blade being sharpened drifted up from the courtyard, punctuating the gravity of their situation. "What bloody good can a key do us when the lock is on the outside?"

Before Maeve could answer, Fiona's frustration exploded.

Drawing her arm back, she hurled the key at the wall with all her might. Sparks flew as metal met stone, and the key clattered to the floor. But she was not done. She spun around, unleashing her rage on the unyielding door with a vicious kick. A shower of dust, grout, and filthy water rained down from the damp ceiling, coating them both in grime.

Maeve sighed heavily, shaking debris from her hair as she cast a somber glance toward her friend. "Fiona, I know it must be hard to believe, but there is so much more going on here than meets the eye."

As if summoned by her words, a lithe shadow detached itself from the darkness outside their window, threaded through the cell's bars and landed gracefully on the floor. With a nimble hop, Nyx mewed as she sat before Maeve, copper eyes gleaming with intelligence as she awaited instructions like a tiny but well-trained soldier.

"Good kitty," Maeve murmured, kneeling before Nyx. She scratched the cat's chin, eliciting a rumbling purr that, for a moment, drowned out the ominous sounds from below. With deft fingers, she plucked one of the rawhide ties securing her braids and threaded it through the key's loop. "Now be a good kitty and take this to your former mistress," she instructed as she affixed the key to Nyx's neck. "And do not dally to chase vermin, my friend. For time is of the essence."

Nyx mewed once, her tail swishing with anticipation.

Fiona gasped as the cat bunched her body, muscles coiling beneath her mottled fur, and leaped back through the same impossibly high bars from whence she'd come.

As Nyx vanished, Maeve turned to face Fiona, whose eyes now glimmered with the faintest patina of hope. "Now what?" Fiona asked.

"Now we wait and hope the gods are still with us."

Too much time had passed.

With Fiona curled on the floor like a pill bug, finally succumbing to a restless doze, Maeve was now the one who paced. She twisted her hair between her fingers as she nervously charted the moon's silver trek. The pale orb cast eerie shadows through the barred window, as if its relentless glow sought to mock their imprisonment. She swallowed hard, knowing tomorrow night, the gilded maiden would rise again, only to shine in her full glory. Then Alaric's time for a cure would be over—a cure she suspected—no, knew—was contained within the glowing pendant she had seen Lady Elora secret into her bodice.

The memory of that moment burned in her mind, its strange luminescence a harsh contrast to the oppressive shadows in their cell. She could almost feel its warmth, imagine its power—so close, yet impossibly out of reach. Even if they were freed, how could they ever convince Elora to part with it without fighting past her relentless horde?

They needed more time.

Tears welled in her eyes as she wrung her hands, their rough skin a reminder of the battles they had already fought. Her throat constricted, a sob threatening to escape. She did not know whether she could stand to wait another second without losing her mind. Where was Nyx? Could she have been intercepted? That was the only reason she could think of to answer why the help they so desperately needed had not yet arrived.

The cold stone beneath her feet seemed to leech the marrow from her bones, the weight of their situation settling on her breast, making it hard to breathe. Yet beneath the fear and despair, a faint glimmer of hope still burned, and she told herself again they were not alone. There were still those who would always stand beside them. They just needed a bit more time. To think. To plan. To slip past Lady Elora's minions, who, by the sound of it, marched through the courtyard in relentless and dreadful numbers.

The rhythmic scrape of undead feet on cobblestones echoed through the night, a reminder of the dark forces arrayed against them. Her ears strained, trying to discern any change in the pattern, some sign of hope they had lost interest in their prisoners and retreated. Instead, she heard the sickening scrape of the guillotine falling once again, this time slicing through the thick air with fluid efficiency. The sound reverberated through her bones, and she shuddered, imagining how it might feel as her life was snuffed out by the blade's deadly bite.

But just as the guillotine's macabre echo faded, another sound rent the silence—the furtive click of a key turning the cell door's lock.

Her heart rose into her throat, a conflicting mixture of hope and dread. Though she longed for it to open on the familiar faces of her friends, a faithless part of her feared Elora had convinced the king to end them now.

Not willing to leave this world without taking a few foes with her, she pressed her back against the rough stone wall next to the door, unthreading the long strap that bound her other braid. The leather was supple from years of wear, yet plenty strong enough to serve as a weapon if need be.

As the door creaked open, its rusty hinges groaning in protest, Fiona startled. Her eyes, wide with fear, met Maeve's as she crept back into shadows that boiled like storm clouds in the farthest corner of their cell. Maeve pressed a finger to her lips, cautioning Fiona to remain quiet. Then she stretched her makeshift garotte taut, muscles tensed, poised to strike.

The door inched open, revealing a scant sliver of torchlight from the dark corridor beyond. Maeve's breath gathered in her throat as a lone, hooded form slipped inside. The figure was much too slight and small to be Lysander's, or even Ingrid or Tilda's. A length of rope was coiled against its side, and Maeve's scrambling mind could only assign it one purpose—to bind her and Fiona's hands behind their backs as they were marched to the guillotine.

Time seemed to slow as the hooded figure took another tentative step into the cell. Maeve's palms were slick with sweat, her grip on the leather strap threatening to slip as she raised her garotte and stretched it tighter still. She could hear her own heartbeat thundering in her ears, drowning out all other sounds.

As she tensed, preparing to lunge at their hooded visitor, her mind raced through a kaleidoscope of emotions. Fear for their lives, determination to fight until the bitter end, and a desperate, clinging hope that somehow, against all odds, this might be the rescue they'd been praying for.

Their strange visitor turned in the nick of time, the dark hood concealing its face shifting just enough to reveal an obsidian glint of almond-shaped eyes. Maeve's breath caught, her muscles freezing mid-motion as recognition dawned.

"*Ilyana?*" she murmured, unable to conceal her incredulous expression. "Why would they send you when you are the smallest amongst us?"

"The way Lysander dotes over you, I am surprised he allowed it." Fiona's expression proved her more concerned than relieved.

Ilyana squared her slim shoulders, her chin lifting to meet Fiona's gaze. "Have you considered my size is exactly why Ingrid chose me?" she snapped as Nyx reappeared in the window above. "As for Lysander, he does not know, for he is... otherwise occupied."

"Doing what, exactly?" Maeve asked.

"Not now," the girl said as she uncoiled her rope and lifted her gaze to Nyx, who seemed poised to pounce. "We only have one chance to break you out, and there is little time before the guards march this way again."

With that said, she tossed her rope high. Fiona gasped as Nyx deftly caught an end in her mouth, letting the rest fall to the floor.

"Now what?" Maeve asked, her voice a hoarse whisper. "Nyx isn't big enough to haul us out of here."

Ilyana's reply came swift and low, her eyes darting nervously towards the cell door. "Nor am I. So we pull until we've dislodged the bars. Hopefully, it will leave sufficient space for us to pass through."

Maeve nodded, wondering how they'd get up there as she wrapped her hands around the coarse rope. But as Fiona followed suit, she could sense the tremors in her grip, her rising fear palpable. "Trust her, Fiona. This is our only chance."

"On the count of three, then heave like all our lives depend on it," Ilyana commanded, her voice tight with tension. "Because they do."

Together, they counted and then pulled. The ancient mortar resisted, but just as Maeve began to despair, the plaster mooring began to crumble. A high-pitched screech pierced the air as the bars began to give way, the sound reverberating in Maeve's teeth. Yet she pulled harder still, muscles burning with effort until sweat beaded on her brow.

Then she heard what they had all been dreading. The rhythmic scrape of undead feet dragging across stone. "The guards!" Fiona said, her breath coming in pained gasps.

"Just keep pulling!" Maeve urged. They were so close, their freedom tantalizingly near.

With a final, desperate heave, the bars clattered to the floor. But the footsteps drew nearer, the sound of jangling keys joining their ominous approach.

"Climb, then hit the ground running. Then head for the old chapel," Ilyana commanded as she knotted the rope around the hand rake and tossed it, once, twice, and then three times until it lodged between the only remaining bars. The makeshift ladder swayed precariously, and Maeve's stomach lurched at the idea of watching her friends scale it. But what other choice did they have?

She stepped back, pushing Fiona towards the rope. "You first," she insisted. "Hurry!" After she watched her friend scramble up, grunting with exertion, Maeve turned to Ilyana. "You next. Go!"

But Ilyana hesitated, her black eyes snapping with emotion. "Maeve, I can't. I'm just a peasant girl. But you—should Alaric perish, are the last hope for all our futures."

"You *must*!" Maeve hissed, her voice raw with desperation. "I am heavier than you. Should the rope break, you would be trapped."

Still, Ilyana hesitated.

"As your future queen, I command it." She grabbed Ilyana's shoulders, locking eyes with her. "Lysander needs you. Alaric needs you. And I know to the pit of my soul I was not meant to die here. So climb, gods damn it! Now!"

An unintelligible shout rang out from the corridor, sending Maeve's heart racing even faster. "Hurry, they're almost upon us."

Her breath caught as she watched Ilyana scale the rope like she'd been born knowing how. The girl's slight frame proved a blessing as she eased through the narrow opening, the sound of her booted feet scraping stone making clear to any who could hear what their intentions were. As she reached the window, Fiona's pale hand reached inside, giving Ilyana the help she needed to haul herself out onto the brambles.

Now, it was Maeve's turn. She grasped the rope, its fragile fibers popping as she hauled herself up. The cell door burst open just as she reached the window's frame, the angry shouts of the guards filling the air.

As she lunged for the dying brambles, thorns tore at her skin. She scaled down as far as she could bear, then let go, tumbling onto the cobblestones below. Pain lanced through her as she hit the ground, the impact knocking the wind from her lungs.

Run, Maeve. Now! For both our lives depend on it! Alaric's distant voice commanded. Pushing past her misery, she scrambled to her feet. A group of patrolling ferals swung their ghastly gazes toward her just as the snowy owl she was coming to believe was a vessel for

Alaric's wandering spirit swooped into their midst, its immense wings beating with fury.

Alaric. Maeve's legs trembled as she forced herself to move, every bone and muscle screaming for mercy. The cold night air stung her face as she willed herself to keep going, the fear of pursuit—and the toll for failure—spurring her on.

With one last glance back at the imposing tower, she plunged into the hedgerows, praying to any gods who would listen that they would all make it to the chapel in time, and she would find the others there, safe and sound.

Maeve was the last of the women to tumble through the chapel door, bruised and battered from her fall, but at least safe.

Isolde was waiting by the door and looking unexcited, as if she had always known Maeve would make it back. "No need to worry about the guards for now," she said with a knowing wink as she turned back to throw the bolt. "Your owl friend has them well occupied."

As Maeve stepped deeper into the dim chapel, she saw that Nyx, too, had made it through their excursion unscathed. The raggedy feline was crouched on the floor behind Isolde, her copper eyes narrowed to half-moons as she nibbled on a strip of dried meat, looking utterly nonplussed.

Maeve's relief rode out with her sigh as she saw the other women, too, were here, looking far better than the last time she had seen them. Though they still appeared weary, they also looked, if not relaxed, at least not alarmed by their circumstances. They sat upon the rough plank floor in a loose circle, also munching on strips of dried meat. Even Diana appeared somewhat revived, supported within the nest of Ingrid's legs, her eyes shining dimly as she leaned back in the protective circle of her beloved's arms. Her leg had been properly splinted and apparently set—Isolde's doing, no doubt.

Only Lysander seemed discontent, looming in the shadows, his freshly shaved face contorted with fury. "What in the gods' name were you thinking, Maeve? You could have gotten yourself and Fiona killed!" His gaze swung to Ilyana. "And you—I distinctly recall telling you to stay put until I returned."

Ilyana bristled, her chin lifting defiantly. "I couldn't just sit here and gnaw on jerky while they were in danger. Once Nyx returned with a key tied around her neck, someone had to act."

Lysander's expression softened slightly, a duel between pride and exasperation crossing his features.

Maeve couldn't help but smile inwardly, heartened to see that Lysander might have met his match in the fiery young woman. Small, yes, but also fierce. "If not for Ilyana's fast thinking, we would still be imprisoned," Maeve added. "But where were you during all this, Lysander? If you were so concerned about our welfare, why didn't you come out into the hallway to check on me like Fiona did?"

"Unlike you and Isolde, I don't have the benefit of foresight," he retorted. "I was busy helping my mother dispose of the belladonna. After we realized you were both gone, I decided to scout the castle so I could know what we were up against. In the meantime, Isolde retrieved the others and took shelter here."

"He speaks the truth," Isolde confirmed as Maeve's gaze sought hers. "Even I was flummoxed as to where you had gone until Nyx appeared with the key affixed to her neck."

"I could only hope that someone would guess it came from me," Maeve said.

Isolde's chin dipped, her expression turning grim. "The second I touched it, I knew it bore your energy. But now that we are all assembled, and, for the moment, safe, you must fill us in on the details behind your capture. There are still far more questions here than answers."

Maeve nodded and took her place amongst the others. For a long moment, she simply stared at the piece of dried meat Ingrid handed her, taking a moment to collect her emotions. "I thought I heard someone cry out in agony," she said, twisting the tough jerky between her fingers. "The second I burst through the door... that's when I saw him."

"Who?" Lysander asked.

"Alaric..."

His brow lofted. "You saw *Alaric*? But that's not possible..."

"I was as shocked by it as you. But he was..." Her voice broke as her mind replayed the image of her beloved locked in an embrace with Lady Elora. Tears pooled in her eyes as she struggled to recount the events she had witnessed in the hallway, for they made little sense, even to her.

As her voice broke in, Fiona scooted nearer and reached out, squeezing her hand supportively. "It's alright, Maeve. Take your time."

But time was a luxury they could not afford. "L-like I said, I saw him... Alaric."

"And you are quite certain it was him?" Lysander's expression was still skeptical. "Because none of that aligns with what I discovered during my advance. I assure you, Maeve, Alaric still lies sleeping in his chambers. I saw him with my own eyes."

"Of course I am sure," she spat. "How could I forget the face of the man I am to marry? But he was also..." Her voice cracked again, her eyes brimming with fresh tears. "He was kissing Lady Elora. And when I cried out, he saw me, and his disdain was... palpable."

"She speaks only truth," Fiona said, furious sparks glittering in her eyes. "And Lady Elora lapped up the way Alaric treated Maeve like a starving kitten does milk."

As gasps rippled through the group, Ingrid's grip on Diana tightened. Even Tilda chuffed, shaking her head in disbelief. "That faithless cur," she spat.

Fiona rubbed small circles on Maeve's back, and she swallowed a fresh wave of emotion. "But you don't understand, Tilda. There was something off about him. He moved... strangely and spoke to me with such ire. And his eyes... when they caught mine, they were empty, as if he were more a puppet than a living being."

"Like an empty husk," Fiona whispered, a thoughtful expression crossing her face as she confirmed Maeve's account.

Isolde leaned forward, her wizened brow creased with thought. "What you describe, Maeve, is not impossible. In fact, it sounds like the work of guise magic. I suspect Alaric's eyes looked empty because whoever you saw wasn't him."

"And who would benefit most from wearing my betrothed's guise?" Maeve uttered, hoping to lead the others to the same conclusion she had drawn.

"King Caligula," Lysander asserted. "Wearing his own son's form?"

Maeve nodded.

"But to what end?" Tilda asked, the edges of her mouth tugging downward.

"To ensure his own coronation... and then his own agenda," Isolde explained, her expression grim. "I have seen the proof of their plan being erected in the courtyard."

"And tomorrow, it will be Caligula who is crowned, wearing Alaric's guise," Fiona added. "And you all know as well as me that man loathes nothing more than he does a human being. He would see them... all of you... if not eradicated... at least subjugated."

"And once the wedding takes place, that would make Elora his queen, and the commander of her feral guards," Maeve added.

Through the chapel's grimy windows, the first rays of dawn began to creep across the sky—a stark reminder that time was running out. "We have until the full moon rises tonight to save him," Maeve said. "But that's all assuming he's not already... gone."

A restless silence fell over the group until Lysander stepped out of the shadows, his golden eyes gleaming. "I assure you, Maeve, Alaric is not dead. His chest still rises and falls with every breath."

Isolde nodded, her hand finding Maeve's shoulder. "My suspicion, too, confirms it, child. Guise magic can only be used if the person whose form has been assumed still lives. And if you think about the events of the last days, you already know he lives... and his spirit thrives."

A heavy silence fell over the group as they absorbed this information. "Then we must find a way to seize the antidote before this scheme can be enacted," Maeve declared, her voice steadying with renewed purpose. "And I am certain it is contained within the pendant Elora wears."

She turned, her gaze pinning onto Isolde's. "Could guise magic be used on more than one person at a time?" she asked, a plan forming in her mind.

Isolde's hand touched her breastbone, concern etching her features. "Exactly what are you thinking?"

"We could have Lysander assume the king's form long enough to seduce Elora into her chambers and lace her wine with a sedative. Then, once she sleeps, he can take the pendant."

Isolde's eyes widened only slightly. "It *can* be done, yes."

"And you have those skills?"

"Yes, thanks to Elora's demands, I do. But just because something can be done does not mean it should be. Dark magic always exacts a toll, Maeve. The price we might pay for invoking it could be steep."

"But what other choice do we have?" she countered, her jaw firming. "If Alaric is to live, if this shattered world is ever again to know peace, we must take this risk."

"Let me be the one then," Lysander said, stepping forward. "For Alaric, for all of us."

Isolde surveyed the eager faces around her, then sighed heavily. "I will do as you ask, Maeve. But let us hope the goddess we serve understands our intent is pure and makes the price for tampering with dark forces one we can all bear."

"You said it yourself, Isolde; love was the only thing that could save Alaric. There could not be any motive purer."

The group exchanged determined nods, the gravity of their situation palpable in the air. Only Ilyana appeared displeased, her expression almost petulant.

"Then let us begin," Isolde said, clapping her hands together. "We have precious little time to prepare."

As the group huddled closer and began fleshing out their plan, the sun continued its relentless climb—a constant reminder of the dwindling hours they had left to save Alaric and the future they all fought for.

Yet beneath the fear and uncertainty, a new hope had sparked to life. They had all come too far, risked too much, to give up now.

THE FIRST RAYS of the setting sun filtered through the chapel's grimy stained-glass windows, casting soft prisms across the weary faces of Maeve's team. Anxiety balled up in her chest as she watched Isolde hunched over a small cauldron, her gnarled hands working with practiced precision. The acrid scent of herbs and something far less pleasant filled the air, making Maeve's nose wrinkle. But it was the strange incantations Isolde muttered as she worked that struck the fear of the gods within Maeve. The very air they breathed now seemed to fester with evil.

"Are you certain this will work?" she asked, her voice barely above a whisper.

Isolde's eyes, bleary with age, yet sharp with wisdom, met Maeve's. "As certain as one can be when dealing with dark magic, child. Remember, certainty and safety are luxuries we can no longer afford. But now it is done."

Lysander stepped forward, his cleft chin set with determination. "I'm ready," he said, though Maeve didn't miss the slight tremor in his voice.

As Isolde handed Lysander a vial of murky liquid she'd siphoned off the cauldron, Maeve's attention drifted to Ilyana. The girl's obsidian eyes were wide with fear, her trembling hands clenched at her sides. Maeve's heart ached for her; she knew all too well the pain of watching a loved one walk into the embrace of a dangerous woman. Especially when that danger involved him giving the appearance that he loved another.

"Wait," she cried, just as Lysander raised the vial to his lips. Fearful of what the dark elixir might do to him, she fumbled in her pocket, withdrawing the talisman Nan had given her. "Take this. For protection."

Lysander's golden eyes softened as he accepted the charm and held it against his heart. "Thank you, Maeve," he murmured, slipping the precious trinket into his own pocket.

With a deep breath, he downed the potion in one swift gulp. For a long, heart-hammering moment, nothing happened. Then Lysander doubled over, his arms clutched around his gut as a strangled cry escaped his lips.

Maeve watched, transfixed, as his body began to change. The transformation started slowly, almost imperceptibly, like ripples spreading across still water. Then, as if some invisible force had taken hold, the changes accelerated.

His bones cracked and popped, the sickening sounds echoing through the chapel. Ilyana screamed as his frame lengthened, shoulders broadening to match Alaric's somewhat more imposing stature. Maeve winced as his jaw dislocated with an audible snap, reforming into the strong, angular shape she knew so well.

She gasped as his skin seemed to liquefy, stretching and shifting like molten wax. The sallow pallor of his complexion waned, taking on the more ashen hue of Alaric's complexion. Even his hair changed, warming from cool black to rich mahogany, the strands lengthening and waving before her eyes.

As his golden eyes clouded over, the irises swirled, boiling with a rainbow of colors until they settled into the familiar cornflower blue of Alaric's gaze. Even the small scar on Alaric's left cheekbone appeared, etching itself into Lysander's transforming flesh.

The process was mesmerizing in its grotesque detail, like watching a sculptor molding clay. When it was over, Lysander gasped, his newly formed body shuddering as if trying to shed the memory of its violent metamorphosis.

When he straightened, it was Alaric who stood before them, his handsome features twisted in a grimace of pain.

"By the gods," Fiona swore, her violet eyes round as coins.

Maeve's swallow felt like a handful of tacks as she forced down the bile that had risen in her throat. The sight of Alaric—or rather, Lysander wearing Alaric's face—drove fresh daggers through her heart. "How do you feel?" she asked, her voice sounding foreign to her own ears.

"Like I've been trampled by a horde of ferals," he replied, his voice now nearly a perfect match for Alaric's familiar timbre. "But I'll manage."

With Nyx sent off to distract the king, the group huddled around Lysander, going over their plan one final time. Maeve couldn't tear her eyes away from his borrowed face. It was uncanny—every detail was perfect, from the set of his jaw to the cornflower blue of his eyes. Yet the expression, the way he held himself, was all wrong. It was Alaric's body, but Lysander's soul contained within.

Unable to look upon him any longer, she turned away, a flutter of white catching her eye. She turned to see the snowy owl's silhouette perched on the windowsill, and she could feel its cornflower blue eyes as they fixed upon her. Whether he was an apparition or real mattered not, for his presence gave her comfort... and hope.

Tread with care, my love, Alaric's voice whispered in her mind. *Isolde was right. Dark magic always comes with a price.*

Maeve's breath caught. She blinked, and the owl was gone, leaving her to wonder if he had ever been there at all.

"It's time," Ingrid announced, her strong voice cutting through Maeve's reverie.

As Lysander steeled himself and made his way to the chapel door, Ilyana rushed forward, catching his arm. "Please," she whispered, tears glistening in her eyes. "Don't let her beauty spirit your heart away from mine."

Lysander cupped her face between his palms, his thumb tracing a scar on her cheekbone. Maeve found the tenderness of his gesture at odds with the man she once believed him to be, and something within her that had been too tightly wound for far too long began to uncoil.

"I swear, Ilyana, that will never happen," he vowed. "For my destiny is already written within the depths of your gaze."

And then he was gone, slipping out into the castle grounds like a wraith.

Now, they could only wait.

Unable to keep company with the others, Maeve slipped away to retrieve her pack. Settling herself between two of the old pews, her fingers brushed against her crystal ball, its surface cool beneath her touch. As the others settled in to wait, she closed her eyes, willing the orb to show her Lysander's progress.

The world around her faded, replaced by hazy visions of stone corridors and shuffling guards. First, she heard the brushing of wings and the hoot-hoot of an owl. Then she saw Lysander striding purposefully through the castle, his borrowed face a mask of regal composure as he rapped on Elora's chamber door.

But then something shifted. The vision blurred, replaced by a scene that made Maeve's blood turn to ice. Lady Elora stood in Alaric's chambers, bent over his sleeping form. In her hand gleamed a wickedly sharp dagger, its blade poised above Alaric's jugular. She didn't think it had happened yet, but she also knew that it soon would.

Her eyes flew open, a cry of terror lodged in her throat. The others turned to look at her, alarm written across their faces.

"What is it?" Fiona demanded. "What did you see?"

Maeve struggled to find her voice, her mind reeling from the vision. "We have to move," she managed at last. "Now. Or all will be lost."

As the group scrambled to gather their weapons, Maeve's gaze drifted to the windows once more. She didn't need to see through the stained-glass panes to sense the gathering storm clouds.

The final battle for Alaric's life—and the fate of their world—had begun.

CHAPTER 25

Elora would have no problem disposing of anyone she believed stood between her and a crown. Maeve knew that. And though her sight had not suggested it, should the guise magic Isolde had enacted come undone before Lysander had procured the pendant, he could be in danger, too.

Once, seeing him at the end of Elora's blade would have delighted her, but much had changed. Now, her breath came in painful pants as she crept through the corridors toward Elora's chambers. Her every nerve was on edge, both hoping and dreading to catch Lysander still in an indelicate situation with Elora. For if he still had her occupied, she could not harm the real Alaric. And even that embarrassment would be better than finding Lysander, too, murdered by that vixen's hand just when he'd redeemed himself.

As she rounded the final corner, she froze. There, just footsteps away, stood King Caligula himself, no longer wearing Alaric's guise. His fleshy hand was poised on the door handle to Alaric's chambers, the same jeweled dagger she'd envisioned clutched in Elora's hand jutting from his boot.

A small cry caught in her throat.

Time itself seemed to slow as the king bent to extract his dagger, then began to turn, his mercurial gray eyes narrowed as they swept the hallway. Maeve flattened herself behind a stone pillar, hardly daring to breathe. If he saw her now, all would be lost. She silently prayed to whatever gods might be listening. But when the king started toward her, she knew no miracle would come. *Alaric, you must help me to help you...*

As if in answer to Maeve's silent petition, a piercing screech rent the air. The snowy owl swooped down the corridor in a blur of white fury. Its vast wings brushed so close to her face that a great rush of air fanned her hair as the creature dove straight for the king, its curved talons extended.

Chaos erupted in the narrow hallway. The king shouted in surprise, ducking and swatting at the owl. As the owl's talons found purchase in the king's arm, his dagger clattered to the stone floor, and he raised both arms to shield his face from the bird's razor-sharp beak.

But the owl was not done yet. His talons raked across Caligula's cheek, drawing blood and a pained howl from the disgraced monarch.

From her hiding place, Maeve watched in awe as the battle unfolded. The owl's movements seemed almost unnaturally precise, as if guided by an unseen force. Its cerulean eyes gleamed with an intelligence that seemed far beyond that of a mere animal. And with each passing moment, Maeve's conviction grew stronger—this was no ordinary bird, but a manifestation of Alaric's spirit, come to protect those he loved.

The king, recovering from his shock, recovered his blade and lashed out at the owl with surprising speed. His dagger connected with the bird's wing, sending him spiraling through the air. But the creature recovered quickly, wheeling around for another attack. As it did so, Maeve could have sworn she saw a flicker of familiar determination in its eyes—the same look she'd seen countless times in Alaric's gaze when faced with a threat.

The owl dove at the king once more, its wings beating furiously as it aimed for his face. The monarch stumbled backward, arms flailing as he tried to fend off the assault. In his haste to retreat, he tripped over his own feet. As he recovered his footing, he fled, his path taking him away from Alaric's chambers, giving Maeve the opening she so desperately needed.

As she darted from the shadows, her eyes met those of the owl for a brief, electric moment. As their gazes connected, a surge of warmth and reassurance washed over her, as if Alaric himself were lending her his strength. At least in his spirit, Alaric was fine and whole. Now, she just needed to see to his physical form.

Heart rising into her throat, she seized the moment. She rushed down the corridor, slipping into Elora's chambers, the door softly shutting behind her.

Inside, she pressed her back against the door, breathing heavily, terror still scalding her veins. The sounds of the ongoing battle between the king and the owl faded into the distance as she focused on the scene before her.

But instead of the enraged zombie courtier she expected, Lysander stood alone and shirtless, the rest of his clothing disheveled. He no longer wore Alaric's guise. His face was a mask of surprise and his cheeks almost florid with... guilt? "Maeve?"

"Lysander?" Maeve gasped, her eyes drawn to the small item clutched in his trembling hand. Hope and suspicion battled within her as she wondered if he was indeed Lysander...or someone else. Elora, perhaps, hiding beneath *his* guise. "You have retrieved the pendant, then?"

He nodded, reaching for his blouse, his eyes reflecting remorse. "Please don't ask what I had to do to get it," he said as he handed the pendant to Maeve and pulled the garment over his head. "But Maeve, why are you here? This wasn't part of our plan."

"I saw something... in my crystal ball, something Elora will do, and I feared we hadn't much time," she said.

"That bitch is indeed relentless," he said, his voice low as his gaze cut toward the window, where the rising moon glimmered over the horizon.

"But where is she?" Maeve asked, the lingering fear Elora might be hiding beneath Lysander's guise causing her to fight tears as her gaze trailed after his.

"When the sedative took effect, I shoved her into the dumb-waiter, naked as the day she was born, and sent her down to the scullery." A near smirk played on his lips. "But she will awaken soon and realize it's missing."

Maeve's mind raced as she affixed the pendant around her neck and tucked it in her tunic. Was she ready to fully trust him with Alaric's life? But the time for planning was over, and as she looked into his eyes, she sensed the same desperation that she felt—the burning need to save Alaric at any cost.

"We should get this antidote into Alaric now," he said.

With her trust in Lysander restored, she pulled open the door and gestured for him to follow.

MAEVE AND LYSANDER raced through the corridor, a winding maze of shadows and wavering torchlight. But Maeve's heart soared with each step that brought them nearer to her betrothed. They were so close now—the door to Alaric's chambers within reach and victory well within their grasp.

The hair at her nape crawled as a guttural roar from behind them stopped them in their tracks, the ghastly sound reverberating off the stone walls. Dread welled in Maeve's chest as she peered over her shoulder. Two feral zombie guards lumbered into view, their decaying flesh hanging in gory tatters, eyes gleaming with inhuman hunger as they readied their filthy weapons.

Maeve raised her dagger, positioning herself against the wall behind her. Lysander stepped forward, his blade glinting in the torchlight as he took a defensive stance beside her. The creatures continued their advance, showing no fear. The first set its sights on Lysander, while the other focused on Maeve.

Lysander engaged his opponent with a series of swift, precise strikes, but the zombie's unnatural strength made it a formidable foe.

Maeve lost sight of him as she engaged her own attacker. As the zombie swung its blade, she countered. But exhaustion had made her too slow. She watched, horrified, as the sword sliced across her forearm, and she bit back a scream, tasting her own blood as she stumbled backward into the wall.

Time crawled as the hissing feral advanced again, shoving her to the floor. With its booted foot on her chest, it raised its blade, seeming to grin as it poised for a killing blow. Her life flashed in slow-motion frames before her eyes—bittersweet memories of Nan and Coralie. Of Alaric, and the grand future they had dreamed of together. Gods damn it, she couldn't die here, not when they were so close.

As the zombie's blade fell, she rolled sideways, casting a desperate glance at Lysander, who was locked in combat with his own undead opponent. His face was contorted with effort as he parried blow after blow. Every counter he made took him further away. As her attacker drew his blade back, two more ferals stepped from the shadows, their putrid stench filling the air.

Maeve's hope faltered, but then a battle cry echoed through the corridor. Ilyana, Fiona, and Tilda burst into the light, their weapons flashing. The torchlight cast fiery halos around their heads, making them look like avenging angels. Blades already swinging, Ilyana and Fiona charged towards the newcomers, engaging them in combat.

Maeve's relief was short-lived. She watched, horrified, as Tilda joined the fray. The woman roared as she threw herself between Maeve and the feral's falling blade. But time seemed to stop as

Tilda's body intercepted the blow that was meant to end Maeve's life.

"No!" she screamed. But it was too late.

Tilda's intervention had done its job, buying her precious seconds. Ilyana broke away, driving her sword through the feral's throat, its head detaching with a sickening crunch.

As the creature crumpled to the ground, Maeve crawled to Tilda's side, cradling her selfless savior's head in her lap. Blood spurted in ruby arcs from her wound, staining her clothes and pooling on the stone floor.

"Tilda, no... please." Maeve's voice broke with anguish as she pressed her hand to the wound to staunch the blood flow. But her efforts were for naught. Tilda's eyes fluttered, the weakest of smiles touching her bluish lips.

"It's okay, Maeve," she gasped, her voice barely audible. "Go now. Save Alaric... then save our people."

Ingrid and Fiona knelt beside them, tears streaming down their faces as Ingrid clasped Tilda's hand. "You brave, foolish woman," she choked out, her voice thick with emotion.

Ilyana rose, her eyes scanning for more threats even as tears glistened on her cheeks. Lysander, having finally dispatched his opponents, joined them, his face a mask of sorrow. Though the women joined hands, uttering petitions to the gods, not even divine intervention could undo the damage. Tilda's breathing soon grew labored, her once vibrant blue eyes losing focus. "Promise me... you'll finish this," she whispered. "Don't let me become one of them."

"We promise," Maeve vowed, her tears falling onto Tilda's face. "Your sacrifice won't be in vain."

With a final, shuddering breath, Tilda's eyes closed, her body going limp in Maeve's arms. A moment of deafening silence fell over the group, broken only by muffled sobs.

Fiona was the first to speak, her voice thick with tears. "There's nothing more we can do for her but prevail. But in order to do that, we must hurry," she whispered, gently touching Maeve's shoulder. "There will be others where they came from."

"Go now," Lysander said. "I will finish this, as was her wish."

Maeve nodded, forcing herself to push through her pain and exhaustion. She carefully laid Tilda's body on the ground, arranging her hands peacefully on her chest. Fiona was right. For Alaric, for Tilda, for all of them—she had to keep going.

With tears streaming unchecked down her face, she rose to her feet, her resolve hardening. She looked at her companions— Lysander, his jaw set as he curled a protective arm around Ilyana. At Ingrid, her eyes blazing with a fierce, protective light, and at Fiona, her face reflecting sorrow and unwavering loyalty.

"For Tilda," Maeve said, wiping her blade on her tunic. "And for Alaric... all of us. We will end this now."

GASPING FOR BREATH, Maeve and the women reached Alaric's chambers. "Guard the door while I administer the antidote," Maeve said. Pushing open the door, she rushed inside.

She found Alaric still lying in his glass capsule, looking as placid and still as the day she had left him. Yet her heart still clenched at the sight of him looking so lifeless. Though she was overjoyed to see the steady rise and fall of his chest that proved him alive, simply breathing was not enough to see his life's dream enacted. For that, she needed his wandering soul returned to him.

"This has to work," she prayed as she lifted the pendant over her head and opened the vial.

Her hands shook as Lysander let himself into the room. After raising the capsule's lid, she leaned in, pressing a kiss to Alaric's forehead. Whispering a silent petition to the gods, she carefully tipped the potion into his mouth, praying to every deity she knew that they hadn't reached him too late. "It is time to awaken now, my love."

The scent of medicinal herbs wafted into the air, mingling with the sulfuric scent that clung to Alaric's bluish skin. Though he swallowed, nothing happened. So she waited, the clock lazily marking every agonizing second that ticked by. Then, miraculously, a hint of color slowly began to infuse Alaric's lips.

She sucked in a breath and held it, eager for his eyes to open, to see with her own eyes the love and recognition she so desperately missed. But the damnable clock kept ticking until too many minutes had crept by. Alaric's eyes remained closed, his beautiful body still as death.

"Maeve," Lysander managed as a sob erupted from her. "You know as well as me he did not want to remain in such a state. If the antidote doesn't work... he left orders. Ones I am obligated to heed."

"Stop!" she spat. "We know nothing yet. It may just take more time."

Lysander's features were drawn with sadness as he approached and took her hand, trying to lead her away.

"Please, just leave me be and go check on the others," she shouted as she drew back her hand, trying to keep the tremors that shook her body out of her voice. "I... you... none of us know how the antidote works. But if you are so certain it will not, I would ask that you let me have some time alone with him. For I refuse to surrender my hopes in the space of a few moments."

"Maeve," Lysander said softly, placing a hand on her shoulder. "I know how much you love him, but the antidote should have done something by now. I fear he is ruined..."

"I. Said. Go."

She pointed at the door, making clear her intentions. Lysander nodded curtly, then moved into the corridor, pulling the door closed behind him. Happy to see him gone, she took Alaric's hand in hers, pressing it against her cheek and wishing that with everything she had in her, she could infuse him with her own life force.

"It is time for you to come back to me," she whispered, her voice cracking with emotion. "Please, my love. I need you. The entire world needs you."

Outside, a sudden blast of wind rattled the windowpanes, as if nature herself sensed the gravity of the moment. Yet the stubborn full moon still crept above the horizon, bathing the chamber in its icy glow. And finally, *finally*, just when Maeve could not stand another second of waiting, Alaric stirred, his eyes fluttering open.

But the sight that greeted her turned her very soul to ice. The gaze that had once been as bright and blue as a field of cornflowers was now as empty and black as a feral's, utterly devoid of the warmth and intelligence she so cherished. There was no spark of recognition, no hint of the brilliant, generous soul she loved more than any other.

Her stomach churned with a nauseating mix of hope and dread. Hands trembling, she caressed Alaric's cheek and ran her fingers through his hair, searching for any hint of the man she loved lurking within the bottomless wells of his eyes. But when she glimpsed nothing but darkness, her cry erupted, strident and shrill.

Lysander burst into the chambers with Ilyana, and she couldn't hold back her fears any longer. "Something's wrong," she choked out, tears streaming down her face. "His eyes are open, but he seems... dazed. Gone. What if he's turning feral, just like Dr. Reinhart warned?"

Lysander leaned over Alaric, speaking clearly, "My prince, can you hear me? It's me, Lysander. You're safe now." But Alaric's vacant gaze showed not even a flicker of recognition.

Ilyana's face grew solemn, her dark eyes welling with a sadness that spoke volumes. "Isolde warned us dark magic exacts a price," she said softly. "But must this be the toll, the life of an innocent man?"

"Perhaps we should summon my mother," Lysander suggested, his voice tight with concern. "She may have insight into the workings of the antidote that we lack."

"Yes," Maeve said, desperate to encourage her friends to believe Alaric could still recover. "Please. Retrieve her."

As Lysander nodded and ushered the others out of the room, Maeve's heart clenched. Alaric's movements grew more restless, his eyes darting around his chambers without truly seeing. Fear raised gooseflesh on her arms as she recalled Isolde's warnings about the unpredictable nature of magic, and a wave of guilt washed over her. Had her actions condemned her beloved to a fate far worse than death? She could not allow her need to hold on to cause her to force him to live like that.

But as she looked at him, wondering whether letting go was the last gift she could give him, a fierce determination sparked within her. This was not the destiny Isolde had foreseen. Their love was what had brought them this far—and if her trials had taught her anything, it was that love's power was the most potent force in the Universe. Surely, if she stopped doubting the veracity of Alaric's conviction, it would prove enough to bring him back completely. She would not give up on him, not now, not ever.

"I won't lose you," she vowed, her voice barely above a whisper as she clutched his cold hand within her own. "Whatever it takes, my love, I will find a way to bring you back to me. Our story cannot be... will not... be over yet. For you know as well as me our tale was written in the stars long before we were born."

Still hopeful for a miracle, she cast her eyes to the window, hoping to see Alaric's owl resting there. But she saw only the moon's mocking eye staring down at her in silent contempt as it limned the edges of the last volume of fairy stories Alaric had read to her. So, not knowing anything else to do, she picked up the book and began to read. "Once upon a time..."

CHAPTER 26

Despite the low growls and grunts that still erupted from Alaric, Maeve pushed past her rising panic and read, though every word she uttered felt like brambles piercing her throat. The familiar tale of love and enchantment flowed from her lips, each syllable a desperate incantation against the darkness that threatened to consume her beloved.

"And the valiant prince traversed the grand courtyard, its alabaster stones gleaming like diamonds beneath his feet. Ascending the winding staircase, he entered the silent hall. There, even the castle guards stood frozen in time, their pikes held aloft, yet they were lost in slumber's embrace..."

A deep silence pervaded Alaric's chamber, and her hopes tried to rekindle as she dared a glance. Did his face appear more relaxed now, or was she only imagining what her heart most longed to see? She did not know. Nor did she dare stop reading him the last fairy story they had shared, for she knew how much he had loved it. Her voice trembled with hope and fear as she continued, clinging to each word as if it were a lifeline that could pull Alaric back from the abyss.

"Through vast chambers teeming with motionless courtiers, he ventured, their elegant forms suspended in repose. At last, he came upon a royal chamber, lush with gilded splendor, where a sight of unparalleled beauty awaited him…"

Alaric emitted the softest of sighs as she'd spoken those words; she was sure of it. Joy ignited in her chest, but was quickly tempered by the cruel voice of doubt that whispered in her mind. "Should I continue, my love?" she asked, hoping beyond hope he would turn toward her and answer. And though he did not, he no longer appeared quite so… restless. So, she indulged her rising hopes and began again, the words flowing more freely now, carried on the wings of her desperate longing.

As Maeve recounted the prince's journey to the sleeping princess, her own emotions mirrored those of the tale. She yearned to break through the spell that held Alaric captive, to awaken him with the power of her love. Yet, with each passing moment, a creeping realization began to take root in her heart—one she fought against with every fiber of her being.

A ruckus sounded in the distant corridors, and the metallic clang of arms striking arms told Maeve her friends were embroiled in combat. Reminding herself they did so for Alaric, she begged the gods to keep them safe and forced herself to keep going, though she feared her voice would betray the panic that stirred within her. Two kind souls had already lost their lives because they believed in her ability to see this cause through.

"T-trembling," she managed, "the prince approached the maiden's bedside and knelt beside her, his very heart aflame with awe." And as she uttered those lines, she heard a soft stirring at the window behind her. The owl had come to roost, his gaze focused and his head tilting as if caught up in her story and urging her to utter the next lines. Were his eyes less blue now, or was that only the moon shadows passing across them? She prayed she wasn't breathing false life into her hopes as she returned to the book's fading pages and began again.

With each word, she poured more of her soul into the story,

willing it to bridge the chasm between her world and wherever Alaric's spirit now dwelled. She recounted the prince's kiss, her voice catching as she spoke of a love so pure and powerful that it could break any enchantment. In that moment, her own desire to bring Alaric back surged within her, a tidal wave of emotion threatening to sweep her away.

Yet even as hope burned bright, a small, quiet voice in the depths of her heart whispered a truth she had been trying to deny. What if Alaric's journey had taken him too far? What if, in her desperation to hold onto him, she was denying him the peaceful afterlife he deserved?

She lifted her eyes and noticed the owl had once again fled. As she turned her gaze onto Alaric, she thought she saw the slightest flicker of blue igniting the vast black pools of his eyes. Her heart leaped, but the fleeting glimmer faded as quickly as it had appeared.

Not knowing why she did so, she rose and bent over him. Though he was still now, she saw only blackness in those once-vibrant eyes. Overwhelmed by the love that welled within her, she pressed her lips to his. Her tears fell upon his face as she silently begged him to let her know if he could ever come back to her.

In that bittersweet kiss, Maeve fell into the bottomless depths of her love for Alaric, the burning intensity of her desire to bring him back. But she also felt something else—a growing understanding that perhaps the greatest act of love would be to let him go. Her heart ached with the realization that the time may have come to release him, to allow his spirit to find peace and move on to the next world without her.

As she pulled away, her tears still fell. "I love you, Alaric. Always and forever. But if you need to go... if it is your time... I understand. I will find a way to see your dream through." Her voice broke on the last words, a mixture of grief and acceptance washing over her as her knees gave way. As she fell into a faint on the stone floor, she realized nothing in her life had prepared her for what she knew must come next, for Alaric had already told them...

MAEVE AWOKE in the garden where she had envisioned Alaric so many times. "Why do you look so sad?" she asked as his gaze poured into hers, his face etched with misery. She looked at him, an unsettling sensation welling up within her. She felt as if she was looking into a wishing pool, seeing only a reflection of his real self.

He dragged a hand through his hair, stammering a little as he searched for words. "For starters, I couldn't find you. No matter how much I have tried to retrace the steps that brought me here, I find myself returning to this very spot. Still alone. Still without you."

"But I am here now," she murmured, cupping his cheek with her hand. Her fingers tingled strangely, as if she was touching mist rather than flesh. "You are no longer lost."

Yet his brow remained pleated with confusion. "But then my owl friend—the one who has been keeping me company as I've wandered these infernal hedgerows looking for a way back to you—seems to have abandoned me. And I don't know why, Maeve, but I feel like he just took a small piece of me with him."

Maeve nodded, swallowing back the sob that tortured her throat, the certainty that he would cross out of this life soon constricting her heart. With each passing moment, Alaric seemed to grow more translucent, his edges blurring slightly. "Please don't worry. I'm sure he'll return soon, if that is your wish."

"Perchance. But even if he does not, all is not lost, for with you as my compass, I'm sure we will be home in no time."

"Then let us try. For together, we have always been more than the sum of our parts." Locking her arm in the crook of his, they began to stroll, but Maeve could not help but sense the dense hedgerows were conspiring against them, shifting behind them as they advanced. The weight of Alaric's arm felt more ephemeral with each step, as if he were fading away. "I understand how you feel about the owl now," she said, willing herself to remain centered in his focus. "For I have an animal friend, too. Did I tell you that?"

He paused and turned to face her, his chestnut brow lofted with surprise. Maeve's heart clenched as she noticed she could almost see through him.

"You most assuredly did not," he said, pulling his hand through her hair. "And here I thought I knew everything there was to know about the woman I am to marry."

"Then allow me to tell you now, for I, too, have grown weary of secrets," she said, pressing a finger to his lips, desperately trying to memorize the feeling of his skin against hers. "My new friend is a cat —a zombie cat—and her name is Nyx. She was given to me by the strangest old woman. Then she told me Nyx had taken to me because she was my familiar..."

An odd light flickered in his gaze as he registered this information. "Your... familiar? So, you've met Isolde, then?"

This time, she was the one whose expression registered surprise, for she had not expected him to be so forthright about where magic was involved. "I have."

"When?"

"Just after you... came out here. And she claimed she knew you, too. So I believe I'm not the only one here harboring a secret."

As their conversation continued, Maeve's dread grew. Alaric's voice seemed to come from farther and farther away, even though he stood right before her, his form shimmering like a mirage.

Just as he bent to press a kiss to the back of her hand, dark clouds blotted the moon, and a stinging rain began to fall. But the only storm that concerned Maeve was the one taking place on Alaric's face as his eyes lifted to hers once more.

"Maeve?" he asked, his expression stricken as he stared down at her hand. "What has become of your betrothal ring? Have you changed your mind about our marriage?"

"No! But there is much treachery afoot, and I haven't been able to tell you," she said, her voice trembling as she realized she could now see the garden through his spectral form.

"Then please, do. I cannot help but sense we are running out of time."

"Perhaps we should go inside first before we both catch a chill?" she said, pulling at his hand as a deep shudder racked her frame. She could barely feel his touch now.

"We're zombies now, Maeve," he said, acting as if he did not know he was vanishing. "What harm can a little cold possibly do us now? If it's your gown you're worried about, we could just take it off and continue our stroll in the nude." The loft of his brow told her he had meant every word. And a part of her longed to do just that, for this might be the last time she ever felt this close to him.

But a flutter of white in the trees caught her eyes just then, and she choked down a sob, knowing their time together was drawing to a close. The pale owl emerged from the branches; its wings spread wide as it swooped towards them. Maeve's heart fell, knowing this moment would decide the fate of a world.

"He's here to lead you into the next life, my love," she said, gesturing toward the owl, her voice breaking.

"But what if I am not ready?" Alaric's voice was barely a whisper now, his form nearly transparent.

"Then you can come back with me, battered but not broken. And once you are well, we shall begin our lives together, just like we always planned."

As the owl drew nearer, its piercing stare fixed on Alaric, Maeve felt a wave of vertigo wash over her. She instinctively raised her arms to shield her head, closing her eyes against the rush of air from the owl's wings. In that moment, she experienced the sickening sensation of falling, as if the ground had disappeared beneath her feet.

When she opened her eyes, Alaric was gone. The owl circled once overhead, seeming to wink at her before disappearing into the night sky.

Maeve fell to her knees, the sob finally tearing from her throat as the crushing certainty settled over her: Alaric's life was over. The garden around her began to fade, leaving her alone in rolling darkness with nothing but the fading echo of their lost dreams.

Maeve swam through layer after layer of churning darkness. She first heard the distant hum of voices. Then she felt warm hands cupping hers as a ring was slipped onto her finger. "It is your turn to awaken, my love," a familiar voice whispered, sending tingles through her body.

Wondering if her heartache had been so deep that it had spirited her away from life, her eyes fluttered open. Her vision slowly focused, revealing not the afterworld, but Alaric's own bedchamber. His pale face hovered over hers, his expression a mix of concern and relief as his familiar gaze poured into hers.

"Your eyes..." she said, her voice thick with emotion. "They're blue again." Her hand trembled as she reached up to touch his face, hardly daring to believe what she was seeing.

Alaric's lips curved into a tender smile. "Of course they are, silly. Your love was the light that showed my wandering spirit the way home." As he clasped her hand against his cheek, his eyes glistening with unshed tears, Maeve noted fresh bruising on his knuckles.

"Then we are not dead?" she asked, her heart thrumming with disbelief.

Alaric's chuckle was low and teasing. "Well, that depends on your definition of dead, I suppose. I'm afraid we are still very much zombies." His tone was light, but his eyes held a depth of feeling that took Maeve's breath away.

Lysander moved into Maeve's field of vision, sporting a fresh black eye as Ilyana clung to his side, Fiona and the others close behind him. She did not need to ask to know where it had come from. Though their faces were etched with exhaustion, their eyes also shone with joy.

"You did it, Maeve," Lysander said, his voice filled with pride. "Peace is being restored, and somehow, your love managed to save our prince. Now get up, both of you. There's a coronation to prepare for, and I suggest we make haste."

"Not just yet," Alaric said, his eyes never leaving Maeve's. "First, I must marry this little warmonger of mine before she gets into any more trouble."

Fiona stepped forward, her arms crossed over her chest, her chin lifting. "But we still have fallen to mourn. And if you were to marry Maeve without inviting her family and friends, they would rightly have your head on a stick. Especially Coralie, who has a very specific gown in mind for your nuptials."

Alaric chuckled. "Of course. And those things must take precedence. But now that your name has been cleared," he said, returning his focus to Lysander, "do you think when the time comes, you could stand up for me as your mother does the honors?"

Maeve's heart soared at his words, but a chill just as soon crossed her grave. "But what of Elora and the king?" Her gaze darted over the faces of her friends, finding them weary but unconcerned.

Lysander's expression darkened slightly. "The king is imprisoned, awaiting execution."

Alaric's jaw tightened as he helped Maeve to her feet, a mix of emotions playing across his face. "And while I should perhaps be saddened, I cannot forget the atrocities my father has committed." Yet his voice was tinged with regret. "His soul was eaten up by evil ambitions. Any grief I might feel will be a long time in coming."

"And Elora?" Maeve asked, fearing her nemesis had escaped their grasp yet again.

Alaric's expression softened as he turned Maeve toward the window. There, in the courtyard below, Elora was being herded across the courtyard by the castle guards, her bare form laden with chains. "As soon as the castle guard awoke, they made short work of chasing off her horde," Alaric said.

"Tomorrow," Lysander added, "she will be en route to an impenetrable tower deep in the Northlands."

"And there she will remain until you can decide what should be done with her," Alaric said.

"Me?" Maeve's eyes widened as she turned to face him. "You would grant me that power?"

"Matters of sentencing are the queen's to decide, my dear. Or at least they will be after I decree it so." Alaric's eyes twinkled with mischief.

"Now there is also a queen we must contend with?" Maeve was certain she had misunderstood. For in this world, women assuming such power was unheard of.

"Not just yet. In order to name a queen, I must first take a wife and be coronated." Alaric's voice was imbued with promise.

"But what about the courtiers? They will never—" Maeve began, only to be cut off by Alaric's soft laughter. He wound his hand around her neck, pressing a finger to her lips.

"How can I kiss you properly if you won't stop talking?" he teased, his eyes igniting with joy.

But he never got the chance, for Maeve was already kissing him, pouring all her love and relief into their embrace. She was vaguely aware of Alaric waving their friends toward the door as he lifted her onto his bed. As he began stripping off his waistcoat, her entire world narrowed to this moment, to the feel of Alaric's arms around her and the knowledge that they had overcome impossible odds to be together.

The rest could wait.

As he peeled off her clothes with a slow reverence that nearly drove her insane with desire, Maeve's heart overflowed with an intense, almost overwhelming joy. When he spread her thighs wide, tears of happiness streamed down her face, and she buried her head in his bare chest, listening to the faint beat of his heart. She felt as though her entire being was suffused with light, radiating outward with the power of their love.

"I love you," she said as his mouth found her center, her voice trembling with the depth of her emotion. "I love you so much, Alaric."

Alaric pulled back, cupping her face in his hands and gazing into her eyes with a love so profound it took her breath away. "And I love you, Maeve," he said softly. "More than life itself. You are my heart, my soul... and now my savior. I owe you everything."

"You owe me nothing," she managed between pants. "Except maybe... this." Lassoing his hips with her thigh, she crawled astride him, taking wicked delight in his surprised gasp as she assumed power.

As they took turns ceding control, teasing and tormenting each other's flesh, Maeve knew that what Alaric had told her was true. No power in the Universe was stronger than love, for when she took him deep into her quaking core, riding him like a steed, the very foundation of their world began to shake.

EPILOGUE

It only seemed right that Tilda would be laid to rest near the former Tributaries' hold, where they could honor and keep watch over the place where her remains would be interred.

On the morning of her burial, winter paid its final respects by releasing its hold on Alaric's kingdom. The brambles that had surrounded the castle were but a memory, and a gentle breeze carried the scent of new beginnings as the somber procession made its way from the castle grounds toward Maeve's village. The air hummed with awakening life after its long slumber. Tender buds unfurled on tree branches, birdsong filled the air, and delicate wildflowers dotted the forest floor with splashes of color.

A flower-adorned cart bore Tilda's body, honoring the sacrifice she'd made so that Alaric could be saved with all the pomp befitting a fallen hero. Maeve and the other women walked alongside the cart, and her heart ached with each step. Tilda's loss felt at odds with the vibrant renewal of the land surrounding them.

"She would have loved this," Fiona said, gesturing to a patch of early crocuses pushing through the earth.

"Tilda always said spring was her favorite season," Ingrid added.

Diana sighed her agreement as she leaned into Ingrid, not just for support, but for solace.

Maeve nodded, a lump forming in her throat. "She deserved to see the victory she made possible."

Ilyana and Lysander had also joined the procession, their faces etched with grief yet holding a quiet dignity. Guards in freshly polished armor surrounded them all, a reminder of Tilda's valor in protecting the royal line.

Lysander and Alaric rode behind on horseback, their presence a testament to the bridges being built between their worlds.

As they passed through the village gates, the human guards demurred, a few even saluting Alaric as he rode by, and Maeve was struck by the change in the villagers' demeanors. Where once there had been scorn and distrust, now there was somber respect. Heads bowed as the procession moved by, and some even stepped forward to lay flowers in their path.

"Look," Alaric said softly, leaning down from his horse to speak to Maeve. "They're beginning to understand we all feel pain at the loss of loved ones."

Maeve felt a new flicker of hope kindle in her chest. "Perhaps peace truly is possible," she said as he lifted her onto his horse. The procession continued, and she leaned back against him, taking solace from his familiar embrace.

When they reached the former Tributaries' hold, a freshly dug grave awaited. Nan, Coralie and Eamon stood nearby, their eyes glistening with unshed tears. As Tilda's body was lowered into the earth, Maeve and the others lifted waiting baskets filled with flower petals —a vibrant mix of blossoms gathered from the castle gardens and the wild blooms Tilda loved most, harvested from the nearby forest.

As they each knelt and scattered the fragrant petals over their friend's grave, the air filled with their sweet perfume, a celebration of life even in this moment of loss.

"Farewell, brave Tilda," Maeve said, her voice carrying clearly in the hushed silence. "You showed us the true meaning of sacrifice and love. May the gods welcome you home, and may your spirit find the peace you helped usher into our world."

Quiet sobs and sob-laced prayers rose around her as they each bid their final goodbyes. As the last handful of petals fluttered down, Maeve caught sight of Eamon and Fiona, reunited at last. She did not miss how tightly their fingers were intertwined, a small spark of joy amidst their sorrow. Maeve did not have to ask to know Fiona would be staying here, at least for a while.

When it was time to depart, Maeve embraced the woman she would lay down her life for with a ferocity that lifted her feet from the ground. "I'll miss you," she said, fighting back tears. "It won't be the same without you by my side."

Fiona smiled through her own tears. "It's not goodbye forever. We'll see each other at the wedding. And with Ilyana staying back with Lysander, perhaps a new friendship will be formed."

"But nobody can ever replace you, Fiona."

Fiona nodded, tears shining in her eyes. "But this time apart... well, it's a new beginning for both of us."

Maeve nodded, then turned to hug Nan and Coralie. "I'll be back soon," she promised, kneeling to look Coralie in the eye. "On the solstice. For the wedding and coronation. And with Fiona so close by, you shall have the prettiest pink dress anyone has ever seen."

Coralie's eyes lit up despite her tears. "Really? You promise?"

"I swear it," Maeve said, managing a smile. "And remember, a princess always keeps her promises."

With one last look at her family and friends, Maeve kissed them each once again, then turned to join Alaric. As they mounted his horse and turned to head home, a gentle breeze picked up, carrying the fresh scent of the land's rebirth.

About the Author

Gentry Lee Burke is a figment of her imagination who resides in a land far, far away.

She's happy to report that like her heroines, she's survived the carnage that man her momma told her not to marry unleashed on her life and made her writing dreams come true. Gentry Lee is also the proud mom of four full-grown, absolutely perfect children, two of them living their best lives with autism.

Though the philandering men have come and gone, the true loves of her life have endured—one teensy papillon, one monster-sized Pomeranian, and two adorable rescue kitties. During the spare time she doesn't have, she's a runner, dancer, artist, and avid cook.

The tales Gentry Lee spins are populated with larger than life heroes and heroines, feminine magic, and sometimes steamy romantic encounters. She swears on a mile-high stack of dogeared cookbooks that any resemblances her villains have to that man Momma told her not to marry are purely coincidental.

Special editions of Gentry Lee's paperback and hardcover books are available on her TikTok shop, where shipping and fun themed swag is always free! Give her a follow on Tiktok @authorgentryleeburke.

www.ingramcontent.com/pod-product-compliance
Lightning Source LLC
Chambersburg PA
CBHW040915010826
48978CB00013BB/1299